DEAD DWARVES DON'T DIE

ANNALS OF THE NAMELESS DWARF: BOOK 8

DEREK PRIOR

Dead Dwarves Don't Die

Copyright © 2021 by Derek Prior

All rights reserved.

No part of this book may be reproduced in any form or by any electronic or mechanical means, including information storage and retrieval systems, without written permission from the author, except for the use of brief quotations in a book review.

ACKNOWLEDGMENTS

Thanks to Cordelia Prior for Purg, Grittel, and Mora, and for all things lily cat.

And to Paula Prior for Igor, and for being my test reader.

1

An enveloping fog, tinged blue by gas lamps on iron posts, muffled the footfalls of the man hurrying along the street.

He wore a fur hat and a long coat. In one gloved hand he carried a staff with a glowing crystal tip which painted thready trails of light through the gloom. His cheeks were pinched, his nose a blade, his pointed chin clean-shaven.

Venton Nap had always said it, and he'd say it again: The afterlife was one big letdown, a tedious, shoddy sequel to the life he'd led on Aosia.

Given half a chance, he'd go back at the drop of a hat, pick up his old life where death had cut it short. But Venton didn't believe in chances, only in hard work and study. When faced with the choice of a bland and changeless eternity, like that embraced by the vast masses of indolent dead, or the chance to make a better future for himself, it was no choice at all.

Pity was, his plans required him to set foot in Scutsville—his name for the depraved region he now walked through. But all progress in Gabala—the Supernal Realm—came with an unhealthy dose of risk: the very real possibility of a second and more permanent death.

He thought he heard footfalls behind him in the fog, but they ceased when he stopped to listen. Probably one of the rancorous souls who haunted the streets of Scutsville, living the same malodorous lives they'd lived on Aosia. Someone once said, "The seeds sown in life are the crop one reaps beyond death." It might have been Venton himself, but he couldn't remember.

Scutsville was where crooks and murderers came after death—those who hadn't signed their souls over to Mananoc. It was home to those too cruel, too self-obsessed, or too lazy to live a second life anywhere other than their own personal Abyss.

Venton plunged into an alley, fanning his nose against the stench of human excrement.

"Be right with you, darling," a whore grunted from where she squatted in the shadows.

Venton hurried on by.

The alley opened onto a rundown road. Thieves and cutthroats mingled with the streetwalkers outside crumbling tenements. Above the glow of the gas lamps, the night sky was a venomous green.

Was that footfalls again, getting louder?

Yes, quite distinct now, picking up their pace. My, they were bold tonight.

Without turning around, Venton reached out with finely tuned senses and siphoned a trickle of essence from the rats that plagued the streets. He drew the essence through his staff and sent a ball of ghostly light over his shoulder.

Someone cursed.

With the merest of thoughts, Venton made the ghost-light burst apart in a myriad dazzling sparks.

The footfalls ran back the other way.

A dog barked in response to his little display. It watched him with big sad eyes from the porch of an abandoned house. Bats flitted from the eaves—the sharp-toothed kind with a taste for posthumous blood—or rather, for the essence it contained.

Venton came at last to a ramshackle townhouse, all crumbling brickwork and missing roof tiles. A cast iron downspout hung at a precarious angle. There were no whores outside, no rogues lurking in the shadows, just an overgrown garden strewn with empty bottles, and a pathway of cracked flagstones scabbed with yellow moss.

He didn't bother to knock. The lock on the door had been broken at some point, but why repair it when there was nothing of value within? Not exactly true, but that was the impression the occupant wished to convey.

There was just the one large room inside. The stud walls had been demolished. Stairs at the far end led nowhere—the second floor had been destroyed by fire. That left the room with an unusually high ceiling, all the way up to the eaves. The rafters were spattered with guano, and bats flitted in and out of the holes in the roof.

Old books were stacked as high as a man all around the floor. There was a fire in the grate that failed to make the place feel homey, a threadbare rug in front of it. Either side of the hearth were long, leather couches, wrinkled and faded with age. On one, there was an iron box with flaking black paint. On the other, a blanket pulled up to his neck, bottle of rum in one hand, lay a wiry old man with a grey-streaked ginger beard and ringlets of the same color that skirted his balding, liver-spotted head.

"You look... well, Captain," Venton said—a well-intentioned lie. The trouble with unpaid penance—and the Captain was bankrupt in that respect—was that it left you as you were just before you died. Worse, in some cases.

"Do I know you?" the old pirate asked, taking a slug of his rum. "You've the look of a lubber about you."

"No names, Captain, as we agreed. But yes, you know me. I refuse to believe you are that drunk."

"Well, you can't have made much of an impression," the Captain said, but there was a glint in his sea-grey eyes.

"I take it my box is no longer empty?" Venton took a seat on the other couch and opened the lid.

Within the box there was moist, ruddy clay that sparkled from the millions of crystalline deposits it contained. It was threaded through with filaments of black flecked with green: minuscule seams of *ocras*.

Venton allowed himself a sigh of relief. It was quickly followed by disappointment.

"Why only half full?"

"It's getting harder and harder to find." The Captain upended his bottle and caught the last drops of rum on his tongue.

"And all this mud and impurity... It'll take an age to get it out."

"Beauty of eternity," the Captain said. "All the time in the world. Unless you were planning on going somewhere else?"

"Maybe I am."

"Well, if you work out where, let me know. Gabala's one great big shog-hole, if you ask me. Supernal Realm, my backside!"

Venton touched his finger to the clay and brought it to his lips. It caused his lips to tingle, and a shiver ran through his veins. "I suppose it will do."

"Said I'd find some for you." The Captain threw off his blanket and sat up on the couch.

"Consider your debt half repaid," Venton said. "I take it the modifications to your ship were successful?"

"Worked a treat." The old man slung his empty bottle aside, then fished about under the couch for another. "Sailed for weeks on the Burning Sea, and nary a char mark on the keel."

"And that's where you found the clay, on one of the husk islands?"

"Only place I could think to look. Blasted stuff's in short supply."

Of course it was. The clay was some kind of residue left over from the creation of Gabala out of pure essence. Witandos had used up all he could find when he created the twelve original dwarven Exalted to answer Aosia's needs at the dawn of history. More recently, Witandos had procured just enough clay for another, seeing as the Exalted bloodline had come to an end. Venton had been present at her creation and ensoulment—he'd still been in favor back then. And it had given him an idea.

If only the Supernal Father had been a more patient "god," he might have discovered more clay. If he'd been as omniscient as he liked others to believe, he wouldn't have had to look.

Still, Witandos's loss was Venton's gain. But it wasn't dwarves *he* was planning to make. Oh, no, his idea was much more daring than that. But even with this new batch of clay, there was still such a long way to go.

"I'm going to need more," Venton said. "When do you plan to set sail again?"

"When I'm good and ready." The Captain pulled the cork from the bottle with a plop.

"Of course," Venton said as he rose to leave, tucking the box under his arm. "But don't take too long."

VENTON LEFT the house and headed down the garden path, back into the fog.

It had grown unseasonably cold, which was an odd way of putting it, since the Supernal Realm had no seasons, save those you brought with you in your memories. Too late, Venton realized the temperature drop was a warning sent up by his preoccupied mind.

Two figures emerged from the fog: a bald man with a cosh, and a woman in high-heeled boots and a coat of scarlet silk. The poor dear must have been freezing. Oh… and she had a staff.

"Venton Nap," the woman said. There was a predatory gleam in her eyes.

"You've heard of me, then. And you're not the teeniest bit afraid?"

"Why would we be?" the bald man said, slapping his cosh into his palm.

"First I heard of you was earlier today," the woman said. "A sorcerer with ideas above his station, was how you were described to me."

"Yes, yes, and now I have to die," Venton said. "Witandos is anything but unpredictable."

The Supernal Father would have killed Venton himself, if he'd not been bound by the law of reciprocity that existed between Supernals. Direct action from one ceded an action of equal gravity to another, in this case Witandos's errant son, Mananoc, the lord of the Abyss.

"You're not the first to come after me."

"No, but we'll be the last," the bald man said.

"Good show," Venton said. "You actually sound half-intimidating. I assume Witandos offered you a reduction in your penance?"

"Then you're not as clever as you think," the woman said.

"Perhaps not," Venton said, "but, I am cleverer than *you* think. Well, it's been lovely meeting you...."

The woman headed him off as he tried to walk past her, eyes flaring as she whispered, "Sleep!"

Venton fanned his hand over his mouth to stifle a yawn. Staggered back a step. Stumbled.

The consummate performance.

With a waggle of his fingers for theatrical effect, he sent her feeble casting back in her face. And *she* really did yawn, before dropping like a sack of potatoes and starting to snore.

The bald man growled something uncouth and charged.

Venton snatched at the man's essence, drawing a little through his staff. Strands of spiderweb streamed from Venton's fingers and entangled the rogue's legs, tripping him, then continued to wrap around him until he was well and truly cocooned.

A scuff came from behind Venton. Before he could turn, a hand clamped a cloth over his mouth and nose. Something astringent stung his eyes. He felt nauseous, then dizzy. His box thudded as it hit the ground.

Someone gasped in his ear. Pressure fell away from his mouth and nose, along with the cloth. Venton turned, just as the body of a man slumped to the ground, and there, behind, blood-stained dagger in her tiny hand, was a child with the head of a dog.

"Grittel Gadfly!" Venton said, coughing against the fumes that lingered from the cloth. "I thought I told you not to follow me."

She had on her leather vest, black britches, and soft leather boots. Her tail thrashed about in agitation.

"Me wasn't following!"

"No, of course you weren't." He gave her an affectionate pat on the head. "But I'm grateful you did."

Venton frowned down at the dead assassin, not sure if that was the right word for the man. He recognized the fumes now: the cloth had been saturated with the sap of the scale-petal orchid. It was supposed to render him insensible, not kill him.

Interesting.

He'd procured a few of the plants from a shady dealer in Vanatus during his life on Aosia. Dried out and blended with tobacco, they made for a relaxing smoke. But scale-petals were indigenous to the underworld of Aranuin. So, what were they doing here in Gabala?

And the other two that had accosted him: a sorcerer who had tried to sleep him, and a man with a cosh—hardly a killing weapon. Last time Witandos had sent assassins, they'd been armed to the teeth with blades and bows.

Grittel stood protectively at his side as Venton knelt beside the sorceress and roused her with a click of his fingers. Her eyes snapped open, wide with fear.

"Calm yourself," Venton said, marking a glyph on her forehead with his thumb. "Now, answer my questions."

She bucked and writhed—that wasn't supposed to happen. Froth spilled from her mouth. Black veins raced over her skin. She screamed, and then collapsed in on on herself.

For a moment she remained, a pile of ash, then even that was gone.

"Sorcery a level above any I imagine she possessed," he said with a glance at Grittel. "Most unpleasant."

As he stood, the same thing happened to the man he'd webbed.

A safeguard against capture, or a punishment for failure? It amounted to the same thing: a second and permanent death.

But who would do such a thing, and why? Sorcery that killed was far too direct for the Supernal Father... wasn't it?

The man Grittel had stabbed was still lying there, choking on his own blood. At first Venton thought Grittel was losing her touch, but then the man went rigid. No black veins this time—there was no need for death magic when the poor chap was already dead.

But he still went the way of all who died a second time: his corpse crumbled into ashes and dust, and his essence leeched away into the Void, lost forever.

Venton picked up the metal box, the lid still securely closed. It had suffered a dent in the fall, but no real harm done.

Grittel looked up at him with her big brown eyes.

"Don't worry, Gritty," Venton said. "I'll be all right."

But would he?

It was perplexing. Nothing like this had happened before, and he'd been an unhappy resident of the Supernal Realm for more than a hundred Aosian years.

"Come on," he said, and together they moved deeper into the fog. "I should get you home."

2

"So, this is what it's like being dead," the Nameless Dwarf said. "I think I'm going to like it."

The sea breeze ruffled his hair and beard. Above, the sky was all the colors of a rainbow, and it was reflected in the waves that caressed the keel of the ship as it glided ghost-like toward the horizon. There was no tang of brine, no squawking of seabirds. Just the waves and the breeze, and a pleasant chill.

Beside him, Cordy looked radiant, her hair golden, her dress the blue of the sky on Aosia. The wind didn't seem to touch her as it did him—or maybe he didn't notice it, on account of his adoring gaze.

Nameless felt underdressed in his brown woolen shirt, goatskin britches, and sturdy leather boots. Where the clothes had come from, he had no idea. He was just thankful he wasn't wearing armor. After all these years, he was done with fighting.

"We should talk," Cordy said. "While we still can."

"While we still can? Lassie, we have all the time in the world."

"We're no longer in the world."

Paxy was watching them from her bench beneath the gunwale. Paxy, who had for so long been ensouled in the Axe of the Dwarf Lords, now every bit as much a dwarf as he and Cordy and the old man piloting the ship. She wore a black cloak over a chainmail hauberk and leather britches—perhaps what she used to wear before she'd been sent to Aosia as an axe. And she looked good for a lassie who was thousands of years old. Despite her silver hair, she could have passed for a hundred and fifty.

The old dwarf stood at the helm, gaze fixed beyond the prow. His white cloak wasn't ruffled by the wind, giving the impression he wasn't quite there, wasn't quite real. That made Nameless look at Cordy again, then at Paxy. Was he the only one affected by the breeze?

"What's up, laddie?" he asked the old dwarf. "You look as though the Sag-Urda monster might burst from the water at any moment and swallow the ship whole."

The old dwarf spared him the merest glance. "Never did clap eyes on that beastie," he said. "I always suspected the stories were made up."

"Some of them were," Nameless said. "But I believed them when I was drinking, same as I did Rabnar the Red's tales of tentacled things from the deep, and flying gibunas."

"Never saw a flying gibuna either," the old dwarf said.

"Then it's a sorry life you must have lived."

"Oh, but it was. I almost saw the end of everything."

"You're not alone there," Nameless said. "I had a hand in stopping the Mad Sorcerer from unweaving all the worlds."

"As did I."

"You did? That's funny, because I don't remember you being there."

"The first time."

"Oh." Nameless swallowed as realization sunk in. To Cordy, he whispered, "Is that…?"

"Maldark the Fallen," she whispered back.

"Legend," Nameless said. "Seems rather sullen. Perhaps the afterlife isn't all its cracked up to be."

Cordy glanced at Paxy before she let out a sigh.

"It's been so long, Nameless."

"Aye, lassie. Two-hundred years."

"I imagined you older." Cordy touched his cheek with her fingertips.

"I was older." But he didn't feel it. His joints no longer ached, and his muscles were firm and full. "How's the beard? Last time I looked, it was mostly grey."

"Not now. It's just as I remember it."

"Must be the sea air."

She smiled, but it looked forced to Nameless. The smile of a stranger he once knew.

"Is everything all right, Cordy?"

"Why wouldn't it be?" She turned her face away, like she used to when she was mad with him.

"Something I've done?" Other than kill her with an axe, that is. But that was a long time ago, and he'd had no choice, considering what she'd become. What the Lich Lord, Otto Blightey, had done to her.

Cordy gripped the gunwale and gazed out to sea. She flinched when he held her shoulders and turned her back to face him.

"Lassie, you're crying."

"No, I'm not." She wiped her eyes with the sleeve of her dress. "I'm so happy to see you again, after…"

"After I died? Aye, and I'm happy to see you too, lassie. But you don't look happy. Perhaps I should ask Maldark to turn the ship around and take me back to Aosia."

"There's nothing left of you there," Cordy said, "save ashes and bones."

"So, they had a pyre for me, then. I always did love a good pyre."

"They forgave you, Nameless. In the end, I think they revered you. They put us together in the same crypt."

"Yes, well, now we're together here."

Cordy shared a look with Paxy.

"What is it?" Nameless said. "I thought you two didn't get on."

"Paxy was sent from Gabala by Witandos the One-Eye, remember."

"Millennia ago, I know. And now she's going back, so why the long face?"

"Me or Paxy?" Cordy said.

"Both of you."

"Just be prepared, my Exalted," Paxy said. "The Supernal Realm is not all gold and glory."

"Are you saying the Beer Halls of Plenty are as made up as the Sag-Urda monster?"

"No, there are beer halls," Paxy said. "Only...."

"Only what? Don't tell me they only serve Ironbelly's!"

"There are still things to be done," Cordy said. "Every thought, every word, every deed we sow in life has a direct consequence in the Supernal Realm."

"And?"

Cordy's eyes glistened with new tears as she placed a hand either side of his face and made him look at her.

"The things you did at the ravine... the massacres at Arx Gravis...."

"You said I was forgiven!"

"And you were. But so many lives taken, Nameless... There are still things you must do. Consequences you must face. And—"

Nameless turned away from Cordy.

"I suppose you're in on this, too, are you?"

Maldark said nothing, merely turned the wheel and kept his gaze straight ahead, where the mist shimmered with bronze and gold and silver.

Nameless could make out the shapes of towers and walls and minarets. There were ships moored at wharves in a harbor.

"It looks no different to Aosia," he said, "save for the sparkles."

When Cordy didn't respond, he turned around. She was gone. So were Paxy and Maldark. It was just Nameless now, alone on the ship as it steered itself into a berth between two galleons.

A man on the jetty—a human, not a dwarf—cast a rope over the gunwale. Mutton-chop whiskers, a really bad combover, and a brocaded red jacket.

As the grapnel bit into the wood, the man hauled the ship toward a mooring post and started to tie the rope off around a cleat.

"Welcome, Nameless," he said in a gruff voice, and Nameless cursed himself for a shogger for not recognizing him sooner.

"Grenic? Gods of Arnoch, laddie, Maldark must have brought me to the wrong place! Send me back, I'm not a shogging Wayist!"

3

Grenic stood to attention and gave a stiff salute. Nothing much had changed about the dragoon, save that he appeared a few years younger and a little less fluffy around the waist. Still had the muttonchops and the bad hair, the purplish nose and the bow legs—from too much horse riding, no doubt, for you had to be a master horseman to be a dragoon, if Grenic was to be believed. And Nameless was always inclined to believe Grenic, a man who was as enthusiastic about his Wayist religion as he was about fighting.

"I didn't expect you to be the one to greet me, laddie," Nameless said.

"Thought it would be your family, wot?" Grenic said. "Your friends?"

"Don't take it the wrong way. I do consider you a friend."

They had gone together on the three quests that were supposed to free Nameless from the curse of the black axe. Grenic had never exactly been a barrel of laughs, but he knew how to use a saber, and he'd shown courage enough to make a dwarf proud. The man had stood toe to toe with the Lich Lord. After that….

"This is hard for me, laddie. I saw you killed by the Daeg."

"Feels like only yesterday," Grenic said. He grimaced as his hand went to his ribs, where the ape-god who slept at the heart of Aosia had crushed them in his massive fist.

"You look younger," Nameless said. "And leaner."

Grenic sucked in his stomach and puffed out his chest, at the same time tweaking the ends of his mustache. "Back to my prime. I'd like to see how the ruddy Daeg would fare against this chap, wot! You, though… I always wondered what manner of face was hidden beneath that great helm."

"A hairy one, laddie, that's what."

"I met your wife," Grenic said, gesturing for Nameless to follow him along the jetty to the wharves. "Said you suffered something terrible after she died, curse that ruddy Blightey. But you bounced back, right? Gave a good account of yourself, too, at the end."

"Bounced isn't the word I'd have chosen," Nameless said. "But I'll not disagree with you about the latter. It was a rare battle, and I'm proud of what Paxy and I did to end it. By the way, where are Paxy and the others? There were four of us in that ship before it docked."

Grenic stopped on the embankment and looked back toward the jetty. The ship was gone.

"Maldark views it as his penance to ferry all the dwarven dead here," Grenic said, "so his ship's never moored for long."

"But he vanished when we were still coming in. Cordy and Paxy, too."

Grenic chewed one end of his mustache as he considered. "The way it's been explained to me, there are as many realities here as there are people. The dead see what they expect to see but—"

"But ultimately we're alone?" Nameless began to panic. That wasn't the afterlife he'd been expecting—drinking for all eternity in the company of old friends. He'd already spent too much time alone: two centuries at the bottom of a fissure in the Southern Crags.

"Not ultimately," Grenic said, turning away and leading Nameless toward a paved street between warehouses. "But like so many of us, you've not fully arrived yet."

"What's that supposed to mean?"

"All of us, save the most holy luminaries, have a debt to repay."

"The consequences of our actions on Aosia," Nameless said. "Cordy said something about that."

"I don't pretend to understand it," Grenic said, "but Witandos says penance is necessary, if we are to ascend."

"Ascend where?"

"Ah, well, that's the thing. It all depends what you're looking for."

They entered a street lined with wooden buildings, many of them with open fronts displaying a bewildering selection of fish and crustaceans on trestle tables. Oddly, there was no stink.

"And you're still doing penance," Nameless said, "two centuries after you died?" How long would it take for his own atonement?

"I am torn. As a Wayist, my heart is set on eternal rest in the Pleroma...."

"But?"

"The Way is hard," Grenic said. "More so here than on Aosia. Witandos tolerates our faith, but he doesn't exactly approve. And he offers enticements to those who would walk the path he sets before us. I dare say you'll start to notice how some haven't changed a jot since death, whereas others are younger, stronger, better looking."

Unconsciously he touched his hair and patted an errant strand back into place.

"Apathy or advancement: those are the two choices Witandos offers. An eternity of repeating the habits we developed in life, or the long, hard road to perfection. As for those who pursue the third alternative—the Way—Witandos says they are wasting their time. Some have the faith to press on regardless. I, however, struggle."

They entered a residential area where the townhouses were packed together in shambling terraces, and rats—yes, rats!—scampered about the gutters.

"People live here?" Nameless said.

"Disappointing, isn't it?" Grenic said. "The afterlife is, nevertheless, life, warts and all."

"But life as we know it...." Nameless said. "I thought it would be..."

"Grander? Cleaner? Purer? And so it will be, the more progress we make."

Nameless let out a world weary sigh—the last thing he had expected to do after death.

"Chin up, old man," Grenic said as they slipped down an alley and emerged from the far end at the foot of a grass-tufted escarpment that climbed in massive steps toward a long wooden building at the top. "There are people waiting to see you."

They followed a zigzagging pathway up the escarpment, stopping once or twice so that Grenic could catch his breath.

"Yes, we get tired here," the dragoon said as he mopped his brow. "We need sleep, and we need food and drink."

"I'll not quibble about the drink, laddie," Nameless said. "But will it taste of anything? Will I smell the hops?"

"In time," Grenic said. "Believe me, Nameless, it isn't as bad as it first seems. Our expectations are set too high. Once reality bites, things start to settle into place."

Nameless was suddenly outside the building at the top—a vast hall constructed from entire tree trunks stripped of their bark and branches. It had a thatched roof and stone chimneys, from which smoke plumed.

"I'm trying not to get my hopes up," Nameless said, "but it looks like the Feasting Hall of Witandos."

He turned to Grenic for an answer, but the dragoon was no longer there.

"And so it is. To you."

The voice was familiar. A man came into focus, seated on a bench outside the hall. A tall man with big ears. He was robed in white, and peering at Nameless over the top of wire frame spectacles he probably no longer needed. For when Nameless had last seen him, he had been an old man, but now he can't have been more than twenty.

Nameless shook his head and started to laugh. "Brother Laranos!

I'm surprised you can still sit, laddie, after what the Lich Lord did to you."

"Best not to remind me of that," Laranos said, face puckered with remembered pain as he stood and gestured toward the open door.

"Shall we?"

4

"Oh!" Nameless exclaimed as he followed Laranos through the open door into the hall. "Oh, my shogging.... Yes!"

He'd not heard it from outside—which seemed odd—but he was hit in the guts by the booming downbeats of a tuba. And there were horns, clarinets, flutes, and trombones. The music came from a band of dwarves decked out in velvet jackets and conical hats, their beards braided with ribbons.

Nameless had only seen such instruments in the dust-covered storerooms beneath Arnoch. No one had been able to get a note out of any of them, save for a raspy farting sound. Even the dwarf lords, after they returned from Thanatos, had forgotten how to play them. There had been no time for music on that miserable death world.

But these dwarf musicians stamped their feet and gyred their hips in time as they played melodies and harmonies that cried out for bawdy lyrics and a flagon of ale.

Beer was flowing, tapped from kegs set on oaken tables around the room, where dwarves feasted on haunches of lamb, rinds of pork, and obscenely large turkey drummers. Tankards clashed, amid the hubbub of chatter and peals of laughter. Nameless's knees grew weak. He wanted to cry.

Fights broke out everywhere, friendly fights with punches in the face and headbutts that broke noses. Winners picked losers up from the floor and fetched them beer. All goodnatured, just as it was meant to be.

The hall was huge, much larger even than it had appeared from the outside. Benches and tables as far as the eye could see, and pipe smoke gathered like clouds beneath the high vaulted ceiling. Wide hearths lined the walls, the burning logs within giving off a hearty blaze.

Nameless wiped a tear from his eye and looked around for someone he might recognize. He wasn't aware he was tapping his foot and swaying to the music till Laranos leaned down to look him in the eye, face etched with concern.

"Are you all right?" the priest asked.

"Never better! Oh, you're in for a rare treat! A dwarven feasting hall! Let's grab a beer."

"Beer? Feasting hall? Oh, of course," Laranos said. "It's what you expect to see. My experience of the Supernal Realm is quite different to yours."

"It is?"

"This is a Wayist temple to me, with fluted pillars and a marble floor. There are priests at rest, contemplating the labyrinth patterns on the walls, or untangling the knots of their prayer cords. And the incense…"

"It's pipe smoke!"

But Nameless could see them now: hundreds of white-robed priests with soppy looks on their clean-shaven faces as they prayed and conversed and sang nauseating hymns. But he could still see the dwarves too, and when he focused on them, the *boom-pah* music drowned out the pious chants, and the priests grew misty like ghosts, very much in the background.

"I'd forgotten how confusing it can be at first," Laranos said. "Because I spend the majority of my time with other Wayists, I seldom have to share realities."

"Is that what this is: a shared reality?"

"Our memories and dreams from life are made manifest to us, and to those we draw close to. You start to see as I see, and I see as you."

"Well, remind me not to hang out with a goat-shagger," Nameless said. "Now, laddie, I've no coins on me, so I have to ask: could you buy me a drink?"

"Beer's free," a ruddy-faced dwarf said, handing them each a flagon. "There's no money here, and no tokens either."

"Obliged to you," Nameless said.

Laranos leaned in to whisper. "There might not be tokens and money, but privileges must be earned."

"Oh aye?"

"This is no static paradise, Nameless. We are called to pass from glory to glory."

"Are we now?" Nameless took a sip of beer. "Tasteless!" he said. "Worse than Ironbelly's."

"The flavor will improve as you progress in glory," Laranos explained.

"And how do I do that, in battle?"

"You work out your penance."

"Penance again."

"I know," Laranos said with a sigh. "It's a Supernal thing. To us it sounds like punishment, but to Witandos its all about balance, and about staking his claim on essence."

"Essence?"

"Ours. Everything that constitutes who and what we are. Witandos desires to purify us, whatever that means. The goal, he says, is for us to perfect our nature, however long it takes."

"Why?"

"I've often thought about that," Laranos said, "and there are several possible answers."

"None of them good?"

"Who am I to judge? I have benefited from playing by Witandos's rules, as I'm sure you can see, but my heart remains set on a better place."

"The Pleroma of the Way. Grenic said the same."

"And you?" Laranos asked. "What do you say?"

"I say there's no better place than where we are right now," Nameless said, gesturing with his tankard to take in the hall. "And if I need to jump through hoops to get beer that actually tastes like beer, I can see myself doing a wee bit of penance."

Laranos nodded, then sipped his beer. "I felt the same way when I first arrived here. And I remember how relieved I was to end up anywhere at all." He coughed to clear his throat. "My faith.... When Blightey...."

"It started to waver?"

"I feared there was nothing waiting for me after death. Or, if there was...."

"An eternity of impalement. Aye, Blightey's a scut-sucking son of a shogger, anyway you look at it."

"All in the past now," Laranos said.

"Let's hope so. Another beer, laddie?"

Laranos drained his tankard and stood. "We probably shouldn't keep our host waiting any longer."

Nameless followed the priest toward the far end of the hall, acknowledging a few dwarves he recognized from that last great battle outside Jeridium.

He jumped as a hand clamped down on his shoulder, then spun around, fist raised.

It was a young dwarf, robed in white.

"You don't recognize me, do you?" the dwarf said.

Nameless squinted at him. "The voice sounds familiar...."

Toe hair and beard, grey eyes—almost blue. He knew that face... only, before, the hair had been falling out in clumps, the beard turning grey. Last time he'd seen that head, he realized with a sickening feeling, it had been on a spike.

"Thumil?"

Nameless looked away, not knowing what to do with his eyes. How could you look at your old best friend after chopping off his head? After killing his daughter—albeit accidentally—and then marrying his wife?

"The Way be with you," Laranos said, raising a hand in farewell as he faded into the background.

"This must be hard for you," Thumil said.

"Oh no, laddie," Nameless said, turning on him. "I don't want your Wayist forgiveness. I want you to hit me. Right here." He pointed to his mouth. "Anywhere you like. Better still, fetch an axe. Do to me what I did to you."

"Do you have any idea how far back revenge would set me?" Thumil said. He was smiling. "I came here as a friend. And because Cordy asked me."

Nameless felt a pang of jealousy. "Cordy asked you?"

"It's not what you think."

"You don't know what I think," Nameless said. Instantly, he regretted his tone. "I'm sorry, laddie. It's you who should be angry, not me."

Thumil remained unflustered, as in control in death as he'd been in life.

"Where is Cordy?" Nameless asked. "Why did she leave me on the boat? Why did she send you and not come herself?"

Thumil drew in a long breath. "She no longer comes here."

"I can understand that. Have you tried the beer? What, laddie? What's wrong?"

"Cordy asked me to let you know that she will wait for you."

"Wait where? For how long? Thumil, what's this all about?"

Thumil put a hand on Nameless's shoulder, leaned in close to whisper. "The Supernal Realm is part of the journey, not the end."

"Spoken like a true Wayist," Nameless said. "Grenic, Laranos, and now you. It's starting to feel like a conspiracy."

"Perhaps it is. A conspiracy of concern."

Thumil opened a door Nameless had not been aware of moments before, and gestured for him to go through.

5

The doorway pitched, and Nameless plummeted across the threshold. His guts flew into his mouth as silver light blazed across his vision.

"Thumil!" he cried out. "What's happening?"

The stench of rot hit him. A great swell of bodies jostled him this way and that as they swept him along in the middle of a stampede.

Thumil was gone.

All around him creatures snarled and howled, things that might have once been men and women, might once have been dwarves. Some were armored, others were naked with livid flesh. Their eyes were crazed and empty, their beards—they all had them, men, women, and children—spattered with blood.

Nameless was carried by the raging tide of horror toward a tower. Demon-dwarves scaled the walls. Glass shattered as they broke in through the windows. The main door hung from its hinges, and the creatures poured inside, snarling and rending.

There were screams on top of screams. Blood misted in the air inside the tower. Screams gave way to howls of triumph as the livid creatures carried a massive body outside—a woman three times the height of a dwarf, though dwarvish in her proportions, her platinum hair drenched in gore, from where her skull had been crushed. Blood soaked the ground from a hundred cuts and bites. A faint glow radiated from her lacerated skin—warm and golden, yet swiftly fading to nothing.

The temperature dropped.

Nameless now stood in a cavern of coal. Frigid mist rose from the ground. Every breath he took constricted his airways and froze his lungs. His teeth chattered, and his knees knocked together. It took all his strength, all his willpower, to remain on his feet.

A vast form resolved out of the gloom: a giant encased in ice, woven from shadow, yet dense, the weight of its presence a relentless tug that seemed to draw all the light to itself and destroy it.

Nameless had seen this very vision before—in a dream a long time ago. He knew, if he looked up, there would be eyes of violet glaring out from the tomb of ice. Eyes that knew him, despised him, mocked him.

Nameless kept his head bowed. He felt tiny, an ant to be crushed. He was worthless, a butcher. Beyond redemption.

A door clicked shut behind him, and the world lurched.

Nameless teetered, throwing his arms out for balance. A room spun around him then settled into place.

"Welcome," a deep voice said.

A single miner's lantern suspended from a ceiling joist gave off a wavering glow. Beneath it, a gigantic figure sat on a wooden throne strewn with furs. The length of his thickly muscled arms, the relative shortness of his legs, marked him as a dwarf, albeit one several times the height of a human. He was as broad as he was tall, his great bulk swamping the chair. A beard of spun gold flowed into his lap, where his hands rested either side of an enormous flagon.

Nameless dropped to one knee—he was compelled to do so. He dipped his head, but not before he glimpsed a scarred and wizened face with one rheumy eye, the other covered by a rusty iron patch.

"Supernal Father?" Nameless muttered into his beard. "Witandos?"

"To you I am."

There was a melancholy edge to the voice, a spell-like quality that plunged Nameless into one of his black-dog moods.

"It is the weight of unpaid penance you feel," the god said.

"Haven't I done enough?"

"Saving the survivors of Arx Gravis from the Lich Lord?" Witandos said. "A monster you provoked."

"Not by choice!" Nameless said. He'd gone to Verusia in his quest to destroy the black axe. That had been the start of Otto Blightey's vendetta against the dwarves.

"And what about when Arnoch was attacked by a five-headed dragon?" Nameless asked. "For my help that time, they made me king." If that wasn't a sign they'd forgiven him, then what was?

"Yes, and then you returned from two hundred years of mourning your wife, in the roots of the Southern Crags, to save the dwarves again. All this I am aware of. But can it ever make up for the thousands you killed?"

The dwarves had come as far as they ever could towards forgiving Nameless, but despite all he'd done to set things right, he had never been able to forgive himself. He'd learned to live with the guilt, even discovered how to laugh again, to drink with friends, and to raise his voice in song.

"I do not blame you for Arx Gravis," Witandos said, the weight of his presence growing heavier with each word he spoke. "But your deeds under the influence of the black axe have reaped dire consequences for us here, and now is the time for you to fix them."

"What consequences?"

"What you saw was just a glimpse."

"The horde of... what were those things?"

"They were once dwarves. The victims of your slaughter. They are demons now."

"My... my victims? No, they've suffered enough. They should be in the feasting hall, drinking and singing bawdy songs forever. Wait! It can't be true. If these demons are my victims, what about Thumil? I just saw him, younger than when he was alive, but still a dwarf."

"Thumil is protected." There was bitterness in Witandos's tone.

"Protected how?"

"It need not concern you."

"And the giant woman? Why would these demons want to kill her?"

Witandos hesitated before he answered, as if he couldn't decide how much to say. When he did speak, Nameless had the sense some important detail had been left out.

"It wasn't demons that killed her. They lack the power."

"Then who?"

"No more questions. For everything I tell you, everything I do, there will be a countermove."

"A counter—?"

"No more now!"

Witandos leaned forward in his chair, his one eye shining like a silver sun, and this time Nameless couldn't look away.

Light flared between them, and within its corona there appeared a cube fashioned from shadows.

It looked like a die without numbers, and Nameless almost said as much, then remembered to hold his tongue.

"I call it a phylactery," Witandos said. "Its purpose is to contain the essence of a living being and to bring them safely home through the Void."

"That's possible?" Nameless quickly clamped a hand over his mouth.

"It was fashioned," Witandos said, "to bring back my daughter, Etala."

According to the old stories, Mananoc had been driven from the Supernal Realm by the Archon and Etala, his brother and sister. The three had fallen through the Void and could never return. The Archon was dead, courtesy of Shadrak the Unseen, and Mananoc remained trapped in the Abyss. But Etala... Witandos wanted to bring her home?

"The phylactery," Witandos said, "has been stolen. Your penance is to return it."

"And if I do this, I'm done?"

"Success here will bring you close, but there is still one more thing I would ask of you."

"Ask?"

"Demand, then. If you are to progress in the afterlife beyond where you currently stand, there is more you must do. Retrieve the phylactery, and your final penance will be revealed to you."

"So, you want to pit me against thousands of dwarves and something so powerful it killed a Supernal?"

"You will not be alone," Witandos said. "You must enlist aid." He raised a finger to forestall Nameless's question. "The nature of that aid, you must decide for yourself."

"Do you have any idea where the phylactery might be, who could have taken it?"

"I can offer no assistance."

"Because you can't take direct action, right? So, where do I start?"

"Where would you normally start?"

"In a tavern, among dwarves."

Witandos allowed himself a chuckle.

"Just don't expect too much of them. A quest like this will advance a soul through glory, but the risks are extreme. Die here—the second death—and there is no coming back. It has proven something of a disappointment to me, that the majority of souls in this realm are afraid of losing what they have. They would sooner languish in apathy, than risk everything in order to ascend."

"I thought the afterlife was for heroes, not cowards," Nameless said.

"The best parts of it are. Do well in this task, and the one after that..."

"And I can drink beer forever?"

"Perhaps one day you will rise to become a Supernal."

Nameless didn't know how he felt about that. Probably not as excited as he was supposed to feel.

"I'm sure Thumil will achieve that before me," he said. "That's the sort of dwarf you want ascending to the heights."

"For Thumil that can never be."

"Because he's a Wayist?"

"Because, like most of your race, he lacks a vital quality."

"Oh, and what's that, then?"

"What is it that sets you apart from most other dwarves?"

"My good looks?"

Witandos's eye narrowed.

"Chiseled abs?"

He knew he was playing with fire, but he couldn't help himself. He flexed his arm to display his biceps. "These?"

"Do not mock me."

"You must be referring to my mother, then," Nameless said. "And the Exalted blood she passed to me. Where is my mother, by the way? And my pa? Yalla and Droom, their names are, or don't I need to tell you that?"

"You will see them soon enough."

"Ah, the carrot to go with the stick, eh?"

"But you are right," Witandos said. "Your mother's blood is what makes you special. Something I added to a very few among your race, a check on the schemes of Mananoc. Here, we call it the blood of the Supernals."

Nameless's mouth hung open as his brain tried to catch up. He looked back at Witandos.

"Did the Archon know? Your son? The one who tried to kill me!"

Witandos made a flicking motion with his finger, and Nameless flew backwards. A brief moment of disorientation, and he was back outside the door he'd entered by.

"Wait! I was going to ask you about Cordy!"

Nameless raised his fist, intending to pound on the door. He hesitated while he counted gibunas jumping into giant tankards of ale—something every dwarf child was taught to do, if they had trouble getting off to sleep.

By the ninth gibuna, he was back in control, and he turned away from the door.

Where the feasting hall had been, there was now a temple with a marble floor, colonnades of fluted pillars, and a high, vaulted ceiling the color of the evening sky, dotted with thousands of stars. There were priest-types everywhere—not all of them Wayists. Clustered together in their own groups, he saw men and women, humans, dwarves, and pointy-eared folk he'd not set eyes on before. White robes, black, red and green. Knotted prayer cords, beads. Some people had leather boxes strapped to their foreheads. Each group was blurry and indistinct, where the spaces they occupied overlapped.

He felt queasy as he stepped away from the door and into the narthex of this impossibly vast temple with no walls to define it—at least no walls he could see.

The sick feeling passed as quickly as it had come, and the serenity of the temple was replaced with the feasting hall once more. The place was again humming with dwarves, drinking and eating, singing bawdy songs.

It was certainly tempting, to remain in the hall forever. But first he had a phylactery to find, and Witandos only knew what next after that.

He passed down the long line of tables. No one offered him a drink. No one met his eye. No one even seemed to notice him. He glanced around for Thumil, for anyone he knew, but all he got for his effort was the conviction that he didn't belong here, and that he wouldn't belong until he had completed his task.

He left the hall and found himself on a street flanked by two-story buildings of wattle-and-daub. Of the hill and the wooden hall, there was no sign. What kind of god would create such a place? And for what reason? Just to confuse people? It was confusing enough being dead and still feeling very much alive.

He saw the glimmer of the rainbow sea in the distance, and the masts of ships moored at the harbor. At least something hadn't altered while he'd been in the hall.

The Supernal Realm was starting to remind him of Cerreth, where the surroundings shifted and changed at the drop of a hat. It felt like Aranuin, the abode of the faen. It felt like the Abyss.

It was to be expected, he supposed. The realms were bound to be similar. They had all been created by Supernals.

It would have been easier with Cordy at his side, with Paxy, Thumil, all his friends of old. But whoever said penance would be easy?

Nameless walked along the street, nodding at passersby and taking comfort from the fact that they nodded right back. Most of them were dwarves, though there were humans dotted about among them. He thought it strange that there were shops here, restaurants, and market squares where traders hawked their wares. He passed among rows of houses, down alleyways and onto more shop-lined streets.

There seemed no end to the sprawl of the city—if that's indeed what it was; no end to the people who lived out a second, more permanent, life here.

He stopped walking to take a good look around. It didn't feel right, all these people, going about their daily business with no sense of urgency, as if they couldn't be bothered to improve their lot.

His eyes focused on the smoke pluming from a chimney, traveled down to the red-tiled roof, the walls of dressed granite, and finally to the wide open door.

He made a beeline for the building, heart skipping as he saw the painted sign outside: a bearded queen standing on her head—Tilba the Legless, patroness of insobriety.

6

It stank of sweat inside, and hops, and weedsticks, and pipe tobacco, and… piss. Just like the taverns back home in Arx Gravis!

Nameless stood in the doorway, a big toothy smile spreading across his face as a troupe of drummers on a raised stage started hammering out a quick, throbbing beat that made him tap his feet.

Strings came next: guitars, mandolins, fiddles, and harps. A fat dwarf took center stage and belted out lewd lyrics in a booming bass, while dance girls with colorful beads in their beards kicked their stumpy little legs high.

The drinkers closest to the door, all of them dwarves, raised their tankards in greeting.

"Laddies!" Nameless said. "Good health to you all."

"Cheers!" came the reply.

Tears stung his eyes—or it might have been the pipe smoke.

On his way to the bar, he walked between long tables that seated shog knows how many dwarves. And what a bar! It extended into the distance with no end in sight. Perfect height for leaning on when ordering a drink, and there were barstools, too, hundreds of them, as many occupied as not.

And it wasn't the only bar, either. There were bars everywhere he looked, and not a wall to be seen. It was a tavern without boundaries, a tavern that could hold as many dwarves as chose to come here.

There were blazing hearths and pigs roasting on spits. There were serving wenches, all chest and beard; warriors with weapons, miners, blacksmiths, rogues, wastrels, tinkers, scholars and scribes. He picked out the white robes of councilors, and even saw a few humans. Shog of all shogs, this was the father of all pubs, a tavern to spend your whole life in, or even your whole death.

"What are you having, darling?" a rosy-cheeked barmaid asked.

"Arnochian Ale."

"Coming right up."

They had it! They actually had Cordy's very own brew, the finest beer a dwarf could drink.

The barmaid plonked a tankard in front of him, and Nameless necked it in one. "Obliged, lassie. Another, if you please."

It didn't taste quite as he remembered it, but it was a shog sight better than the beer in the Feasting Hall. Did that mean he'd started his penance, simply by accepting Witandos's task?

"Oh, shog," he said, patting down his pockets. "I've nothing to pay for it with."

"On the house," the barmaid said. "Everything's on the house. Always."

"I think I'm going to like it here," he said as she handed him his refill and he sipped it more slowly than the first.

"That's what they all say. If you're anything like this lot, you'll never want to leave."

Wasn't that just the truth? He didn't. He could happily sit at the bar for all eternity, drinking the beer, listening to the music, chatting to everyone he knew.

But that was the thing. Where was everyone he knew? He didn't recognize a soul. Perhaps he wouldn't, until he'd fetched this shogging phylactery Witandos had gone and lost.

"Nameless Dwarf?"

He turned to the dwarf beside him at the bar, a wily looking shogger with knotted muscles and a beard in good need of a comb.

The dwarf wore a dented breastplate of iron, a moth-eaten cloak, and stained britches.

"Do I know you, laddie?"

"No, you don't know me, and I don't know you. But I've heard a lot about you. They said you was on the way here. Whole place has been buzzing about it all morning."

"You drink in the morning?"

"And why ever not? Stann's the name. My friends call me Shogwit." He took a swig from a bottle, then sighed and wiped his mouth. "Old Frufty's Chili Moonshine."

"You're shogging me!" Nameless said. "That stuff will rot your guts and addle your brains."

"Join us," Shogwit said, indicating a table with drinkers packed along both of its impossible lengths.

"Know anyone?" Shogwit said as they took their places on a bench.

"Afraid not," Nameless said. "Actually, I was just thinking…."

He trailed away. He hadn't recognized any of the other drinkers at the table, but suddenly he did. Several of them, in fact. Quite a few:

Muckman Brindy and Ming, who had died in the mines when the golem attacked. Both raised their tankards to him. Togal Grimwart, who liked to be known as Duck.

"No Kal?" Nameless asked.

Duck gave a pained expression and shook his head.

Of course there was no Kal. Kaldwyn Gray had remained behind on Thanatos, in the Forest of Lost Souls.

"So, you made it here at last," a shabby old dwarf said.

Old! He was still as old as when Nameless last saw him, maybe even older.

"Someone's not been doing his penance!" he said, leaning across the table to shake Rugbeard's hand.

"Why, this is great," Nameless said. "All of you here, drinking together."

It could have been perfect, if Cordy had been there, with Thumil

—the way the three of them had been before it all went wrong. And if Droom and Yalla and Lukar had been there too.

But if they had been, why would he ever strive for more? Witandos must have known that.

"I have to say, I like this tavern way better than the Feasting Hall of Witandos."

"That place!" Shogwit said. "Bunch of stuck-up glory-seekers. Think they're better than us. Always going somewhere, and never arriving. Well, we have arrived, and we ain't moving, eh, lads and lassies?"

"Aye!" Tankards were clashed against the tabletop.

Nameless caught sight of someone else he knew.

"Councilor Yuffie!"

Yuffie the Corrupt, as they called him behind his back, looked grey-faced and ancient, his robe threadbare and grimy, scarcely any white left in it.

"How did you avoid the Abyss, laddie, a bribe?"

A dwarf in black stood up from the table, and Nameless's good humor evaporated.

Coalheart, the dwarf's name was. A Svark from Arx Gravis. An opportunist and a toe-rag, who had colluded with Nameless's reign of terror.

Coalheart looked older even than Yuffie, though he had died a young man. His cheeks were sallow, the skin of his face taut and parchment thin, giving the impression of a fleshless skull.

"My Lord Corrector," Coalheart said.

"Sorry, laddie, you must have mistaken me for someone else."

"Like that, is it?" Coalheart said, then stalked away.

"I assume this means trouble?" Nameless said.

"You won't get any trouble here," Duck said. "Coalheart won't do anything. None of us ever do."

"Remember how the Council of Twelve used to be?" Rugbeard said. Yuffie looked up at that, as if he missed those days—or, more likely, the backhanders he received. "Well, that's us now. Frozen. Scared to act, in case we lose what little we have left."

"The dead who can't be arsed with rising through the degrees of glory stay put right here," Shogwit said. "We neither go up nor down, and that's the way we like it."

"And you're all right with that: set in your ways, nothing ever changing, for all eternity?"

"Reckon we are," Duck said, taking a long pull on his drink.

Grunts of agreement sounded up and down the table, though to be honest, no one looked exactly happy about it, and there was a definite chilling of the atmosphere.

"Well," Nameless said, rising, "I suppose that means none of you would be interested in coming on a wee adventure with me?"

"Adventure?" Muckman sounded more horrified than when the golem crushed the life out of him.

"More of a quest, actually. Witandos has asked me to retrieve something that was stolen."

"He gave you a choice?" Rugbeard asked.

"Not exactly. But he did say it would account for the bulk of my penance."

"No disrespect," Shogwit said, "but what good's working out penance if you end up dead again—permanently this time? No thanks, sonny. We've all we need right here. You don't want to be worrying about all those levels of glory and shite like that. Shog Witandos, and you can tell him I said that. See if I care. Stay here with us. Go on, I'll introduce you to the lads you don't know."

He turned to the dwarf on his right—a young fellow so big he almost didn't fit the description of a dwarf. He had a thick, unruly beard, a freckly face, and a gormless grin.

"This is Purg."

"Who's Purg?" the big dwarf said.

"You are, idiot. Reckon he must've suffered a blow to the head," Shogwit said. "Some big battle long ago, no doubt. Left him thick as two short planks, an affliction that seems to have followed him here, though shog alone knows why."

"Not a very dwarvish name: Purg," Nameless said.

"Some scutting human gave it him," Shogwit said. "Took Purg in and made him part of his crew, the way I understood it."

"Who was that, then?" Nameless asked.

"No one you've heard of. Moving on: this is Master Munzark, Pikwin Sump, Rorsk Ironbelly..."

"Not *the* Rorsk Ironbelly, founder of Ironbelly's brewery?"

"Aye, that's me, matey."

"Forgive me if I don't clash tankards with you," Nameless said. "I'd never hear the last of it."

Purg was frowning at Nameless, then his eyes lit up, as if he'd just thought of something—which seemed unlikely.

"Purg go."

"Go where, laddie?"

"On quest."

"Do us a shogging favor, Purg," Shogwit said. "You don't even know what a quest is."

"Purg know."

"Bollocks, you do!"

"Purg know!" His eyes had turned bloodshot, and the veins on his neck stood out in ridges.

"Laddies, laddies," Nameless said. "Forget I ever mentioned a quest." He was going to have to look for help somewhere else. He upended his flagon and downed the contents in one.

Purg stood and did the same, then banged his flagon on the table: a challenge.

"You don't want to be having a drinking contest with me, laddie," Nameless said.

"Do."

"Some other time, maybe. I've a quest to get on with."

"Chicken," Purg said.

Shogwit slapped himself on the forehead and rolled his eyes.

The rest of the dwarves at the table cheered, goading Purg on.

"Chicken, now, is it, laddie?"

Purg flapped his arms and made clucking sounds.

"Bar wench," Nameless called out. "Arnochian Ale for me and my friend here. Line them up!"

∼

When Nameless came to, Purg was still drinking.

The rest of the dwarves had gone.

"Something I said?"

Nameless's head pounded and he wanted to be sick. Some afterlife this was turning out to be.

"They went to another table," Purg said. "Called Purg stupid. Said you stupid too."

"Laddie, I have to go."

The big dwarf had a fresh tankard halfway to his lips. "Purg win?"

"Yes, Purg, you won. Now, if you'll excuse me, I have to find a sorcerer."

"What's that, then?"

"A wizard."

"Purg know a wizard."

"Yes, I'm sure you do."

"Cleverest wizard who ever lived. Come with Purg. You see."

7

Purg led Nameless out of the tavern through a side door that hadn't been there before. At least, Nameless thought it hadn't. But neither had there been any walls. One minute, the tavern had been boundless, extending into infinite space, the next, it had been a cozy little pub. Maybe that's the way Purg saw it.

He followed the big dwarf down a long, winding lane flanked by hedgerows and lit by glowstones atop iron posts.

"Where did you live on Aosia?" Nameless asked, panting with the effort of matching Purg's pace. The lighting reminded him of Arx Gravis, and the hedgerows evoked the Sward, where his family had lived for centuries.

"Can't remember," Purg said, without slowing down.

"What do you remember?"

Purg stopped and frowned. Tugged his beard. Frowned again. "Nothing much."

"But you do remember where we're going?"

"Where's that, then?" Purg said, but then he clapped Nameless on the shoulder with a big, meaty hand. "Hah, Purg fool you!"

"You did there, laddie, and after you drank me under the table too. I'm starting to take a dislike to you."

Purg's face dropped, and his eyes glistened.

"Just joshing!" Nameless said, returning Purg's shoulder slap with one of his own.

Purg stared blankly at him for the longest time, then suddenly burst into laughter. "Purg like you, silly dwarf. Purg's family like you, too."

"You have family here?" It was all right for some! Witandos might have been top dog in the Supernal Realm, but he had a mean streak a mile wide, keeping Nameless from his wife, his brother, his ma and pa. It was easy to see where Mananoc got it from.

They walked through pasture where a flock of sheep grazed. A startled rabbit hopped from their path as they entered in among trees —oak, ash, rowan, and yew. Sunlight splashed the leaves and dappled the ground.

More and more it reminded Nameless of the Sward, or the imaginary landscapes he'd dreamed up as a child when his pa read him stories. He spotted a doe watching them from behind a fallen trunk, a fawn teetering on its birth legs beside her. A flash of white drew his eye toward thicker brush some way off: a stag with huge antlers, pink eyes tracking them as they passed.

Purg seemed oblivious, or perhaps he was just used to seeing all this idyllic beauty.

They crossed a stone bridge over a brook and followed the forest path down into a valley. The hillsides were striped with yellow and mauve crops, and the valley opened onto grassland splashed red with strawberries. There were mushrooms and toadstools everywhere, gilled and spotted, scarlet, white, purple, pink and blue. They passed among vegetable patches overrun with ducks pecking for slugs. Fruit trees in blossom ringed a neatly partitioned herb garden, beyond which Nameless could see grape vines, beehives, a crop of what looked like tobacco.

"Are they hops?" Nameless asked, pointing out the looming bines, green and full-grown, ripe for harvesting.

"Purg pick hops and put them in barrow."

"You make beer?"

"Purg not make. Purg drink."

"I'm with you there, laddie. And all this is part of the Supernal Realm? This is your reality?"

"Purg don't know what you mean."

The big dwarf stooped to pick up something from the ground: a white paper bag. He brought it to his nose then grinned. "Chocolate truffles!"

Before Nameless could even take a look, Purg upended the bag into his mouth and chewed greedily.

"You have truffles here? In paper bags?"

Purg shook his head, cheeks big as a hamster's, brown drool trickling into his beard. He grunted something that might have been, "Not usually."

They entered a hedge maze taller than both of them, and Nameless trusted Purg to get them to the other side, which he did with surprising ease. As they exited the maze, Nameless could smell woodsmoke, then he saw a one-story house in the shape of an L, with a thatched roof and a pluming chimney.

Purg started towards it along a winding gravel path, but Nameless put a restraining hand on his shoulder.

"Eh?" Purg said.

Nameless pointed at the ground to the right of the path, where the grass has had been trampled, and huge hoof-prints were pressed into the mud. Cloven hooves.

"You have overgrown cattle here?"

"No."

"Monster pigs?"

"No monsters here."

Purg's massive hands bunched into fists, and his entire demeanor changed. Gone was the affable idiot. In his place, something that reminded Nameless of the battle goats they bred at Arnoch: muscled, ill-tempered, and extremely dangerous.

Like a billy-battler staking out its territory with stomping and pissing, Purg strode toward the lone tree that overlooked the house—a massive yew with iron struts supporting its enormous limbs.

And then Nameless saw him, beneath the tree, back to them: a hulking man, tall even for a human, and wider than a heavily muscled dwarf. He wore a dark tunic, split around the arms, and only half covering his muscular arse. There was something about his head: broad and covered with shaggy hair....

Were those horns?

The man must have heard Purg closing in, because he started to turn, but then a woman's voice off to the right startled him.

"Oi, you, whoever you are, get off my bleedin' mushrooms!"

A woman came barreling out of the trees, face red with fury. Middle-aged or older. On the short side for a human. Patched and tattered clothing, unkempt hair, festooned with different colored… mushrooms? She stopped in her tracks as the horned man bellowed at her and charged.

Purg charged too.

The big dwarf slammed into the man-beast and knocked him flying.

The monster got to his knees, and Purg punched him in the snout, spinning him back to the ground.

Nameless could see more clearly now: a barrel-chested man with knotted thews, cloven hooves, and the head of a bull.

Purg delivered an almighty thump to his face, and the bull-man squealed like a pig, then started to moan and complain as he clutched his nose.

"Oh, my nares! My olfactory protuberance!"

"Your what?" Purg said.

The bull-man turned blurry and started to shrink, until his tunic was an ankle-length robe on a much smaller man. A man with two slippered feet and a human head, craggy and wizened, long nose angled off to one side and pouring blood from where Purg had broken it. Grey hair, grey beard, and a snowfall of dandruff on his shoulders.

Chocolate truffles! Of course!

"Magwitch?" Nameless said as he approached. "Magwitch the Meddler? I hope this isn't the wizard you were going to take me to, Purg."

"Purg never see him before."

"You!" the wizard said to Nameless, hands protectively covering his nose as he sat up on the ground. "The perspirator of the massage at the ravine."

"The what?" Purg said.

"Them's not real words," the little woman said, hands on hips.

"If they are, he's not using them in the right way," Nameless said. "Wizards and academics are like that, but this one's the worst offender."

Magwitch's voice was muffled by his hands. "Shadrak the Unseen brought you to see me, but I cannot reconnoiter your name."

"Reconn-what?" Purg asked.

"It means nothing, laddie. It's not a real word."

"Wizard-speak?"

"Aye, wizard, academic, politician. They're all the same, bunch of pretentious shoggers. There's a reason you can't remember my name, laddie," Nameless told Magwitch. "But I'm more interested in what you're doing here."

"Purg want to know too."

"And so do I," the little woman said. "And who the shog is this, Purg?"

"My friends call me Nameless," Nameless said.

"So what should I call you, then?" the woman asked, before letting out a shrill laugh. "Don't mind me, love. Name's Mora."

"Ah, of course," Magwitch said. "The dwarf in abscess of nomencaricature!"

"Ignore him," Nameless said.

Purg made a circle of his finger beside his head.

"Like you can talk," Mora said. "So, what do we do with the scut?" She prodded Magwitch with her boot.

Before anyone could answer, a thunderclap split the air, carrying with it a man's softly spoken but waspish voice:

"For pity's sake, keep the noise down out there! I'm trying to work!"

8

Purg pressed a finger to his lips and crept on tiptoe towards the part of the house that formed the base of the "L", beckoning for Nameless to follow.

"Where do you think you're going?" Mora said, grabbing Magwitch by the earlobe before he could slink away.

Flames danced on the tips of Magwitch's fingers, and only Nameless seemed to see.

"I wouldn't, laddie. Remember what happened last time you tried that around me?" The sorcerer had tried to burn Shadrak, so Nameless had crushed his hand and snuffed out the flames.

Magwitch grimaced, then waggled his fingers to show the flames were gone.

"Good lad."

They entered a workshop with walls of uncut stone, exposed joists, and stained wooden beams that made the ceiling look lower than it already was—no bad thing to Nameless's mind. An arched opening led to the main part of the house.

A hawkish man with slicked-back hair sat erect on a stool in front of a lumpy, child-sized statue on a potter's wheel. He wore a patterned dressing gown over an ankle length black robe, like the kind worn by the sorcerers at Jeridium's Academy, only fancier, with ropey brocading and subtle embroidery. He smoked a pipe as he worked at the clay with a steel scraping tool. His back was to a game board with alternating black and white hexagons, atop which were brass figurines, many of them armored, a couple with crowns.

On the other side of the game board was a girl in a leather vest, black pants, and calfskin boots. At least, Nameless thought it was a girl. She had the head of a dog, and her tail patted the chair as it wagged. Her doe eyes were narrowed in concentration, her hand hovering over one of the figurines, as if she were afraid to commit to moving it.

"Uh, Venton…" Purg said.

"I'm working!" the sculptor snapped without looking round.

"Me thought we were playing Empires," the dog-girl said in a squeaking voice.

"Some of us can do two things at once," Venton said. "Have you had your turn yet?"

The dog-girl's hand moved to a different piece—that of a robed woman—and she placed it on an adjacent hexagon.

"Priestess to Goat-Rider four," she said, at the same time palming another piece.

"Goat-rider?" Nameless said. "You have dwarves in this game?"

Venton flashed a look at him, then got straight back to his sculpture. "Purg, you know the rule about bringing friends home. I'm too busy for entertaining."

"Your turn," the dog-girl said.

"Priestess to Goat-Rider Four, eh?" Venton said as he turned to face the board. "Then I'm sorry to inform you, but that is victory to…. Where's my Empress?"

The dog-girl threw up her hands. "It wasn't I!"

"It never is!"

"Did me win?"

"Yes, Grittel, you won."

With a squeal of delight, the dog-girl jumped out of her chair and proceeded to dance around the room.

Venton gave a quick appraisal of Nameless, then his eyes came to rest on Magwitch.

"What's he doing here?"

"Sneaking," Mora said.

"I do not sneak!" Magwitch said.

"Indeed," Venton said. "But you have been known to meddle, have you not? I assume you didn't come here to pick Purg's brains, so what is this about?"

"He was after my mushrooms," Mora said.

"Was not," Magwitch said. "How dare you recuse me!"

Nameless rolled his eyes.

"I tell you, he was pilfering my mushrooms," Mora said. "Disguised as a giant with a cow's head."

Magwitch puffed out his chest with pride. "A polymorphosized renditioning of the bovinian hominoidius husk."

"Words of one or two syllables only," Venton said. "Otherwise you make as much sense as Purg."

Purg looked up at mention of his name but didn't seem to have been following the conversation at all.

"And to what end did you change yourself into a cow-headed giant?" Venton asked.

"Bull," Nameless said, tapping the top of his head. "It had horns and pecs and a great big thingy."

Venton surveyed him for the longest time. "I'm sorry," he said, "but we've not been properly introduced."

"Purg try—"

"I am Venton Nap. I expect you've heard of me?"

"Can't say I have, laddie."

Purg sniggered. "No one ever has."

"Thank you for that, Purg," Venton said. "Your wit is rivaled only by your intellect."

"Eh?"

"And your name, sir dwarf?"

"Nameless."

"I see. Like that, is it? Another of Witandos's thugs come to punish me?"

Magwitch shifted nervously from foot to foot. Without him seeming to notice—though Nameless did—the dog-girl, Grittel, crept behind him. She stood stiller than Venton's sculpture, dagger gleaming in her fist.

"No, my name really is Nameless. As in a dwarf with no name."

"Such a sense of irony your parents must have.... Wait! It's you, isn't it!" Venton stood. "I hope I'm not expected to bow... Lower back pain from too much time sitting and reading."

"I was only king for a wee while," Nameless said.

"Yes, you abdicated. Something to do with your wife. Didn't the Lich Lord—?"

"My wife's here in Gabala," Nameless said. "She's quite all right now." Well, perhaps not all right. Something was wrong, he was sure of it.

"Good," Venton said. "Pleased to hear it. And what about you? Are you all right?" He sounded wary, as well he might, if he knew his history.

"Aye, laddie, I'm all right. But it's this skulking shogger you need to be concerned about. He was spying on your house, and not with good intentions, I'll wager."

"Yes, but in the guise of a bull-headed husk," Venton said. "Whatever was that about?"

"I connived that the aspect of the morphasosius would frighten you," Magwitch said.

"What's he say?" Purg said. "Them wizard words?"

"*Them,*" Venton said acerbically, "are made up words, when they are not merely malapropisms."

"My biographer used a lot of big words," Nameless said, "and knowing him, they were made up: *Aureate*, for shog's sake! *Argent!* And what the shog is *bedizened*?"

"The first is gold, the second silver, and the third, all that glitters," Venton said.

"Oh, so he wasn't making them up, then?" Nameless said. "Guess I really am an uneducated grunt, after all."

"Let me get this straight, Magwitch," Venton said. "You thought that, by polymorphing yourself into a bull-human hybrid, you would frighten me. But frighten me into what? Making a mistake that a half-rate wizard like you could capitalize on?"

"Frighten you into peeing your pants!" Purg said.

"Shut up, Purg."

"Sorry."

"He was after my mushrooms!" Mora said. She squared up to Magwitch, and the wizard took a step back, then yelped when the tip of the dog-girl's dagger touched him between the shoulder blades.

"It was Witandos!" Magwitch wailed, throwing himself to his knees and clasping his hands. "He made me do it!"

"Made you?" Venton asked.

"Told me to extinguigate you."

"Why would you do it, laddie?" Nameless asked. "You might be a shogger, but you're no killer."

"Said he'd eradish my penultinance. Said I'd burgeon in glorification, be young again and strapping."

"So," Venton said, "Witandos doesn't plan to give up. I am to be punished, wiped out, cast into the Void, after all I did for him!"

"You did something for Witandos?" Nameless said. "Something he couldn't do for himself?"

"Interesting, isn't it?" Venton said. "A god who is not quite all knowing, not quite all powerful."

"But he knows I'm here!" Magwitch said, rising to his feet.

"And will do nothing to help you," Venton said, reaching for a crystal-tipped staff in the corner by his chair. "Because he can't, not unless he wants Mananoc to take a direct action in proportion to his own."

The crystal atop Venton's staff glowed blue, and in response, the air around Magwitch grew cloudy and opaque, then resolved into grey bars of stone that hemmed him in.

"Feruveal polymorphosis!" Magwitch said. "Stolen knowledge!"

"But of course. Why do you think Witandos wants to kill me?"

"Laddies, laddies," Nameless said. "I'm not sure I want to get mixed up in this. Thanks for the recommendation, Purg, but it's probably best I find another sorcerer."

"Shroud of you to realize," Magwitch said. "You should have approached a reprehensible conjurateror, like me, not a fool who concocts a cage without a roof."

Magwitch began to rise into the air, then dropped on his arse when his head collided with the cage's iron roof, which hadn't been there a second ago.

"Just be thankful I didn't give it spikes," Venton said.

Magwitch shimmered as his body began to shrink. Venton gave a lazy wave of his hand, and the gaps between the bars closed, until Magwitch was trapped within a prison of solid stone and iron. His muffled cries came from inside.

"If I may, before you go," Venton said to Nameless, "why do you seek a wizard?"

"A task I must perform."

"Need I ask for whom?"

"Witandos."

"Of course. And in return, you will be absolved of your sins and granted an eternity of glory?"

"I was hoping for beer," Nameless said, and Purg guffawed, slapping him on the back so hard Nameless almost chucked his guts up.

"Dwarves!" Venton said. "Personally, I can think of nothing more tedious than sitting in a beer hall for all eternity. So, what does that solipsistic tyrant want you to do?"

"He wants me to find something for him."

"What kind of something?" Venton's eyes narrowed. "No, wait. Don't answer that yet. Purg, do be a good chap and carry our visitor to the edge of the smallholding. Not that visitor!" he said when Purg reached for Nameless. "The one encased in stone."

Purg hefted the stone prison to his shoulder as if it were nothing.

"Is it just an illusion?" Nameless asked.

"Illusion? Hah! No, it is quite real."

"How much does it weigh?"

"Oh, four-hundred pounds, give or take."

"Purg," Nameless said, "you and I will have to get together for some deadlifts."

"Eh?"

"A competition, laddie, to see who's stronger."

"Silly dwarf," Purg said. "Purg strongest there is."

And with that parting shot, he left, taking Magwitch with him.

"I'll bring you some mushroom tisane, Venton," Mora said. "For his nerves," she explained.

"Am I being irascible?" Venton asked.

"A little."

"Duly noted. I'll have it in the main house. Mushroom beer for Nameless, too, if you have any."

"Mushroom?"

"You'll love it," Mora said. The look on her face said he better had.

"And Grittel Gadfly..." Venton said.

The dog-girl sheathed her knife and smiled, as if butter wouldn't melt.

"Go play now. Nameless and I have to talk."

9

Nameless followed Venton down the single slate step into a lounge that positively glowed orange with warmth.

"What do you think?" the wizard asked.

"Small," Nameless said. "But I like small."

The low ceiling was divided by dark wooden beams. A threadbare rug of faded reds and browns covered the entire floor, save for the edges, where the oak boards beneath were exposed. At the center of the room, an iron stove with a cylindrical flue gave off a homey heat, flames licking over a log in the grate, spitting and crackling. A leather chair sat either side of the stove, beside each a low table with a pipe and a jar of tobacco.

There were books on knotty wooden shelves, paintings on the walls, a hatstand in one corner, with a long black coat and a fur hat hanging from it.

"Modeled after my home on Aosia," Venton sighed. "Every last detail."

"In case you forget?" Nameless asked.

"In case I forget."

Venton seated himself by the stove and gestured for Nameless to do the same.

"But is it real?" Nameless asked. The leather chair creaked when he sat. "Is any of this real?"

"That all depends on your definition of reality," Venton said, popping a pipe in his mouth and stuffing the bowl with tobacco from the jar. "Help yourself," he grunted around the stem.

And so Nameless did.

He smelled the tobacco before he filled his own pipe: fruity and laced with... "Rum?"

"Made it myself," Venton said. "One of many varieties. I used to have a little shop in Vanatus City, you know, until I moved away."

"Where did you go?"

Venton didn't answer at once. He leaned out of his chair and plucked a brand from the grate to light his pipe.

Nameless accepted the brand next, then drew on his pipe with quick, sharp puffs until the tobacco smoldered in the bowl. He coughed and spluttered as he flipped the brand back into the fire. "Been a long time since I smoked," he said.

"I moved to Medryn-Tha, south of the Farfall Mountains." Venton blew out a smoke ring and settled back in his chair, focus turned inwards, remembering. "You might ask why. I was in my nineties at the time. I had always collected stories of the magic of Medryn-Tha, more specifically the region I am sure you are acquainted with, being the former King of Arnoch."

"Cerreth," Nameless said.

"I sought the prolongation of my life among the husks of those nightmare lands."

Nameless frowned.

"Not, I might add, like some have done. I am no Lich Lord of Verusia, if that's what you're thinking."

"Thank shog for that," Nameless said, relaxing and taking a puff on his pipe.

"You have heard the legend of the lily cats?"

"Can't say I have, laddie. Why lily?"

"Haven't the foggiest, and the literature doesn't say anything about it. They literally do have nine lives, according to the accounts left by Bellosh the explorer. Utterly unique, even among husks. I suspect they have a foot in both worlds—here and on Aosia. I may never know. It was the last quest I went on."

"What happened?"

"I died. And my companions died with me. I blame myself, of course."

Venton withdrew into himself, and Nameless felt it best not to probe further. They sat smoking for the longest while, Nameless watching the flames dancing across the logs in the grate.

"But back to your question about reality," Venton said, as if there had been no break in the conversation. "You might ask if Aosia is real. It was dreamed by the Daeg, after all. Even the life forms added by Etala—the Aculi, the ancestors of all humans—are constituted of the same substance. I never knew it at the time, but I picked up a lot when I was helping Witandos. We are all *essence* in varying degrees of density. Ultimately, that's all everything is."

"And the essence comes from?"

"Ah!" Venton said. "A metaphysician and a dwarf! That's a rare combination."

"Oh, I'm no metaphysician, laddie—if I even knew what that was. But it does make you wonder, doesn't it? The essence has to come from somewhere."

Venton stuck out his bottom lip, as if he'd never considered the idea before, but there was a wicked glint in his eye. He was playing with Nameless, the condescending shogger.

Nameless had never liked sorcerers. Well, save for Nils, perhaps. He was all right. But the others he'd known: Jankson Brau, who'd run an outfit of rogues outside of Malfen; Silas Thrall, possessed by a dodgy grimoire that had led him to his grisly death; and Otto Blightey, the author of that grimoire, the Lich Lord himself.

He opened his mouth to say something he'd probably regret, but Mora chose that moment to enter with a mug of steaming liquid for Venton and a flagon topped with froth for him. Beer always improved his mood.

Nameless reached for the beer, but Mora turned her back on him, tending to Venton first.

"Get that down you," she said. "Settle the cockles."

"Thank you, my dear," Venton said.

"Cockles?" Nameless said.

"Think of them as humors," Venton explained.

"I never did understand what humors were either."

"Cockles is cockles," Mora said, "and I'll not hear another word about it."

Nameless recoiled from the ferocity of her tone, but Venton merely winked and smiled to let him know it was all right.

"Beer," Mora said, thrusting the tankard in his face."

"Obliged, lassie."

"Too right, you are."

She stood watching him, hands on hips, as Nameless took a tentative sip.

"Well?"

It was fruity, with an aftertaste of loam and mushrooms.

"Beats Ironbelly's," Nameless said. "And it has taste—real taste, not like the beer in Witandos's Feasting Hall."

"So, you like it?"

"Aye, lassie. I love it."

Mora gave him a narrow-eyed look, and at first he thought she didn't believe him; but then she smiled, before scurrying out of the room.

"You have some interesting friends," Nameless said.

"I consider them my family." Venton grew swiftly morose, dipping his eyes and chewing on his pipe stem. "It was a spell that killed us. One of my own that backfired."

Nameless set down his pipe. It had gone out, in any case, and he really wasn't much of a smoker. He took a discreet sip of mushroom beer and waited for Venton to say more.

"You know how Cerreth can be," Venton said at last. "At least the parts between the stepping stones."

"Ah, you know about the stepping stones," Nameless said. Arnoch was one of the permanent fixtures in that ever-shifting land of nightmares. He'd visited several others.

"Bellosh mentions them in his book," Venton said. "But there are gaps in his knowledge, uncharted areas where we were forced to walk across the chaos. Out of the blue, if you can believe it, we were attacked by a dragon."

"Oh, I can believe it, laddie."

"A magnificent wyrm, it was, ancient and quite ill-tempered. Grittel, bless her, got behind it and stabbed it in the rump, but her dagger shattered on its scales. Mora tried to intimidate it, but intimidation doesn't work on dragons, especially when they're fifty times the size you are. Purg grabbed it by the tail, intending to swing it around his head..."

"He did?"

"Purg really is incredibly strong, you know," Venton said, sighing as he sipped his mushroom tisane. "But not that strong. He neither knows his own strength, nor its limitations. The dragon flicked him off with ease and raised a claw to stomp on him. Which is where I, unfortunately, came in."

"Why unfortunately?"

Nameless took another sip of beer, then a long pull. His head already felt woozy, and he'd not even downed half the flagon.

Venton might have winced. A tic started beneath his right eye, but he covered it with his fingers. The bones on the sorcerer's other hand stood out from where he gripped his mug so tight. Seeming to realize, he took a big gulp of his tisane, and now he really did wince, as if the contents were as bitter as a battle goat's rancid scrotum—not that Nameless knew about such things, but he'd heard from an old dwarf who used to train the goats at Arnoch... over a pint of Ballbreakers... during one of the rare occasions he'd snook off alone and pretended he wasn't king for an hour or two.

Venton rested his mug in his lap, as if he wasn't quite ready to let go of it; as if he might need an emergency top up of Mora's calmative at any moment. "I panicked," he said, more to himself than to Nameless. "It was a complex spell—a spell that should have incinerated the dragon and left the four of us unharmed. A degree of difficulty above most spells I was wont to cast, but nothing I shouldn't have been able to handle. I mistimed a gesture, garbled the odd word… The long and the short of it is, the spell backfired. And that, my friend, is how we all came to be here."

"And the dragon?" Nameless asked.

Venton shrugged, then finished off his tisane. "Who can say? I imagine I gave the beast a good chuckle, if nothing else."

Venton seemed to sink deeper into his chair, taking some of the warmth in the room with him. For the moment, at least, the talk had gone out of him.

Silence was an old friend to Nameless; he knew when to give it its head, and so he let the conversation go.

He looked around at the pictures—portraits in oil of Venton's odd little family: Mora, Purg, and Grittel. Venton appeared in none of the paintings, even the group pictures. Maybe he was the artist.

He half rose from his chair, intending to peruse the books on the shelves, lowered himself back down again when Venton glanced at him, one eyebrow raised.

"You like books?" the sorcerer asked.

"Just appreciating your room, laddie. Can't say I'm known for my reading, if I'm honest."

"That's probably a good thing. Half the reason for my stooped shoulders and dismal eyesight is too much reading."

"But worth it, though?" Nameless asked.

"Pah," Venton said with a dismissive wave. "The alleged wisdom contained in most of those books—in most books ever written—is so much straw. Experience is the great teacher in sorcery."

"But the books provide a starting point, surely?"

"Perhaps. Of course. I'm willing to concede that. But tell me this: how good a fighter would you have turned out to be, if you'd only ever studied books on fighting?"

"And not practiced with an axe? Never sparred in the Slean? Never cut my teeth in battle? Dead's what I'd be. Ten times over."

Venton gave a thin smile. "Yes, well, fortunately we don't get to die ten times. Only twice. And after more than a century in this infernal place, one begins to understand why so many embrace the second death… by their own hand."

"Suicide? That's possible here?"

"It's something of an epidemic."

"But that can't be right," Nameless said.

"Very little is right about Gabala, or Aosia, for that matter. But of the two, I know where I'd sooner be."

"Reality's a shogger," Nameless said, raising his flagon, only to find it empty.

"Reality's an onion with more layers than you'd believe," Venton said. "And don't let the Daeg or Witandos convince you otherwise. Gabala, Aosia, the Abyss—they are all but bubbles in reality, creations of false gods."

"You mind telling me who the true gods are, then?" Nameless said. "Because I've been having doubts of my own about Witandos and his kind. I mean, take the Daeg, for example: a dog-headed ape, the creator of Aosia!"

Venton chuckled. "Plagiarizing demiurges, is what they are. Where they come from, I imagine Witandos and his ilk are no more than third-rate magicians."

"Where do they come from?"

"Ah," Venton said. "Now, isn't that the question. Much as I hate to admit it, the Wayists know a thing or two on the subject, if you can cut through the myths that smother the truths in their holy scriptures like weeds."

"You're not going to tell me you're a Wayist now, laddie, are you? I was just starting to warm up to you."

"Good grief, no! For better or worse, I've more in common with these solipsistic Supernals."

"You want to create your own world? Because I knew a man who tried that, and it didn't end well."

"Rest assured, I am no Sektis Gandaw. The Mad Sorcerer was more of a credulous moron, as far as I'm concerned. What was he thinking, accepting the lore of the faen as a gift! Did he believe they had abandoned the very thing that defines them—deception—in order to give him a leg up in the old empire of Vanatus? No, I merely wish to control my little domain, provide for myself and my family, and be left alone to delve deeper into the mysteries of this most mysterious of existences."

Some of the warmth had returned to the room as they spoke, and Nameless felt uncharacteristically contented.

"This place," he said, indicating the room, but meaning the house and the grounds, "it seems so…"

"Stable? Compared with the rest of the Supernal Realm, it is. That's because I will it to be so. Everywhere else is an amalgam of the overlapping experiences and expectations of those unfortunate enough to reside here."

"You *will* it?"

"A trick I learned when I worked for Witandos. I am observant, you see, and I have a nose like a bloodhound for the truth. Everything is essence, ultimately, more so here than on Aosia. The lower one descends through the realms—figuratively speaking—the denser the essence, and the less malleable. It can still be shaped, but at a much greater cost."

"So, you shaped the essence here… to surround yourself with all this?"

"We, all of us, reshape the essence of Gabala constantly, but unconsciously, and usually only as far as we can see—and even then, only if our expectations don't collide and overlap with someone else's. Where people congregate—and the dead do love to congregate, just as they did in life—the surroundings can get a bit confusing."

"You don't say."

"I started out quite small," Venton said. "Just this room, in fact. But over time I expanded my control. It's more or less permanent. This place exists even if I sleep or if I am away from it. I find that rather comforting."

"So," Nameless said, "is that what you did to Magwitch: reshaped the essence around him to form a cage?"

"Clever, wasn't it?"

"So why can't Magwitch do it?"

"Magwitch the Meddler," Venton said, "is more of a muddler."

The wizard stiffened and raised a hand for quiet. Nameless had heard something too… a titter, he thought. He started to run his eyes round the room, but Venton gave a subtle shake of his head, then proceeded to go on with what he'd been saying.

"But perhaps Magwitch has learned to do something similar. What was it he turned himself into? A bull-man? Same principle, only even more localized. I wouldn't put it past Witandos to have let slip the secret to give Magwitch a better chance of killing me. But there are levels to sorcery, even here, where mind is key."

He lashed out with his hand and grabbed thin air. There was an answering yelp, and the dog-headed girl appeared out of nowhere.

Venton let go of her ear.

"Grittel Gadfly! I thought I told you to go play, and here you are listening in to my private conversation."

"It wasn't I!" the dog-girl said.

"Of course it wasn't."

Eyes downcast, tail tucked between her legs, she picked up Venton's pipe from the table.

"Me gave you a pipe once."

"I know, and it was a far finer pipe than this. You should have seen it, Nameless: the stem was *ocras*, and the bowl was carved ivory from the tusk of a nietan."

"Me didn't steal it!"

"Of course you didn't. And it was the best present anyone's ever given me."

"Promise?"

"I promise. Now, do be a good girl and run along. Nameless and I still have much to talk about. Alone."

"Okay," she said, and promptly vanished again. This time, padded footfalls moved away from the room.

"Invisibility," Venton said. "She was born in a laboratory, poor dear. Her parents were meldings, held in captivity. Goodness knows what was done to Grittel when she was in the womb."

"Sektis Gandaw?"

"Not him personally. Fanatical followers. But that's enough about me and mine. You were going to tell me what Witandos wants you to do, and why you came looking for a wizard."

"Ah, now where do I start? Before I arrived in the Supernal Realm?" *The seeds we sow in life....* But how far back should he go? The twin massacres at the ravine? How could he avoid it, if Venton was to comprehend what was happening here and now?

The sorcerer was wringing his hands, sharp eyes flashing with impatience.

"I grew up in Arx Gravis..." Nameless started, but Venton waved him off.

"I know all that."

"You do?"

"Got it here, somewhere," Venton said, gesturing at the books on the shelves. "The story of your life. I forget the author's name...."

"Nils," Nameless said. "Nils Fargin."

"The most appalling grammar," Venton said. "But if you can get over that, not a bad book. What I need from you is a concise account of what is happening now, and what exactly Witandos wants from you."

"Well, uh..."

"If you'll permit me," Venton said, rising and coming to stand over Nameless, "it would save time if I see for myself. Speech can be so inefficient."

He extended his hands toward Nameless's face, fingers splayed. Without a thought, Nameless grabbed him by the wrists and squeezed, and Venton's lips quivered as he tried not to cry out.

"I hope for your sake you're not thinking of using magic on me, laddie...."

"With your permission."

"And why would I grant that?" But already, he had relaxed his grip.

Venton smiled his thanks. "Because you came seeking a sorcerer's help, that's why. And you'll be hard-pressed to find a better sorcerer than me."

"You want to read my mind?" Nameless asked. "Because it makes for some pretty dark reading."

"I only need to see the most recent interaction between you and Witandos. I am fully conversant in his methods, and he's bound to have left a trace."

Nameless nodded warily as he released Venton's wrists. "Go ahead, laddie. Be my guest."

The sorcerer touched his fingertips to Nameless's face then closed his eyes. His mouth twitched. The tic once more started up under his eye. Warmth suffused Nameless's skin from Venton's touch, seeped into his mind.

"Mananoc," Venton muttered. "Encased in ice at the heart of the Abyss." He drew in a deep and shuddering breath. "And what's this? The Tower of Making. I used to work there."

Venton used his thumbs to close Nameless's eyelids, and now they saw together: the horde of dwarvish demons; the gigantic form of the Supernal woman bleeding out on the ground, or rather slowly dissolving into it. There was something about her... something vitally important, but Nameless had no idea what it was.

"I..." Venton said. "She used to greet me when I turned up for work at the tower. We were not friends exactly, but I wouldn't have minded if we were. How can this be? Who could slay a Supernal? Not demons, certainly. Then who, or what? Wait, there's something else. One last thing I've yet to see."

Venton gasped. His fingers left Nameless's face.

"The phylactery!" the wizard breathed. "Stolen from right under Witandos's nose."

"You know what it is?"

Venton's eyes were wide, their focus turned inwards, as if he sought an answer to an impossible question.

"We must go to the tower. There may be clues as to where the phylactery has been taken."

"You sound worried, laddie."

"Because I am worried. This is bad. Very bad indeed."

10

Venton didn't like it. Not one little bit. The phylactery was a vehicle to bring a Supernal being back through the Void. He should know: he'd been the one to design it. It was meant to bring Witandos's daughter Etala home. But if it could work for her, it could work for her brother. And Etala only had one brother left alive: Mananoc the Deceiver, Lord of the Abyss. Of course, he was getting ahead of himself. Speculation without corroborating evidence was a waste of a good mind. And if they were going to find evidence, it was at the Tower of Making.

He strode ahead of Nameless and Purg, leading them through the strangled forest of bracken and briars that encroached on his smallholding, the little bit of Aosia he'd reconstructed from the essence of the Supernal Realm.

Purg had brought his woodcutting axe. In these parts, you could never be too careful.

The untamed woodland was the product of those who lived like animals among the trees: outcasts, hermits, unrepentant brigands.

It was also a shortcut.

"Why we go to tower?" Purg asked for the umpteenth time. "Venton not work there anymore."

Venton let out a sharp breath through gritted teeth. He was trying to think!

"You tell him," he said, then noticed that Nameless had fallen behind.

Nameless had barely hinted at it as they left the house, but it was plain he was missing his wife. Venton had heard what had happened to the Queen of Arnoch, and if he'd been the shuddering kind, it would have made him shudder. But now that the nightmare of what the Lich Lord had done was supposed to be over, Nameless was being kept from her side.

Witandos was heartless like that. It wasn't the first time he'd used loved ones as the proverbial carrot, to ensure he got whatever it was he wanted.

"Purg ask three times. Why Venton not answer?"

"Three?" Venton said without slowing his pace. "I'm surprised you can count so high."

"Hah! Purg can. One, two, three!"

"And what comes next?"

"Five. No four."

That, at least, brought a smile to Venton's face. But this was no smiling matter. It was bad enough languishing in Gabala for an eternity, but if he was right, if the phylactery had been stolen as the prelude to a coup by Mananoc, there would be suffering, there would be pain, and there would be countless second deaths. And as to the effect it would have on Aosia! Witandos had always been the balance to Mananoc's influence in the lower world. If he was ousted—if he was killed—everything would become one vast Abyss.

"Clues," Venton said, pausing to let Purg catch up.

"Eh?"

"Clues," he said again. "Where else would you find them, save at the scene of the crime?"

"What crime?" Purg said.

Venton ignored him and instead turned back to the trail—a snaking dirt track through the woods.

"By the way, Nameless," he asked over his shoulder, "how were you planning on finding the phylactery before you met me?"

"No idea," Nameless said. "Witandos was no help at all. He said he can't take direct action."

"What if he's acting indirectly?" Venton asked. "What if he knew you would run into Purg, and that Purg would bring you to me?"

"Silly Venton," Purg said. "Even Purg don't know what Purg going to do, so how Witandos know?"

"How exactly, I'm not certain. But every now and again he raises that eyepatch he wears, and he sees things others can't. Things that haven't happened yet."

"So, he really is all-knowing," Nameless said.

"I didn't say that. But at the very least, Witandos is an arch-manipulator. Where do you think Mananoc gets it from?"

Nameless sniffed then fanned his nose. "What the shog's that smell?"

"Purg?" Venton asked. "Have you been eating Mora's stew again?"

He was joking, of course. The odor was of an altogether different kind: pungent and sickly sweet.

A blurry porch resolved out of the undergrowth, then the rest of the house behind it—more of a hovel, actually.

A skinny man sat on a rocking chair, stringing a guitar. Greasy hair, rabbit-skin coat, and, as ever, he was smoking somnificus. He looked up as he tightened a string.

"Venton Nap. Always a pleasure, geezer." He nodded at Nameless and Percy. "Geezers."

"Elias," Venton said. "I trust you are well."

"You know me, Venton. I'm always well." Elias took a puff on his weedstick. "Toke on the ol' spliff?"

"Forgive me," Venton said, "but we are in somewhat of a hurry."

"Slow down, Venton. Stress will shog with your heart. You don't want to end up like Baz."

"Baz?" Nameless asked.

"Friend," Purg said. "Purg like Baz."

"More of a work colleague, actually," Venton said. "Thank you,

Elias, advice duly noted."

He waved without breaking step, and Elias and his house faded into the background.

"Who was that?" Nameless asked.

"That, my friend, was Elias Wolf, the Bard of Broken Bridge. He spent his life in Sahul, the land of the Aculi."

"I had a friend," Nameless said, "whose foster mother was Aculi."

"Idol-worshipping savages," Venton said. "Did you know they revere Witandos's daughter Etala as a goddess?"

"Kadee was no savage," Nameless said, "and I'll give an Arnochian kiss to anyone who says otherwise."

"Kiss?" Purg said.

"Head-butt," Nameless said. "And you call yourself a dwarf!"

Venton slowed to a stop. "It wasn't my intention to offend," he said. "Purg will be the first to tell you, I have a runaway tongue that constantly gets me into trouble."

Purg folded his arms across his barrel chest. "Make Grittel Gadfly cry. Purg not like."

"I am also irritable, obsessive, and an opinionated bigot," Venton said.

Nameless smiled. "A man who knows himself. I like that. There's no crime in being a shogger, if you've the balls to admit it."

Purg nudged Nameless and whispered, "And he does smelly farts."

"Unfortunately for you," Venton said, "I am not deaf." He waggled his fingers and Purg yelped. "Don't worry, I'll not turn you into a turnip this time. Last warning, though."

He turned back to the path, indulging in a satisfied smile. Purg would sulk for at least an hour, which would allow Venton more time to think. *Oh, good grief, what now?*

"Something's been troubling me," Nameless said. "If Witandos wanted you to help me, why did he send Magwitch to kill you?"

"If you were serious about killing a sorcerer of my ability," Venton said, "would you send a halfwit like Magwitch the Meddler to get the job done? Magwitch was a diversion. He wasn't supposed to succeed."

"Witandos is trying to keep the enemy guessing?"

"I call it an oblique play. If Witandos takes too direct an action, he'll cede an unchallenged move to Mananoc, who already holds the upper hand. The Deceiver was owed a major move, you see, on account of...."

"On account of duping me with the black axe and having me slaughter thousands of innocent dwarves."

"A major victory for him, and although you did much to remedy it on Aosia..."

"The consequences still need to be addressed here."

"Exactly," Venton said. "Those consequences provide Mananoc with a very real foothold in this realm."

"So, Witandos already knows who took the phylactery?" Nameless asked.

"And where it is, but he can't say. Hence the need to manipulate us on the sly."

"And you're all right with that, are you?"

"Oh, I fully intend to use it to my advantage."

"Look!" Purg said. "What is it?"

He was stooped over a pile of dirt swarming with red ants.

"That," Venton said, "is an ant mound. Fire ants, at a guess. Don't touch! They have a nasty sting."

Purg stood up straight and backed away, eyes roving the undergrowth. "There's another," he said. "And another."

"What's that in the distance?" Nameless asked.

"Either it's a hill I've not seen before," Venton said, "or it's a very large ant mound. It doesn't concern us. Come along."

Venton turned at the crunch of deadfall underfoot.

"Funny looking ants." Nameless said.

Purg shook his head. "They not ants, stupid!"

"You don't say," Venton said.

They were men.

Hard-looking men.

Six of them.

With dozens more skulking amid the trees.

11

But they weren't ants!

Purg's head started to throb. Nameless was wrong.

He leaned in close to Venton, so he could whisper his concerns.

"Two legs, like us."

"Your point?" Venton said.

"Ants have six legs." Or was it seven?

"I think Nameless knows that, Purg. He was being sarcastic."

"You were?"

"It's a fault of mine, laddie. Sorry for any confusion."

"You!" one of the ants who wasn't an ant said, stepping towards Nameless. "I know you!"

Looked like a big human to Purg: shaggy hair, stubbly face, piggy eyes. Chainmail shirt that looked too tight and left his hairy belly exposed.

Purg narrowed his eyes at the cleaver in the man's hand.

"A lot of people know me," Nameless said.

"Indeed," Venton said. "While everyone I meet claims never to have heard of me."

"Malfen," the man said, the others with him moving to block the track, two in front, three behind.

"Shog-hole of a town," Nameless said.

"Couldn't agree more," Venton said. "You remember it, Purg. The gateway into Cerreth. We passed through it on our last fateful trip."

Purg frowned. He had no memory of the place, but then again, it was a struggle even remembering his own name. Not that it was his own name—his real name. He'd forgotten that too, so Venton had given him a new one.

"Of course you remember," Venton said. "The whole place was full of cutpurses, waghalters, and pox-ridden whores."

"I used to rule Malfen," the man said.

"King of the dungpile, eh?" Nameless said. "Back in the day, Malfen used to be ruled by the Ant-Man. What was his name again?"

Nameless was looking at Purg for an answer, and that only made the throbbing in Purg's head grow stronger.

"Shent," the man said.

"Shent!" Nameless said. "That was it! Did you know him, laddie?"

"I am him!"

"You are?"

Nameless ran his eyes over the man, from head to toe. "The Shent I knew was all mandibles and carapace. And he had these flimsy wings he used to buzz around with."

"The Ant-Man was one of Sektis Gandaw's meldings," Venton said. "He must have reverted to his original form when he arrived here. That happens sometimes."

White light flashed behind Purg's eyes. Red-hot needles pierced his brain and he lurched, clutching his head.

∼

He lay on a cold metal table, naked. Leather straps held his arms and legs.

He struggled to free himself, but he wasn't strong—not like he was now.

Something growled. Rattling, shaking, groaning.

Heart thumping in his chest, he turned his head. There was a table alongside his, a huge mannish thing strapped to it, bristling with hair all over. Thick cords of vein stood out on its neck as it strained against its bonds. Not a dwarf, like him: it was too big for that. Too big even to be a human. It thrashed and spat and cursed in a tongue he didn't recognize.

A blood-filled tube came out of its arm. The other end was in the crease of Purg's elbow, inserted into the vein.

What was he doing here? What were they doing to him?

They?

He didn't even know who "they" were.

The monster roared. One of its restraints snapped and its massive arm came free. It reached for the tube siphoning blood from its other arm, but men in grey tunics were suddenly all over it, pinning it down on the table.

A woman passed across Purg's field of vision, her back to him as she jabbed a needle in the monster's shoulder. It shrieked and roared then started to cry. Within moments it was fast asleep and snoring like a pig.

The woman turned to Purg, a mask covering her nose and mouth, eyes narrowed as she examined the tube in his arm....

∽

WITH A JOLT, he was back in the forest, Venton gripping his wrist, a concerned look on his face.

"You zoned out again, Purg. Are you all right?"

Purg licked dry lips. Already, the vision was fading from memory. In a moment or two, it would be gone.

Until the next time.

More and more people crept from the trees—dozens of them. They formed a cordon around Purg, Venton, and Nameless, closing like a noose.

"Sorry," Shent said. "But what's yours is ours."

Nameless laughed. "And what exactly might that be? Nothing's real here. Even the clothes on my back are—"

"Essence," Venton said. "They want our essence—everything that defines us."

Shent bared his teeth. He had two long fangs, like a wolf's. All around them, the other people did the same, hissing, fangs glistening with saliva.

"We're gonna drain you dry," a thickset man with a net and a sword said. "Ain't that right, Carl?"

"That's right, Venn," a lean man said. He held a dagger in either hand.

"With all our essence taken, we'll enter the second death," Venton explained, "where we'll drift in the Void forever, mindless as...." He glanced at Purg for some reason, but didn't finish what he was saying.

"Wait a minute," Nameless said. "Venn the Ripper and Carl the Cat's Claw? The pair of brigands I killed before I killed Shent?"

"Scut," Venn said. "You was just lucky, wasn't he, Carl?"

"Lucky," Carl said. "But now it's our—"

Purg's axe came down before he'd even thought about swinging it. Split Carl's head right down the middle, and there was a spray of bright blood. Pretty.

The Ripper's mouth dropped open, but before his shock could fully register, Nameless surged forward and punched him on the jaw, spinning him from his feet. The Ripper hit the ground hard and didn't get up.

The cordon slackened a little. Men and women cast nervous glances at Shent. The former Ant-Man looked less certain of himself now.

"Before Purg and I go all baresark on you," Nameless said, "and Venton here fries you with magic, answer me this: Why would you risk your afterlife trying to deprive us of ours? Isn't it enough to live here for all eternity?"

"And do the same crap things we did in life," Shent said, "only forever? Who wouldn't want a leg up in this shithole? Essence is power here. It's the key to progress."

"A shortcut with unproven results," Venton said. "One is supposed to nurture, enrich, and expand one's own essence, not steal the essence of others."

"Is that a fact?' Shent said. "And how long does that take? How many centuries?"

"In your case," Venton said, "I imagine we're talking in terms of millennia."

Shent stuck his face in Venton's, and that made Purg growl and raise his axe. Shent took a step back.

"You've seen how the Supernals live," Shent said, and he was whining now, like Grittel Gadfly when she had to go to bed. "You've seen them twats who feast in the hall of Witandos, acting like their shit don't stink. People like us don't get that, not in a hundred years. Not in a thousand. So, why wouldn't we take it for ourselves?"

"You've not changed, laddie," Nameless said. "Well, you have: I think I preferred you with the mandibles and the wings."

"You think I give a shog what you like?" Shent said.

"Purg like wings," Purg said, advancing on Shent. "Purg like butterflies. Purg don't like you."

"Kill them!" Shent yelled, raising his sword.

Rage burned through Purg's veins, turning his vision red, but before he took his first swing, music floated out from the trees, stopping him in his tracks. Soothing chords on a guitar, a plucked melody, like the kind Purg sang to Grittel Gadfly to help her sleep. A man's crooning voice—or was it an angel?

Shent's sword hung limply at his side. Purg lowered his axe. Everyone turned to look back down the trail. Purg turned too.

Elias Wolf, in his rabbit skin coat, walked lithely towards them on the balls of his feet, guitar in hand, lips moving impossibly slowly as the words of his song washed over his captive audience.

Purg tried to focus on the words, but they scrambled his mind and made him yawn. Something about peace. Something about making love not war....

He heard the sound of dozens of weapons thudding as they hit the ground, and then his eyelids grew heavy and closed.

"Night, night, Grittel Gadfly," he said in his mind. "Nighty, night...."

12

Nameless watched in a daze as naked dwarf women sat all around him on plush cushions, their beards oiled and braided with silver and gold. They were all drinking. He was drinking too, from a never emptying mead horn, such as the dwarves of the most ancient legends were said to use.

And he could hear music, faint at first, in the background of his mind. But as he focused on it, the music grew louder: fingerpicking on a guitar, hypnotic crooning, exhortations to love and be at peace.

Ordinarily, he'd have called it a shog-awful song, but right here, right now, it was the most beautiful sound he'd ever heard.

And this place! High vaulted ceiling, frescoed walls and fluted pillars. Quality dwarven craftsmanship. There was nothing quite like it.

Nothing quite like stout dwarven women, either! He had to swig his mead to stop from ogling the girls. That wouldn't have been right. The only woman for him was Cordy.

Just thinking of his wife snapped him back to the present.

He stumbled as if he were drunk, but there was no mead horn in his hand, and he was surrounded by trees, not bearded women.

Elias Wolf continued his song as Shent and his goons slunk away into the woods, walking like zombies. Purg was snoring on his feet.

Not Venton, though. He was leaning on his staff and shaking his head with amusement.

"That won't work on me, Elias. You know how I abhor folk music."

The dog-girl, Grittel Gadfly, lay curled up at the wizard's feet. Venton met Nameless's enquiring look with a roll of his eyes.

"She's been following us, the disobedient pup. Her invisibility wore off when she lost consciousness. You can stop that awful racket now," he told Elias as the last of the brigands disappeared into the trees.

"Purg and I would have handled them," Nameless said. "Wouldn't we, Purg?"

The big dwarf came to with a yawn. "Purg smash them," he said, then a soppy look came over his face as he spotted Grittel Gadfly. He knelt beside the dog-girl and stroked her ears till she woke up.

"Me have such nice dreams," she said, then covered her mouth as she saw Venton giving her a stern look. "Me wasn't following!"

Venton smiled and offered her a hand up. "You never are."

Elias slung his guitar over his shoulder and headed back the way he'd come from. "Anytime, geezers. No need to thank me. Actually, you could tell Mad Mora to forage me some more mushrooms... the happy kind. Laters."

"Bye, Elias," Purg called.

Grittel Gadfly took hold of the big dwarf's hand and waved at Elias's retreating back. "Bye, bye."

Venton turned away and continued briskly along the track. Purg kept up with ease, as his legs were longer than a normal dwarf's. Nameless found himself lagging behind with Grittel. He smiled and tried to think of something to say as they scurried to keep up, but she stuck her tongue out at him.

Venton veered off into the undergrowth, seemingly following a new trail that Nameless couldn't see. They pushed their way through ferns and thorns as the ground dipped into a valley. Shapes moved in the underbrush, and Purg stopped to point at them.

"Keep moving!" Venton said without even looking back.

The greenery fell away, until it became clear that what Nameless had taken for a valley was more of a gulley with sheer granite walls either side. They followed the path through the gulley until Venton held up a hand.

There had been a rockfall that had blocked the way ahead.

"Why are we stopping?" Nameless asked. "You don't need to be a ravine goat to clamber over those boulders. Here, I'll show you."

He started toward the rubble.

"That won't be necessary," Venton said.

The wizard stood in front of a particularly massive boulder and lit a weedstick. With a puff and a satisfied sigh, he said, "Purg, would you mind?"

The big dwarf seemed to know what he was doing, and when Grittel Gadfly did a happy jig and clapped her hands, Nameless had the distinct impression they'd been here before.

Purg set down his axe and crouched in front of the boulder, as if he were going to dead lift it. That would have been absurd: the rock was as tall as Purg, and five times as wide.

Nameless's jaw dropped as Purg found purchase with his fingers and leaned his shoulders into the rock.

"Do you want a hand with that, laddie?"

Purg grunted with effort, and the rock shifted a hair's breadth. "Why Purg want hand?" He heaved again, and the rock moved an inch this time. "Purg already got two hands."

And he got both hands under the boulder now, bent his knees, and extended his hips.

"Well, I'll be shogged!" Nameless said, as Purg lifted his end of the boulder then flipped the entire thing and sent it crashing to the ground. It bounced and rolled, then slammed into a pile of smaller rocks amid a cloud of dust.

In front of Purg, where the boulder had stood, was a perfectly circular hole in the ground, big enough for even the fattest of dwarves to fit into.

Nameless peered over the edge then stepped quickly back. The hole dropped away into the dark as far as the eye could see.

"I'm not going down there," he said.

"Brave dwarf like you?" Venton said. "Oh well, children first, then."

"Yay!" Grittel Gadfly said as she skipped to the hole and flung herself in head first.

Purg stood on the brink, watching as Grittel plummeted and then vanished from sight.

"Purg not like."

Venton shoved him in the back, and Purg yelped as he fell into the hole.

"He always says that," Venton said. "See you on the other side."

And with that, the wizard hopped in and dropped from view.

Nameless teetered on the edge, willing himself to jump. He'd been the same around water, until Rabnar had finally taught him to swim. He smiled at the memory: the old Captain had pushed him over the gunwale of the *Watchful Wake*.

"Sink or swim," Rabnar had called down to him as he spluttered and splashed. "And be quick about it. There's sharp-tooths in these waters."

And with that thought in mind, Nameless jumped.

∽

"WEE!" Grittel cried as she dropped like a stone, gold and silver hoops racing past her.

Head over heels she tumbled, wind tickling the hair on her face and stinging her eyes.

"Wee!" she cried again as the ground rushed up to meet her, smelling of grass and flowers and sheep.

∽

Purg squealed as he plunged into the hole. Naughty Venton had pushed him—again!

Circles of sun-fire shot past him, segments of a shaft of silver and gold. His guts flipped into his mouth and he tasted bile. He badly needed to pee.

∼

Venton went feet-first, drifting gently down, now that he'd learned not to fall. He took the time to study the rings of silver and gold that formed the concentric circles of the secret gateway. He'd come to think of it as a liminal space that connected the outer world of the penitent dead to the inner paradise of the Supernals and their favorites.

And then there were the most capable among the dead sorcerers, like Venton himself, like Baz and a handful of others, whose services were indispensable. Or had been, in Venton's case, until Witandos decided he was getting too big for his boots.

∼

Nameless squeezed his eyes shut. He hated magic, and the night-black hole in the ground had the stink of sorcery. Wind tugged at his beard and ruffled his clothes. Light flashed behind his eyelids, and within its glare he could see Cordy's face.

Cordy!

He thought her name so hard, hoping he might reach her. It sounded daft as shog, but this whole place was daft as shog. There was no rhyme or reason to it, nothing a dwarf could take hold of and shake or hit or drink by the pint.

Gabala was driving him mad, and he'd only been here a matter of… How long had he been here? Time seemed to pass in a blur. A couple of hours, a thousand years? How could he know, and what did it matter?

His feet touched solid ground, soft and yielding. There was no jolt, no heavy landing, merely the sense that he had arrived.

He opened his eyes onto lush green meadowland speckled with buttercups. All around him, the buzzing of bees, the bleating of sheep.

"Tranquil, isn't it?" Venton said as he lit a weedstick and shook the match out before flicking it on the grass. "And compared to everywhere else in this unimaginative and somewhat tedious afterlife, as stable as rock."

"Is that where you got the idea for your homestead, laddie?"

"My little bubble of perfection? I might have stolen the method of constructing it from here—or, rather, from there," he said, pointing out a tower in the distance, high up on a craggy hill. "But the design is entirely my own."

Grittel Gadfly entered Nameless's field of vision and grasped the tail of Venton's coat. Someone sniffed, and he turned to see Purg dabbing at his eye with a dirty, fat finger.

Nameless's gaze returned to the tower on the hill.

"Behold," Venton said, "the Tower of Making. Pretentious bloody name. I can't say I relish the climb. My knees couldn't have been more grateful when Witandos and I parted ways and I no longer needed to trek there daily."

13

The smell of sheep dung was the most wholesome thing Nameless had yet come across in the Supernal Realm. In an earthy sort of way, it evoked the life he'd left behind.

Grittel Gadfly skipped through the buttercups, Purg strolling along behind her, axe over one shoulder.

"They always loved coming here to visit me at work," Venton said.

"I can understand why," Nameless said. "The parts of Gabala I've seen to date—save for your place, that is—don't feel natural."

"Because they're not," Venton said. "But then, neither's Aosia; it's just a more familiar kind of unnatural. The worlds created by the Supernals, like my own little creation here, are but bubbles in reality, closed in on themselves, self-contained ecosystems formed from the essence of their makers. The really clever thing is how their essence keeps growing. Here, the dead arriving from Aosia add to the sum total of essence, which enriches Gabala's diversity and complexity, and expands Witandos's domain. Oh, it's still a drop in the ocean of all there is, but it keeps him feeling important.

"Aosia is another thing altogether. The Daeg has a genius for creation that Witandos can only dream of. Which is ironic, considering the Daeg's dreams are the medium of his creativity. Fear of

Mananoc and longing for his mother have conspired to make the Daeg the most fecund of beings."

At the edge of the meadow, they began the long climb up the stairway hewn into the cliff face. Grittel said she was tired, so Purg carried her on his shoulders.

"We are now at the core of Gabala," Venton said as he followed Purg, and Nameless came up behind. "The part that most resembles our old life on Aosia. None of that overlapping of realities here. It's all terribly stable."

"Why do you think that is?" Nameless asked.

"I suspect it's because it more closely mirrors the reality Witandos originally came from: the Pleroma of the Way."

Halfway to the top, Venton paused to smoke a weedstick. Purg continued on ahead, Grittel twiddling with his hair as she sat happily on his shoulders.

"Are you all right, laddie?" Nameless asked. The climb barely affected him: gone was the knee pain and lack of endurance he'd suffered in his final years of life. His body felt young again, full of strength and vitality. Venton, on the other hand, was sweating profusely and struggling to catch his breath—even more so now that he was smoking.

"Baz—the colleague I mentioned—nearly died climbing these blasted steps. He was always sickly, even as a child, and as an adult he was a virtual invalid. You know what finished him off and ended his life on Aosia? He was helping me out on an expedition—I forget what it was about. All I remember is the entrance corridor to some tomb or other. Filled with traps it was, and poor old Baz fell into a pit."

"Nasty," Nameless said. "How deep was it?"

"Only three feet. It was designed to hinder, not to kill. It was the shock that killed Baz. Weak heart. Weak lungs, for that matter. Weak kidneys, weak liver, and don't get me started on his pancreas. He only had to look at sugar and he'd be passing water the rest of the day."

Nameless looked up the steps. Purg and Grittel were nearing the top.

"Another second or two," Venton said, puffing on his weedstick and coughing his lungs up.

"And this Baz worked here with you?" Nameless said. "Does that mean he made this climb every day?"

Venton flicked his weedstick over the edge of the steps and watched as it was picked up by the breeze and drifted to the ground hundreds of feet below.

"He did not. After that first time, Witandos took pity on him and gave him a room in the tower. It would drive me mad being around Supernals all the time, but Baz has always been so reasonable."

"So," Nameless said, "Witandos lives here?"

"No one knows exactly where he lives. The tower is more of a gigantic workshop on many levels. Ready to go on?" Venton asked, as if he'd been doing Nameless a favor by stopping.

At length they reached the sprawling plateau at the top. Purg and Grittel now walked hand-in-hand, half a mile ahead. The tower loomed over them, though it was still some way off, and in the distance beyond it, the placid waters of a sapphire sea sparkled—not the multi-hued ocean Nameless had sailed to get to the Supernal Realm.

He squinted at what he thought was mist on the horizon.

"Smoke," Venton said. "The start of the Burning Sea."

"Oh? And what's that, then?"

"Think of it as a barrier to keep the undesirables out: the dead creatures who owed their existence to the Daeg's nightmares."

"There are husks here."

"There are husk *there*," Venton said, pointing into the far distance. "Islands of them. Entire continents. And other, far worse things besides."

"I assumed husks went to the Void when they died, or the Abyss."

"Witandos has first pickings," Venton said. "Despite the rebellion of Mananoc, Witandos is still top dog among the Supernals. The Void gets the leftovers—after the second death, one has to assume. As to the Abyss: it takes a contract to go there, a contract very few are willing to sign."

On the approach to the tower, the ground had been churned up by hundreds of boots.

"The dwarf-demons?" Nameless asked.

"And something else," Venton said, pointing out some massive footprints.

Purg and Grittel Gadfly had stopped and were staring at something on the ground. As he and Venton drew nearer, Nameless saw it was the gigantic corpse of the Supernal woman Witandos had shown him. A steady discharge of golden mist effused from her armored body, evaporating into the air. Surrounding the body, there were wildflowers, some as much as two feet tall. Rabbits grazed among them, and bees buzzed in search of nectar.

The woman had long arms like a dwarf, and dwarvishly short legs; but she was bigger than any dwarf Nameless had ever seen—other than Witandos. Bigger than any human. Standing, she would have been at least fifteen feet tall. Every inch of exposed skin was torn or bitten or cut, the open wounds glistening with dried, golden blood. Her platinum hair was more iron now, its tangled ends disappearing into the earth like roots in search of water.

But it was her face that set Nameless's heart thumping. He'd not seen it clearly in the vision back at the feasting hall, and in life he'd only seen it in the painting Droom had commissioned from Durgish Duffin—an image that had burned itself into his mind. But in the painting she'd had black hair, not platinum, and she'd been a third of the size.

"What is it?" Venton asked.

Purg was frowning at Nameless. Grittel watched him closely, her dog-head cocked to one side.

Nameless tried to answer, but he couldn't feel his lips. Couldn't feel anything save the hardening of his skin as the black dog mood came over him and turned him to stone.

"Nameless?" Venton asked.

"Yalla," Nameless breathed. "My mother."

14

Venton didn't bother asking for clarification. What would be the point? Nameless was stiff as a board, corpse-rigid, vacant as Purg on a good day.

He'd seen this sort of thing before, oh, several hundred years ago, during his otherwise forgettable youth. His mother would sometimes sit for days on end without moving. Father used to hold a mirror to her lips to make sure she was still breathing. That was in between the times she ran about all over the place, talking so fast it made his head hurt, and spending the meager household savings on stuff they neither wanted nor needed. Mother's fluctuating mood was a large part of why Father had taken a rope out to the big oak tree on their land. Venton had been the one to find him.

"Run on ahead," he told Grittel. "After the attack on the tower, the doors are probably barred from the inside. You know what to do?"

"Me know."

Grittel let go of Purg's hand and turned invisible.

"Oh, and Purg..."

"Purg know!"

Loyal as a dog, the big dwarf ambled towards the tower... just in case. Venton breathed a sigh of relief. Purg would look after Grittel, and that left him free to think.

Quickly, he ran his eyes over Yalla's wounds. There were certainly a lot of them, but there was no doubt it was the head trauma that had killed her for a second time. If she'd not been changed into a Supernal, there would have been nothing left of her by now. She'd already have gone to the Void. According to the legends, her first life had been ended giving birth to Nameless.

He crouched down next to her head for a closer look. The skull had been crushed by a massive blow. No easy thing when she must have stood over fifteen feet tall. If it wasn't a Supernal that killed her, it had to be a giant... some manner of husk, or a creature that could fly.

But therein lay the mystery: it wasn't just anybody who could enter the inner realm, and the husks were confined to the islands of the Burning Sea. So, it had to be a Supernal. Except that wouldn't account for an army of dwarf-demons approaching the tower undetected. A feat like that would require a sorcerer on a par with Venton himself. Well, almost on a par. Not Magwitch the Meddler, that was for certain.

Nameless was a statue, staring through glazed eyes at the corpse of his mother. Venton didn't relish dealing with the dwarf's grief. His own had been bad enough after Father's suicide. If Venton hadn't packed his few things and left home that very day, he'd have been the next body swinging from the tree.

The melancholy was still there inside him somewhere, only kept at bay because he never sat still long enough for it to take hold. Always busy, always studying, always making progress—even here, so long after his natural death.

Venton turned out his coat pockets on the ground: ball of string, weedstick, pipe, tin of tobacco, flask of brandy, mushroom snuff—for which he had Mora to thank. Finally, he found what he was looking for: a rolled up leather pack, which he unfurled to reveal half a dozen glass tubes the length and thickness of a finger, each sealed with a cork. He squinted at the labels (Mora's handwriting was so bad she could have had a career in medicine in Vanatus, where they had met). "Powder of black trumpet, pepper cap, and yellow skull-ripper," he read. That should do the trick.

Unstoppering the tube, he held its open end beneath Nameless's nose. The dwarf's nostrils flared, then they twitched. His eyes instantly streamed tears and he gasped like a drowning man snatching at air.

"Shog!" Nameless cried, spluttering and coughing. "Shog, shog, shog!"

He clutched his guts. "Think I'm going to...."

Nameless promptly threw up, then wiped the vomit from his beard.

"My apologies," Venton said, "but you seemed in a bad way."

"What the shog was that, powder of Ironbelly's?"

"Just something Mora put together for me, in case of emergencies. Now, listen Nameless...." Venton was useless at sympathy, and he was as empathetic as a brick. *I'm sorry for your loss?* Is that what people said. He was sure he'd heard it somewhere.

Thankfully, Nameless spared him the trouble.

"Why has she just been left here? Don't they have pyres in Gabala? Couldn't they at least have buried her?"

Venton placed a hand on his shoulder—something he'd picked up from Purg, who had a knack of making Grittel stop crying with such simple gestures. Obviously, consoling the afflicted had nothing to do with a brain.

"She's a Supernal, Nameless. The essence that made her so was drawn from the realm. To the other Supernals, leaving her here like this is a mark of reverence."

"Huh," Nameless snorted.

"I only spoke with her once or twice," Venton said as they both stared at the gigantic body, its essence settling above the ground like mist, slowly evaporating. "Baz knew her better. She was the guardian of this place. I knew she'd been a dwarf of some renown before she became a Supernal. But your mother?"

"I never knew her in life," Nameless said. "But when I died I hoped I might.... How did she even become like this?"

"A Supernal?" Venton said. "She was one of the few to rise through the degrees of glory, all the way to the top... at least, the top of this self-contained so-called reality."

"And for what?" Nameless's voice broke, and he dropped to his knees beside his mother's giant corpse. He didn't cry, though, from what Venton could see, merely rested his forehead on her chest and grew still once more.

Just as Venton was starting to fear the dwarf had grown catatonic again, Nameless spoke in a quavering voice.

"So that's it? She's gone forever... into the Void?"

"Yes, I'm afraid so," Venton said, immediately kicking himself for his lack of compassion. He tried to soften it with an added, "Maybe."

"Maybe?"

What did he have to go and say that for? Now he needed to confabulate. And to do so, he adopted his most kindly tone—something else he'd stolen from Purg.

"No one knows where the Supernals go when they die. We assume the Void, like the poor creatures they create, but the original Supernals came from the Pleroma of the Way. Perhaps that's where they return."

"But my ma was a dwarf by nature, not a Supernal."

"Is there any distinction to be made between a Supernal born and a Supernal evolved?" Venton asked. "I'll leave that to the theologians to decide." There, that should get him off the hook, at least for now.

"So, there's hope?" Nameless said.

Hope he would see her again? Get to know the mother he'd never known?

The cynic in Venton—which admittedly was the greater part of him—didn't think so, but he wasn't just a cynic. Indeed, he'd spent his whole life on Aosia trying to prove his cynical self wrong. And here he was still doing it!

Venton hadn't encountered his father in the century or so he'd been in Gabala. Did that mean he'd been claimed by the Abyss?

Probably. And if not the Abyss, the Void. But he liked to think there were other possibilities, even for suicides.

As for his mother: he'd seen her the day of his arrival, and he had walked the other way.

"I thought I'd made my position clear on the concept of impossible things." He clapped Nameless on the back—because that's what dwarves did, wasn't it? "Live for today, my friend. Let the future take care of itself. But it never hurts to hope."

"What about my pa?"

"I'm sure he's quite all right. Come on now, we should leave her."

Nameless climbed to his feet like a dwarf twice his age—closer to the age he'd been when he died.

"Let's get to the tower," Venton said.

"Why? What's the point?"

Well, Purg and Grittel were waiting, for one thing. Venton managed to stop himself from saying it, though. He'd been insensitive enough for one day.

"Clues," he said. "Clues as to what happened to your mother." There, he was getting the hang of this.

"She was killed," Nameless said flatly. "That's what happened."

"And we will find out who's responsible."

And once they did, Venton was sure there would be retribution. Probably quite a lot of it, if the stories of the Ravine Butcher were anything to go by.

"Plus, the original reason we came here: there may be a way we can trace the phylactery. If it should fall into Mananoc's hands...."

"Aye, he'd come here and turn this place into a second Abyss. You said that before. But would we notice any difference?"

A huge one, Venton wanted to say. But this was hardly the time.

The last few hundred yards to the tower felt like a hundred miles. The broken windows had recently been regrown from the surrounding essence (Venton could tell because they still shimmered to the trained eye). The door looked sturdier than when he'd worked here: black *ocras*, riddled with green veins. Nothing was getting through that. Once bitten—

"They have *ocras* here?" Nameless asked.

"Why wouldn't they? They have beer, don't they, and anything else you might find on Aosia."

"I thought it seeped into Aranuin from the Abyss?" Nameless said.

"Beer?"

"*Ocras.*"

Venton stopped briefly. Considered a quick lecture on the relationship between realms. *Ocras* might indeed have originated in the Abyss, but the Abyss was an emanation of Mananoc, and Mananoc was the son of Witandos....

He decided against it. Far better just to agree with Nameless in this mood.

It was a relief to find Purg waiting outside. He might have a brain the size of a pea, but he possessed the strength of an ogre, which was more than a little reassuring.

"Venton right," Purg said with a roll of his eyes that, coming from him, seemed ridiculous. "Door locked. Purg smash?"

"An *ocras* door is beyond even you, my friend. Fortunately, I anticipated trouble getting in."

The tip of Venton's staff glowed as it siphoned off the essence of bees and butterflies.

"Grittel Gadfly," Venton whispered, and her name skirled like the wind through the gap between the door and the ground.

"And what's that supposed to do?" Nameless growled.

Venton was about to explain, when he was saved the trouble by the click of the lock and the door swinging open.

Grittel slipped out.

"Good girl!" Venton said. Her skills at burglary were only slightly less impressive than her ability to slit throats.

"It wasn't I!" she said in her shrill voice.

"What do you mean it wasn't...?"

A man in a wooden wheelchair rolled out from behind her. He was stick-thin, with skin like a mummy's. Snub nose, jaundiced eyes, a pathetic wisp of beard. When he smiled in greeting, there were more gaps than teeth.

"Baz the Conniver!" Venton said. "Am I glad to see you!"

And he was.

Really, he was.

15

"Conniver?" Nameless said. "Sounds like an epithet for a faen."

"A term of endearment," Venton said. "I've known Baz a long time. He's many things, but a faen he most certainly is not."

Baz gave a mock sly smile. "I assume you're here about the phylactery, Venton?"

"Can you think of anything else that would bring me back to this place?"

"And there I was thinking you missed me," Baz said. "Come on in."

He turned his wheelchair and led them into an entrance hall with a thirty-foot ceiling. An iron statue twice Venton's height stood on the inside of the doorway. Its head swiveled as they entered, the ruby eyes flashing. It held a scimitar in one rusty hand.

Nameless stiffened.

"Act like you own the place," Venton said. "It won't attack unless we look suspicious. I assume Witandos brought it out of mothballs after...."

"After the tower's Supernal guardian was killed." Nameless said. His ma, Yalla.

He feared mere mention of her name would bring on the black dog once more, and so he didn't say it aloud.

They followed Baz's wheelchair through an arched opening into a cathedral-like chamber. The floor was tiled with jade.

A bald man with a plaited mustache gave them a disapproving look as they passed. Black britches, shiny black shoes, black tailcoat with silver buttons, starched white shirt, and a necktie shaped like a butterfly.

"Master Venton," the man said. "Forgive me if I appear inattentive, but I neither see you nor hear you."

Venton tapped the side of his nose. "Understood, Seldon. If you have nothing to report, Witandos can maintain his facade of ignorance regarding our involvement. That way, he doesn't have to cede a move to Mananoc. Is that a fair assessment?"

Seldon put his nose in the air and walked right on past.

"All this subterfuge makes my beard itch," Nameless said.

"What's that, then?" Purg asked.

"It's the long hairy thing that dangles from my chin. Look, laddie, you've got one too!"

Purg glanced from Venton to Baz, and finally to Grittel, who tugged his beard to make it easy for him.

"That's a subterfuge?"

"No, Purg," Venton said. "It's a jar of fermented cabbage."

Grittel let out a high-pitched yip.

"Have you noticed the ceiling?" Venton asked Nameless.

It was painted with the scene of some titanic clash of armies, Witandos in the thick of it, axe in one hand, spear in the other.

"He has two eyes," Nameless said.

"Observant of you. The painting depicts the Battle of the Pleroma, just before the Supernal Mundartha blinded Witandos in one eye with the very spear you see him holding."

"Not an easy feat to poke a man in the eye with his own spear."

"The spear was Mundartha's. Witandos took it as a trophy. Mundartha took it back."

Baz feigned a yawn, then grinned at Grittel.

"Race I!" she said.

"Not sure my old ticker can take another race," Baz said, emphasizing the point with a wheezing cough. "Oh, go on, then!"

Baz spun his wheels and sped across the jade floor with Grittel barking as she chased him.

Nameless and Venton followed at a more leisurely pace. Purg just stroked his beard as he stared up at the ceiling.

Grittel overtook Baz and came to a stop before a silver door set into the far wall.

"You beat me again!" Baz said, breath rattling in his throat.

"Baz's constitution is a far cry from that of an ox," Venton explained. "It's more like the founding document of the Quilonian Republic."

"Oh hoh!" Baz said. "I see your wit hasn't improved." He passed his hand in front of the door, and it slid open onto a silver-walled cubicle that seemed too big for the space it occupied.

"Reminds me of the warrens beneath Sektis Gandaw's mountain," Nameless said. "Not to mention a lore craft I once rode in. Several times, actually."

"Comes from the same place," Baz said, as he wheeled himself into the cubicle and the others followed him inside.

"Aranuin? You have faen lore here?"

Baz let out a sigh and rolled his eyes.

"Best not to ask," Venton said. "Let's just say, Baz and I both advised Witandos against dealing with the faen when they turned up here in a lore craft one day—and I suspect it wasn't the first time."

"Perhaps he's soft on them," Nameless said. "Technically, they are his grandchildren. What I don't understand, though, is why Witandos didn't just conjure up a contraption like this by himself."

"Because he lacks imagination," Venton said. "Witandos is a pretender god. He doesn't create from scratch, merely reproduces what is already familiar."

"From the Pleroma?"

"Where else?"

The door slid shut, and the cubicle juddered as a low drone started up.

"Going down," Baz said.

Nameless's guts hit his throat, and he retched.

"Thank shog for that," he said when the door slid open. "Thought I was going give the old Ironbelly's yawn."

"Purg like Ironbelly's," the big dwarf said, then promptly threw up all over his boots.

"Aye, laddie, I can see that."

"Don't expect any sympathy from me," Venton said. "All the times you've been here, Purg, you should be used to it by now."

Quicksilver seeped up from the floor and oozed over the contents of Purg's guts. Within moments, it melted back into the pristine floor, leaving his boots shiny and clean.

"They missed the puke in your beard," Nameless said.

Purg wiped it away with his hand, then licked his fingers.

"I have to say, Baz," Venton said as they exited the cubicle, "I was worried you might have been killed in the attack."

Baz stopped his wheelchair to grasp Venton's gloved hand. "I slept through the whole thing. It's the remedy Mora made for my ailments. Ten minutes after I drink it, I wouldn't hear a trumpet if you blew it in my ear."

They entered a circular chamber lit by tall candles that gave off no smoke, paper lanterns, rose-tinted glowstones, and violet phosphorescence from what at first glance looked to be wallpaper, but on closer inspection proved to be a furry fungal growth.

"Mora found the spores for the wall covering deep underground," Venton said. "They insulate as well as illuminate."

"Missing the old place, Venton?" Baz asked.

"Not at all. Regrets are about as helpful as Purg in a debate."

"A what?" Purg said.

The sorcerers shared a smile.

"I never told you at the time," Baz said, "but it was wrong the way Witandos fired you."

"I was not fired! It was a mutual parting of ways."

Grittel wandered the room, trailing her hand over the continuous workbench that ran around the walls. It was broken only by the door they had entered by.

Nameless couldn't make sense of much of the paraphernalia on the workbench: glass jars half-filled with soil, pinprick holes in their metal lids; wooden boxes with muslin covers; diagrams etched into metal slates; books of bound parchment open to reveal pages crammed with symbols; spools of copper wire; others of silky thread. Tall mushrooms with luminous caps were stationed at regular intervals, shedding a clear and unwavering light.

"Mora again?" Nameless said.

Purg guffawed. "Mora and her mushrooms!"

"You never complain when she makes mushroom pie for you," Venton said.

"Purg like pie."

"Don't we all? Mora's always had a thing about fungi, Nameless, and quite right too. Did you know, every fungus that grows on Aosia is also found here in Gabala and, allegedly, in the Abyss? According to no lesser authority than Witandos himself, all fungi have their origins in the Pleroma."

"Some fungi are highly intelligent," Baz said, "and instrumental in maintaining the integrity of all that exists. They also constitute the heart of the phylactery and enable it to travel between the realms, while communicating what lies outside to the occupant."

"Baz's main area of research is mycology," Venton explained.

"Still in its infancy," Baz said, "but there's lore in mushrooms. The ancients of Vanatus knew a lot more than we do, thanks to the faen."

"You're talking about Sektis Gandaw?" Nameless said.

"Don't get him started," Venton said. "The records of Sektis Gandaw's experiments provided a stimulating point of departure, but the phylactery was my brainchild. Witandos thought there was no way for his children to come back through the Void. That's the sad thing about Supernals being devoid of imagination. No intuitive leaps for them. He tells every dead sorcerer who comes here about his dilemma, hoping against hope they can come up with a solution."

"And then you did," Nameless said.

"It took a while. A few decades, in fact. But once I get a bee in my bonnet about something, I don't let up."

"If you two know so much about this phylactery," Nameless said, "why don't you just make another one?"

"If this was simply about returning Etala to her father, we might," Venton said, "though it would take decades of hard work, and there's no guarantee of finding more of the materials we would need. But this is not about Etala. Whoever stole the phylactery has another use in mind, and I have a very nasty suspicion as to what it is."

"Me bored," Grittel said. She'd plonked herself on the workbench, feet dangling over the edge.

"I'm sorry, my dear," Baz said. "You know how sorcerers like to talk."

"Buzz, buzz, buzz," Purg said. "Like flies in Purg's ears."

"I'm sure Nameless understands the need for context," Venton said.

"Laddie, all I've heard so far is a lot of waffle about mushrooms."

"Without fungi," Venton turned to an empty pedestal in the center of the floor space, "we'd never have been able to make the phylactery."

"It was virtually finished when the buggers stole it," Baz said. "Only needed fine adjustments and testing. Rigorous testing—you know how I am, Venton. Sorcery this complex can't be rushed."

Venton took a magnifying glass from his pocket and stooped to examine the top of the pedestal.

"As I'd hoped," he said, inviting Nameless to take a look.

Through the lens, Nameless could just make out tiny black dots.

"Dead fleas?"

"Spore print," Baz said, wheeling himself closer and taking a turn at the magnifying glass. "Even honeycombed into the phylactery's essence chamber, the fungal matter remains active."

"Meaning," Venton said, "we have what we need to trace the phylactery."

"You lost me at honeycombed," Nameless said, then, with a glance at Purg, "You lost him a while before that."

"It's easier if I show you," Baz said. "Grittel, dear, be a good girl and fetch me that box from under the bench, would you?"

Her eyes lit up and she jumped down. "Which box?"

Venton sighed. "How many boxes do you see under the bench?"

"One," she said.

Baz took a gentler tone. "The black one with the green veins. There you go, sweetheart. Bring it over here."

She handed Baz the box, then stuck her tongue out at Venton.

Baz opened the lid to reveal a tiny black cube that didn't quite look solid—as if it were woven from shadows.

"This was the prototype," Baz said. "Intended for the Archon, before he was lost to the Void."

He tapped the top of the cube three times, and it opened like the lid of a box—only, there were no hinges. The inside surfaces were creamy in color, and they looked smooth, until Venton prompted Nameless to look through the magnifying glass.

"It's porous," Nameless said. "Speckled with holes."

"Allow me." Venton twisted the handle of the magnifying glass. "Look again."

Now, Nameless could see it clearly: every surface was comprised of impossibly small, perfectly formed honeycomb, each of the cells lined with filaments of some glistening material.

"The honeycomb is fungus," Baz said, "grown within the web of a bee-spider—so named for the hexagonal pattern it weaves its threads into. The webs are ephemeral, lasting less than a day before dissolving into the Void. But they possess a strange, symbiotic relationship with fungus."

"I found a way to petrify the webbing," Venton said, "without destroying its properties. Hence the honeycomb template for the fungus to grow within."

"One of our earliest discoveries," Baz said, "was that the honeycomb configuration enhances the fungi's natural ability to absorb and discharge essence, and to remember."

"It has memory?" Nameless asked.

"Given the right cues," Venton said, "the fungi will absorb the essence of any object, any being, and retain the pattern of its form. When the cube passes through the Void and arrives at its destination, it opens and the fungi restores whatever it absorbed."

"But nothing can exist in the Void," Nameless said.

"A common misunderstanding," Venton said. "Your own Axe of the Dwarf Lords was sent from Gabala to Aosia via the Void. The children of Witandos fell through the Void and survived. The clay sculptures—Witandos calls them golems—that encased the souls of the first Exalted…"

"He made dwarves out of clay?" Nameless asked.

"Not all dwarves, stupid," Purg said.

"Just the first twelve Exalted," Venton said. "The rest were dreamed by the Daeg."

"The Void is not nothingness, as most assume," Baz said, "but an ever-expanding colony of dark fungi, too small for the eye to see, which has the inverse properties of what we call matter. Dark fungi should not exist. Sektis Gandaw's paradox, they used to call it, after the Mad Sorcerer harnessed dark fungi to make the null sphere that was supposed to unweave all things."

"Many times," Venton said, closing the cube so only its shadowy outer shell was visible, "Witandos has sent his creations through the Void, but it is a one-way trip. Without a phylactery, only the dead can return."

"The outside of the cube is comprised of dark fungi," Baz explained. "Venton had the idea of harvesting spores from the Void to fashion the cube's outer casing—no easy feat, I can tell you."

"Spare him the details, Baz," Venton said.

The old sorcerer looked affronted. "You tell him, then."

"The dark fungi, like the honeycomb within, had to be forced into a particular shape: the cube. It took decades of work."

"Which is why my explanations can't be rushed," Baz complained.

Purg's eyes lit up, as if he'd just caught up with the conversation.

"Purg carry big spoon to portal and fish for Void-stuff."

"Another oversimplification," Venton said, "but Purg is correct in principle. We fashioned a scoop attached to a telescopic rod of *ocras*."

"You know how to make things out of *ocras*?" Nameless said. "Only the dwarves of old knew how to do that, and they had help from the faen."

"Venton asked for their input," Baz said. "Which I found rather hypocritical."

"The faen were already here, working on projects for Witandos," Venton said. "No harm came of it."

"I assume there's a reason you can't use this prototype phylactery to bring Etala back," Nameless said.

"You are correct in that assumption," Venton said. "It doesn't work, due to a mishap in the preparation. The fungi inside the cube has petrified to the point that it is incapable of absorbing or discharging essence."

Nameless found himself flagging, and it was an effort staying focused on the conversation. The effects of the mushroom powder he'd inhaled were starting to wear off. He kept seeing his ma, his gigantic Supernal ma, with her head caved in.

"Nameless?" Venton asked. "What is it?"

"I know what you said, but it's not right to leave my ma lying on the ground like that. A dwarf should have a pyre. There should be a wake with food and grog."

Nameless didn't miss the concerned look Venton exchanged with Baz.

"Perhaps you'd be so kind as to collect enough particles of dark fungi from the phylactery for me to attempt a locating?" Venton asked. "I'd like to take Nameless and see if we can pick up some more... clues. You know...upstairs."

Baz stuck out his bottom lip, then nodded that he understood.

There was something neither wizard was saying.

"Grittel can stay and help me," Baz said. "And Purg can keep guard in case the thieves come back."

Purg slammed the haft of his axe into his hand. "What thieves?"

16

As Nameless and Venton exited the cubicle onto the jade floor of the cathedral room, the iron giant came stomping in from the entrance hall. The glare of its red eyes gave the impression of anger, as if it had made a mistake letting them past the first time. The massive head swiveled to toward Venton, then immediately switched to Nameless, where it lingered.

"Useless, brainless, piece of junk," Venton said, and the giant sagged as if ashamed. "It's no wonder Witandos replaced you with a Supernal guardian. The only pity is, he saw fit to bring you back."

"Maybe he thinks this thing's more reliable," Nameless said.

"Don't," Venton said, and the severity of his tone was like a slap in the face. "Don't even think such a thing. I didn't know her well, but your mother was both capable and loyal. More than capable. Whatever got past her would have defeated this rust-bucket golem with ease."

A metal groan came from somewhere within the iron giant. Chin on chest, it turned away and lumbered back into the entrance hall.

Venton chuckled to himself.

"What's so funny?" Nameless asked.

"Oh, nothing really. Just reminded me of Purg, that's all."

"Big and dumb, eh?" Nameless wasn't laughing. "Laddie, I get the impression Purg's not as stupid as he wants us to believe."

"Hah!" Venton said. "Not as stupid as...."

When Nameless still didn't laugh, Venton dried up, and he didn't look so sure of himself.

"You really think that... about Purg?"

"I remember a young friend of mine being mocked by a wizard because he couldn't read."

Venton swallowed, then glanced nervously at Nameless's hands, as if he expected them to clench into fists. "What happened?"

"The wizard died, and my friend was accepted into the Academy at Jeridium. Went on to be Principal."

"How..." Venton said. "How did the wizard die?"

"You mean, did I kill him?" Nameless shook his head. "If you must know, I tried to save him." Silas had been his name. Such a distant memory. Silas Thrall. Another victim of the Lich Lord. "My point is, my friend surprised a lot of people who had written him off as a nonce."

"And you see similar potential in Purg?"

"I think he's faking it."

"Faking his stupidity? You mean, all these years, Purg has been pulling the wool over my eyes? But why? What does he hope to gain from...?"

Nameless tried to suppress it, but his chin quivered, and his beard only emphasized the fact.

"You're pulling my leg!" Venton said.

"Ah, laddie, you should have seen your face!"

Venton strode across the chamber to a door that blended in with the wall panels. "And there I was thinking you were grieving for your mother."

"I am!" Nameless said as he hurried to catch up. "I just can't—"

Venton stopped and put a hand on his shoulder. "You can't give into it. Believe me, I know just how you feel."

"Joking staves off the black dog mood," Nameless said, "in the absence of beer."

"Beer," Venton said, opening the door and leading the way into a long corridor with white-painted wainscoting and sky-blue walls, "generally makes depression worse."

"Only when you stop drinking."

They proceeded along the corridor and up a winding staircase. At the end of a carpeted landing, they came to a door.

Venton knocked three times with his staff.

"Has someone else moved in?" Nameless asked. *Already?*

The door opened and a young dwarf poked his head out. He wrinkled his nose at Venton, but when he saw Nameless, his eyes lit up, then he started to cry.

"Pa?" Nameless said.

He looked at Venton for confirmation. The dwarf in the doorway looked young enough for Nameless to be *his* father.

"I got younger," Droom said.

What a stupid shogger Nameless had been! Of course his ma and pa would have lived here together, once they were reunited in death. He'd not considered the possibility, because Droom was the only parent he'd ever known. After Yalla died giving birth to Nameless, Droom had never remarried, and he'd have clouted anyone who dared suggest that he did.

"Son," Droom said. "I heard you'd…"

"Heard I'd kicked the bucket, pa?"

Tears streamed down Droom's face, soaking into his beard. "I wanted to be there to greet you when you arrived, only…"

"Witandos wouldn't permit it?"

"He means well, boy."

"Maybe."

Droom took Nameless's hand in both his own. "Was it a good battle?"

"It was a scut of a battle."

"But you did good, eh?" Droom said.

"Aye, Pa, I did you and Ma proud." Himself too, if he was honest.

Droom embraced him, causing Nameless to grunt. His pa was still broad-shouldered, with shovel-sized hands, and he had a squeeze like an alpha gibuna.

"And this is?" Droom said, holding Nameless out at arm's length.

Venton doffed his hat. "My condolences, Droom."

"Do we know each other, son?"

"We are acquainted. I used to work downstairs. Venton Nap?"

"Never heard of you."

"Oh…"

Droom winked as he put his arm round Nameless's shoulder and led him inside.

Clothes were strewn about the place, some giant-sized, some regular. There were pots and pans, books and scrolls—a whole bunch of mundane things Nameless had never expected to find in the Supernal Realm.

"I'm in the middle of packing my stuff," Droom said. "Now your ma's gone, there's no sense in me staying here."

"Gone? Pa, she was murdered."

"Murdered? Killed? She'll be over it by now. Your ma was never one to hold a grudge."

"I wish I could say the same for me," Nameless said.

"Leave it be, son."

"Leave it be!"

Venton slipped past them and crossed to the window, where he ran his hand along the sill before rubbing his fingers.

"They broke in through windows all around the tower," Droom said. "Climbed like spiders. Witandos called them demons, but they were dwarves, I tell you. I even recognized a few."

"Aye," Nameless said. "They were dwarves once upon a time."

"Me and your ma were sleeping." Droom opened a door to show the bedroom.

"Big bed…" Nameless said.

"Your ma was a big woman. Least, she became one. Come on in," Droom said as he sat on the bed. He patted the mattress, and Nameless sat beside him.

Outside, in the living room, he heard Venton strike a match. Soon after, he smelled the aroma of weedstick smoke.

"She was big enough in that painting you used to have on the wall, Pa."

"Ah, the one by Durgish Duffin." Droom indicated a rectangular patch of discoloration on the wall above the headboard. "Used to hang right there. First thing I did, when your ma didn't come home, was to vanish it."

"How'd you do that, then?"

"Same way we create all the junk that makes us feel at home," Droom said. "The stuff I'm packing to take with me."

"You create it?"

Droom thumped his chest. "Comes from here: memories."

"Made manifest by one's own essence," Venton said. The wizard was standing in the doorway, examining something in the palm of his hand with his magnifying glass. "Like our bodies, our clothing.... You don't think you passed over from Aosia fully-clothed do you?"

"Not if they had a funeral pyre for me."

Venton resumed looking through his magnifying glass.

"Anything interesting?" Nameless asked.

"You recall how the outer casing of the phylactery left a spore print?" Venton said. "Well, the long-suffering dead of this realm—all of us—leave a similar residue. I don't fully understand the mechanics, but it's bound up with how we move about from location to location. There is no real distance in the Supernal Realm. There is no space at all, in one sense."

"That'd be 'no sense'," Droom said.

"I see where Nameless gets his wit from. But look here. Tell me what you see."

Venton crossed to the bed and held his hand out for Nameless to inspect.

"Specks of dirt?"

"Now look through the lens."

Nameless took the magnifying glass and looked again. This time, the specks were larger: knotted clumps of fibers too small to see with the unaided eye. Threads of black and brown and green and blue, all bundled up together in a tight and infinitesimal ball.

"What are those little red dotty things?" Nameless asked.

"Spoors," Venton said.

"Mushrooms again?"

"The spoor print of the Abyss."

"These dwarves—these demons—came from the Abyss?"

"Impossible," Venton said. "At least, without the phylactery. No, they came straight here from Aosia, the same way you did."

"Maldark's wee ship?"

"You kept him extremely busy."

"And they weren't demons when they arrived?"

"No," Droom said. "They weren't. I knew a bunch of them, recognized them when they came in. Only…"

"Only, you were ashamed to greet them?" Nameless said.

The dip of Droom's head was all the confirmation he needed.

"I don't blame you for what you did at the ravine, son, and neither did your ma. But when the victims came in, it was… awkward."

"If I may return your focus to the issue at hand," Venton said. "Or rather, in the palm of my hand…. This red spoor print, this residue of the Abyss: there is only one way it could have come here, to my mind."

He raised an eyebrow, waiting for Nameless to come up with the answer, as if it were perfectly obvious. Which, of course, it was.

"The faen," Nameless said.

"I warned Witandos not to permit their presence here," Venton said.

Nameless stood and started to pace. The faen again. It was always the faen—creatures begotten of deception itself, fallen like turds from the arse of Mananoc. Always tricking, always lying, always betraying. Well, not all of them: the Sedition were trying to make amends. And then there was Shadrak, who Nameless had long considered a friend. Shadrak, who had put a bullet through the eye-slit of the *ocras* great helm Nameless once wore, bringing an end to the Corrector's reign of terror. Shadrak, who had been at his side in that last terrible battle outside the walls of Jeridium.

"What is it, son?" Droom asked, rising and resting a hand on Nameless's shoulder.

Nameless tried to explain, but his voice cracked. His joints were growing stiff again, his skin hardening like clay in a kiln.

"Shock," Venton said. "He's not even had time to start grieving yet."

"Oh, son," Droom said. "Your ma. You would have seen her on the way up."

Nameless couldn't keep the anger from his eyes, so he looked away.

"I wanted to give her a pyre," Droom said. "I really did, but—"

"It's against the rules for Supernals," Venton said.

"Rules!" And now Nameless couldn't stop himself from unleashing his anger. "So you just left her there to dissolve into the ground?"

"Aye," Droom said, so quietly Nameless almost didn't hear. "I left her there."

"He had no choice," Venton said.

"Shut up!"

Nameless's fists shook from where he clenched them so tight. "No wake, pa? You didn't even have a wake?"

Droom dipped his head, and Nameless instantly regretted speaking to his pa the way he had. He knew it wasn't Droom's fault.

"Look, Pa…" Nameless said, chewing over the words of his apology.

Droom's head snapped up, his eyes bright with excitement. "We could have one now, if you like."

"A wake?"

"I have just the thing."

He almost knocked Venton over in his rush to get through the doorway.

"I'm intrigued," the wizard said, as he and Nameless followed

Droom into the living room, and found him rummaging through his packed-up possessions.

"Shog's bloody law," Droom said. "It's underneath that lot."

Nameless lent him a hand re-stacking the boxes until they reached a crate at the bottom. It had no lid, and inside were a dozen brown bottles packed with straw.

"Love the detail," Venton said.

"Aye, just like how they packed the crates back home."

"Is that beer?" Nameless asked, his mood already lifting.

"Not beer. Your ma gave it to me last anniversary of my snuffing it." Droom handed Nameless a bottle and took one for himself. Venton declined, then produced a slender flask from his robe.

"I'm more of a brandy man," the wizard said.

Nameless almost choked as he recognized the label on the bottle. "Taffyr's Golden Honey Mead!"

"Essence," Venton said. "Beautifully formed, though. Exquisite."

"Shogging well should be," Droom said. "Yalla got them from Taffyr himself."

"Taffyr's here?" Nameless said. "And you've met him?"

"Too right I've met him. Old Taffyr died when I was a boy, but that man was always a legend to me. Still is. I got all tongue-tied when your ma introduced us, but then the mead started flowing and now we're good mates."

Nameless was almost too worried to try his mead, in case he was disappointed, as he'd been with the beer.

"Go on," Droom said, taking a swig of his own. "Tell us what you think."

"For ma," Nameless said, then took a sip. He let out a long, satisfied sigh. "Smooth as silk. Velvety. Honey-sweet, but not at all syrupy."

"Just like in life, eh?" Droom said, raising his bottle. "To Yalla."

"To ma," Nameless said.

Venton raised his flask. "Yalla. Wife, mother, and Supernal guardian."

"You had to go and ruin it, didn't you?" Nameless said. "Why'd you mention the last bit?"

Before Venton could make his apology, Droom said, "He was right to mention it. A wake's not just for happy memories. It's for a whole life, truly lived, the good and the bad."

Nameless winced. "Aye, pa, you're right. Venton, forgive me for being such a shogger."

The wizard clapped him on the shoulder.

"So what happened, Pa? What really happened?"

Droom clutched his bottle to his chest. "The dwarf-demons coming through the window woke me up. By the time I realized what was happening, Yalla had already killed three of them. Instantly awake, she was. Shoggers didn't know what hit them.

"We heard hundreds of them downstairs, rampaging through the tower. Yalla didn't hesitate to go down there—it was her duty—but when I tried to follow she slammed the door in my face and locked me inside. I didn't even know we had a key!"

"She was protecting you," Nameless said.

"Aye, I know, and we'll have words about that when I see her again."

"When you see her again? Pa, she's—"

Venton waved Nameless quiet. "Your wife was a dwarf lord. She was Exalted. And she was a Supernal. It would take more than demons to bring her down, no matter how many there were."

"Outside," Nameless said, "there were huge footprints—and they weren't Ma's." In the vision, Yalla had been carried outside the tower by the demons.

Droom sniffed and wiped his nose. "Locked in like I was, I didn't see the end, but Witandos said something big killed her."

"And he didn't say what?" Venton asked. "Because I find it hard to believe he doesn't know."

"I still don't understand why she became a Supernal," Nameless said. "Did Witandos force her?"

Droom shook his head. "No, he didn't force her. Floated the idea, maybe. Actually, quite a lot. But it was your ma's choice."

"Why, though?"

"Hope, I assume," Venton said.

"Hope of what?"

"Getting out of this place," Droom said. "Witandos told your ma that Supernals were originally the Archons of the Pleroma—hence the name of his own son. It would take time to grow into her powers, he said, but once she did, she would be capable of ascending to the Pleroma, and she could take me with her."

"A likely story!" Venton said. "I'll tell you what I think. I think Witandos saw Yalla's potential. He vowed never again to take a mate after Gabala's death, yet all he does is pine for her and his children, all three of whom were lost to him when they fell through the Void. So, he creates surrogates whenever he deems someone suitable."

"How did she die?" Nameless asked. "Witandos's wife, I mean?"

"Suicide," Venton said, then upended his flask and took more than a sip.

"The first of many," Droom said. "Sad, really. So sad. But despair finds us all sooner or later, in this place."

"The dwarves in the pub seemed fine to me," Nameless said.

"They might pretend to be," Droom said. "Might even believe they are for the longest time. In my case, the first century was all right, but when the second started, and all I was doing was drinking away the hours with the same boring shoggers night after night... You can see how it might dampen a dwarf's good humor."

It was hard to imagine for Nameless, but he conceded the point.

"You've been here a long time, Venton," Droom said. "You must know what I'm talking about. Tell me you've felt the despair."

"Not a bit of it," Venton said. "I've never had any intention of remaining in this place."

"And yet you're still here..." Nameless observed.

"But not forever," Venton said. "That's the key. All manner of suffering can be endured, so long as it doesn't last forever."

"I agree," Droom said. "Which is why I've decided to walk the maze."

"You won't catch me doing that," Venton said. "If you'll excuse the pun, I'll find my own way."

"Maze?" Nameless said. "What maze?"

"Think of it as a ghetto," Venton said, "where the Wayist dead wander interminably, in the hope they'll come out the other side into a paradisal eternity."

"And will they?"

"Thumil says so." Droom sighed then looked Nameless in the eye. "Cordy too."

Nameless shook his head. "Cordy, a Wayist! You're yanking my beard."

"She's new to it," Droom said. "Same as me. But we'll walk the maze beside Thumil, and together we'll find a better place."

Thumil and Cordy had been married before, but when she'd died, she'd been Queen of Arnoch. She'd been Nameless's wife!

"So, that's why she was so shogging cryptic on the ship ride to the Supernal Realm. I knew something was up."

"Death has a way of changing us all," Droom said.

"Speak for yourself," Venton said.

"Aye," Nameless concurred. "You'll not catch me wearing a white robe and spouting all sorts of nonsense about love and peace."

"Well, I'm sorry if I disappoint you, son," Droom said, "but my mind's made up."

"Reckon I could change it with a bottle or two more of Taffyr's...."

Droom chuckled. "Go on, lad, crack a couple open. But even Taffyr's won't change my mind."

Nameless opened two bottles and passed one to Droom.

"Ah, laddie," Droom said, "it's good to see you. One of the hardest things was not seeing my boys."

"You've not seen Lukar?"

"Why would I?"

"Pa, Lukar's been dead more than two-hundred years."

"That's not possible," Droom said, the color draining from his face. "Witandos would have told your ma. We'd have known."

"He went into Aranuin, Pa. He was killed by the seethers."

Droom looked to Venton for help.

"I'm sorry, Droom. Your son may never show up here. The

seethers absorb all essence that comes into contact with them. They feed it directly into the Abyss."

"Oh, my boy!" Droom said. "My boy!"

He set his mead down and turned a slow circle, shaking as sobbed.

Nameless's eyes were dry. Coming here, finding Yalla outside, seeing Droom.... It had all been too much for him. All he felt was numbness, and not even Taffyr's was going to fix it.

The door opened and Grittel Gadfly slipped inside.

"You have the spoors?" Venton asked as he crossed the room towards her.

"Lots of them," she said. "Hundreds and hundreds."

Venton accepted a slender tin from her and opened the lid to see. "Excellent. That should do nicely. Nameless...." The way the wizard shuffled from foot to foot, he was itching to leave.

Droom sniffed back tears. "It's all right, son. I'll be fine once I get to the maze. Who knows, in a thousand years I might become a luminary. A thousand more, maybe I'll join your ma in the Pleroma."

"If she's there," Nameless said.

"She shogging well better be, if I'm going to all that effort!"

Droom smothered him in a bear hug, and now it was Nameless's turn to cry.

17

Purg tramped along behind the others on the way back to the portal. Venton's voice was a constant buzzing in his ears. The wizard never stopped talking, and most of what he said made no sense.

Normally, Grittel Gadfly would've hitched a ride on Purg's shoulders, but she was prancing and skipping circles around Venton and Nameless, excited to be going home. It wasn't normal, the way she acted. She might've looked like a child, but Grittel was more than a hundred years old. They all were. Most of those years had been after death, but still, it was time she grew up.

And as for Nameless, he'd seemed all right when Purg met him in the tavern, but ever since he'd been a right miserable shogger. Yes, his big Supernal ma had died, but everyone died. Everything. Least he still had a pa. Purg didn't have a pa or a ma, or if he did, he couldn't remember them.

All that remained of his childhood were fleeting images of the sea and a crumbly cliff. And sometimes there was a city with big walls and guns on the parapet.

After that, the memories were of bright lights and metal walls, and masked faces staring down at him.

"Coming?" Venton said.

The wizard had walked back to Purg, leaving the others waiting outside the portal—a whirling patch of glittery air.

"What is it, old friend, flashbacks again?"

"Purg fine."

"Talk to me, Purg. It might help."

"Purg fine."

"Suit yourself," Venton said. "But I'll have Mora rustle up some mushroom tisane for you. It helped last time."

"Purg don't need it."

"You might, Purg. If I'm right about what's going on, we all need to be at our best."

"What is going on?" Purg asked.

"I'll tell you, if I'm right."

Purg put an arm around the wizard's shoulders and they walked together towards the portal. "Thought you were always right."

"That's the impression I like to give," Venton said. "Now then, everyone, who wants to go first?"

⁓

Going up was better than going down. It felt like flying.

The portal spat Purg out, and he tumbled head over heels, coming to a stop on his back.

Grittel pointed and laughed.

Nameless and Venton had gone through first, and were seemingly waiting for him to do something.

"What?" Purg said as he picked himself up and dusted himself down.

Venton nodded toward the boulder.

"Why Purg always have to cover portal with rock?"

"You seriously think I could shift that thing?" Venton said.

"I reckon I could give it a go," Nameless said, rolling up his sleeves.

Purg folded his arms across his chest.

Dumb dwarf. Let him try.

"You'll do yourself an injury," Venton said. "Best let Purg do it. He really is unusually strong."

"Ah, but does he have the blood of the Exalted?" Nameless asked.

Purg didn't even know what that was.

Nameless limbered up with some side bends and shoulder rolls, then he spat on his palms and leaned into the rock. He grunted and heaved, but the boulder didn't budge.

"Hah!" Purg said.

"Just gauging the weight," Nameless said. "Now for the real attempt."

This time, he bent his knees and got his fingers under the rock. His face reddened as he drove his feet into the ground.

The boulder wobbled. For a second, Nameless got his end half an inch off the ground, then he dropped it back down with an earth-juddering thud.

Venton shook his head. "Purg, would you be so kind?"

"Oh no," Nameless said. "I've got this now."

He took up the same position as before, hands under the boulder, but this time, before he drove with his hips, he bashed his head into the rock.

"Does that help?" Venton said with a roll of his eyes.

"Considerably more than you do."

Nameless smacked his forehead into the boulder a second time, opening up a crimson gash. "Oh yes!" he cried. "Oh, shogging yes!"

He heaved, and the boulder rocked. Leaning his chest into it, he roared as he thrust with his hips, sending the boulder rolling over the portal, where it wobbled for a few seconds before settling into place.

"Pah!" Purg said.

Grittel yipped as she clapped.

"Bravo," Venton said. "Now, can we get underway?"

"One moment," Nameless said. He was bent double, hands on thighs. "I'm a wee bit…" He pitched face-first to the ground. "Dizzy," he mumbled through a mouthful of dirt.

Purg helped him into a sitting position. "Stronger than you look," he said.

"Maybe, but next time, you can move the shogging boulder. The problem with Exalted blood is that it thinks the rest of me can keep up."

∽

THE WALK back home through the woods wasn't as long as Purg remembered. Or was it? It didn't matter. His mood picked up considerably when Grittel took his hand and sang one of her silly songs:

> *I love my Purg, he is so strong,*
> *But Mora's barking mad.*
> *Old Venton Nap is never wrong,*
> *But Nameless looks so sad.*

Purg knew the melody but not the words. Grittel had a gift for making them up and finding the rhymes. Not the refrain, though. She never changed the refrain, and so Purg joined in:

> *With a mushroom tea and a yip yap yo,*
> *And a dog without a bone.*
> *And a dog without a bone.*

"I am not sad," Nameless called over his shoulder. "And what's all this about 'barking mad' and 'a dog without a bone'? I've sung some nonsense verse in my time, but I had the excuse of being drunk."

"Grittel doesn't drink," Purg said. "She's not old enough."

"Not old enough! How long have you all been here?"

"Nigh on a hundred Aosian years," Venton said.

"I rest my case."

"You sing a verse, Nameless," Grittel said. "Go on, sing. Sing!"

"Not without beer. And if you really are as young as you act, you'd want to cover your ears."

"Duh," Purg said. "How Grittel hear song with ears covered?"

Nameless didn't answer. Venton had said something to him, talking right over Purg like he always did, and Nameless's attention switched.

"Stupid dwarf," Purg mumbled. "Cover your ears!"

"So me don't hear the rude words," Grittel said. "But me do hear them, all the time, at the tavern."

"Grittel go to the tavern?"

"Me follow you whenever you go."

"Purg never see you there."

"The tavern's not the only place you don't see I."

Purg frowned as he imagined all the times she might have been there when he thought he was alone. For weeks, he'd thought a mouse was stealing the food from his plate whenever he looked the other way. Or a ghost. Now he wasn't so sure. He gave her a narrow-eyed look.

Trust was such a brittle thing when you had no idea who you were or where you came from; when you couldn't remember what you were doing this morning, let alone yesterday.

He let go her hand and hung behind the rest of the way, even when Grittel sang a new verse about him sulking.

"Maybe we see Elias again," Purg said, "and hear real music." He liked the bard's music; it helped him forget he couldn't remember.

Grittel stuck her tongue out at him.

But then Purg did remember something: the ant-fellow and his goons who'd waylaid them on the way to the portal. After that, he gripped his axe tight and kept scanning the woods left and right, but the only thing he saw was a hedgehog. Purg liked hedgehogs. He waggled his fingers at it and smiled.

∽

AT HOME, they all sat around the long table in the kitchen while Mora prepared her "funny" mushrooms to help Venton with his scrying—whatever that was.

"You look like you could use some too," Mora told Nameless. "Not you, though, Purg. Remember what happened last time I gave you the red toadstools with the white warts?"

"No."

"Probably just as well," Venton said as he checked his reflection in the bowl of water in front of him on the table. It was a big bowl, made of bronze.

Nameless refused the sliced toadstool. He looked preoccupied, and Purg knew there was a reason. Something or other....

Venton leaned away from the bowl and bit into the toadstool slices with relish, which was unusual, considering how rarely Venton seemed to eat.

"Here's your tisane," Mora told Purg. "And Grittel, here's your mushroom milk."

Grittel wagged her tail and smiled sweetly, then snatched the cup from Mora. She'd fallen into one of her sullen strops. Purg caught Grittel glaring at Nameless, and when he shook his head at her to tell her to stop it, she glared at him instead. After that, she splayed her hand on the tabletop, took out her knife and stabbed the point between her fingers. Faster and faster she went, till Purg worried she might cut herself. When Venton sighed—which meant he wanted her to stop—she twirled the knife on her fingertip, flicked it into the air, and caught it by the handle. She wrinkled her nose at Purg, then turned invisible.

Purg hated it when she did that. He couldn't relax. At any moment she might creep up behind him and bark in his ear.

He took a sip of tisane and tried to relax. Mora had made the drink for him so often, he actually did remember what she put in it: candy-cap mushrooms gave it its sweetness, then there were dull-caps to calm his nerves, and silver trumpets to sharpen his wits.

"Where did I put the tin?" Venton asked. When no one answered, he said, "The tin from the tower... with the spoor print."

Just then, the tin floated through the air and landed in Venton's lap. Purg guffawed, then covered his mouth. No one else seemed to find it funny. Save Grittel Gadfly. He heard her snigger, then the sound of her footfalls running away.

"You'd better not have been messing with the phylactery spoors!" Venton called after her.

The wizard's eyes looked strange to Purg: almost totally black, from where the pupils had grown large.

"Here," Mora said as she came up behind Nameless. "I poured you a mushroom beer."

Nameless snapped out of his stupor. "Thank you, lassie. I was just thinking about beer."

Venton opened the tin and upended it over the bowl. What looked like black dust felt into the water, and he stirred it in with his finger.

"What Venton doing?" Purg asked.

"What does it look like?" Immediately, the wizard winced and apologized. "Forgive me, Purg. The toadstool makes me irritable, but it's a necessary evil. I'm steeping the phylactery spores in the water."

"What's steeping?" Purg asked.

"Soaking," Mora explained as she took her place at the table.

"Why?"

"To mix the spoors with the water, to help him scry the location of the phylactery."

"What's that, then?"

Venton sucked in a breath through gritted teeth. "Mora, I thought you said the tisane sharpened his wits!"

"There's only so many times you can hone a blade with a whetstone," Nameless said, before taking a sip of beer.

Purg guffawed.

"You liked that one, did you, Purg?" Nameless asked.

"Woof!" Grittel barked in Purg's ear, making him jump. She appeared beside him and whispered: "He means the tisane can only do so much, Purg, and that you're still dumb."

Purg glared at Nameless. "No, Purg not like."

"If you've quite finished," Venton said, "I am trying to concentrate."

The wizard's face was pressed up close to the bowl. Purg suppressed a giggle. It looked as though Venton was going lap up the water like a dog. Either that or wash his face in it.

"See anything?" Nameless asked between sips of beer. "Other than water, that is."

"Vague impressions," Venton said. "Someone is warding against my scrying. A flaming sea, a craggy isle. Wait, what's this?"

Purg leaned across the table to see, but Venton swatted him back.

"I can see the demons," Venton said. "Thousands of them."

"Dwarves?" Nameless asked, sitting forward.

Venton nodded. "The same as we saw before. Pallid, wasted. Dead eyes."

"Through no fault of their own," Nameless said. "This was my doing."

"I hardly think so," Venton said.

"And you'd know how?"

"Did you willingly slaughter them? Back at the ravine city, was it your intention to murder thousands of your own kind?"

The beer in Nameless's tankard was spilling from where the hand holding it shook.

Purg reached over and pried the tankard from his grasp, setting it down on the table.

"I thought they were demons," Nameless said.

Venton sat back in his chair and pushed the bowl away from him. "And now they really are."

"I won't fight them," Nameless said. He looked at each of them to make sure they understood what he was saying.

"Purg won't fight them neither."

"Oh," Venton said, "and why's that, then?"

"Purg dwarf. Purg like dwarves."

"Even when they are no longer dwarves?" Venton asked. "Nameless, think of your mother, lying on the ground. You want to avenge her, yes?"

"It wasn't dwarves that killed my ma. You said as much yourself.

Even demon dwarves. I'll not fight them, I say. I was possessed last time, tricked into seeing what they wanted me to see."

"They?" Mora asked.

"The faen?" Nameless said. "Mananoc?"

"Good!" Venton said, standing abruptly. "Excellent! So, we are agreed on one thing."

"We are?" Nameless said.

"The demons are victims every bit as much as your mother. Every bit as much as we all might be, if we don't put a stop to this. And no, I don't mean the demons are your victims, Nameless. They are the spoils of Mananoc's victory over Witandos, when he used the faen to trick your brother into going after the black axe in Aranuin."

"And then tricked me into going after Lukar," Nameless said so quietly, Purg almost didn't hear.

"The Deceiver turns our best qualities against us," Venton said. "Just look at Sektis Gandaw and his inflated intellect, or the Lich Lord's passion for occult knowledge. In your case it was loyalty, love for your brother."

"And hope," Nameless said. "I hoped for a return to the days of glory, for a way out of the fossilized existence in Arx Gravis."

"Well, don't abandon hope, whatever you do," Venton said. "Because there's nothing Mananoc feeds on as much as despair."

"So, it's him, is it?" Mora said. "That big stinking turd at the heart of the Abyss is behind these shenanigans?"

"Isn't it obvious?" Venton said.

Purg shook his head, but no one seemed to notice.

"The phylactery was intended to bring a Supernal back through the Void," Venton said. "It was stolen with the aid of demons who were once the dwarves...." He winced and glanced at Nameless.

"It's all right, laddie, you can say it: the dwarves slaughtered at Arx Gravis. What else?"

"Well, the Burning Sea narrows it down, if not by much. But then there's the craggy isle with the black mountain. It can only be the Isle of Mananoc, home of one of the three Void portals in the Supernal Realm. Either someone plans to escape—"

"Or they plan to bring someone here," Nameless said. "I have a nasty feeling I know just who."

"Mananoc has an island here?" Mora said.

"He used to live in the Supernal Realm, remember, until his rebellion against his father went too far and he was driven out—and only just. He'd never have entered the Void willingly. His brother and sister dragged him into it, kicking and screaming."

"Lost forever," Grittel said with a sniffle. "All three of them."

"Lost to the Supernal Realm," Venton said. "But not to Aosia. And the Archon managed to trap Mananoc in the Abyss, with no way out. Until now."

Silence fell over the room.

Purg didn't like silence. It made him look for some way to fill it, inside his own head. And there was nothing much there, save for half-formed thoughts that never reached completion, and masked faces peering down at him, and a knotty clump of rage and hunger.

He belched. Not because he needed to, but because it might prompt someone to say something, even if it was just to tell him off.

Nameless took it as a cue to drink some more beer, and that seemed to get his mouth working again. "I assume it's not Mananoc himself who killed my mother. In the vision—you've seen it, Venton—he was still encased in a block of ice."

"Mananoc always works via proxies," Venton said. "For two reasons. One: he remains frozen at the core of the Abyss. Step outside his own creation, and he will be lost to the Void forever. Two: every move he makes cedes an equivalent move to Witandos. But in the peculiar world of Supernal justice, Mananoc holds the advantage on account of his success at Arx Gravis, with the black axe. He must have claimed the slaughtered dwarves as his due."

"But..." Purg said, surprising everyone, even himself.

All eyes turned on him, and Purg was suddenly tongue-tied. It felt important, what he was going to say, but what if he didn't know what the shog he was talking about and they mocked him for his stupidity?

"But what?" Venton asked.

"Purg thought...."

He backed out when he heard Grittel snigger.

"Be quiet, girl," Mora said. "Let Purg say what's on his mind."

Grittel shrieked with laughter, then promptly turned invisible when Mora stood and gave her the crazy-eyed look.

"Well?" Venton prompted.

Purg's cheeks started to burn. "Purg forgot."

"Typical," Venton said.

"No, wait. Purg remember. If Mananoc stuck in Abyss, and you say dwarf things too puny to hurt Nameless's ma…"

"We're still no closer to knowing who or what could have killed Yalla," Venton said. "I was just coming to that bit. But thank you, Purg. And thanks, Mora: the tisane may still be effective after all."

"Do we need to know?" Nameless said. "My task is to retrieve the phylactery for Witandos. I'm sure whoever killed my ma will try to stop me from succeeding. And I hope they do. We'll see how that works out for them."

"There's still the matter of the sorcerer," Venton said.

"Venton a sorcerer," Purg said.

"I am aware of that, Purg. Mora, you might want to up the dose next time. There is, however, another sorcerer, one working for the other side. A sorcerer powerful enough to bring the dwarf-demons to the vicinity of the tower undetected. A sorcerer with the ability to thwart my scrying, and presumably a sorcerer with the nonce to work out how to operate the phylactery."

"Or maybe not," Purg said, his insight escaping his lips before he could doubt himself.

"Oh?" Venton said. "Do enlighten us, Purg."

"If this sorcerer knows how to use phylactery, why he not done it already? Why not Mananoc back here and turning Supernal Realm into Abyss?"

Venton's cheek twitched. He held up a finger as he struggled for something to say, then finally settled on, "That, my dear Purg, is a very good question. The answer, one must assume, is because the puzzles I placed on the phylactery to prevent its misuse require a genius to solve them." He gave a polite cough. "Presumably, our mysterious sorcerer is not as clever as I first took him to be. Nevertheless, to be on the safe side, we had better get going."

Everyone stood.

"Not you two," Venton told Purg and Mora. "And don't even think about following!" he yelled so that Grittel Gadfly would hear, wherever she was. "Just me and Nameless."

"Laddie, this is my penance."

"I'm not so sure," Venton said. "I'd say it's much more than that, and I think Witandos is fully aware of the fact."

"You think he knew you'd become involved?"

"I have no doubt about it. He's playing his cards close to his chest, and I suppose he has to, if he's not going to give away any moves."

"So, why can't we come?" Mora said, folding her arms over her chest.

"Because...." Venton said, his voice cracking. "Because I'm the reason you all ended up here before your time, that's why. I'll not risk losing you to a second death."

"It's that dangerous?" Mora asked.

Venton merely nodded.

"Purg come with you."

"No, Purg, I forbid it."

Purg retrieved his axe from beside the kitchen door.

"Purg come!"

When he turned to glare his defiance at Venton, the wizard's eyes were glistening. Venton forced a smile and nodded his assent.

"Look after Grittel," Venton told Mora.

"You don't have to tell me that."

"Now," Venton said, "Purg, Nameless, let's go see a man about a ship."

18

The harbor was empty when they arrived, only a single longboat moored at the jetties. The sky was overcast, and a thick mist rose from the water, which was grey, not the rainbow hues it had been when Nameless arrived.

A little way out to sea, a three-masted carrack waited at anchor. He could make out sailors in the rigging, unfurling sails from yards. The bowsprit—a big bellied woman wearing a crown—seemed familiar.

"Looks like the Captain got my message," Venton said.

Before they left, Nameless had observed the wizard standing by one of his beehives, surrounded by the swarm. When he'd come back inside, the bees had undulated away through the sky to do his bidding.

"So, where is he, then?" Nameless said, casting another look out to sea. There was something about that ship....

"Where he always is, when he's not tucked up in bed with a bottle of rum."

Venton led them across the wharf toward a tavern.

Purg clattered ahead in his armor, which he'd insisted on bringing—rusted plates that covered his chest, thighs, and forearms.

The big dwarf half jumped out of his skin as the door swung open and a man in a maroon coat and tricorn hat stumbled out. He had a beard a dwarf would die for, red streaked with grey, and it hung to his knees. His face had been turned leathery by the wind and spray, but his bloodshot eyes still found room for a sparkle. He wore a solitary turned down boot, his other leg a false one carved from the bone of a whale—a flying whale, if the owner was to be believed.

"Rabnar the Red!" Nameless said.

Rabnar and Venton exchanged a look.

"Well, so much for anonymity," Venton said. "You two know each other?"

"Know?" Rabnar said. "Know! This dwarf crewed with me for nigh on three years. We sailed the Sea of Weeping from Medryn-Tha to the Empire of Vanatus. And what adventures we had, eh, lubber!"

"Aye," Nameless said. "Till you went and died on me. I knew there was something familiar about that ship."

Rabnar followed his gaze out to sea. "I brought the *Watchful Wake* with me. After I died, I woke up still on board. The ship was empty, all the crew gone. I looked all over for you and Nils and that pretty lass that could change into sharks and seabirds and all manner of things."

"Ilesa," Nameless said.

"Aye, that's the name. I thought at first you'd all abandoned ship, daft as it sounded, so I took hold of the wheel and steered a course, as if I knew where I was going. Somehow, the *Wake* brought me here."

Nameless gazed out over the water, remembering his own arrival. "The sea was all the colors of the rainbow when I came in."

"Same for me," Rabnar said. "Same for all of us who come by ship. But the rainbow sea's a one-way sea, lubber. Once you dock here, there's no going back. Set sail the same way you came in, and you'll end up someplace else in Gabala. Good thing is, it's a great big ocean out there, and there are islands a-plenty to explore, whole lands, entire continents."

"And sharks as big as houses?" Nameless said with a wink.

"Them too."

"Purg bored," Purg said. "Purg get beer." And with that he went inside the tavern.

"Make sure you bring me one," Nameless called after him. "Rabnar?"

"I'm fine thanks. Had my fill of rum for now, and there's plenty more aboard the *Wake*."

Nameless shook his head. "I don't understand, laddie. You look the same as you did when I last saw you, right down to the grey in your beard and your false leg."

"I don't believe in penance," Rabnar said. He hawked up phlegm like he used to, then realized he wasn't at sea and couldn't spit over the gunwale. He wrinkled his nose and swallowed. "And besides, this place is about as honest as my tall tales, and you know how tall they can get. A bit of grey in my beard and this ol' peg-leg keeps me real."

"The Captain here," Venton said, "may be the only man who can get us across the Burning Sea."

"Well, I can think of no one I'd rather sail with," Nameless said, pulling Rabnar into a hug. The Captain stank of rum and brine and moldy fish, so Nameless decided it was better to hold him out at arm's length.

"When them bees of yours came to see me," Rabnar said, "I knew you was after more clay."

"Clay?" Nameless asked.

"For my sculpting," Venton said.

"He thinks he can make a new body for himself," Rabnar said, "so he can return to Aosia through the Void!"

"There's no reason why it shouldn't work," Venton said. "I pinched the idea from Witandos. He let slip while I worked for him that he used a special kind of clay to create dwarves."

"He made the dwarves out of clay?" Nameless said.

"The first twelve Exalted, yes. It's also why there's so little clay left, and one of the reasons why, when he sent more aid to the dwarves, he had to meld souls with divine alloy."

"The Axe of the Dwarf Lords and her brothers," Nameless said.

"Well," Rabnar said, "if it's more clay you want, it's going to take awhile. That stuff ain't exactly easy to find."

"This isn't about clay," Venton said. "Our business is rather more urgent."

"Is it now? Urgent, you say? That's a word you don't hear bandied around in the Supernal Realm. It undercuts the concept of eternal life."

"Listen, Captain—"

"Go on, don't be shy, lubber. You may as well call me Rabnar now Nameless has let the cat out of the bag."

"And I am Venton Nap, although you probably already worked that out for yourself. I am somewhat well known, hence the need for secrecy."

"Venton who?" Rabnar said.

The wizard looked crestfallen. "Never mind. I need you to take us somewhere. Considering the work I did augmenting your ship, I'd say you still owe me."

"I'm in debt to no one," Rabnar said. "Save Nameless here. He has my debt of friendship. So, I'll take you lubbers where you want to go."

"Good enough for me," Venton said. He glanced around, scowling. "Where the blazes is Purg?"

"He went for a beer," Nameless said.

Venton rolled his eyes. "See what I have to put up...." He stopped mid-sentence, frowning back towards the buildings that hemmed the harbor.

A group of men were approaching the tavern, and it didn't look like they were coming for a drink. Nameless did a quick head count: twelve, all humans, save the one at the front, who was most definitely a dwarf. A dwarf in the black cloak and *ocras* breastplate of a Svark, the shifty shoggers who acted as the Senate's enforcers back in the bad old days of Arx Gravis. He actually looked dead, a bandy-legged corpse walking: grey skin, grey beard, liver-spotted head.

As the mob drew nearer, hands resting on the hilts of scabbarded swords, recognition crawled through Nameless's guts.

"Coalheart," he muttered to himself. "I knew he was going to be trouble."

Eleven hard-eyed humans and one evil-eyed dwarf came to a stop mere yards from Nameless, Rabnar, and Venton.

"My Lord Corrector," Coalheart said.

"Not any longer," Nameless said. "I left that shogger behind at Arx Gravis, along with the thousands he slaughtered—him and the Ravine Butcher."

"Sorry to hear that," Coalheart said. "But you'll always be the Corrector to me."

"I wasn't myself, laddie. I was possessed."

"We're all of us possessed by something," Coalheart said. "Tits, arses, beer...."

He glanced at his companions, as if he expected them to laugh, but their eyes were fixed on Venton.

"Possessed!" Coalheart said. "You think that makes a blind bit of difference to the thousands you killed? Because I can tell you, it don't."

"You know that for certain, do you?" Rabnar said.

"I know what they've become," Coalheart said. "Because of him."

"Because of Mananoc," Venton corrected, "and the ludicrous game of tit for tat the Supernals play."

"Oh, it ain't no game, wizard, as you're about to find out. Now, we can do this the easy way—"

"Or?" Rabnar said.

"This don't concern you, old man. It's the wizard we want."

"Is it now?" Nameless said, stepping in close to Coalheart. "And why's that, then?"

"Don't think you can intimidate me," Coalheart said. "In case you ain't noticed, Corrector, you ain't got no black axe no more, and you ain't got no fancy armor neither."

"Laddie," Nameless said, "all I need's these two fists to beat a scutbag like you. So, I'll ask again: What do you want with Venton Nap?"

"I don't answer to you," Coalheart said. "Not no more. I serve a new master, one who could've kicked your shogging arse even if you still had the axe and the armor."

"Oh, and who's that, then?"

"That, shogger, ain't none of your concern. Same as it's none of your business what we want the wizard for."

"Need I remind you," Venton said, "what happened to the last thugs who tried to abduct me?"

"Which is why I've got this," Coalheart said. He took a faceted crystal from his pocket. "Any magic you sling at me, this beauty sends straight back at you."

"Ah," Venton said. "Decent of you to warn me."

"What's in this for you, Coalheart?" Nameless asked.

"Leg up in the new world order that's coming. Reckon I did all right for myself last time, back at the ravine, till you went and shogged it all up. But I didn't come here to reminisce about the past. Lads...."

The thugs with Coalheart drew wicked looking cleavers with serrated edges.

"Would you look at that, Rabnar," Nameless said. "Those are some fancy swords."

"Still prefer a cutlass," Rabnar said, drawing his. As in life, it was brown with rust, but Nameless knew from experience it always had a keen edge, and he'd seen Rabnar use it often enough to know Coalheart's goons were in for a spot of trouble.

"Don't suppose you have a spare?" Nameless asked.

"Here, use this." Rabnar produced a bottle of rum from his coat pocket.

"Don't you want to finish it first?"

"A moment, lubbers," Rabnar said, and the thugs looked at Coalheart for instructions.

Rabnar pulled the cork with his teeth and took a long, glugging pull on the rum. He sighed and belched then handed the empty bottle to Nameless, who upended it for use as a club.

"Take the wizard alive," Coalheart said. "As for you, Corrector, I ain't forgotten how you watched me die and did shog all to prevent it. So, now I'm gonna return the favor."

Purg chose that moment to emerge from the tavern carrying a couple of beers.

"Laddies, laddies," Nameless said, as the thugs edged forward. "Why so tentative? There's nothing to be frightened of."

"Save the second death," Venton said.

"Well, there is that."

Purg eyed the scene as if it were the sort of thing he encountered every day. He sipped his beer and handed the other to Nameless.

"Be with you in two shakes of a gibuna's knackers," Nameless told Coalheart as he downed his beer.

And still the thugs didn't attack.

"Oh, for shog's sake," Coalheart said. "Do I have to do everything myself?"

He drew his sword and came straight at Nameless, but before he got there, he tripped on something and landed face-first on the ground, sword clattering away from him.

Purg hurled his tankard, and it struck a goon on the forehead, dropping him like a sack of spuds. That freed the big dwarf up to take a double-handed grip on his axe.

Rabnar's peg-leg rat-tat-tatted on the ground as he darted forward and swung his cutlass. Steel met steel as the thug he was aiming for parried, but before the man could recover, Rabnar head-butted him in the face. There was a sickening crunch, and blood sprayed from the man's broken nose. That was all the incentive the thugs needed to flee.

"Come back," Purg said. "Purg promise to be gentle."

Coalheart got to his knees, a scarlet graze above one eye. Venton loomed over him, misty tendrils effusing from the tip of his staff.

"I warned you," Coalheart said, reaching into his pocket. "Didn't I shogging warn you?"

His eyes widened and he swallowed, before checking his other pocket.

"Looking for this?" Venton asked, holding up the crystal.

"How the shog?"

Grittel Gadfly appeared out of thin air, dagger in hand, a wicked glint in her eye.

"Sorry me tripped you," she said, not sounding at all like she meant it. Then to Venton: "And sorry me followed you again."

"No you're not. I am, however, relatively pleased to see you."

The misty tendrils from Venton's staff shot towards Coalheart, solidifying into web-like strands that smothered him. Coalheart struggled in vain to free himself, then gave up when he realized he was surrounded, Venton and Rabnar in front, Purg one side with his axe raised, Nameless the other with a bottle and a tankard, and Grittel behind, looking like she was about to fillet a fish.

Nameless slammed his tankard into Coalheart's mouth, and a tooth rattled to the ground. He raised the rum bottle, causing Coalheart to cower behind his arms.

"This new master you mentioned," Nameless said, "I'd like to know who it is."

"Believe me," Coalheart said, gingerly dabbing at his bleeding mouth, "you don't want to know."

"Someone killed my ma. Is this master of yours responsible?"

"Shog you!"

Old darkness flooded Nameless's mind. The rum bottle in his hand might just as well have been the black axe.

"Who's your master?" he said. "I won't ask again."

Coalheart started to laugh. "You ain't changed, Corrector. But I'm gonna have to disappoint you. So long, scuts."

The sorcerous webbing that covered Coalheart sagged as his body turned instantly to black dust.

"Someone doesn't want us to pry too much," Venton said. "Same thing happened to me when I was attacked by thugs in Scutsville."

"Scutsville?" Nameless asked.

"Home," Rabnar said. "When I'm not at sea. So, lubbers, does anyone want to tell me what's going on here?"

"Once we're underway," Venton said.

"Best get a move on, then," Rabnar said, leading them towards the jetty. "Urgent business, you say. Where'd you want me to take you so urgently?"

"The Isle of Mananoc," Venton said.

The Captain drew up sharp and Nameless almost bumped into him. "Lovely spot for a picnic."

"Picnic?" Venton said.

Rabnar nodded toward the longboat, where Mora stood waiting on the jetty, a wicker basket clutched in either hand. The first was stuffed with bread, cheese, honey, and fruit. The second was filled with mushrooms.

Grittel squealed in fright and turned invisible.

"Don't think I didn't see you," Mora said. "Running off the way you did! You and I are going to have words, Grittel Gadfly. And as for you three"—she meant Purg, Venton, and Nameless—"what were you planning on eating on this bleeding voyage? Fish?"

Venton looked like he'd seen his worst nightmare, but when Purg lay a big hand on his shoulder, Nameless realized the wizard's fear wasn't for himself.

"You shouldn't have come," Venton said. "None of you should have come."

"Is that a fact?" Mora said. "Well, we're here now, so deal with it."

19

"Hoist them squares and catch us some breeze!" Rabnar the Red hollered. "And give me some lateens on the mizzen, boys."

The Captain took a swig of rum and saluted Venton with the bottle. "Tide's with us, lubber, and there's a west wind blowing."

"And that's a good thing, is it?" Venton said, tasting bile as he swallowed another wave of nausea.

"You want to stand at the prow, lubber. You'll feel the sway of the ship less there."

"Thank you for the advice," Venton groaned as he headed toward the front of the ship. He muttered under his breath, "Call me lubber again and I'll turn you into a bowl of soup."

Venton adored the sea. Unfortunately, the feeling wasn't reciprocated. Motion had never sat well with him—any motion, other than the action of his own legs.

But the Captain was right, he quickly discovered as he reached the prow and looked out over the bowsprit. He found instant relief watching the waves break around the keel, feeling the wind in his hair, the spray of brine on his face.

Last time he'd been at sea had been with Mora, aboard one of Vanatus's famed iron ships on the way to the Azarot Archipelago, a cluster of islands that had been taken over by fanatical disciples of the Mad Sorcerer, Sektis Gandaw. No seasickness that time, just a droning background hum and the smell of heated metal.

Rabnar's ship, by way of contrast, was a big-bellied carrack with a big-bellied bowsprit, all wood and canvas and barnacles, and stinking of fish and rum. In place of the background hum, there was the constant cursing and ribbing of the sailors, the squawk of seabirds, the scamper of rats down below—every last little detail so very perfectly Aosian. It made Venton wonder how Rabnar did it. Had he painstakingly reconstructed the ship from materials found in the Supernal Realm, or had he discovered the same secret Venton had used to create the facsimile of his Medryn-Tha smallholding? That didn't seem likely, unless master of sorcery could be added to the list of feats and talents the Captain had done nothing but boast about since they came aboard.

"Rabnar said I'd find you here," Nameless said, full of an unusual amount of cheer for a dwarf who'd recently lost his mother—for the second time. Venton guessed it was on account of the half-drunk bottle of rum he clutched in one hand. "Shog, you look green, laddie. Not half as bad as Purg, though. I've never seen such a bad case of the gravelly brown yawn."

Venton winced at a gripe in his guts. "Boats don't bother me. A wizard is master of all modes of transport, all manner of discomfort. You are mistaken about my complexion. I was merely thinking."

"And thinking makes you green, does it?" Nameless took a swig from his bottle. "Try some, if you like. Rabnar's always sworn it helps with seasickness."

"I am not…" Venton covered his mouth as he belched.

"All that contemplation's giving you indigestion," Nameless said. "Go on, laddie, a wee dram of rum will see you right."

Venton accepted the bottle. "Just a sip, then."

"Finish it. There's plenty more where that came from."

Venton shrugged then took a long pull on the bottle.

"Does it help?" Nameless asked.

Venton wasn't sure, so he took another drink, then poured the remains of the bottle down his throat.

"Tell the Captain his nautical wisdom is much appreciated. I feel right as rain."

"I'm not surprised. That was a lot of rum. Perhaps you should come away from the gunwale. Last thing we want's a drunken wizard overboard."

"Drunken! My dear Nameless, you really think half a bottle of rum's going to affect me? I've built up a tolerance to alcohol from Mad Mora's mushroom moonshine."

"Hmm," Nameless said. "About all this mushroom stuff...."

"Don't knock what you don't understand."

"But you did say she was mad."

"Ah, but mad crazy, or mad angry? Word of advice." Venton hiccuped. "Don't let her hear you speak badly about mushrooms. It's a religion to her. Literally."

"I'll keep that in mind."

Nameless leaned over the prow beside Venton, staring out to sea.

"You'll get salt in your beard," Venton warned.

Nameless gave a distracted smile. He seemed fixated on the sharp-tooths weaving through the waves. He let out a sigh and shook his head. "Gabala's not what I expected."

"Too similar to Aosia?" Venton said. "There's a reason for that. Each of the known worlds—Aosia, Gabala, and the Abyss—were shaped from the essence of Supernal beings."

"Aye, but what exactly is essence?"

"Formless, is what it is, when left to its own devices. According to Sektis Gandaw's extant writings, there is something called the *feruveum*, a fabric or structure of infinitesimal fungi underlying the cosmos, and this is what gives essence its form."

"And where does this *feruveum* come from?"

"If Gandaw says anything about that, it must have been in one of the chapters I skimmed. His prose style is not the most engaging."

"Now why doesn't that surprise me?"

"Mora believes the *feruveum* was dispersed throughout the

cosmos in a once-for-all creative act—like spermatozoa, or the spores of an infinite puffball. The way she speaks about it, you'd think it was sentient."

"Mushrooms again," Nameless said. "I'm seeing a theme here, laddie."

"Indeed, Mora's something of a religious monomaniac, but you get used to it."

"But where does Witandos fit into all this? I thought he was supposed to be the supreme god."

"Supernal beings are not creators out of nothing; they are manipulators of the fungal fabric, and thereby shapers of essence. All life on Aosia was given form by one Supernal or another, but not created."

"So, not much difference between the Supernals and sorcerers," Nameless said.

"You make an astute observation. Supernals, however, are able to effortlessly access the essence they are constituted from, and unlike us, they suffer no physical cost for doing so. If I were to use my own essence for sorcery, I'd end up as decrepit as Baz in next to no time. Hence the reason sorcerers generally take essence from the environment, but even then there is a cost—in blood."

"My friend, Nils, the Principal of Jeridium's Academy, told me some sorcerers made use of... conduits—is that the right word?"

"To weather the flow of essence, yes. Or rather, to redirect the corrosive side-effects of sorcery away from the caster. My staff, for example"—Venton thumped its butt against the deck—"functions in a similar way to a lightning conductor."

As if in response, something huge slammed into the prow. The ship pitched, and Venton yelped as he flipped over the gunwale. Nameless grabbed him by the back of the coat and hauled him back.

"Reckon they thought it was dinner time," the dwarf said.

"Who...?"

The dwarf nodded at the waters below and Venton gulped.

There were three dorsal fins keeping pace with the ship.

"You can relax your grip on the staff now, laddie."

Venton looked in a daze at his white-knuckled hands wrapped around the staff, and only then did he realize how close he'd come to dropping it overboard.

"Oh, thank goodness," he said. "And thank you, Nameless. You have no idea how much effort and time went into constructing this staff. Materials of this nature are not at all easy to procure in the Supernal Realm." Which is why several of the staff's components had been 'borrowed' from the Tower of Making, courtesy of Grittel Gadfly, who is a dab hand at such things.

"What do you think hit us?" he asked. "It felt like we ran into a whale."

"Maybe it was," the dwarf said, though he didn't sound convinced. He studied the waves for the longest while, as if he expected the culprit to surface and swallow the ship whole.

"Come on, laddie, let's sit down in case there's another impact."

They moved away to the port gunwale, where they sat on the long bench that ran all the way along the side.

Over on the starboard gunwale, Purg cut a sorry figure as he leaned overboard to be sick. Had he even noticed the collision?

Wind swirled across the deck, bringing with it the smells of baking from the galley.

"Is that Mora?" Nameless asked. "Smells good, whatever it is."

"Oh, yes, that'll be Mora." She'd headed to the galley the moment they came aboard. "Always on the go, that woman. She never stops." As if Venton could talk. "If she isn't foraging, she's cooking or concocting teas and tisanes. The only time she sits still is when she's smoking dubious looking mushrooms in order to commune with her god."

"If you don't mind me asking," Nameless said, "is there anything…"

"Romantic? Between me and Mora?" Between him and anyone! "Good grief, man, I was in my eighties when we met, and while Mora and I have an understanding, we are not exactly cut from the same cloth."

"I'll say," Nameless said. "So, how did you meet?"

Venton smiled. "Back then, I used to run a pipe and weedstick store in Vanatus."

"In your eighties?"

"I retired from sorcery, but not from life. Indeed, I was just getting started with normal living. The shop was my way into society. Mora came in one day, looking for a quality tobacco with which to lace her powdered mushrooms. We hit it off straight away—the beginnings of a fruitful, if not always easy, partnership."

"And the others?"

"Purg and Grittel? You've heard of the Azarot Archipelago?"

"Can't say I have, laddie?"

"Course you have, lubber," Rabnar the Red said, coming over to sit with them. "After Verusia, when we went sailing around the Empire. You remember, those islands we was warned away from by an iron patrol ship. Forbidden, they was. No one allowed to go there."

Rabnar held two bottles of rum. He handed one to Nameless and took a swig from the other.

"What did we hit back there?" Venton asked.

"Oh, don't trouble yourself about it, lubber. Probably just the sharp-tooths getting ornery."

"Big sharp-tooths," Nameless said.

"Did I tell you about the one that leapt right out of the water and swallowed me whole?" Rabnar said.

"Aye, you did, laddie."

Rabnar looked crestfallen. "Course, it could have been a dragon turtle we ran into."

"Dragon turtle?" Venton said, glancing about, half-expecting to see a scaly head rising above the gunwale.

"Aye," Nameless said, "or that faen Ahab you once told me about. You remember, the one who rode on the back of a flying whale."

The Captain chortled, then noticed the empty bottle in Venton's hands. "If I'd known you was a drinking man, I'd have brought another."

"Really, I'm fine," Venton said.

"I vaguely remember those isles," Nameless said. "Something to do with Sektis Gandaw."

"That's the Azarots all right," Venton said. "For years, the abode of the fanatics I told you about, who followed the teachings of the Mad Sorcerer. Hidden right at the heart of the Empire, they had networks of underground laboratories within which they conducted all manner of vile experiments."

"And that's where you found Purg and Grittel?" Nameless asked. "But Purg's a dwarf. There are no dwarves on Aosia outside of Medryn-Tha."

"Mora and I found an abandoned lore craft on one of the islands—no easy feat, considering it was invisible, but we had help, companions with rare skills. Judging from the trophies we found inside, I'd say the fanatics had been traveling all over the world picking up specimens."

Venton noticed Purg had stopped throwing up over the side and was crossing the deck towards them.

"That," Venton said, "is all I'm at liberty to say. Purg is a little touchy about his past, and Grittel gets paranoid if others talk about her. Knowing her, she's probably been listening in."

"Grittel's the little girl with the doggy head, is she?" Rabnar said with a chuckle

Venton touched a finger to his lips and whispered, "She's knifed people in the back for less than that, Captain."

Rabnar swallowed the rum in his mouth and glanced around fearfully.

"Grittel stab Purg once," Purg said as he drew near. "Purg love that scar. Purg's favorite."

"It's all right, Captain," Venton said, "I was joking. Grittel ran off with her tail between her legs. Giving Mora the slip like she did, in order to follow us…. that was a brave—or foolhardy—act of disobedience. I wouldn't want to be in her shoes."

20

The den was so cold, Grittel's breath misted in the dank air. It was sleeting outside the hole in the ground she and Mama and Papa lay in. The shiny people had found them there. Not Grittel: she'd made sure they couldn't see her. But they'd seen Mama and Papa. And then they'd gone away.

Shivering, Grittel snuggled into Mama for warmth, but felt only ice. Mama had lain face-down for days, feathers sticking out of her back. Feathers on a stick.

Papa was face-up, a feather-stick jutting out of his eye. There was dried blood around the site, but he'd be all right. Mama and Papa were only sleeping.

They smelled, though. Like off-meat. The stench made her queasy, but she had nothing left to throw up.

Grittel's belly began to ache again. She was hungry. She tried to shake Mama awake, but Mama was too tired to rouse. Giving up, she scratched around in the soil of the den, but all the earthworms had gone. She'd already eaten them.

Outside, the sleet had petered out, and she could hear the sea now, and birds squawking overhead. The sound frightened her, and she squeezed into the gap between Papa and Mama and cried herself to sleep.

A BANG WOKE HER. The den pitched to one side then rocked itself steady again. In a panic, she sat up—and hit her head. Above her, the wooden slats of a bench, not the dug-out roof of the den.

And she remembered.

She was on a ship—Rabnar's ship. Ever since they'd left the harbor, she'd hidden away beneath a bench, invisible. And she understood at once why she'd been frightened in her dream: Mad Mora had shown up at the dock, and she was angry with Grittel for running off from the smallholding.

But me only wanted to help, Grittel imagined herself saying.

She winced at the response she would get.

Her stomach rumbled. She was as hungry as she'd been in her dream, and she could smell cheese and dough and mushrooms baking in the galley. Perhaps if she went to Mora and explained herself, said she was sorry....

But she couldn't do it. Wouldn't. It wasn't fair. She'd done nothing wrong!

And so she curled up on the deck beneath the bench, checked her hand to make sure she was still invisible, and went back to sleep.

"GRITTEL'S the little girl with the doggy head, is she?"

She became aware of voices up above her bench. That sounded like Rabnar. He chuckled afterwards, and Grittel bared her teeth. He was mocking her.

Sleep still held her in its clutches, and she tried to shut the voices out, but then she heard her name again:

"Grittel stab Purg once."

Me didn't do it, she wanted to call out, but that would have given her away. And besides, she did do it, sort of. But it wasn't her fault!

"Grittel ran off with her tail between her legs."—Venton. "I wouldn't want to be in her shoes."

That made her tummy clench. Mora again! Why had she run off without saying anything? She hated it when Mora was in a strop. There was nothing worse.

Her tummy switched back from clenching to rumbling, and the smell of baking made drool trickle from her jaws.

Actually, there was something worse than Mora's fury.

Hunger.

Grittel was briefly back in the den with that thought, an old man reaching inside to pull her out, commenting she was all skin and bones. She remembered a big strong dwarf with a bloodstained beard filling the den with rocks and soil and self-consciously mumbling a prayer for Mama and Papa, still inside.

That was the day Venton and Purg found her and took her over the sea to Vanatus.

To Mora.

The memory brought tears to her eyes. She suppressed a sniffle in case the three sitting on her bench heard. Quiet as a mouse, she slid along the deck beneath the bench and came out the end. No one saw her.

Plucking up her courage, she took a deep breath, then, head bowed, tail between her legs—she could almost hear Venton saying, "Told you so!"—she made her way to the galley.

Mora was stooped in front of the open oven as Grittel came down the steps and through the doorway. Hands encased in filthy oven mitts, Mora removed a tray of cheese and mushroom scones and set them on a mat to cool.

She looked old from worry. Mora was odd like that: when she was in her element, working in the garden, tending the bees, foraging in the forest, she was rosy-cheeked and vibrant, full of vigor and life; but give her something to fret about, and she became a wizened crone.

Her mousy hair was all mussed up, and the dried mushrooms she decorated it with—pretty reds and blues and yellows—were in disarray. She muttered constantly to herself in her secret language. It might have been the mushrooms in the scones she was speaking to— Mora did that: apologized to the mushrooms for cooking them, or thanked the big puffball in the sky for its providence. To Grittel's ears, the utterances sounded spiteful. Angry. Perhaps now wasn't the best time. She started to back up the stairs.

"I ain't stupid, girl," Mora said. "That invisibility don't work on me."

Grittel winced then showed herself. "Did the mushrooms tell you me here?"

Mora's eyes were bloodshot, the pupils massive. "They're everywhere," she said. "Maybe now you'll believe me. In the air you breathe, the earth, the sea, even amid the stars. There's nowhere you can hide from the *feruveum*, Grittel, and the *feruveum* talks to me."

Only when Mora had been smoking, and come to think of it, there was a background smell of burned tobacco and powdered redcap. She must have been seriously angry to use some of her most cherished supply.

"Come here," Mora said.

Grittel hung her head. Her tail went limp.

"Come here!"

Trembling, Grittel did as she was told.

"Now, before you go making apologies neither of us believes," Mora said, "have a scone. I expect you're hungry."

21

It was an odd thing to Nameless when night fell and a single gibbous moon washed the decks in silver. He was used to there being three moons.

He sat by himself at the stern, looking back at the ship's wake through the choppy water. Thinking, brooding, trying to get his head straight.

It had all seemed so simple on the ship ride from Aosia with Cordy and Paxy, but then they had disappeared, and the peace of death he'd just started to enjoy was filled with all the uncertainties of life.

"Cordy," he muttered.

Would they see each other again? Would Witandos permit it? Would Cordy want it now she was a Wayist?

He caught a whiff of fish—and not the background odor of the *Watchful Wake,* either. Cooked fish.

Sailors were congregating on the benches around the gunwale, eating and drinking. How long had it been since all work on deck had stopped? And how had he not noticed? The black dog mood? Hardly. He'd been maudlin, but not in the depths of despair.

He stood and stretched out his legs after sitting so long. His arse was numb, his joints stiff, and a chill had crept unnoticed into his bones. His stomach let out a long, gurgling grumble, and so he followed the smell of the fish.

Rabnar had brought his grill on deck—an upturned bronze shield filled with coals, set atop an iron-rimmed barrel. Above the smoking coals was a metal latticework, upon which lay four headless and filleted fish.

Purg stood over the grill with a fish slice and tongs. A group of sailors waited, plates in hand, drinking ale and talking. Mad Mora sat at a low table, gutting another fish.

"Ah, Nameless," Venton said. The wizard was standing apart, smoking a weedstick. "We were beginning to think you'd fallen overboard."

"I think that's your purview, laddie. No, I just needed some time to think."

"Understandable. It's a big adjustment, arriving in Gabala. Takes most of us decades to get used to it."

"Aye, laddie, well I'm not sure I want to get used to it."

Venton opened his mouth to respond, but Mora abruptly stood and shoved a plate of fish in his hand. "Don't," she said.

"I can assure you, I wasn't going to," Venton said.

"He's always getting people's hopes up," Mora told Nameless. "Whatever he says, don't believe a word of it. Same as them Wayists, walking their bloody maze in the hope of reaching the Pleroma, it's all nonsense."

"Just because your efforts came to nothing," Venton said.

"You tried to leave Gabala?" Nameless asked. "Let me guess: using mushrooms?"

"Don't be so bloody impertinent," Mora said. "And technically, they was toadstools. Waste of bleeding time."

"I beg to disagree," Venton said, passing his plate of fish to a sailor, as if he drew all the sustenance he needed from smoking. "Without your early attempts, I'd never have had my intuitive leap and come up with the phylactery."

"Which is for Etala, not any of us," Mora said. "A sodding Supernal. Go on, why don't you tell Nameless about the lily cats?"

"He already has," Nameless said.

That didn't seem to register with Mora.

"He had this book he picked up on one of his trips to Malfen. It said these lily cats possessed the secret of life, so he set off to find them and dragged us along with him. Only, he left the bleeding book behind, so we got lost in Cerreth. Till the dragon took care of that particular problem."

"It wouldn't have made one jot of difference if I'd brought the book," Venton said. "It only mentioned the lily cats in passing. Which is why, when we got lost, I wanted to return to Malfen to search for the companion volume, but you refused to let us go back there."

"I don't blame you, lassie," Nameless said. "Does anyone even read in Malfen?"

"You have to understand," Venton said, "I was a very old man at the time. I thought the secret of the lily cats might prolong my life."

"What is it with wizards and prolonging their lives?" Nameless asked.

"My only motive," Venton said, "was to be able to continue looking after these reprobates."

"As if we couldn't manage without him!" Mora said. "And, do you know, he still goes on about the bloody lily cats."

"I suspect they have some means of shuttling essence between worlds," Venton said. "Else, how do you account for their nine lives?"

"You're asking the wrong dwarf, laddie," Nameless said.

"He thinks he could use the power of the lily cats to get us all back to Aosia!" Mora said. "Only, he's no closer to knowing what their secret is, and he hasn't found a single lily cat in all the time we've been here. You ask me, there's more chance of finding the mother of all mushrooms."

"Haven't I already found her?" Venton asked, and Mora gave him a vicious slap on the arm.

"Ho, lubber!" Rabnar called out as he crossed the deck with a netful of fish and a fishing rod over one shoulder. "Thought you'd smell the grub sooner or later." He passed the basket to Mora, who smiled sweetly, all her belligerence gone in an instant. "Rum or beer?"

"You know me, laddie," Nameless said. "If there's beer to be had...."

"Coming up."

Rabnar scuttled off to his cabin, leaving an uncomfortable silence between Venton and Mora. Nameless tried to think of something to say to Purg, but the big dwarf was still staring wide-eyed at the fish he was cooking, as if they might leap off the grill and bite him.

"Are they supposed to be black like that?" Nameless asked.

"Eh?"

"Purg, you lummox," Mora said. "I told you to turn them!"

"Purg forgot."

"I'll do it," one of the sailors said, a big strapping lassie Nameless thought he remembered from their adventures on the Sea of Weeping. He was about to ask her name, but Rabnar returned with a bottle of rum and handed him a flagon of ale, and that was that.

"Where's Grittel?" Nameless asked.

"Probably right behind you with a knife," Venton said.

"Grittel's all right," Mora said. "She'll come round, you'll see."

"Mind if I take that?" Nameless asked, indicating one of the char-blackened fish.

The sailor slid the fish onto a plate for him.

"I like the crispy bits," Nameless said, as he bit off a piece of fish and washed it down with a swig of beer.

"I know." She looked him in the eye, as if to ask if he remembered who she was. And he did, sort of.

"Don't tell me your name," he said. "It's on the tip of my..."

"Ash," she said.

"I was going to say that."

"You don't remember, do you?"

Nameless grimaced. "Sorry, lassie, I can't even remember my own... Ash! Of course I remember. The lassie who harpooned that big scaly monster and saved the ship. That was some shot."

He also remembered that she'd been there when the *Watchful*

Wake returned to Medryn-Tha after Rabnar's death. Nameless had lost touch with the crew when he'd gone into the Southern Crags. That made him wonder what had happened to Ash all those decades ago, how her life had ended.

"Here, Purg," Ash said, "let me show you how to grill fish."

"Purg like that." He watched her with the same attentiveness he'd watched the fish—for all the good it had done.

"Eyes on the fish," Purg," Venton said, causing Ash to chuckle.

The wizard flipped something into the air and caught it. Something that glinted in the moonlight.

"Is that...?" Nameless started.

"The crystal of spell turning that Coalheart fellow had. Might come in handy if we run into this enemy sorcerer."

"Assuming he doesn't have one himself," Nameless said.

"Ah..." Venton said, pocketing the crystal. "I wonder how that would work: a spell bouncing from one crystal to the other till... till what? Mora, what effect would that have on the structure of the local fungal matrix?"

"Buggered if I know."

"Helpful as always," Venton said.

After they finished eating, Purg helped Ash clean the grill, while Mora's pupils swallowed up the rest of her eyes as she smoked some foul-smelling muck in a pipe.

"Best stay out of her way," Venton said. "Grittel," he called out. "Keep an eye on Mora."

"Me know!" a squeaky voice said from right behind him, making the wizard jump. The dog-girl appeared out of thin air. "You don't need to tell I."

"There's no predicting how the mushroom pipe's going to affect Mora," Venton explained to Nameless. "Sometimes she has visions, others she hears voices—and not pleasant ones, either. She's been known to fall into a trance, soil her clothes, vomit all over herself, or grow rabid and violent." He rubbed his chin, frowning at some raw memory. "I wouldn't put it past her to leap over the gunwale in the belief that she can fly."

"So why do it?" Nameless asked.

"It's how she communes with her god."

"The giant puffball in the sky? Well, to my mind, any god that requires its devotees to smoke that stinking muck is one you won't catch me worshiping."

"On that, we are agreed," Venton said. "But is it true, you dwarves still worship Witandos?"

"Personally, I used to curse by his name, but worship? I didn't see a whole lot of that going on at Arx Gravis under the Council of Twelve, and when we got to Arnoch, we were too busy fixing the citadel up to give religion much thought. *The Chronicles of Arx Gravis* make mention of a cult of Witandos in the days before King Arios of Arnoch, according to my brother."

"Which is to be expected," Venton said, "given that Witandos made them the gift of the first twelve Exalted. I wonder if they worshiped him before that, or some other god?"

"Who cares?" Nameless said, "Maybe they didn't bother with gods back then. A good pint of beer's always been enough for me."

"Are you lubbers done talking?" Rabnar asked. "Because I've something to show you."

The Captain led Nameless and Venton into his cabin, where threads of black smoke plumed from an oil lamp that hung from the ceiling.

Spread out on the square table—at which Nameless had spent many an evening playing seven-card and getting drunk—was a stained and crinkled map.

"Got it from Maldark the Fallen," Rabnar said, "who does nothing but sail these waters, when he's not ferrying folk over from the other side."

He jabbed a finger at the central land mass, a vast continent with edges that seemed to blur into the sea.

"That's where we set out from," Rabnar said. He moved his finger to a small island dominated by the picture of a black mountain. "And this is where we're going."

"The Isle of Mananoc," Venton breathed.

"What's this?" Nameless asked, indicating a far bigger island to the west.

"No idea. Never been there."

There were words scrawled over the island, the handwriting sloppy and illegible, though Nameless was sure the letters were Old Dwarven. Probably Maldark still wrote in the ancient tongue. Now, there was a dwarf who hailed from a different era.

"But this," Rabnar said, tracing a red line that split the ocean midway between their starting point and their destination, "is where the Burning Sea begins—and the fun."

"Fun?" Nameless said, recalling how, when Rabnar had used that word in the past, disaster usually struck.

"Them seas are full of husks that passed over from Cerreth," Rabnar said. "All manner of beasties with tentacles and teeth. And some so fair, that just to look on them will strike a man dumb, or have him leap into the waters just to get a closer look, only to be dragged under forever."

Nameless laughed and clapped the Captain on the shoulder. "Death hasn't curbed your enthusiasm for tall tales, laddie."

"I'm serious. When it heats up outside—and it will when the waves are crested with flame—we'll all of us have to keep our eyes peeled. We won't be making a stop till we reach the Isle of Mananoc. The sea's bad enough, but by far the worst of the husks, in my experience, live on land. All I can say is, I hope we don't get shipwrecked."

"That happens?" Nameless asked.

"There are storms here that would make a hurricane seem like a mouse's fart by comparison," Rabnar said.

Nameless started to relax. Now he knew the Captain was back to his old ways.

"And great big leviathans that could crush a ship like the *Wake* with one swish of their tales."

"Like whatever it was that hit us earlier?" Venton asked.

Rabnar didn't answer, merely looked at them both with wide eyes.

22

Purg was tired after the barbecue. It took a lot of concentration to watch the fish, and the cleaning up afterwards went on forever. He snuggled under the blankets in the dormitory he shared with Nameless and a bunch of sailors. Venton had a cabin with Mora and Grittel.

It had been a hard day but a good one. A day to make Purg smile. Ash had been nice to him: told him when to turn the fish, then shown him how to clean the grill with wire brushes and soapy water. And she was so beautiful... Ash... Ash....

Purg's teeth started to chatter as sleep clouded his mind, and a lone tear bled from his eye to dampen the pillow.

"Leave Purg alone," he muttered. "Leave Purg...."

∽

P<small>URG LEFT</small> *the citadel with two other dwarves. They were all armed to the teeth. A battle goat had been snatched from the pens overnight, and it hadn't lifted the latch on the gate and let itself out. Footprints led away from the goat enclosure. Massive footprints.*

They followed the trail up into the hill country, and the goat was there waiting for them. Or rather, its remains were, every last scrap of meat picked from the bones.

"Hungry shogger," one of the dwarves said—Purg couldn't think of his name. Couldn't even recall what his own name was, but he knew it wasn't Purg back then. "That was a big goat."

"Come on," the other dwarf said—he seemed to be the leader. "The prints don't stop here. Whatever killed the goat will kill again, if we don't do something about it."

"Something that could do that to a battle goat..." Purg said. For a moment, he became aware that he was dreaming, and that he spoke so much better in his dreams. "We should go back for reinforcements."

"Where's the honor in that?" the leader said.

The dream skipped ahead like it always did—and always to the bad bits.

The leader's screams were terrible as the ogre ripped his arm from its socket in a shower of blood. The other dwarf dropped his hammer and backed away, the seat of his britches sodden and bulging and stinking like a cesspit. The ogre lunged for him, grabbed his head in a massive hand and squeezed. As the skull cracked and gore slopped through the ogre's fingers, Purg charged. The ogre's eyes widened. Purg's axe arced toward its belly....

And froze.

Light blazed around them—Purg, the ogre, the dead dwarves. A column of light from above.

Purg strained with all his might, but he couldn't move a muscle below the neck. The ogre growled and roared and spat, but it was as paralyzed as he was.

A low drone started up, then Purg drifted into the air, along with the ogre and his dead comrades, rising within the column of light.

Next came the silver room, and he could hear his teeth chattering even in his dream. He heard his moans and whimpers too, as he tossed and turned on the bed.

The ogre's eyes were rolled up and white like a baresark's, as it fought against whatever invisible force held them both.

Purg's axe remained frozen in mid-swing. He couldn't move a muscle, but out of the corner of his eye he saw the blood of his dead companions puddling on the burnished floor. Liquid metal bubbled up out of the floor and smothered the blood, before draining away, leaving pristine silver in its wake.

Doors slid open all around the room. Men and women entered, masked, dressed all in grey. They brought leather restraints and shiny implements.

Purg shook all over as a masked woman stood before him, in her hand a long needle with a bead of fluid glistening at its tip. His guts clenched. Tears of frustration welled in his eyes. And then she plunged the needle into his neck.

∾

"Laddie, it's all right. You're just having a bad dream."

Someone cradled Purg's head as he screamed and sobbed.

"You're onboard ship, laddie. I can fetch Venton, if you like."

"Nameless?"

"Aye, Purg, it's me. Do you want me to get one of the others? Mora? Grittel?"

"No," Purg said, sitting up. "Grittel not see Purg like this. Grittel scare easy. Grittel dream bad, like Purg."

"You're still trembling," Nameless said. "I stowed some of Rabnar's beer under my bed. I'll open one for you."

"Purg like beer."

"Course you do, you're a dwarf."

The beer helped. The first bottle took the edge off. The second had Purg yawning and ready to go back to sleep.

"You need me to stay by your bedside?" Nameless asked.

"Purg fine now," he said around a yawn. "You see Ash, how she nice to Purg?"

"She's a fine looking woman, laddie."

"Beautiful," Purg said, as sleep closed around him. "And Nameless…"

"Laddie?"

"Thank you."

23

Nameless left Purg snoring peacefully and tramped up top. He just couldn't sleep. The dorm was oppressive, and it stank of sweat and flatulence.

The night air was biting on the quarterdeck, the smell of brine a relief.

He found Rabnar with one hand on the ship's wheel, other holding a steaming mug. Apart from the Captain, the decks were empty. It had been that way every night when they'd sailed together before, the crew taking a well-earned rest while Rabnar kept watch through the night.

"Hot toddy?" Rabnar asked.

Nameless accepted the mug and took a sip—whisky and honey in hot water.

Rabnar lifted his tricorn hat and let the breeze blow out his straggly hair. "Not sleeping, eh? Well, I'm glad of the company." He crammed the hat back on his head and grinned. "It's good to see you again, lubber. We had some adventures, you and me. Good times, eh?"

"When they weren't bad." Nameless handed him the mug back.

"At first they were, but you pulled yourself together, son, and it's not every man that can do that."

"I gave up," Nameless said. "I let Cordy go."

"No, lubber, you accepted a hard truth."

They had gone looking for Cordy. Nameless had been convinced the Lich Lord had taken her to his castle at Wolfmalen in Verusia. But in reality, she'd died at Arx Gravis. The Lich Lord had turned her into a still-living corpse. She'd come at Nameless in a frenzied rage, and he'd cut her down.

"I couldn't accept she was gone," Nameless said. "Couldn't accept it was my axe that ended her. I made myself believe Blightey had tricked me, and Cordy was still alive."

"I wish we could have found her for you," Rabnar said. "But you've found her now, right?"

"Aye, I found her."

He told Rabnar that Cordy had traveled with him and Paxy on Maldark's ship, only to disappear once he arrived in the Supernal Realm.

"Happens all the time, " Rabnar said. "Everyone has penance of their own to do. Personally, I can't be bothered, There's enough to take care of today without moping about what I did yesterday, or worrying about what I might do tomorrow."

"You haven't worked out any penance?" Nameless asked. "Witandos didn't make you?"

"He can't. Oh, he likes to give the impression he can, but even dead, we still have free will, and I exercise my free will to tell him to stick it. Course, there's no progress without penance. No rising from glory to bleeding glory. But that's all right with me. I'm happy with what I've got." He gave the ship's wheel an affectionate pat.

"So, I could just tell Witandos to go shog himself?"

"You could, but you won't. You really see yourself sitting in one of them fake taverns drinking beer day after day, with the same company?"

Nameless tried to imagine that. Was it so bad? There were far worse ways to spend the afterlife. But Rabnar was right: a year or two in a tavern had a certain appeal, but after that....

"I could sail with you, like in the old days...."

"Aye, you could," Rabnar said. "But sail where, and why? Sure, there's a lot of places in this realm I've yet to discover, but discover them I will, and then what? I'm all right with sailing aimlessly forever. I can't think of anything better I'd be doing. But you, lubber, you don't belong here."

"Course I belong. I died." Wasn't that the badge of membership everyone shared in Gabala?

"And what's that mean, exactly?" a voice said out of the dark. It came from the bench along the starboard gunwale.

"Mora?"

She struck a firestick, touched it to the bowl of her pipe, gave the stem three sharp sucks, and the contents smoldered red. A pungent odor wafted over Nameless, and it wasn't just tobacco.

Mora's face was half in, half out of shadow, lit only by tiny phosphorescent motes that drifted up from the bowl of her pipe.

"Death on Aosia is life here," Mora said. "It's just essence moved from one place to another."

"And death here?" Nameless asked.

"Leads either to the Void or somewhere better," Mora said. "Better than any of us could imagine. Depends on what you desire more. You decide. There ain't no other choice."

"Venton wants to return to Aosia," Nameless said.

"Venton wants a lot of things he can't have. How about you, Nameless Dwarf? What do you want?"

"Cordy," he said without thinking. "I just want to be with my wife."

"Forever?"

"Yes. I think."

"Having second thoughts?" Rabnar asked.

"I don't know. If I knew where she was, what she was up to...."

"I could show you, if you want," Mora said. She patted the bench she was seated upon.

"Go on," Rabnar said. "Maybe she knows a thing or two—certainly more than I do. Don't worry, I'm not going anywhere. I'll be right here, if you need to talk more."

That should have been a comfort to Nameless, but as he clapped Rabnar on the shoulder and moved to the gunwale, he couldn't help wondering if any of this was real.

"I did die on Aosia, didn't I?" he asked Mora as he seated himself beside her—then shunted himself away a little. She stank of loam and mold.

"You must have done, if you're here," she said.

"And there's definitely no way of going back?"

"Would you want to? How is it any different, save on the surface? Still the same problems, the same kinds of people, lying, cheating, stealing. Like mirror reflections they are, Aosia and Gabala. Air bubbles in the cosmos, connected by the essence they share."

"The essence of their Supernal creators?"

"You're not as slow as you look. And there was me thinking we'd found us another Purg."

"Lassie, you're the Ironbelly's of charm. Now, you said you could show me Cordy."

Mora set her pipe down on the bench and produced a flat metal case from her pocket. She opened it to reveal dried mushrooms of dubious appearance—red, blue, green.

"What I can do is put you in touch with the *feruveum*. What happens next depends on how dense she is."

"I wouldn't let Cordy hear you say that, lassie."

"I don't give a stuff what she hears. My point is, most people have cut themselves off from the fungal matrix that shapes all life. Most don't even know it exists."

"And these mushrooms will help me see the *feruveum*?"

"They'll awaken whatever dormant ability you have to connect with it. All you gotta do is flood your senses with things you remember about your wife: sights, sounds, smells, taste...."

"Steady on," Nameless said.

"Oh, and don't forget touch."

"As if I could. Cordy used to show affection by punching me in the face."

"I can see the appeal," Mora said, handing him a piece of red mushroom. "Chew on this and concentrate on your wife—every sense, got it?"

"Got it," Nameless said.

The mushroom was surprisingly sweet. As he chewed, a pleasant fizzing sensation filled his mouth. He held an image of Cordy in his mind, as she'd been on the ship from Aosia: fresh-faced and golden haired. He clung to the sound of her voice, but when he tried to recall her scent, there was nothing. On the boat he'd smelled nothing but brine, but before, when they had trained together in the Slean, or when they had lain together as King and Queen.... He knew she'd smelled of musk and honeysuckle and a healthy dose of sweat, but all he could smell was rot—the stench of a putrefying corpse.

"Anything yet?" Mora asked.

"I can't smell her." Only the thing she had become before he ended her life.

"Then don't try. Work with what you have."

"I can see her, hear her...."

"Touch?"

"Cold, clammy," Nameless said. Just as bad as the smell. "I can't remember what she felt like." Warm, sensual, soft in all the right places—they were just words to him. He couldn't dredge up the sensation.

"Try this," Mora said.

Her fist slammed into his teeth, splitting his lip. He tasted blood in his mouth.

"Feel her now?"

"Yep," Nameless said. "You certainly know how to bring back old memories."

"But can you see her yet? Really see, not just remember? Close your eyes."

Nameless did so, and his mind threw up random images: Cordy, Thumil, Duck, Kal.... But then he saw a hall with walls of mother-of-pearl, a marble floor, a high, vaulted ceiling painted midnight blue and dotted with stars.

And there she was: Cordy, dressed in a white robe, hair and beard unbraided, unkempt—as if she no longer cared about appearances. Her eyes were closed, her hands clasped in... prayer?

"I see her," Nameless said. "I think."

"You think?"

"I saw her in this place before, in a dream or a daydream, sometime before the Battle of Jeridium." He'd assumed it was a vision of the Feasting Hall of Witandos. "It's not working, lassie. This is just another memory."

"Is it?" Mora said. "What if it was more than a dream before? What if you glimpsed her as she is here in the Supernal Realm?"

"No," Nameless said, but then Cordy opened her eyes and she smiled at someone he couldn't see. Suddenly, there were corridors—hundreds of corridors—leading away from the hall. He relayed all this to Mora.

"You know what it sounds like?" she said. "The maze the bloody Wayists walk around, seeking the entrance to the Pleroma."

Nameless opened his eyes, the vision fading but not quite disappearing from his mind. Hearing about Cordy's conversion from Droom was one thing, but seeing it for himself....

"Why'd you open your eyes?" Mora said. "You're wasting a perfectly good mushroom. Get back to it. What's she doing now?"

Nameless shut his eyes again.

Cordy moved towards one of the corridors, where a dwarf was waiting. A hooded man, also robed in white. Nameless's heart clenched as Cordy took his hand. Acid burned in his veins. Before he could see what happened next, Rabnar's voice snapped him out of the vision.

"Oh, ho, you two lubbers! Come take a look at this."

Nameless swayed as he stood from the bench. It felt as though his bones had been removed, leaving him half floating, half floppy.

"That'll be the mushroom," Mora said, taking his elbow and

guiding him to the helm, where Rabnar was pointing out to sea, past the prow.

Smoked crept and curled above the water, and there was a continuous line of flames on the horizon.

"The Burning Sea," Rabnar said. "I hope you're duly impressed."

Nameless just stared ahead blankly. All he could think of was his seething rage, and the dwarf holding hands with Cordy.

He was sure it was Thumil.

24

After completing his morning review of the sorcerous forms in his considerable arsenal, Venton went up on deck, shielding his eyes against the glare.

The sunrise spoke to him of forge-heated iron—not an image that would normally emerge from his mind. Probably, it was evoked by the sweltering heat rising from the sea. Tendrils of smoke curled above the gunwale, dissipating as they climbed toward the sails. The waves were aflame as far as he could see in every direction. Every now and then, a red dolphin would break the surface and roll back under, and for a brief moment reveal the grey water beneath.

The acrid fumes coming off the sea made Venton cough. He reached for his brandy flask, then remembered it was empty.

"Here," Mora said, coming from the galley, steaming cup in either hand and passing one to him. "Mushroom tea. Your favorite."

Venton winced. He'd never plucked up the courage to tell her it tasted like she'd steeped sweaty socks in water. But he couldn't deny that it perked him up every morning. Goodness only knew what was in those mushrooms. Ignoring the taste—a feat at which he'd become remarkably adept—he took a sip and relieved the irritation in his throat.

"Mora, you look terrible."

"Must be catching, then," she said as she sipped her own tea.

Her eyes were bloodshot, set in deep cavities, and her pupils were almost permanently dilated these days.

"Mushroom-induced visions again last night?" Venton said. "I'm worried we're losing you to the *feruveum*, Mora. You can't keep going on like this."

"You ain't no better when you're learning a new form for your sorcery."

"That's different."

"Inferior, maybe, and so doesn't warrant the same risks." She became suddenly animated—manically so. "My control over the *feruveum* is growing all the time, and to my mind that's a good thing. It's the only hope we have. You have to be realistic, Venton. Aosia's gone. No matter what you say, we can't go back, only forward."

"To the Pleroma?"

"Call it that, if you must, like all them other arseholes."

Venton shook his head. "And what if you get there and find your omnipresent mushroom brain or great puffball in the sky or whatever it is? How does that help you, let alone the rest of us?"

"In the mushroom," Mora said, and now she sounded every inch the sage, "we can all be one."

"What if I don't want to be one? And I think we can agree that neither of us would be happy about being one with Purg!" He finished his tea and handed her back the cup. "No, Mora, leave it to me to find us a way out of Gabala. You just concentrate on cutting back on the mushrooms. For Grittel's sake. For all our sakes."

He left her muttering under her breath and headed towards his spot at the prow—only to find Purg had gotten there first. The dwarf was still wearing his armor, axe slung over one shoulder.

"I hope you didn't wear that to bed," Venton said, holding onto his fur hat with one hand, in case the breeze whipped it from his head and it burned up in the sea.

"Course Purg didn't. Purg not stupid."

"Far be it from me to contradict you," Venton said. "But you'll roast in all this heat."

"Purg fine."

He didn't look fine, the way his eyes never left the flaming water.

"What is it, Purg?"

"Something down there."

"They're called dolphins."

"Something else."

Venton watched the fire-capped waves until it hurt his eyes. Nothing.

"Don't worry, Venton. Purg keep everyone safe."

"I know you will, old friend."

He left Purg standing there and moved into the shade beneath the foremast. Rabnar waved from the aftcastle, where he was drinking from a bottle and keeping an eye on the quarterdeck below. Venton raised his staff in acknowledgment.

"How are my modifications to the *Wake* holding up, Captain?" he hollered.

Venton had spent weeks reshaping the essence that comprised the hull, imbuing the wood with the heat retardant properties—if not the density and appearance—of granite.

"Perfick!" Rabnar called back, saluting Venton with his bottle.

Nameless was a brooding presence, slumped on a bench, leaning back against the gunwale. His beard and hair were smoldering, although it might have been an effect of the heat haze.

"Second thoughts?" Venton asked as he joined the dwarf. Using his staff for support, he lowered himself to sit on the bench, still surprised after all these years in Gabala that his knees no longer hurt.

"Don't see the point of second thoughts," Nameless said, "when our choices are still the same."

"No choice at all, you mean. Witandos really has his claws into you, doesn't he? You could just refuse to play along. I did. I mean, who does he think he is, meting out penance to all and sundry? Penance, for goodness' sake! It's all about manipulation of essence. Ours!"

"I can't refuse him," Nameless said.

"Why not?"

"Cordy. He took her away until after I completed this quest. I reckon he didn't expect me to see what she was up to, though. So, maybe we do have a choice."

"Oh?" Venton rubbed his chin as he tried to make sense of Nameless's utterances. "Ah, Mora, of course. She put you in touch with the *feruveum*."

"I wish she hadn't." Nameless sighed. He swiveled on the bench to look out at the fiery sea. "Ignore me, laddie. I'm just ornery about what I saw. Now I know why my pa always warned me and Lukar not to eat the mushrooms that grew on the ravine walls."

"You want to turn back?" Venton asked tentatively.

"You sound worried that I might, laddie."

"Oh no, not really. It's just, I put a lot of work into that phylactery, and I'd hate for some charlatan to break it in his ham-fisted attempts to use it."

"Personally," Nameless said, "I'd be more worried about what happens next: when Mananoc comes through from the Abyss. The sooner we get this over and done with, the sooner I can…." He dried up, leaving the thought unfinished.

The dwarf was agitated. Tormented, even, the way he gripped the gunwale so hard his knuckles turned white.

"It doesn't burn?" Venton said.

Nameless stroked the gunwale. "Not even hot. How's that, then?"

"That, my friend, is the result of a lot of hard work."

"Rabnar said you augmented the ship so he could sail these waters in search of more clay. That little statue you were working on when I first met you…"

"It's a golem. Or it will be when I finish it. If." Hopefully he wouldn't need it now. He would have to see how things played out.

"What's it for exactly?" Nameless asked.

"Oh, this and that. Helps me to while away the time."

"Speaking of which," Nameless said, "how long do we have?"

"Until this wizard or whoever works out how to use the phylactery? Weeks, months, years? It would take a genius to solve the puzzles I built into it any faster than that. Even Baz couldn't do it."

"Don't be so sure of yourself," Nameless said. "What if this sorcerer's cannier than you think?"

"If he is, I'll eat my hat. I put all my considerable mind into the puzzles, and no sorcerous hack is going to crack them anytime soon, mark my words."

"Laddie," Nameless said, "you sound angry. What's going on?"

"I am not angry," Venton said as he stood, emphasizing the point with a thump of his staff against the deck.

"Anyone would think it was your phylactery we were after, not Witandos's."

"Anyone incapable of thought," Venton muttered.

Nameless's eyes narrowed, and Venton raised his hand in apology. There was fire in the dwarf that hadn't been there before. Suppressed anger. It made him… dangerous.

In his hurry to turn away before Nameless could respond, he bumped into something and yelped.

"Grittel!" he growled, and she instantly appeared out of thin air, tail tucked between her legs.

Behind him, Nameless chuckled. Well, at least he seemed to have cheered up.

"Me sorry," Grittel said, and all Venton's frustration and anger melted away. Of course, he didn't want her to know that.

"Is there anything else you want to apologize for, while we're on the subject?"

She nodded.

"Well?"

"Me sorry for running away from Mora and following you."

"Has Mora forgiven you?"

Another nod.

"Well," Venton said, "I'm not happy about it. You've placed yourself and Mora in harm's way."

She started to say sorry again, but Venton stopped her with a raised finger and the sternest look he could manufacture.

"But," he said soberly, "I will do everything in my power to keep you both safe, and I'm sure Purg feels the same."

"You will?"

Venton tickled her behind the ear. "What do you think?"

Grittel's nostrils flared and her ears twitched.

"What is it?" Venton asked.

She emitted a whine as her hand went to the hilt of the dagger in her belt.

Something huge struck the ship, causing it to lurch. Sailors cried out. One man fell away from the rigging but managed to hook his legs in the ratlines and hung there upside down.

Nameless stood from his bench, looking around for the threat. Mora swilled the remains of her tea overboard. Rabnar hollered from the aftcastle steps as he made his way down: "All hands, battle stations!"

"Battle...?" Venton said.

At the prow, Purg climbed over the railing and balanced precariously at the base of the bowsprit, above the figurine of the pregnant woman. He'd seen something in the waters below, but what the blazes was he doing?

The boat juddered at a second, lesser, impact. The sailor in the crow's nest cursed. Fire and water showered over Purg and rained down on the foredeck as a massive, flame-wreathed tentacle reared above the prow.

"Oh, my shogging...." Rabnar cried. "Kraken!"

The tip of the tentacle turned this way and that, as if it were feeling the air, searching for something. Someone. Ignoring Purg, it curled down to slap into the deck in a hissing rush of steam, then undulated across the planks... straight toward Venton.

Purg bellowed and swung his axe. Blood misted the air. The tentacle backtracked to the prow and slid out of view. A second later, there was a plop and a splash.

Purg cast a look at Venton, gave a nod that seemed to say everything was going to be all right—*Purg keep everyone safe*. And then the dwarf turned and leaped into the burning sea.

"Purg, no!" Venton cried out—too late.

The idiot must have forgotten he was wearing his armor.

25

Purg's axe bit into the tentacle, showering him with blood. The tentacle slid back into the water, but there was something else there now. Something massive.

"There you are!"

The thing Purg had seen earlier: a hulking mass in the sea, amid the smoke and the flames. An island of livid flesh with a great lidless eye, and lots of tentacles that thrashed beneath the surface.

"Purg got you!" he muttered.

He glanced round at Venton and gave a nod: *I told you so.*

See, he wasn't stupid. He'd bided his time, watched the waters, and now he was going to make this monster pay. No one—no thing—was going to hurt his friends.

Venton cried out as Purg leapt from the base of the bowsprit, swinging his axe. The creature suddenly dived beneath the ship, and the axe connected with nothing but fire and water.

Purg hit the sea next: scorching heat, smoke in his lungs, then he was through the flames and plummeting like a stone through the cold water beneath. He thrashed about, refusing to let go of his axe as he kicked for the surface, but the weight of his armor dragged him down.

Through the murk and a rash of bubbles, he glimpsed a tentacle, then saw the barnacles on the underside of the ship. Down and down he went, lungs burning for air, forcing him to gasp. He swallowed saltwater.

And he knew then he had failed. Stupid, dumb fool that he was, he had failed to protect Venton, Mora, and poor little Grittel....

∼

Purg's heart *thudded in his chest. There had been a boom, an explosion. One of the metal walls of his cell had a smoking hole ripped into it. Masonry cascaded from the ceiling. He could hear shouts and cries, the blare of a klaxon, the clash of blades. Screams.*

Frantic, he turned to the hole in the wall. It was big enough to walk through. And so he did, into the wind and the rain and the cold of night. The stars above were obscured by rising smoke.

He froze in place as three of the grey-clad wizards ran past. An armored woman gave chase, white cloak flapping in the wind. She hurled something like a club at the fleeing wizards. There was a flash, a concussive blast. Clumps of smoking flesh spattered the ground. Blood rained down.

More armored figures joined the woman. Some had bows. Others had long-barreled weapons of grey metal. They conferred then disappeared around the side of the building.

And he ran then. Really ran, as fast as his legs could carry him. Out into the dark, tripping on roots, crashing through underbrush, flinching at every flash and every boom, always moving away from the buildings of the wizards, where he'd been imprisoned. Where they had done things to him, though he couldn't remember what.

∼

Something caught Purg's wrist, slowing his watery descent. He opened bleary eyes upon froth and bubbles swirling around him. It was a hand that had caught his wrist—a hand formed from water. Watery arms wrapped around his chest pulling him into a hug. He glimpsed a man's face in the chaos of bubbles, a tail like a fish's, also made of water.

And then he was moving upwards, carried in the water's arms, rushing towards the surface.

26

"Give me that, laddie."

Nameless snatched a harpoon from a sailor who looked too scared to use it. Someone needed to protect Venton.

The wizard stood at the prow, staff raised, eyes shut in concentration. Below him, beneath the ship's big-bellied bowsprit, the water churned, dowsing the flames. Bubbles raged, and Nameless glimpsed a mannish shape formed from the water itself, diving for the depths.

The hairs on Nameless's arms stood on end as he came to stand beside the wizard. Whatever sorcery Venton was working, it was potent. He only hoped it would be enough to save Purg.

Nameless leveled the harpoon at the water, but the tentacle had vanished beneath the waves, and he'd lost sight of the watery man now. All he could see was a chaos of bubbles in the agitated sea.

He flung himself back as a wave crashed over the foredeck. Hair and beard sodden, Nameless spat out water and wiped his eyes. Rapidly, unnaturally, the water reversed course, leaving Purg, unmoving, on the deck, axe clutched in a white-knuckled hand, just like Nameless would expect from a dwarf. The retreating water flowed upwards over the gunwale, then cascaded back into the sea, sizzling and steaming as it passed through the flames.

"Thank goodness," Venton said, stooped over and leaning on his staff for support.

Mora and Grittel scurried to Purg, and together rolled him onto his side. Water spewed from his mouth, and then he coughed. Mora half-cursed, half-sobbed as she cradled Purg's head.

Grittel turned to the prow, ears twitching.

All around the deck, sailors gripped spears and clubs, daggers and swords. Rabnar met Nameless's gaze, then turned to take in the crew, finger pressed to his lips, cutlass ready in his other hand.

Silence, save for the creak of the yards and Purg's retching. Then even Purg seemed to hold his breath.

Nameless could hear his heart pounding in his ears. Venton looked ready to collapse. He was exhausted from whatever sorcery he had worked.

Still nothing.

Rabnar let out a long sigh, echoed by his crew. Nameless released the throttlehold he had on the harpoon. He was about to suggest everyone deserved a stiff drink, but then a thud sounded from below.

Something scraped along the belly of the ship.

Purg rose unsteadily to one knee.

Venton started to edge back from the prow, but the ship reared, pitching him on his arse.

Nameless staggered back a few steps, throwing out an arm for balance.

A tentacle whiplashed over the gunwale, snatching Venton by the ankle and hoisting him thirty feet into the air. The immense bulk of the kraken rose from the sea, great, lidless eye glaring, three more tentacles weaving into the sky, half a dozen more writhing through the waters below.

Venton cried out. A spark started at the tip of his staff, but the tentacle shook him, and the staff clattered to the deck.

And Nameless was running, blood burning in his veins. The blood of the Exalted. He slipped on the water-logged deck, but went with it, sliding towards the prow and launching the harpoon with all his might. Crimson burst from the lidless eye, the harpoon buried deep in the pupil. The great bulk shuddered. Tentacles thrashed.

"Venton!" Nameless cried as the wizard fell.

Halfway to the deck, Venton drifted down, light as a feather. He teetered on his feet, haggard and drawn, then he collapsed.

Nameless caught Venton and dragged him back. Grittel grabbed the wizard's staff.

"Keep him safe," Nameless said as he shoved the unconscious Venton beneath a bench at the gunwale. "Shog knows why, but it's after him."

With a skull-shaking roar, the kraken surged out of the water, the front half of its bulk crushing the bowsprit and landing on the foredeck, pitching the nose of the ship into the sea.

A sailor slid toward the monster's hideous beak, but Ash caught the man's arm and hauled him back. Tentacles crawled over the deck, blindly feeling, searching, hunting.

Rabnar's cutlass bit deep into one, then an axe came down and cut the limb in two. Purg was up and fighting.

Slipping and sliding, sailors came on, advancing on the central mass of the beast with swords and spears. A tentacle brushed against a sailor's shin, coiled around him and dragged him screaming aloft. Nameless winced at the crack of the man's spine, then watched helplessly as the tentacle slung the sailor into the burning sea.

"Your dagger, lassie," Nameless said to Grittel. "Give it to me."

"So long as you give it back," she said.

Then he was charging down the slanting deck straight at the kraken, wishing he still had Paxy.

Sailors hit the great central mass with everything they had. Swords bounced off the kraken's glistening hide, spears snapped. About the only parts vulnerable seemed the tentacles and the eye, and that was already gushing blood. Rabnar slammed his cutlass into the creature's beak, maybe chipped it a little.

And then Nameless was there, stabbing over and over with Grittel's dagger, puncturing the skin but rewarded only with quickly clotting drops of blood.

He was distracted by a crack from behind. One of the snaking tentacles had struck the foremast, splitting it in two. The yards and the sail pitched toward the sea, stopped only by the ratlines and the forestays. The top of the mast hung at a diagonal to the bottom, and the ship started to list.

The sailor beside Rabnar screamed as he lost his footing and slid toward the beaked maw. Rabnar lunged for the man in vain, then backed up to avoid the spray of gore.

Nameless gave up on the kraken's body and switched his attention to a tentacle—and just in time. As he stabbed into the tentacle's base, the far end crept towards Venton—still unconscious beneath the bench.

Another tentacle struck Nameless in the back, slinging him against the teetering foremast. Grittel's dagger went skittering away across the deck.

The creature's bulk shifted, causing the ship to drop down in the sea. Flaming water flooded the foredeck, and Nameless rolled to his feet, backing away onto the quarterdeck. Sailors stamped out the flames. Someone tipped over a rainwater barrel.

"Put out the fires!" Rabnar cried, boots smoldering. "Without the ship, we all die."

The questing tentacle touched Venton's back, then slid under him and started to wrap around his body.

Grittel snarled and leapt onto the tentacle, biting and clawing, eyes rolled up into her head. A second tentacle whiplashed over the gunwale and flicked her high up into the ratlines, between the shrouds on the half-toppled foremast.

Nameless ran toward Venton, but Purg got there first, slamming his axe into the tentacle coiling around the wizard and cleaving it in two. The second tentacle slapped the big dwarf down, and this time Purg didn't get up.

Nameless grabbed Purg's axe, ducked beneath the flailing tentacle, and hacked into its underside, spilling blood.

Sailors retreated from the foredeck, putting out fires, yelling and cursing. Shog only knew what would happen if the sails caught.

That left only Rabnar and Ash facing off against the kraken.

Four more tentacles rose from the sea in a shower of flaming water. The great beak snapped, and a sinuous tongue darted out, but even with his peg-leg, Rabnar was nimble enough to side step. The Captain's cutlass sliced into the tongue, and the creature let out a gurgling roar.

Ash hacked into a tentacle, deflecting its attack as it lashed toward Rabnar, and then Nameless was there one side of the Captain, Ash on the other.

"Just like old times, eh, lubber?" Rabnar said.

"Except back then I had the Axe of the Dwarf Lords."

Tentacles took hold of the gunwales both sides and propelled the central bulk forward, pitching the ship into a nose dive. Nameless slipped onto his arse and slid toward the beaked maw. He dropped Purg's axe, and two cutlasses went sliding after it, toward the kraken. Rabnar caught the back of Nameless's shirt, and Ash caught Rabnar. But who had Ash?

Slowly, painfully slowly, Purg heaved all three of them up the slanting deck, one hand gripping Ash's wrist, other grasping the rope of the forestay.

The kraken heaved again, and timbers groaned. Flaming water flooded over the crushed prow. Smoke plumed into the sky. Tentacles swayed above the central bulk: one, two, three, four....

"I'm out of ideas," Nameless said.

"Me too," Rabnar said, "but what a fight, eh, lubber? Launch the lifeboats!" he hollered to the sailors on the quarterdeck. "Abandon ship!"

"I'm slipping!" Ash cried.

"Purg... got you," the big dwarf growled. "Purg not let go."

Venton was up, crossing from the gunwale to help Purg. Grittel Gadfly was climbing down the ratlines, but suddenly stopped and started to bark.

"Mora, no!" Venton cried.

Mora slid past Nameless on her backside, a rope fastened around her waist. He thought at first she was shooting straight into the creature's maw, but the rope pulled taut mere feet from it.

Mora was between them and the kraken.

"Get back!" Nameless yelled.

Mora rose to her feet, held in place by the rope. The kraken's truncated tongue lashed toward her, but withdrew when the air around Mora flared. Thousands of infinitesimal motes sparked into existence. Light spread outward from Mora toward the beast, the motes connecting with each other, forming threads, patterns, a net of glittery radiance. When the net touched its hide, the kraken shuddered and roared. The web of light spread throughout the monster's body—beneath the flesh, it seemed, though shining so bright it revealed the kraken's underlying... structure?

Mora cried out, the words guttural, incomprehensible. Tentacles thrashed wildly. The central mass trembled. Then, with a terrible, keening wail, the creature burst apart in a shower of gore that fell sizzling into the hot sea.

The ship's prow sprang up out of the water. Cheers rolled out across the decks.

And Mora collapsed in a heap.

27

She was soup, bubbling in a pan. Tea steeping in a mug. She was scones and muffins and sardines on toast. She was a forest of toadstools, the earth rich with truffles, the shade of a parasol mushroom, the gills of a chanterelle, warts on a fly agaric, the poison of a death-cap. She was the discharge of spores from the primordial puffball, dispersing throughout the universe. She was the strands of the fungal matrix, the *feruveum,* that gave shape to all essence. She was the omnipresent mind and the insignificant speck, the all and the nothing. She was hollow. She was full. She was... she was...

"Mora," she muttered, still half asleep. She was in bed? "Mushroom Mora. Mad Mora. Mora Muscaria." The things people called her!

Her?

As in me?

I?

"Come back to us, Mora. Please, come back."

"Venton?"

"I'm right here."

She felt him squeeze her hand. Tried opening her eyes, but it was too painfully bright. Even with her eyelids shut, she could see motes like tiny suns, burning, blinding, excoriating.

"Whatever you did, Mora, you shouldn't have done it. You almost killed yourself."

"You'd rather the ship went down?" she rasped. "Rather I let that thing take you? Because it was you it was after, no one else."

"I know," Venton said. "But we should be thankful for small mercies."

"We should?"

"The enemy sorcerer must be having all sorts of trouble working out how to use the phylactery, if he has to go to such lengths to force me to help him. You'd think a wizard powerful enough to control that tentacled monster would have the requisite intelligence to solve the puzzles I wove into the phylactery. But alas, no. Yet again, I have sold my genius short."

"Prick," Mora said.

"At least that brought a smile to your face. Feeling better?"

She risked opening her eyes again. Shut them once more. Filaments of iridescent light ghosted behind her eyelids. They surrounded her. They were within her. They *were* her.

"It's the *feruveum*," she said in a querulous voice. "All around me. Everywhere. It's all I see, and it burns!"

"Give it time," Venton said. "You'll recover."

"And you know that how?" Mora growled. Her eyes stung the way they did when she cut onions.

"What's this?" Venton said, dabbing her cheek with his finger. "Tears, Mora? Whatever is the world coming to?"

"I'm scared, Venton."

"Scared you might not see again?"

She shook her head. "Scared I've offended the *feruveum*. Scared it has hold of me now and won't never let go."

"Then do what you would tell me to do, were our positions reversed."

"Stop whining about it?"

"Pray."

"Don't mock my faith. Not now. It ain't right."

Venton grew stern. Serious. "I am not mocking. You, however, are demonstrating a decided lack of faith. Pray, I tell you, to your great mushroom in the sky."

"I'll try," she said.

"Don't try, just do. What you did up on deck, Mora, it was more than mere sorcery. Beyond anything I've ever achieved. It was... a miracle."

"Miracles don't exist," Mora said. "Only science and sorcery. Isn't that what you say?"

Venton chuckled. "If they're not one and the same."

"At some point they are," Mora said, drifting back to sleep. "We all are: one and the same. One."

"Spoken like the Mora of old," Venton said. "See! Already getting better. Now, pray and sleep, then pray some more."

"And you'll stay with me?"

"I'll stay."

⁓

Mora woke this time to the smell of pipe tobacco.

"What is that, breakfast?" she asked blearily.

"This," Venton said around the stem of his pipe, "is rum-soaked shag. Appearances can be deceptive. The Captain's a man of exquisite taste."

"So, where are we?" Mora asked, sitting up in bed and wiping the sleep from her eyes.

"Currently limping toward land. The ship sustained structural damage from the kraken, and the foredeck was badly burned. Not the hull, I might add. My augmentations have proven a great success, though I'm sure they are nothing compared to whatever you did up top."

He eyed her expectantly.

"What land?" Mora asked. "The Isle of Mananoc?"

"Rabnar says we'd never make it so far in this state. We're heading for a bay on the closest island, although I'm inclined to call it a continent, if the Captain's map is to be believed. Mora, what you did... to the kraken... I have to know what it was."

"Why? You jealous?"

"Not in the slightest. But I am curious. You know me. I won't rest now until I know every last detail."

"I don't know how to explain it," Mora said. "I got scared. Scared for Grittel and Purg. Scared for you. All I could see was the ship burning and that monster thrashing, and all of us going down into the flames and the water."

"And then?" Venton leaned forward on his chair, pipe in one hand, pluming smoke.

"I felt the *feruveum*... like never before. Under my skin, in my veins, my marrow. And there was this... presence."

Overshadowing. All-encompassing.

"Your puffball god?"

Mora shrugged. "All I know is that it was a mind. A massive mind. I'm sorry to say, it was bigger than yours, Venton."

"Now I know you're exaggerating."

Mora smiled, but it was a weak smile, all for the wizard's benefit. She still trembled within, still wanted to abase herself before the power she had felt—power she had communed with. All the interwoven strands of the *feruveum* that sustained the universe emanated from that mind. Even now she could feel the echo of its pulsing omnipresence.

"But what you did," Venton said, "how you destroyed the kraken... Admit it: you could do it again, couldn't you? I take back what I said about a miracle. It was either science or sorcery, because there's no such thing as prayer on demand. So, think, Mora. It's important to me. What exactly did you do?"

"How did I kill the kraken?" She wasn't sure she did anything more than will its destruction. The rest: it had been done through her, not by her. She had been one with the *feruveum*.

"I pulled apart the fungal matrix that gave it its form," she said.

"Its essence collapsed in on itself?"

Mora nodded.

"But how did you do it? How did you know what to do?"

The question hit at the core of her trembling. She didn't know. But Venton would never accept that as an answer. He'd keep wheedling away at her till she gave him what he wanted. The acquisition of knowledge was an obsession for him, every bit as compulsive as smoking.

And so she tapped the side of her nose and uttered the one word that would bring his probing to an end:

"Sacred."

"Oh, for goodness' sake!" Venton said.

But he knew better than to press her now. Last time he'd tried to wrest the sacred mysteries of the mushroom god from her, she'd kicked him in the fruits.

As Venton opened the cabin door to leave, Grittel Gadfly came scampering inside.

"You're awake! Me was so worried."

Grittel climbed into bed and lay her head on Mora's breast. She smelled of cooked fish.

"You been stealing again?" Mora said. "The Captain will throw you overboard for the sharp-tooths."

"It wasn't I!"

28

Rabnar stood on the bench at the gunwale to relieve himself over the side. He shook off the drops and gave a shudder, then turned as he fastened his britches.

"Always need to piss when we approach land."

"I remember," Nameless said.

Rabnar sat beside him, looking out beyond the ruined prow, where the mountains they had been heading toward these past several hours shimmered in the heat haze coming off the sea.

"Should be turning into that big bay on the map any minute now," Rabnar said. "Hopefully, before the storm breaks."

Clouds had been gathering overhead for some hours, and thunder rumbled in the distance.

The Captain's eyes lingered on the carved figurehead of a pregnant woman now lying on the foredeck. It was spotted bobbing in the sea after the creature died. Rabnar had ordered it salvaged.

"Lick of paint and she'll be good as new, eh?" Rabnar said.

It would take more than paint, but Nameless didn't say so. He knew how much the figurine meant to Rabnar. She was the heart and soul of the ship.

"I never told you who she was, did I?" Rabnar said. "Nella Beritt.

The only woman I'll ever love—besides the few hundred that came before her."

"What happened?" Nameless asked.

"Died in childbirth."

"The baby was yours?"

Rabnar smiled. "I like to think it was. Ah, she was a fine woman. Queen, they used to call her. Queen of an island of pirates off the coast of Scaythe. Woman like that, should've died in battle on the Sea of Weeping."

"Aye," Nameless said, but his mind had already strayed. He was thinking of Cordy, who had also died pregnant.

He started at Rabnar's hand on his shoulder.

"Don't you go getting all maudlin again, lubber. It's why I never told you before."

"You think she still... Cordy, I mean?"

"Still loves you? I never met her. It's not me you want to listen to. It's what you know"—he patted his chest—"in here."

"That's the thing of it," Nameless said. "Since coming to Gabala, I don't know what to think anymore, about anything."

"But what do you feel, lubber? What do you *feel*?"

Nameless didn't answer that. He felt jealous, angry, confused. He felt alone. And though it was hard to admit it to himself, he felt scared. This wasn't the afterlife he'd hoped for, full of old certainties, and friendships that would never end. It was as messy as life on Aosia, and after the fight with the kraken—the sailors who had died a second death—it felt just as fragile.

He glanced at the crew sitting around, exhausted, subdued as they snacked on grilled fish the cook had rustled up for them. There was a woman up in the crow's nest, a man at the helm, but other than that all activity on deck had ceased. Rabnar knew sailors. Knew when to push them and when to give them a break. They'd have their work cut out for them making repairs once they reached the lee of the bay.

Venton emerged on deck from down below. He looked agitated, muttering under his breath as he fished about in his coat pocket. He pulled out his weedstick case and flipped it open.

"How's Mora?" Nameless asked.

Venton popped a weedstick in his mouth and lit it, then exhaled a long stream of smoke before he replied.

"She'll recover."

"And you?"

"How am I? Same as I always am." When Nameless raised an eyebrow, he added, "Well, a little irritable, perhaps, but that's to be expected."

The wizard had been beside Mora's bed all day.

"The little lassie did well," Nameless said.

"Aye," Rabnar said. "I can't thank her enough. We'd have lost the ship without her. The rest of us was worse than useless against that thing."

A cheer went up from the sailors at the stern, and Nameless turned to see Purg holding a rainwater barrel above his head. The barrel was taller and wider than the dwarf.

"Is that full?" Nameless asked.

"Aye," Rabnar grumbled. "Don't you drop that now! It's all we have left!" The sailors had used up the other rainwater barrels putting out the fires on deck.

Purg slammed the barrel down and uprighted it, causing Rabnar to pinch the bridge of his nose and wince.

"Please tell me it's not leaking," the Captain said.

Sailors clapped Purg on the back as he swaggered toward Ash seated at the gunwale. She gave a polite clap—or was it sarcastic?

"Well, Purg looks proud of himself," Venton said as he took a drag on his weedstick.

"And so he should," Nameless said. "I'd like to see you lift that barrel."

"Why would I want to?"

"Because..." Nameless said. That was the funny thing: all those years of deadlifting heavy weights, and he still didn't know how to explain why he did it. Testing himself, he supposed. Proving he wasn't old. Until he was.

"Purg's showing off," Venton said. "I just hope she lets him down more gently than he did that barrel."

"Ash?" Rabnar said, pushing down on his thighs to stand. "I'd say Mora's more her type. Right, I'm due back at the helm."

"Poor old Purg," Nameless said as Rabnar scuttled away, peg-leg clacking on the deck.

Purg sat beside Ash and she promptly stood.

Nameless looked away. "I don't think I can watch. But that was some feat of strength, eh? He's unnaturally strong."

"You could say that," Venton said. "While Purg was incarcerated on one of the isles in the Azarot Archipelago, they did things to him."

"Sektis Gandaw's fanatics?" Nameless asked.

Venton flicked the stub of his weedstick over the gunwale. "Don't tell Purg this, but I went back long after I found him. I went through the records the Mad Sorcerer's disciples left in their laboratory. They had commenced melding Purg with an ogre, when the Church's Elect knights raided the isles and shut the enterprise down. After only three procedures, Purg had the strength of ten men, but alas, his brain atrophied and he suffered major memory loss."

"And Grittel?" Nameless asked. "You found here there?"

"On one of the smaller isles, where they ran a different set of experiments. Grittel is a second generation melding. Her parents were humans, melded with dogs. Grittel was their only child. Her parents died when the knights came. The only thing that saved Grittel was her invisibility. I assume the ability was grafted onto Grittel from some sort of husk—I never did find her notes, and she doesn't remember. According to a book I read, Sektis Gandaw used to perform such operations when the fetus was still in the womb."

"I'm guessing Purg didn't remember his real name," Nameless said. "Did Grittel have one before you came along?"

"Purg was my grandfather's name: Purgivius Nap. Taught me how to box, bless him."

"You can fight?"

Venton flung out a jab, a cross, a left hook.

"Good form," Nameless said.

"But alas, I lack the stamina to make much use of the skills," Venton said.

"You need to run, laddie."

Venton grimaced. "I think not. Mora came up with the name Grittel Gadfly after smoking a particularly virulent mushroom."

"So, you found them both and took them in, eh? Not quite as irascible as you'd like others to believe, are you, laddie?"

"What else should I have done? I gave them food, a home, and they helped me as best they could—a good deal, actually, seeing as I was an old man at the time."

"Well you're not old now," Nameless said.

"This is how I looked and felt in my fifties—a darned sight better than ninety-seven, the age at which I died. But, do you know, I never liked being young. All that passion! All that being right all the time, despite being objectively wrong."

"If you don't mind me asking, laddie, how did you die? I'm guessing heart failure."

"Then you guess wrong. That was Baz. In my case...." The wizard gazed out over the burning sea. "A spell backfired when we were on an expedition. Killed all four of us."

"Laddie, I'm sorry. And you feel responsible?"

Venton clenched his jaw. "Let's just hope the dragon my spell was intended for was caught in the blast—so long as it doesn't show up here seeking revenge."

Venton stiffened as Mora and Grittel Gadfly came up on deck. When Mora waggled her fingers at him, he sighed and raised his staff in acknowledgment.

"Ships ahoy!" the woman in the crow's nest called down. "Galleys of some kind. And they don't look natural."

Nameless glanced at Venton, then stood and crossed to the helm as Rabnar took out his spyglass and extended the tube.

"No stranger than iron, I suppose," the Captain said, peering through the lens.

He passed the spyglass to Nameless.

The *Watchful Wake* was heading towards a massive harbor, where dozens of single-masted ships were berthed. A lone galley was leaving the harbor, oars cutting the water and sending up sparks and steam. It was coming straight at them.

"No stranger than iron," Nameless concurred.

The ships were made of stone.

∽

THE STONE GALLEY closed distance with the *Watchful Wake*, its lone sail furled on the yard. A sculpted goat's head adorned the prow, eyes glittering and golden. A long black cylinder was mounted on a platform above the figurehead; in the firelight coming off the water, it sparkled green.

"*Ocras*," Nameless muttered, watching the approaching ship through Rabnar's spyglass.

A squat figure climbed up to the platform, holding a flaming rod. Some kind of creature made of grey stone, with two arms and two legs.

"Wait a minute," Nameless said, as the creature touched the flame to the back of the cylinder. "That's a canon!"

He'd seen how devastating such a weapon could be, when a dwarf named Grok the Garrote had used a canon to decimate the Lich Lord's feeders, who had pursued the survivors of Arx Gravis on the way to Arnoch. "I suppose it's too late to turn us about?"

"Everyone down!" Rabnar yelled, then just stood there himself, staring down the muzzle of doom.

There was a boom and a flash. Smoke spewed from the barrel of the canon, followed by an almighty splash fifty feet off the *Watchful Wake's* prow.

"Warning shot," Rabnar said, hands on hips. He frowned at Nameless. "Too proud to take cover?"

"I could ask you the same question, laddie."

The galley raised oars and coasted, still some few hundred feet from the *Wake*. More stone creatures appeared on deck, armed with shields the color of slate, axes, hammers, crossbows.

"What are they waiting for?" Nameless said. He passed the spyglass back to Rabnar.

"Buggered if I know."

A shadow fell over the deck. Sailors cried out, and Nameless looked up as a massive balloon dropped down beneath the clouds, till it hovered above the ship, its underside almost grazing the crow's nest.

It was an airship, twice the length of the *Watchful Wake*, bigger even than the dirigible Nameless had flown in at Arnoch, when he'd faced the five-headed dragon. Portholes ran along the side of the craft, and there was a gondola beneath the balloon, where dozens of grey-stone—were they people?—stood at the rails. Traps sprung open in the floor of the gondola, and three ropes dropped down to the deck of the *Watchful Wake*.

One of the stone people at the rail shouted something. Sailors turned to Rabnar with baffled looks on their faces, but the Captain only shrugged. Nameless recognized one or two of the words, and started to say so, but Venton got there first:

"Prepare to be boarded!" the wizard said. "In Ancient Vanatusian."

"What should we do, Captain?" Ash asked.

All around the deck, sailors watched Rabnar for instructions.

Rabnar glanced toward the galley off the prow, its *ocras* cannon aimed at the *Wake*. "We're in no state to fight."

Nameless snorted at that, but the Captain was right. He turned when he felt a presence lurking at his shoulder: Purg, axe gripped in both hands.

"Nameless fight, then Purg fight," the big dwarf said.

"Aboard the *Wake*, we do whatever the Captain says, laddie. Understood?"

Purg didn't answer. He gazed skyward as three stone people slid down the ropes and landed heavily on the deck. If they'd come to fight, why leave the bulk of their force on the gondola?

The sailors surrounding the ropes towered over the stone people, who were no taller than Nameless. And they weren't made of stone, he could see now. They were armored in it. Carved breastplates, intricate greaves and vambraces, pauldrons and gorgets, only a hair's breadth between the plates.

Rabnar approached the trio. "Rabnar the Red, Captain of the *Watchful Wake*. We're in a bad way and could use some help."

Venton translated for him, and when one of the three stone-clad people answered, he translated her reply.

"Apparently, we are trespassing in Kunagosian waters, and will explain ourselves—or, rather, you will, Captain."

The stone-clad woman removed her helm to reveal a blunt face and a braided beard.

And it made an obvious sort of sense. Ancient Vanatusian was the same language as Old Dwarven.

Purg rushed toward her. "Dwarves! Purg a dwarf."

She backhanded him in the face with a stone gauntlet, and Purg dropped on his arse.

"Lowborn scum," she said in the common tongue.

Fire surged through Nameless's veins, and he stepped toward her, even as Purg climbed unsteadily to his feet and wiped blood from his mouth.

"If you can speak the common tongue," Nameless said, "what's with the Old Dwarven? Nowadays, that's a language only for scholars and pretentious shoggers."

"Or dwarf lords," she said, hands on hips. "There was no common tongue when I walked Aosia, and speaking it offends my lips."

"Well, lassie, hit my friend again and it'll be my fist offending your lips, and you'll be shitting teeth for a week."

The other two stone-clad dwarves moved beside her, and all three drew shortswords.

Nameless scoffed. "Show them, Purg, what real dwarves use."

Purg raised his axe.

The woman glanced up at the airship, where dozens of armored dwarves watched from the gondola. "You don't want to be fighting us."

To Nameless's way of thinking, there was only one way to handle belligerent dwarves. "Oh, but I do, lassie. And Purg does too, don't you, Purg?"

"Purg like fighting."

"Captain?" Nameless asked. "With your permission...."

"Granted," Rabnar said.

The fire in Nameless's blood turned to lightning. He took a step forward, and all three dwarves stepped back.

The dwarf woman's eyes widened. "You have the blood of the Exalted!"

"Aye, lassie, I do. You, however, do not."

"I assume you've heard of Arnoch?" Venton said. "Because, my dear, you are talking to a former king. Somewhat disrespectfully, I might add."

"King of Arnoch?" she asked.

Lightning forked across the sky, illuminating the clouds.

Nameless narrowed his eyes, and all three dwarves dropped to their knees.

"Not you, Purg," Nameless said. "You can get up now."

"But Nameless king," Purg said as he stood.

"Not anymore, I'm not."

"Once a king, always a king," the dwarf woman said. The muffled roll of thunder punctuated her words. "Platoon Leader Hala Griff, at your service, sire."

29

Venton had never cared much for watching others eat, and so he gazed out of a porthole at the clouds as Nameless and Purg tucked into the bread, cheese, and ale the dwarf servers brought them.

Mora picked at the fare. She looked almost as tired as Venton felt.

As to Grittel Gadfly: either she'd stayed on the *Watchful Wake* as it was escorted into harbor by the dwarf galley, or, most likely, she'd followed them on board the airship, invisible. Grittel was paranoid like that, always seeing threats, always taking measures in case something went wrong. The thought that she was even now watching over him and the others made Venton smile. For all her strange ways, Grittel was fiercely protective, and loyal to a fault.

Off-duty dwarves were seated at round tables the length and breadth of the dining room, which took up an entire side of the dirigible. The center was apparently for crew quarters, the opposite side an armory and training room. There was a brig at the back and the helm at the front.

It was odd: besides a little turbulence, the only indication they were moving—that they were hundreds of feet in the air—was the scud of the clouds past the portholes.

Venton had read about balloons that could carry people, but nothing on this scale. It was a testament to the proto-science that had existed before Sektis Gandaw, and evidence that the Mad Sorcerer wasn't the only one to have been approached by the faen. But it also seemed a gentler kind of science, more in harmony with the world around it.

"Nameless fight well," he heard Purg say. The two had been bantering incessantly since they came aboard. It was nice for Purg to have a friend.

"Thanks, laddie. So did you."

"Purg fight better. Purg best there is. When monster attack ship, Purg chop off tentacle."

"And who do you think stabbed it in the eye?"

Venton yawned into his fist. He was drained from his spell-casting against the kraken and had been too concerned about Mora to rest. If not for his staff weathering the flow of the essence through him, he'd probably not have survived the use of so much sorcery. He'd either have had to pay back the essence he wrested from the fish in the sea and the birds that followed the ship with his own blood, or he could have used his own essence, that which constituted who he was and gave him form. In short, he could have eaten himself up. And yet, that's what happened to so many sorcerers: always cutting themselves to pay for borrowed essence, or suffering terrible contortions as their bones warped and their muscles atrophied.

Venton looked round as the helm door opened and shut. Platoon Leader Hala Griff entered the mess, armored in stone, helm tucked under her arm. She made a beeline for their table.

Venton rummaged about in his pocket for a weedstick and popped it in his mouth.

"Laddie, you might not want to be doing that," Nameless said as Venton went to strike a firestick. "Last airship I flew in blew up—with a little help from a five-headed dragon, mind."

"His Highness is right," the Platoon Leader said.

Nameless grimaced at the title, then shrugged and swigged his ale.

"The gas that makes the dirigible lighter than air is highly combustible. Probably, you would be all right, but all it takes is a tiny leak...."

"Then I shall forego smoking until we arrive."

"You want to eat and drink instead," Mora said—not that she was doing much of either. "Get any skinnier and people will mistake you for a lich. Here, I've got something for you."

She took a jar from her basket and passed it across the table.

Venton frowned at the contents: a viscous, creamy discharge. "Mushroom milk," he said without enthusiasm. "You're too kind."

He unscrewed the lid and sipped on it anyway. There was no point arguing with Mora.

"How's it taste?" Nameless asked.

"Bitter, as always." Venton gave Mora his most appreciative smile. "But it has the desired effect."

Already his brain was fizzing, and he could feel the pulse on the side of his neck.

"And how is the beer, sire?" Hala Griff asked.

"Grainy," Nameless said, as if that were a good thing. "Earthy. You don't use hops in your brewing?"

"That there's ale, pure and simple, sire, the way we used to brew it when I was alive. There were no hops in Arnoch in my day."

"Nor mine, more's the pity," Nameless said. "I thought of sending for some from my home city, Arx Gravis, but...."

"But?"

"It was too soon," Nameless said, speaking into his tankard. "To soon for anyone to go back to the ravine."

"And you?" Hala Griff asked Purg. "What do you think?"

Purg looked at Venton, as if he needed permission to speak.

"The ale, Purg," Venton said. "Do you like it?"

Purg nodded and took another swig.

"I must ask your forgiveness," Hala Griff said.

"Eh?" Still Purg couldn't meet her eye.

"I was wrong to strike you, Purg. I was also wrong to speak down to you. The friend of a king is no commoner. Please accept my apology."

"Okay," Purg said, as if no harm had been done. And in his simple, happy mind, it hadn't.

Mora caught Venton smiling, and she smiled too. Not for the first time, he felt like they were a couple of proud parents.

"A dwarf lord apologizing, Platoon Leader?" Nameless said. "That's not something you hear every day."

"It is a matter of pride to admit when we are wrong," Hala Griff said.

"Ah, of course, lassie. You were a dwarf lord from before the Destroyer came to Arnoch. Before Thanatos changed the last of the dwarf lords."

"Tell me about it," she said.

"Oh?"

"I was thinking of a couple of newcomers who joined us recently. Too stubborn and too proud to play along with Witandos, and so he exiled them to Kunagos. You'll meet them soon enough."

Nameless frowned. "I'm not sure I want to."

"So," Hala Griff asked, "are you both from Arnoch?"

"Arx Gravis first. You've probably never heard of it. But then Arnoch. Purg?"

This time, the look Purg gave Venton was a helpless one. Purg had been known to panic when people asked him questions he couldn't answer. On occasion, he'd grown violent. It was a terrifying thing to him, not knowing who he really was, where he had come from.

"Tell them what you told me," Venton suggested.

"You tell them."

"Very well." For Hala Griff's benefit, Venton explained, "Purg has a severely impaired memory. He does, however, have recurring dreams. In one, there is a citadel with immense walls, and in the distance, cliffs that crumble into the sea, only to re-form."

"Arnoch," Hala Griff and Nameless said at the same time.

"But Arnoch when?" Nameless asked. "Do you remember, Purg, was there a king or a queen? A Council of Twelve?"

Purg's grip on his tankard tightened so much the handle snapped off.

"I should not have pried," Hala Griff said. "Once again, I'm sorry."

"He'll be all right," Mora said. "Time for your medicine, darling." She pressed a dried blue-cap to his lips and Purg accepted it into his mouth without thinking. Even as he chewed, his eyes crossed. By the time he swallowed, they rolled up into his head and he fell back in his chair, snoring.

"Poor old Purg," Venton said.

"Did I offend him?" Hala Griff asked.

"If you did, he'll have forgotten by the time he comes round," Mora said.

"He feels threatened by too many questions," Venton explained. "The curse of having no memory."

"Head injury?" Hala Griff said. "Something similar happened to my uncle during the war against the Ravener."

"Not exactly," Venton said. "Mora and I found Purg wandering and alone on one of the isles of the Azarot Archipelago. We'd gone there looking for mushrooms that had been augmented by a group of self-styled scientists who followed the teachings of the Mad Sorcerer, Sektis Gandaw. The Church of the Way had recently driven the scientists out and ruled the isles off-limits, but I can think of no rules that will come between Mora and mushrooms.

"Purg was no more than a wild beast. He'd escaped captivity during the battle for the isles, but with no one to feed him, he was starving. He was also covered in blood—none of it his own. We suspect he had hunted and killed some of the other victims of the so-called scientists who had experimented on him."

"You're lucky he didn't attack you," Nameless said. "Strength like that, he could rip you in half."

"He did attack us," Mora said.

"And I charmed him with sorcery," Venton said. "Mora later calmed him with a tisane—the first of many."

"What experiments?" Hala Griff asked. "What did they do to him?"

"The scientists were three steps into the process of melding him with an ogre," Venton said.

An invisible hand gripped his beneath the table, causing Venton to smile. "After Purg, we found Grittel Gadfly." Snuggled in the den with her dead parents. He gave her hand a reassuring squeeze.

"Grittel Gadfly?" Hala Griff said.

"Oh, you haven't met her yet, have you? She must have stayed behind on the ship."

Mora winked at Venton and shook her head.

"And what exactly happened to the ship?" Hala Griff asked.

"A big tentacly thing is what happened," Nameless said.

Venton told her about the kraken's attack, about the damage it did to the prow, the foremast; the flames that blackened the deck.

"And it just attacked for no reason?" Hala Griff asked.

"I imagine it was following instructions," Venton said.

Before Hala Griff could ask whose instructions, Mora stood and pointed out the porthole, as the airship began a slow descent toward the most massive structure Venton had ever seen.

"The Citadel of the Conclave," Hala Griff said with pride.

"Citadel?" Nameless said. "Lassie, it's bigger than a hundred Arnochs."

"And it needs to be. All the deceased kings and queens of Aosian history find their way here sooner or later," Hala Griff said. "And now we get to welcome one more."

30

"Welcome to New Arnoch," Hala Griff said as she led the way down the airship's gangplank. "Capital of Kunagos."

"About that name..." Nameless said.

"Our founder was Kunaga, one of the Twelve, the first of the Exalted."

According to legend, he was also the first baresark.

"Kunaga's here?"

"I am not authorized to say more."

Nameless shivered. The hangar was open to the sky, and they were above the clouds. Purg was still drowsy from the mushroom Mora had given him, so Nameless lent him the support of an arm. Venton and Mora came next, and behind them an escort of ten dwarves armored in stone.

"Standard procedure," Hala Griff explained. "Until Your Majesty can be formally confirmed."

She brought them to a raised square set into the floor of the hangar, with stone balustrades on each of its four sides. When everyone had entered through the narrow gate, Hala Griff pulled a lever and the square platform descended through the floor.

Nameless clutched the railing as the platform picked up speed, taking them down through level after level of the citadel. They passed hall after vast hall, each with a different statue of a dwarven king, queen, or hero. One level served as a parade ground, where phalanxes of stone-armored dwarves performed disciplined maneuvers.

They stopped briefly at an enormous space dominated by an artificial waterfall that cascaded into a reservoir. There were pillars instead of walls, between which Nameless glimpsed the expanse of the city below, a sprawl of roads and aqueducts, towers and dwellings that seemed to have no end.

Here, Hala Griff told Venton, Mora, and Purg to wait, and she directed five of the guards to remain with them.

"I assume I'm allowed to smoke?" Venton called out, as the platform continued down.

Nameless lost count of how many levels they descended, until Hala Griff pulled the lever again and brought the platform to a stop. Thirty levels? Forty?

He followed Hala Griff into a hall with a marble floor and granite pillars, the five remaining guards keeping tight formation behind. He felt more a prisoner than a king. Tapestries covered three of the walls, each depicting scenes of battle, of fire and blood.

Hala Griff led him through an archway and along a broad corridor. Ensconced glowstones at ten-foot intervals cast an unwavering glow. At the far end, two dwarves in suits of *ocras* plate armor stood in front of double doors, also of *ocras*. The guards each carried what look to Nameless like a dragon gun, only smaller than the ones mounted on the battlements at Arnoch.

The guards stood aside as the doors swung inwards of their own accord, and red mist spilled out into the corridor.

"Please," Hala Griff said, gesturing for Nameless to enter.

The mist was so thick, Nameless could only see a few inches in front of his face. It prickled his skin and put an itch in his beard. Had he been too trusting, he wondered, as he heard the muffled thud of the doors closing behind him? Too late to worry about that now.

A shadow appeared the mist: a horned giant, bigger even than Yalla had been.

The giant loomed over him, reaching down with a hand. Nameless backed away, and the hand didn't follow him, just hung there, fingers splayed.

Silver motes ignited in the mist around Nameless. They swarmed over his skin, burning, causing him to cry out and swat them away. Only, the motes weren't just touching his skin; they were inside him, and he could see them through his flesh, which had grown translucent. His hands, his arms, his legs and torso—all defined by glittering silver dots. He didn't need to see his face to know it was the same. Just like whatever Mora had done to the kraken. He could see the very structure of his own being, the *feruveum* that gave form to the essence that defined him.

He tried to turn back to the door, but he was locked in place, unable to move. His heart—a shimmering cluster of silver sparks that he could actually see—thumped within the glittery lines of his ribcage. At any moment, he expected the same fate as the kraken, but then the sparks winked out—or at least grew invisible to his eyes. He was solid once more, a thing of flesh and blood and bone.

The mist dispersed, revealing a gigantic woman with curling ram's horns that grew out from a shock of grey hair. She had a wizened face, impossibly ancient. Her grey beard was braided into a trident, her eyes black orbs that sparkled with silver flecks. She wore a robe of crudely stitched animal skin, and a bearskin cloak over her shoulders. Despite her immense size, her thickset features, her long arms and short legs marked her as a dwarf.

"I know you," she said in a voice that evoked granite. "I have seen you. Watched you."

"Then you know what I am," Nameless said—a butcher, a husband who failed to protect his wife, a drunkard grieving in a cave for two-hundred years.

"You are Exalted, a hero, a king."

"You're missing out the bad bits," Nameless said.

"Because they do not matter. You were deceived, preyed upon by the Abyss, and you prevailed."

"There we'll have to disagree," Nameless said. "It was a bullet between the eyes that stopped me, or didn't you see that bit?"

"I saw. And I saw what you did next, how you saved the survivors of Arx Gravis from the Lich Lord. How you brought them home to Arnoch. They forgave you. Made you their king."

"And I abandoned them," Nameless said.

"You were broken. You went to the mountains to die. I watched as the dwarven armies came together at Jeridium, both under the influence of ancient evil. One wrong choice, and our race would have ended there. You knew this, and still you chose. A decision that cost you your life."

Nameless opened his mouth to object, but she spoke right over him.

"And so I say you are Exalted, a hero, a king. I will not be swayed in this."

"Are you a Supernal?" Nameless asked.

"What the Supernals possess by nature, I earned over millennia."

"Who are you, a goddess?"

"Do not blaspheme! I am one who cast auguries from the entrails of beasts before Arnoch was coaxed out of the bedrock of Cerreth. I am one who was taken up into the Pleroma in a vision and returned with the runes that formed the first language of Aosia. I am one who served the kings and queens that history has forgotten. I am one who serves still, until the end of time."

"And your name?"

"I have none."

"That, at least, we have in common," Nameless said.

"Indeed. But I will call you King, and you may call me Oracle."

"I prefer Nameless, but whatever. I assume you were expecting me, Oracle?" Nameless said.

"I was informed by the Platoon Leader while you were yet aboard the dirigible. *We* were informed."

Silver motes reappeared, this time around the gigantic woman, and she started to shrink.

Nameless had to look away. Watching was almost painful. It felt as though his eyeballs were being stretched.

When he looked back, the Oracle was the same size as any other dwarf woman. She raised her hands, and once more Nameless glimpsed the fabric of reality: patterns of motes that slowly resolved into a background he had not discerned before.

Arranged in a horseshoe around him were tiers upon tiers of thrones, each of them occupied by a king or a queen. Dwarves, every last one of them, bearded, dour-faced, and robed in the different styles of all the ages of Aosia.

"Eternal Majesties," the Oracle said, "it is him."

And with one voice they all cried, "Hail, brother! Hail King Nameless of Arnoch!"

31

Grittel sat on the low wall between two pillars, where the hall they'd been told to wait in opened onto the sky. Her feet dangled over the edge, and she could see right through them to the city far below. She'd been toying with the idea of showing herself to the others. After a time, invisibility could get so boring. But what if something happened? What if this was a trap?

Nameless had been gone for an hour or more, and the five dwarf guards in their stone armor had done nothing but stand and stare, eyes tracking every movement Venton, Mora, and Purg made. Grittel had snook up behind them several times and worked out just where to plunge her dagger.

Venton did nothing but sit on a stone bench by the reservoir, eyes shut as he smoked one weedstick after another, thinking, rehearsing his spells in his mind, contemplating new ones. She'd known the wizard so long, she knew exactly what he was doing.

Mora lay curled up on the hard floor, snoring like a pig. She was still drained by whatever she'd done to the kraken, and Grittel was worried about her. Worried she might not fully recover, but also worried about what Mora might become.

Grittel looked round at the scuff of boots on stone—Purg coming to take yet another look outside, as if he, too, were bored out of his mind. She kept perfectly still and held her breath, until Purg stepped right up to her wall, and then she blew her most massive raspberry.

Purg squealed and stumbled back, tripping over his feet and pitching to his butt. His axe clanged against the floor and skittered away.

That got the guards' attention. As one, they advanced a step, half-drawing their swords.

"Hey," Purg said. "That not funny, Grit—"

"You are such an oaf!" Venton snapped, before Purg could give the game away. The wizard stood and turned to the guards. "Forgive his clumsiness. I can't take him anywhere."

Mora sat up and stretched. "What's all the noise about?"

Grittel's nostrils flared and her ears twitched as the platform came back up.

Nameless stepped off into the hall. There were two dwarves with him, a man in a robe and crown, and a woman in a bearskin cloak, with ram's horns poking up from her wild hair.

Grittel rolled from her perch and crept in a wide arc in order to get behind them.

"Well?" Venton asked as Nameless approached.

"Did I ever mention how much I hate meetings, especially meetings of dwarves?"

Purg collected his axe and went to stand at Venton's side. Mora just stared at the dwarf woman, who suddenly turned her head and glared right at Grittel. She made a clutching motion with her hand, and Grittel could see herself once more. As, apparently, could everyone else.

The guards rushed to surround her, and Grittel snarled as she drew her dagger.

"It's all right," Venton said, "she's with us."

"Platoon Leader Griff mentioned only four arrivals," the woman in the bear cloak said. "Can you vouch for her, Highness?" she asked Nameless.

"Aye, lassie, I can."

At a nod from the dwarf in the crown, the guards backed away toward the platform.

Grittel sheathed her dagger then sidled up to Mora and held her hand.

"These are the companions I spoke of," Nameless said.

"Venton Nap," Venton said. "I expect you've heard of me?"

The dwarf king shook his head.

"Oh, well, never mind," Venton said. "This is Mora. The lummox with the axe is Purg, and the disobedient pup is Grittel Gadfly."

Grittel felt heat rise to her face, and she narrowed her eyes at Venton.

"This," Nameless said, introducing the man in the crown, "is King Arios, the last king of Arnoch—at least, until I came along. He was a crumbling skeleton the first time we met, not this strapping fellow you see before you."

"*The* King Arios?" Venton said, more impressed than Grittel had ever seen him. He even gave a slight bow. "I am beyond honored."

Mora did a poor impression of a curtsy. Purg just gawped, as if he didn't know what a king was. And Grittel… she didn't know what she was supposed to do or say, so she just gripped Mora's hand tighter and felt her tail curl between her legs. In the background, she heard the platform descend again. No one else seemed to notice.

"And this," Nameless said, "is the Oracle."

The dwarf woman in the bearskin cloak ignored everyone except Mora, to whom she gave a nod of respect.

"Sister," she said.

"You ain't my sister," Mora said, "so I ain't yours."

The Oracle smiled. "We are sisters in kind, if not in blood. I sense you have seen much. *Felt* much. But there is more for you to discover. Take courage. Do not fear. Every sacrifice will be worth it."

"So," Venton said, "this meeting you alluded to…."

"A conclave, they call it," Nameless said, "of every king and queen of Arnoch, and even before."

"And?" Venton said.

"I told them our story, laddie, and they are sympathetic…."

"But?"

"We're on our own."

"I am sorry," King Arios said, "but the majority are against direct action. If the Oracle is right in her reading of your situation, there is too much at stake."

"This land—Kunagos," Nameless said, "is named after its founder, Kunaga."

"One of the original twelve Exalted," Venton said. "I gathered as much. But why would he come here? Why is he not with his maker, Witandos?"

"Because Kunaga rejected that demiurge," the Oracle said. "That false god."

"Kunaga refused to play Witandos's game," King Arios said, "and so he sailed the seas until he found a land to call his own."

"And Witandos permitted that?" Venton asked.

"He preferred Kunaga's self-imposed exile to a direct confrontation," King Arios said. "But he didn't reckon on the popular support Kunaga enjoyed. Millions of dwarves followed Kunaga, and the realm within a realm, Kunagos, was born."

"Witandos feared that Kunaga would one day lead the dwarves of this land against him," the Oracle said, "and so he set the sea afire. He claims it is to keep the husks out, and perhaps that is a part of the truth."

"And where is Kunaga now?" Venton asked. "Is he here?"

King Arios looked at the Oracle. "Not here."

"Kunaga grew obsessed with usurping Witandos," the Oracle said. "He was contacted by the faen, who helped him develop a fleet of stone galleys, but there was opposition to Kunaga's plans for conquest. He became tyrannical, insane. He considered himself a god. At last, the kings and queens of the Conclave waged war against Kunaga and drove him into exile."

"Exile where?" Venton asked.

It was Nameless who answered: "The Isle of Mananoc."

Venton's eyes widened in surprise. "Kunaga is behind the attack on the Tower of Making?"

"I can only assume," the Oracle said. "I cannot see. Kunaga's rage shields him from me. And there is another: a sorcerer who has woven an obscuring cloak about the Isle of Mananoc."

Nameless nodded, as if he'd seen this coming. "He's called Jankson Brau."

"I've heard of him," Venton said. "A rank amateur."

"He might once have been," Nameless said. "I put him in his place fairly easily when I ran into him outside of Malfen more than two-hundred years ago. But it would seem his powers have grown in the intervening years, and more so after death."

"So," Venton said, "we have our sorcerer, and, forgive me for saying it, we have a likely suspect for your mother's murder."

"Kunaga," Nameless said.

Grittel hid behind Mora. She didn't like the change that had come over Nameless. He was no longer the amiable dwarf she'd first met at the smallholding.

"I assume you told them about the demons?" Venton said.

"Aye, laddie. That I did."

King Arios rested a hand on Nameless's shoulder.

"Before the coming of this Jankson Brau," the Oracle said, "I used to feel the torment of these former dwarves. In death, they passed to the Isle of Mananoc, the spoils of the Deceiver's victory over Witandos in the proxy war they continually fight on Aosia."

"Because I found the black axe," Nameless said. "Because I did his bidding."

"Witandos lost the battle for the ravine," the Oracle said, "but, with the way you found your redemption at the last, he did not lose the war."

"And now he wants me to go up against Kunaga?" Nameless said. "The most powerful of the Exalted, and the father of all baresarks."

"It is worse than that," the Oracle said. "Before Kunaga's self-imposed exile, Witandos made a grave mistake."

"Let me guess," Venton said. "The faen?"

The Oracle nodded. "Witandos granted them access to the Supernal Realm, in return for lore he did not need, but they persuaded him otherwise. Before this Jankson Brau put an end to my scrying, I learned that the faen brought with them fungal spores from the Abyss, which they gave to Kunaga. The spores made him grow in power and size, till he resembled a Supernal. And I suspect it was the faen who told Kunaga to steal this phylactery you mentioned."

"If Mananoc is freed from the Abyss," Nameless said, "Kunaga will have his victory over Witandos."

"Indeed," Venton said, "but at what cost?"

"You still have not told me what you will do," King Arios said to Nameless. "Even before the faen altered Kunaga, he was almost too much for the entire Conclave to defeat. Hundreds of Exalted were sent screaming into the second death during that terrible civil war. You must understand why we cannot help you. And I urge you even now: stay here with us. If Kunaga is successful, if Mananoc comes, there is no place more defensible than Kunagos—our strongholds, our fleet, our thousands of stone-armored dwarves. And we will be allied with Witandos."

"What if that's not enough?" Nameless said. "No, I need to see this through. And I don't care how big he is, how tough, that shogger Kunaga's going to pay for what he did to my ma."

"I feared as much," King Arios said. "If only you still had the *Paxa Boraga*."

"You don't want to know how many times I've thought the same thing," Nameless said.

"Purg smash Kunaga," Purg said.

Nameless nodded gravely. "Aye, laddie, you might." He didn't sound convinced.

Grittel's ears twitched as she heard the platform return. She picked up the scent of unfamiliar sweat, laced with beer.

Two dwarf women stepped away from the platform, and the guards parted to admit them. They wore black armor—greaves, vambraces, breastplates. Both wore golden circlets over their helms. One had a black scimitar hanging at her hip, the other a scabbarded broadsword.

Nameless's jaw dropped as he turned to face them.

The woman with the scimitar glared at Nameless and then approached Purg. "Smash Kunaga, would you?" she said. "Brave words for a commoner." She looked him up and down and pursed her lips. "Such a big boy. Shame you're not Exalted."

The other woman stopped in front of Nameless.

"I bet you thought you'd seen the last of us outside of Jeridium."

"Hope has a habit of disappointing me," Nameless said.

32

Last time Nameless had seen Thyenna Ieldra, Queen of Arnoch, was when she lay dead upon the battlefield outside Jeridium. Actually, she was the last thing he saw in life, eyes rolled up in her head, blasted from her feet when his Axe of the Dwarf Lords had struck her ruby scepter, and both scepter and axe had broken.

"It's not a rematch I'm looking for," Thyenna said.

"I wouldn't blame you if you were," Nameless said. "Both of us dying like that, you'd have to call it a draw."

"You won, Nameless," she said. "And I want to thank you for that."

"You what? Thank me?"

Her sister Gitashan was studying Nameless with feral eyes. Last time he'd seen *her* she'd had blood frothing from her mouth. Shadrak the Unseen had stabbed her in the back—which was a good job, considering Gitashan had been about to cut Nameless down.

"What you did that day," Gitashan said, "the last day we three drew breath on Aosia, was a sacrifice that had to be made. A sacrifice you were the only one courageous enough to make."

"Lassie, if I didn't know better, I'd say you were gushing."

"Do not make light of our praise," Thyenna said. "Nor our apology."

"Now I know you're up to something," Nameless said. "The Thyenna and Gitashan I know apologize to no one."

"We should have been able to resist the Lich Lord and the Witch Queen," Gitashan said.

The admission clearly caused her pain, but it made Nameless look at her anew. She'd always been hard, implacable, which was to be expected. Gitashan and her sister had been born and raised on Thanatos. The only law they knew was dominate or die.

But it was an undeniable fact that Gitashan, more so than her sister, was exquisite. If a sculptor needed a model for the perfect dwarf woman, lean, muscular, perfectly proportioned, Gitashan was the lassie for the job. Oiled black hair, kept civilized by her coronet; the tawny eyes of a predator; features like chiseled granite, yet somehow still sensual. She was refined, regal, and feral rolled into one, a lioness among dwarves. And that one time she had tried to seduce him in the Dark Citadel on Thanatos! He'd tried to forget the urge she aroused in him, out of respect for Cordy, but it had been a prodigious task. A more prodigious task refusing her—a slight Gitashan had never forgotten, and which Cordy had paid for with her life.

"Queens Gitashan and Thyenna are here to help," King Arios said.

"We heard your speech to the kings and queens," Gitashan said. "We were seated at the back."

"They have not yet been inaugurated into the Conclave," Arios explained.

"Which," Thyenna said, "means we are not bound by its rules."

"Nor will we ever be," Gitashan said. "Not if those cowards will do nothing but hide behind their walls."

"Just like Arx Gravis under the Council of Twelve," Nameless said. "What is it about dwarves and inaction?"

"It shames me," Arios said. "As I know it shames many of my fellow kings and queens. But how else can we govern, save by majority consent?"

"How about a tournament?" Gitashan said. "To the death. Last woman standing."

"Do not be so certain you would win," Arios said. He was no old man to be trifled with, no crumbling skeleton perched on a throne. This was King Arios in his prime, a match for any dwarf. Still, Nameless wouldn't want to bet against Gitashan.

"Forgive me for pointing it out," Venton said, "but we seem to be straying from the point. The phylactery? Kunaga? The Isle of Mananoc?"

"One moment," Nameless said, his eyes meeting Gitashan's. The breath caught in his throat, and he had to force himself to hold her gaze. "You really want to help?"

Shog only knew they could use the help. He'd fought alongside Thyenna and Gitashan on Thanatos—before he fought against them in the Jeridium war. The three had been unstoppable, their Exalted blood singing as they battled in close proximity, binding them together in a harmony of death.

"King Arios has already told you as much," Thyenna said.

Gitashan said nothing, but her lips parted a hair's breadth, revealing a flash of white teeth. Her breath was sweet and laced with beer. The musk of her sweat was almost too much to bear.

"We're hardly in a position to turn down help," Venton said.

"Purg say yes," the big dwarf said, staring stupidly at Thyenna.

"I agree," Nameless said, still holding Gitashan's gaze. "But first, Queen Gitashan and I need to talk."

She started to smile, as if she knew she had him hooked. On Thanatos, she'd been obsessed with finding a worthy mate, and she'd decided that Nameless was the one. The smile melted from her face when she realized he wasn't being flirtatious.

"About my wife," Nameless said. "About Cordy."

Gitashan's chin dropped to her chest.

"You don't have to do this, sister," Thyenna said.

"Yes," Gitashan said. "I do."

"Do we really have time for this?" Venton asked.

Nameless flashed him a glare.

"Oh well," Venton said. "If you must."

Nameless gestured to the low wall at the edge of the floorspace, where the hall opened to the clouds, and Gitashan followed him there, walking like a woman on her way to the gallows.

They stood side by side in silence at first, gazing down at the cityscape below. Dimly, Nameless was aware of Venton speaking to the others, planning, thinking out loud, worrying. Purg was right: it was like the buzzing of insects.

"I was jealous," Gitashan said at last, eyes tracking the movement of something in the street hundreds of feet below. "Angry. Disappointed."

"You didn't think Cordy was fit to be my queen?"

Her jaw clenched, but she didn't answer.

Nameless caught sight of the dirigible that had brought them to the citadel. Watched as it slid in between the clouds, beginning another patrol. He wondered if Hala Griff was aboard, not that he gave a shog either way. He was just distracting himself, acting like a coward. And so he said what needed to be said.

"And after Cordy became Queen... after what Blightey did to her..."

"I didn't know what he had in mind," Gitashan said. "If I had known..."

"You'd have what? You'd have warned me?" He shook his head. Tasted blood on his lower lip as he bit into it.

"What the Lich Lord did to her..." Gitashan started, but stopped when Nameless narrowed his eyes.

"You'll not speak of what that monster did. But I want you to name her."

"I—"

"Go on, name her. Name my wife."

"Cordana," she said as if she were chewing gristle. "Cordana Kilderkin."

"Cordana Kilderkin, Queen of Arnoch," Nameless said.

Gitashan turned to look at her sister, and Nameless feared he had gone too far. He hadn't intended to torture her like this. It had been two-hundred years ago, for shog's sake. But his blood boiled and acid tears welled in his eyes. It was then he realized his fist was clenched. Gods of Arnoch, had he been about to hit her?

"Cordana Kilderkin," Gitashan said, in a tight voice. He hadn't noticed her turn back to face him. Her lip trembled, and her tawny eyes glistened. "Queen of Arnoch."

It was like a needle lancing a boil. Rage sloughed away from Nameless. His shoulders dropped down from his ears. His hand was stiff when he splayed the fingers, from where he'd clenched it so hard.

"You must believe me," Gitashan said. "I didn't know what Blightey planned. I wanted to kill him after. Ask Thyenna. I wanted to kill myself."

"And yet you still went to him. Served him."

"I returned to Arx Gravis, not to Blightey. I had no idea he was there, until he started whispering to me. At first I thought it was the guilt, and the voice was my imagination. But the whisperings grew clearer, more insistent."

"And you listened?"

"I was weak."

Nameless studied her for a long while, and she held his gaze, even as a single tear tracked down her cheek and lost itself in her beard.

His anger had gone. Completely gone. He wasn't even sad. He'd done more than his natural share of mourning in his cave in the Southern Crags. Cordy was all right now. She was safe. And she was where she wanted to be, he thought bitterly. With Thumil.

"You weren't weak, lassie. You were born and raised on Thanatos, used to threats that come at you head on—and you faced those threats like a dwarf should. But Aosia's a different world, its dangers more subtle. How could you defend yourself against the Lich Lord? That shogger's had millennia in which to perfect his particular brand of evil."

It's not as if he'd done any better against the deception of the black axe. Gitashan's failure had led to a single death. His had led to thousands.

"But..."

"No buts," Nameless said. "We are dwarves. We are Exalted. Our past does not define us, only what we do right now."

"You will accept our help?"

"If you make me, I'll beg for it."

She let out a sharp exhalation and sagged. Nameless caught her by the elbow.

"If I could change the past..." Gitashan said.

He placed his hands either side of her face, touched his forehead to hers. "You can't, lassie. None of us can."

He wiped a tear from her cheek with his thumb, and she managed a feeble smile. She closed her eyes as she drew in a deep breath. When she opened them again, she held Nameless out at arm's length.

"Thank you," she whispered, then turned and started back toward the others.

"Oh, and Gitashan," Nameless said.

She looked over her shoulder at him.

"Nice arse."

Her eyes flashed with indignation, but then she blushed and gave a coy smile. "Glad you noticed."

And then Thyenna embraced her, and it looked to Nameless as though the queens were both sobbing.

"How could I not notice?" he muttered under his breath. "That there is the arse of a dwarf lord. An Exalted arse. The queen of all arses. Uh oh," he said as he saw Venton approach. "And here's the king."

"So, you've accepted their help?"

"Aye, I accepted it."

"They may prove useful against Kunaga, but it's the wizard I'm more concerned about, this Jankson Brau."

Nameless clapped him on the shoulder, causing Venton to wince. "From what I've seen of you, laddie, and what I know of him, I'd say we hold the advantage in that department."

"I'm not so sure."

"As to Kunaga... He was a handful before he received power from the Abyss. If the Conclave and all the Exalted they commanded struggled against him then, I don't fancy our chances now, even with Gitashan and Thyenna."

"Perhaps my sorcery…." Venton suggested, sounding anything but convinced.

"Perhaps. But it's the demons we need to think most carefully about. How to save them."

The others had drifted closer, listening intently.

"Thousands of demons," Nameless said, making sure everyone heard him. "Dead dwarves who've suffered enough already. They aren't to blame for what they've become. If anyone's to blame, it's me, for allowing the black axe to dupe me." He looked from Thyenna to Gitashan. "I was too weak."

"But are they capable of suffering anymore?" Venton asked. "Can they even be described as dwarves?"

"What else would you describe them as?" Nameless said. He checked himself. He was getting too angry again, and it wasn't fair to take it out on Venton. "Sorry, laddie. No matter how much time passes, it's still raw."

"I understand," Venton said. "And I apologize. Sometimes I get so concerned with the facts that I come across as insensitive. Just ask Mora. She'll tell you."

"Sensitive as a brick," Mora said.

"But what I still haven't grasped," Venton said, "is how the dwarves were changed into demons, creatures more suited to the Abyss. Mananoc holds no sway here."

"He still has his isle in this realm," King Arios said. "A place to keep his spoils of war."

"The faen must have introduced Abyssal spores on the Isle of Mananoc," the Oracle said. "For that is the only thing I can think of to effect such a vile transformation."

"But for the dwarves to change so radically…" Venton said.

"They would have to breathe the spores year in, year out," the Oracle said, with a glance at Mora. "Ingest them. Be continually exposed to them. If I could go with you—"

"But you cannot go," King Arios said. "The Conclave has spoken."

"Tell me," Mora said. "Whatever you've got in mind, perhaps I could do it."

"You are not ready," the Oracle said.. "Such a direct contact with the *feruveum* would kill you."

"She's done it before," Venton said. "We were attacked at sea—by a kraken. Mora did something to the *feruveum*, and the kraken collapsed in on itself."

"Impressive," the Oracle said, "but compared with what must be done—"

"Just shogging tell me," Mora said.

A sudden yapping drew everyone's attention. Grittel Gadfly was hopping from foot to foot, pointing at the sky outside.

An iridescent column of light—violet, blue, and gold—rose from the sea to penetrate the clouds. It flickered for a few seconds and then was gone.

"It's coming from the isle of Mananoc," King Arios said.

"The phylactery," Venton said. "The first of its puzzles has been solved."

"I thought you said we had nothing to worry about," Nameless said.

"I've changed my mind. Didn't I just tell you I was concerned about this Jankson Brau. A wizard capable of controlling a kraken should not be underestimated."

"How many puzzles does the phylactery have?" Nameless asked.

Venton grimaced. "Baz wanted there to be seven...."

"How many?"

"Three's what he told me," Mora said. "So we'd better get a move on."

Venton was still wincing. "Actually, it's more like two. I was in a hurry. Projects of my own to work on. I assumed Witandos would keep the phylactery safe."

"Then you need to go," King Arios said. "I may not be permitted to accompany you, but the Conclave said nothing about lending you my personal stone galley."

"I was hoping we might travel by airship," Venton said.

"A dragon lives high up on the isle's lone mountain," King Arios said. "Last time we sent airships to spy on Kunaga, two were shot down in flames. The third only just made it home."

"You're going to tell me the dragon arrived about a hundred years ago, aren't you?" Venton said.

"Even if it's the same dragon you ran into on Aosia," Nameless said, "I doubt it knows you're coming."

"Just don't stay long in the open," Arios said. He deferred to the Oracle.

"Before the wizard blocked my scrying," she said, "I saw a vision of dwarves—I assume they are demons now—scurrying like ants through the warrens beneath the mountain."

"And Kunaga?" Nameless asked.

"I did not see him, but I felt his rage."

"That's baresarks for you."

"He is no mere baresark," Arios said.

"I remember," Nameless said. "Exalted, baresark, and something like a Supernal all rolled into one."

"Something Abyssal," the Oracle said.

"Call it what you like," Nameless said, "but Purg's still going to smash him, aren't you, laddie?"

It did nothing for Nameless's confidence when the big dwarf dipped his eyes and swallowed.

"There's something I'd like you to have," King Arios told Nameless. "I'm sure a few more minutes won't make much difference."

"It might," Venton said, then rolled his eyes and sighed.

"The rest of you go with the Oracle down to the harbor," King Arios said. "Nameless and I will meet you at my galley as quickly as we can."

"Hopefully, quicker than Jankson Brau can solve the final puzzle," Venton said. "But I have to say, in my defense, it was rather a devious one. He's probably spitting and cursing with frustration as we speak."

"Or not," Mora said.

33

King Arios's chambers weren't what Nameless had expected. His own as King of Arnoch had been sumptuous to the point that he'd never felt comfortable in them, and Cordy had considered them gaudy. Arios's were plain by any standard. Walls, ceiling, and floor of undressed granite, heavy wooden doors with iron handles, a modest hearth. There were stone couches festooned with dour-colored cushions, a stone bed—without a mattress. There was even a stone bar atop which were kegs of mead and ale.

Arios opened a large chest and handed Nameless a single-bladed battle axe.

"It's not the *Paxa Boraga*, more's the pity," Arios said, "but it served me well in the war against Kunaga."

"You forge weapons here?"

Arios reached back inside the chest and pulled out a breastplate, then a horned helm, both made of stone.

"Aren't they a wee bit heavy?" Nameless asked.

"Put them on and see."

Arios helped him to buckle on the breastplate. It was like wearing a silk shirt, it was so light. The helm was no heavier than a hat.

"Please tell me it's not magic," Nameless said.

"In a way, it is. The Oracle's gift to me. She manipulated the structure that gives shape to essence. You could swim in armor like that."

"Thank you," Nameless said.

"Least I could do. I only wish I was coming with you."

"I always said dwarves did better with kings than councils," Nameless said. "But this: a council of kings and queens!"

"I know, I know. We'll work it out eventually, given another few thousand years."

"If you have that long," Nameless said, slapping the axe haft into his palm. "If Mananoc doesn't return."

Arios clasped him by the shoulders. "You must stop him in his tracks, and that means you must go up against Kunaga."

"You're not exactly filling me with confidence," Nameless said.

"If there's a way to win," Arios said, "you will find it. When the Destroyer came close to ending our race all those centuries ago, thousands stood against it and failed. But when you found Arnoch at the bottom of the sea, you faced the Destroyer and prevailed."

"With Paxy!" Nameless said. "With the Axe of the Dwarf Lords!"

Arios nodded gravely. "I know. But you have friends, and Queens Thyenna and Gitashan will not let you down." He gripped Nameless's forearm. "Do not forget, you were once King of Arnoch, Nameless. Abdication counts for nothing. You are still a king of Arnoch and always will be. Go with my blessing, brother, and with the blessing of every other ruler of our race."

"I thought they didn't approve of going up against Kunaga."

"Do not mistake prudence for disapproval. The majority were against starting another war because of how many dwarves were lost to the second death last time. But fight they will, if you fail and Mananoc comes."

∼

WHEN NAMELESS ARRIVED at the harbor, Venton was waiting impatiently, weedstick in his mouth, the butts of several others littering the jetty. The wizard arched an eyebrow at Nameless's new armor and axe.

Purg was grinning from ear to ear. "Good to see you, Nameless," he said.

"Laddie, I've not been gone two shakes of a gibuna's knackers, but it's good to see you too. You like the armor?"

"And the axe," Purg said. "How come Purg not get new axe?"

"What's wrong with the one you've got? That, Purg, is a legendary weapon: the axe that cut a tentacle from that big tentacly thingy."

Purg's mouth dropped open, and he gazed in awe at his axe.

The Oracle was deep in conversation with Mora, who did nothing but twitch and fiddle with her hair. Maybe she'd just started to realize how badly it needed to be washed.

Nameless didn't see Grittel Gadfly at first, but then he heard her yapping excitedly and saw her coming across from the neighboring wharf, where the *Watchful Wake* was undergoing repairs. Rabnar was with her, handing her slivers of jerked beef and laughing each time she yapped for more.

"Been waiting to see you off, lubber," Rabnar said as he approached.

Grittel's tail hung between her legs, and she whined at Rabnar's empty hand.

"All gone, puppy," Rabnar said. "I'll dig out some more treats for when you come back."

If we come back, Nameless thought. He didn't need to say it out loud. He could tell from the sober look Rabnar gave him the Captain was worried.

"How are the repairs to the *Wake* going?" Nameless asked.

"Faster than I could've hoped. There's a team of dwarves helping us. Ash is overseeing the work, so I asked the dwarves where I could find the best taverns. Research. You know me."

"I wish I could stay," Nameless said.

"Aye," Rabnar said. "We'd have a laugh, wouldn't we? Drinking, singing filthy shanties, whoring—dwarves do have whores, don't they?"

"None you'd be able to handle, old man. They've granite thighs, and beards you could get lost in."

"Perhaps I'll stick with the drinking and the songs, then. What is it, lubber? You don't look yourself."

That's because he wasn't.

"I didn't think I'd need armor and an axe after I died."

"I know, lubber. I know. That's probably why you turned up in Gabala without them."

"This was supposed to be an end to fighting," Nameless said. An end to heartache and conflict of all kinds. "I thought I'd be living it up in Witandos's feasting hall with Cordy, you know, forever."

"Aye, well I can understand how you might feel cheated."

"Used, is how I feel."

He became aware of Venton looming behind him.

"That's how we all feel sooner or later," the wizard said. "Those of us with any sense. If you ask me, Witandos is as bad as his son, Mananoc. They're nothing but stealers of souls, the pair of them."

"That's a bit harsh," Rabnar said.

"Tell me how he's any different? Mananoc rebelled against Witandos, but why wouldn't he, when Witandos himself rebelled against the Pleroma? Like father like son, I say."

"And the Daeg?" Nameless asked.

"A different case entirely. Mananoc raped his sister, Etala, the Daeg's mother. Aosia's a very different world to this one. It's a protective bubble thrown up by a terrified child."

"You sound like you miss it," Rabnar said.

"And you don't?"

"There's no going back for us," Rabnar said.

"And there's no going forward!"

"Sooner here than the Abyss," Nameless said. "Or Thanatos."

"There's no difference!" Venton said. "A prison is still a prison, no matter the cosmetic differences."

"Perhaps there is a way forward," Nameless said. "The maze of the Wayists."

"I'm a wizard. I do not put any stock in blind faith. Rats in a cage is all those deluded Wayists are, on a road to nowhere. Save for your family members, of course, and your friend Thumil."

"Don't hold back on their account," Nameless said. "I'm inclined to agree with you. Even if they're right, who would want to end up in the Pleroma? I mean, what do they even do there? Do they have beer?"

"How would I know?" Venton said. "Walking the maze in search of the Pleroma is about as enticing to me as throwing myself into a bottomless pit. I refuse to speculate on what might or might not lie ahead. Witandos stokes our hopes and fears. This is his realm. Everything is ordered to benefit him, to prop up his delusional belief that he is a god—*the* god! I tell you, Witandos is in denial about where he comes from. He's a creature like the rest of us. Bigger, maybe, more powerful, but he's still just essence coerced into form by the *feruveum*."

"So, why are you doing this?" Rabnar asked. "Why go after this phylactery, when it only benefits Witandos?"

Venton pursed his lips as he thought about that, but whatever he had been about to say, he abandoned and said instead, "To prevent the return of Mananoc."

"And you don't think Witandos could do that himself?" Nameless said. "And don't give me any of that bullshog about maintaining balance between Supernals. If Mananoc invades, that's a direct attack on Witandos. Those rules no longer apply."

"You would think," Venton said. And Nameless could tell from his demeanor that the wizard had done a lot of thinking about that very subject.

"So, what's going on here?" Nameless asked.

"How should I know?" Venton said. "But understand this: I do not risk my friends—my family—lightly. I was responsible for their first death. I will not be responsible for their second."

Purg and Grittel moved closer to Venton in a show of solidarity. Mora came to join them.

The Oracle was nowhere to be seen. One moment she had been there, the next... gone.

"I suppose we should be off, then," Nameless said.

"Aren't you forgetting something?" Venton asked.

Nameless followed the wizard's gaze to a quayside tavern, outside which Thyenna and Gitashan sat at a stone table, drinking. They raised their tankards to Nameless, downed the contents, then stood and started towards the jetty.

"I see you've found reinforcements," Rabnar said. "Just make sure you come back, lubber. Maybe then we'll do a tour of the taverns."

"I'd like that," Nameless said, clasping the Captain's hand.

"You're shaking," Rabnar said.

"It's just withdrawals, laddie. I've not had a drink in hours."

34

Splash, sizzle, hiss. Catch, drive, release. The rhythm of the stone oars hitting the burning water had been an irritation at first, but with time it lulled Venton inside his head and made it easier to think. Of course, he wasn't pulling on the oars himself: the four dwarves took care of that.

The shame of it was, he had the space in which to think, but none of it was clear thinking. It was tainted by emotion. By a burgeoning sense of inadequacy. By fear.

The Jankson Brau he'd heard of on Aosia had been little more than a prestidigitator who'd headed a bunch of rogues outside of Malfen. Yet, if Brau had solved the first of the phylactery's puzzles, he was clearly no fool.

Venton fingered the spell-turning crystal he'd taken from Coalheart. Had Brau made it? Did he have another?

"Worried, laddie?"

"A little concerned, perhaps," Venton said, though it felt an enormous understatement. "How did you defeat Jankson Brau before?"

"He tried some kind of magic on me," Nameless said. "His hands caught fire, so I shoved them in his face. But let's not bank on that happening again. He's bound to have made adjustments."

"Undoubtedly," Venton said. But what kind of adjustments? How much had Jankson Brau improved as a sorcerer in the years since his death? If he was indeed behind the kraken that had attacked the *Watchful Wake*, a considerable amount, it would seem.

※

It wasn't as if Mora didn't believe anymore. She just didn't know what it was she believed in, and that scared her. She had always felt the unified power that encompassed the universe—well, at least since she'd had her first taste of red-cap. In a way she didn't understand, it had spoken to her, revealed its interconnectedness with all life. And she'd known it was natural and good, and that, above and beyond the false creations of the Supernals, everything was as it should be.

But what if she was wrong? What if there was no gigantic puffball at the heart of the universe, the father and mother of all life, sending out the spores that constituted the *feruveum*? Or what if there was, only it was far more than she had ever dreamed?

Because she had felt something of a different magnitude when the *feruveum* had flowed through her, when she had directed it to destroy the kraken. Something—some intelligence—had granted her the power as a gift, a favor. It had approved of her actions. And it had known her, deeper than she knew herself.

Were the Wayists right? Was there a supreme being behind all the worlds? A god that nevertheless permitted suffering? Permitted evil like Mananoc, the Witch Queen, and even Otto Blightey?

How could she accede to the call of this... thing, this entity, this intelligence, if she didn't know what it was, what it stood for?

The Wayists acted as if they were certain, but then the Wayists she'd met were insipid and ineffectual, children when it came to wisdom, prone to abandon their beliefs at the slightest whiff of sex, or booze, or money.

She should never have opened herself to such power—even if it had meant the loss of the ship and everyone on board. She could still feel it thrumming through her marrow, still feel its hunger for her, as if it were a pack of hounds with the scent of her blood.

She only had herself to blame. She'd gone too far with the mushrooms. And she should never have followed Venton on this foolhardy quest. But therein lay another power that disturbed her. It hadn't just been the fact of Grittel Gadfly slipping away and Mora following. They had both, in their own ways, been compelled to come. Families stayed together.

She flinched as something big surfaced off the gunwale in a spray of water and steam. She turned to look too late and saw only flickering flames above the ripples.

Had anyone else noticed? If they had, they showed no sign of it. Purg, Nameless, and the two dwarf sisters were consumed by their rowing, matching each other stroke for stroke.

She watched the fiery water until it settled, praying there were no more tentacled beasts. Because she wasn't ready to open herself to the *feruveum* again. Perhaps she never would be.

And yet, that's exactly what she was going to have to do once they reached the Isle of Mananoc. The Oracle was convinced it was the only way of breaking the hold of the Abyss over the demons who had once been dwarves. Everyone was counting on her, especially Nameless, because they were his victims, his responsibility.

Why couldn't they just turn around and go back home, refuse to do the bidding of Witandos? She almost spoke the thought aloud, demanded an answer… from Venton, from Nameless. *Let Witandos fight his own battles,* she wanted to say. He's the shogging Supernal!

~

Purg was the best rower. Purg was the strongest. Nameless's hair and beard were drenched, his mouth open as he sucked in air. Gitashan gritted her teeth as she pulled on her oar, too proud to admit she was tiring. Purg focused on the pair of them in an effort to avert his eyes from Thyenna, seated on the rowing bench opposite him. She had stripped off her armor, and was naked from the waist up. It wasn't right. People should wear clothes. Purg tried not to think about her skin glistening with sweat, but once seen it was hard to forget, hard not to sneak another look.

"Keep your eyes on the sea, commoner," Thyenna growled.

"Purg look at sea! Why you call Purg commoner? Platoon Leader Hala call Purg commoner too. It's not nice."

"But it's what you are," Thyenna said. "A commoner from Arx Gravis."

"Actually, he's from Arnoch," Nameless said with a glance over his shoulder. "If he's been here a hundred years or so, I'd say that makes him one of your subjects, Thyenna. Hopefully, from before the time the Witch Queen possessed you with the ruby scepter."

"One of my subjects?" Thyenna swallowed. "Forgive me, Purg," she said. "I have not acted as a queen should."

It was a struggle keeping his eyes level with hers, when all Purg could think of was her sweaty chest. Somehow he managed it, though the effort made his head hurt.

"Queen remember Purg from Arnoch?" he asked.

"I'm sorry, I do not. There were so many subjects, so much to do. But if Nameless is right, and you lived during my reign, you fall under my responsibility. My protection."

Purg's eyes dipped for an instant, but he pulled them back level with hers.

"Purg like Queen."

She smiled and shook her head. "Look, if you must, so long as you keep rowing."

"Down, Purg!" Venton said from behind.

∼

GRITTEL GADFLY KEPT her eyes on the flames and the water, watching for the things that sometimes broke the surface, only to slide away back under: red dolphins mostly, but she'd seen an eel with the head of a rat, and a huge cloak-like creature with a scorpion's tail and banks of glittery eyes.

Watching the sea was the only way to keep out of her own head, away from the memory of the den and the cold bodies with the arrows sticking out of them. She knew what they were when she was awake. Knew, and hated arrows for what they'd done to her mama and papa.

It had grown quiet on the deck once more, everyone back inside their own heads, frowning, muttering, twitching—in Mora's case.

Mora wasn't right. She looked scared. So did Venton, and he wasn't scared of anything. Purg didn't know what it was to be scared. He probably couldn't remember where they were going or what they were doing. He had eyes only for Thyenna, flaunting her muscular arms and her big boobies. If she didn't cover herself soon, Grittel was going to stab her.

"What is it, Grittel?" Mora said. "Worried?"

"No."

"It's all right to be scared."

"Me not."

Mora nodded. Tried to smile, but it was more of a grimace.

"Your hands are shaking," Grittel said.

Mora shoved her hands in her pockets. "No, they're not."

Venton let out one of his irritable sighs. "I'm trying to concentrate," he snapped.

"Try harder," Mora said. "Grumpy old scut."

"I am not...." Venton stopped and pinched the bridge of his nose. "You two should have stayed home. You know how I worry about you."

"Don't you worry about us," Mora said. "Worry about this wizard that's got your knickers in a twist."

Grittel pressed up close to Venton and gave him a hug. "Me keep you safe," she said.

"No, you will not. You will make yourself invisible the second we reach the isle. Keep Mora safe, if you must. And Purg. But I will not have you risk yourself on my account. I'd never forgive myself if anything happened to you again. To any of you. Do I have your word on that?"

"Me promise."

"Grittel..."

"Me said me promise!"

Venton's sigh this time was a world-weary one. He didn't believe her.

Grittel scooted down the bench, away from him, and folded her arms across her chest.

∼

THE BRIEF SNATCHES of conversation were balm to Nameless's agitated mind, but each time the silence returned, so did the images that had been burned into his mind: Cordy and Thumil's wedding day back in Arx Gravis—he couldn't picture his own. And he imagined them walking hand in hand through the Wayist maze, stopping from time to time, embracing, kissing.

Unbidden, a sound part anguish, part anger burst from his lips: "Gah!"

"Are you in pain?" Gitashan asked, glancing his way from the opposite bench. "Want me to rub it better?"

He stared at her blankly, still lost in his dark ruminations, but when she turned back to face the prow, he didn't look away. He was mesmerized by the economy of her movements as she pulled on the oar. She wasn't even breathing hard—shog knows he was. About the only sign of exertion was the veins popping out on her biceps, and the faintest flush to her face.

He found himself relieved she had kept her breastplate on. He'd glimpsed what Purg had been gawping at—Thyenna's sweaty tits— and to be honest, they were a sight a dwarf could sit and ponder happily throughout the afterlife. But for all her dwarf lord magnificence, Thyenna wasn't half the specimen her sister Gitashan was. He tried not to think about what lay concealed beneath her armor. Cordy was still his queen, he told himself, then started to repeat it in his mind. Whatever was happening between her and Thumil—if it was anything at all—Cordy wasn't to blame. He was the one who had failed to keep her safe from the Lich Lord. He was the one to bury his axe in her chest. Just as he'd taken an axe to her first husband, Thumil, before ramming his head on a spike.

All forgiven!

All in the past now!

Like shog it was.

No wonder she'd gone back to Thumil. No wonder she'd embraced his Wayist nonsense.

If she had.

He tore his eyes from Gitashan. He refused to be an animal drawn by lust—no matter how much Gitashan invited it. He owed it to Cordy to hear what she had to say. Perhaps there was a reasonable explanation for what he'd seen in the mushroom-induced vision.

A dwarf as prone to delusion as he was, he should never have accepted mushrooms from Mora in the first place.

He glanced behind at Mora, as if it were her fault now, not Thumil's or Cordy's, not his own. She was staring at him, and Nameless immediately looked away.

He'd glimpsed madness in her eyes—more so than before. Emptiness. Chaos. Despair.

She looked like a woman who had seen the outcome of their quest, and had realized the futility of going up against Kunaga. She looked like a prophetess of truth.

On instinct, he reached for Paxy's haft, but found only air.

The images in his mind of Cordy and Thumil gave way to an aerial view of the battle outside Jeridium. It was as if he were a bird, or his spirit drifting free of his body.

He saw himself lying dead on the field of battle, the haft of the *Paxa Boraga* in his hand, her broken blades on the ground beside him.

His death that day had been a choice he'd made, a choice that had saved the dwarven race from extinction. But now? The only choices seemed those made by Witandos, a being who acted as if he were a god.

Save the choice to avenge his mother.

Aye, he could at least act on that choice.

35

Fog again, just like in Scutsville, when the rogues had accosted him, only this time rising above the smoke and the fire of the sea, obscuring the beach they were nearing.

Standing at the prow, Venton could make out the smudge of a jungle in the near distance, silhouetted trees trailing vines and creepers. Looming over the trees, the dark bulk of the Isle of Mananoc's only mountain. But of the beach before them, nothing, only fog.

Red and yellow flashed above the mountaintop, the orange of fire that for a moment backlit the clouds. It was followed by the rumble of thunder. Or was it a roar?

"Volcano?" Nameless said.

Venton glanced behind at the dwarf, still rowing, along with the three other dwarves, though much more slowly now. The stone galley slid through the smoke and the flames and the water with reluctance, it seemed, an overabundance of caution.

Grittel Gadfly stood amidships, tail rigid, nostrils flaring.

"What is it, Grittel?" Venton called to her. "What do you smell?"

She shrugged as she sat back on her bench. "Sweaty dwarves. Smoke from the water. Seaweed."

Venton rolled his eyes. "Helpful as ever."

Grittel folded her arms across her chest. The way she kept glancing up at the distant heights, he could tell she was spooked. He felt it himself: a niggling worry that clawed its way up his spine.

"Leave her be," Mora said. "It's just a bleeding volcano."

"And that doesn't bother you?" Venton asked. "What if it's about to erupt?"

"I seriously doubt Kunaga would take up residence in a volcano," Thyenna said.

"I met a fire giant once," Nameless said, "who lived in a volcano. Poor old Sartis."

"Why poor?" Gitashan asked. "What happened?"

Nameless briefly met her gaze but gave no answer.

"It's getting shallow," Thyenna said. "Ship the oars and coast in with the tide?"

"We're going to beach the galley?" Venton asked.

"How else were you planning on getting ashore?" Thyenna said. "Swim in the flaming water?"

"Oh," Venton said. "To be honest, I hadn't given it much thought." Any thought, actually. He'd been too distracted worrying about what lay ahead: thousands of demons, Kunaga himself, and the wizard, Jankson Brau. And now he was worried about the roar from the heights. He sincerely doubted it was thunder, or the grumble of a volcano.

Water sprayed from the oars as the dwarves rowed into the mist. Gitashan swore when her oar struck something solid, and then everyone raised their oars in the tholes. A few moments later, the prow ran aground amid the crunch and clack of gravel on stone. The ship lurched, and Venton steadied himself by gripping the gunwale.

It was like disembarking blind, the fog was so thick. As his feet touched the beach, Venton drew local essence through his staff and set the tip blazing with violet fire—it may have been the essence of crabs or shellfish, seabirds or insects; he couldn't see and he didn't care. He felt the others pressing in around him.

Grittel whined. Venton saw her outline in the mist, and then even that was gone.

"Good girl," he muttered. "Be safe."

A sphere of golden light flared into existence at the edge of the jungle ahead of them.

"What the shog is that?" Nameless asked.

Another sphere appeared beside it, then a third, a fourth. All along the tree line that hemmed the far end of the beach, golden spheres blazed until there were more than a dozen.

As one, the spheres rose steadily into the air.

"Everybody down!" Venton cried, realizing too late what it was.

Balls of golden flame streaked toward them, leaving fiery trails in their wake. Nameless, Gitashan and Thyenna flung themselves down before anyone else reacted. Purg just stood there like a lemon. Mora hesitated a spit second too long. Grittel was nowhere to be seen. And Venton: he'd never been a quick man....

The golden spheres converged upon his position—as if he were the only one they were after. He raised his hands in a futile effort to protect his face, but then the spheres reversed course and went streaking back the way they had come.

Concussive blasts shook the beach, illuminating the jungle beyond in a blinding flash. And then there was nothing, save the obscuring fog, the pounding of his heart in his ears, and the surf hitting the shore.

"What the shog just happened?" Nameless said, climbing to his feet. "Those things came straight at you. I thought you were dead, for sure."

Venton reached into his coat pocket for Coalheart's crystal. It effused a ghostly blue light. He began to chuckle.

"Someone went to a lot of trouble setting those magical wards," he said, "but the crystal drew the sorcery to me then sent it back to its source. I imagine the wards were destroyed when the golden spheres returned to them and exploded."

Mora marched up to him and slapped him in the face. "You could have told us!"

"I forgot," he said. "There's so much on my mind."

"You could have died!"

"We could all have died," Gitashan said as she helped her sister to her feet. "But we didn't, so now we move on."

"Uh, Venton...." Purg said.

"What now?"

Purg frowned as he pointed through the fog toward the mountain.

Above the summit, a dark shape undulated through the sky. It had wings the size of sails, a sinuous neck, and a snaking tail.

"Dragon!" Nameless bellowed, already running up the beach toward the trees.

Everyone followed the dwarf's lead.

Everyone except Venton.

He just stared at the great wyrm circling overhead, wings stirring up a hurricane.

"I just knew it!" he muttered.

It wasn't fear he glared up at it with. It was anger. Because if the dragon hadn't surprised them that day in Cerreth, appearing out of the storm, he would never have panicked. His spell would have gone right. And Mora, Purg, and Grittel wouldn't have died so long before their time.

"Venton!" Mora screamed. She was halfway to the jungle. The others were already in among the trees, though Nameless had started back toward her.

"Keep going!" Venton cried. "I'll not lose you again."

"You'll come here right now!" Mora yelled.

"I can do this!" Venton called back, eyes fixed on the dragon above him, descending in a lazy spiral.

A sudden fear unmanned him and he yelled at Mora, even as Nameless dragged her away up the beach.

"Where's Grittel?"

Mora answered with a shriek of warning as the dragon swooped down at Venton, jaws open and spilling smoke, underbelly glowing like forge-heated iron.

Venton raised his staff.

36

"I'm coming, laddie!"

Nameless shoved Mora toward the trees and tore down the beach toward Venton, axe in hand.

"Don't you shogging push me, you hairy-faced midget!"

He glanced over his shoulder to see Mora hurrying after him. And not just her. Purg shook his axe and roared as he charged, Thyenna on one side, Gitashan the other. He should have known no dwarf would stand by while he grabbed all the glory.

Not that glory was there for the grabbing. More likely, they would share a martyrdom of ashes.

Fire spewed from the dragon's maw as it dived straight at Venton. The crystal atop the wizard's staff flashed, and a disk of scintillant blue light appeared between him and the dragon. Flames struck the disk, painting its surface orange. Venton looked away, covering his eyes, and then the flames rebounded from his magical shield, morphing into shards of blue lightning that ripped through scales and wings.

The dragon corkscrewed as it plummeted earthwards, then crashed into the ground in a hail of scree. It shrieked in pain and rage as it thrashed its tail to right itself.

Venton's disk winked out and he slumped to his knees. The dragon roared and took a lumbering step toward him, one leg lame and riddled with smoldering holes. Its wings trailed behind, a tattered mess.

And Nameless powered into it, swinging his axe in a murderous arc. Steel met scale and bounced off, but at least he had the dragon's attention. Its massive head veered toward him.

Then Thyenna, Gitashan, and Purg were there, hacking with all they had. Gitashan's *ocras* scimitar bit deep, and the dragon screeched. Its tail lashed toward Gitashan, but Purg timed his swing perfectly and chopped right through it with his axe. The end fell writhing to the beach in a shower of steaming blood.

A claw bashed Thyenna aside, but she rolled with it and came straight back up to her feet. Nameless hacked into the underbelly, where there were no armored scales, and the dragon reared up, emitting a skull-splitting roar. Its head darted down, and he threw himself aside, but the dragon hadn't been going for him. It was aiming at Venton, still on his knees.

But somehow Purg was there, between the dragon and the wizard, as if he'd anticipated its attack. The dragon's jaws gaped, fire burgeoning in its gullet, but Purg stood his ground and met the attack head on, swinging his axe two-handed with unbelievable power. Steel shattered teeth the size of Gitashan's scimitar, and the dragon shrieked as it backed away.

Purg followed, chopping into its neck as if it were a tree he were trying to fell.

"Let it go, laddie," Nameless said, Thyenna and Gitashan either side of him, wide-eyed with awe.

But Purg was relentless, hacking into the dragon's neck over and over. Sizzling blood rained down on him, but that only served to fuel his rage.

And when he'd finished, when his axe cleaved right through the dragon's neck and both head and body hit the ground, causing the beach to bounce, Purg just stood there glaring, eyes bloodshot, teeth bared. He resembled nothing so much as a baresark. Worse, Nameless realized: Purg looked as though he wanted to rip into the dead dragon and devour its flesh.

"Mora..." Venton gasped from his knees. He raised a shaky finger to point at Purg.

"He was only trying to save you from your own stupidity!" Mora said as she crept toward Purg's back, untying the pouch in her hand. She balked as Purg turned at the sound of her voice, eyes burning with rage.

Mora flung the contents of the pouch in his face—some kind of powder, it looked to Nameless. Or spores.

Purg gasped, then coughed, then sneezed, until he was bent double and shuddering. When at last he recovered enough to push down on his thighs and stand straight, his eyes were watery, but at least they were no longer bloodshot. The rage had left him, replaced by a bemused look.

"It's his ogre blood coming to the fore again," Venton explained. The wizard tried to stand but couldn't manage it, so remained on his knees, leaning on his staff.

Purg turned to gaze proudly at the dragon's still-twitching body and its severed head. "Purg kill dragon," he said with a satisfied nod.

"Aye, you did," Nameless said, "but it was only a wee nipper compared to the one we faced at Arnoch, eh, lassies?"

"It was big enough," Thyenna said.

Nameless helped Venton to his feet. "You do realize we've still got Jankson Brau to deal with. Are you going to be up to it, laddie?"

Mora roughly shoved Nameless out of the way and took hold of Venton's elbow. "What were you thinking, exhausting yourself like that, when you could have just run with the rest of us to the trees?"

For once, words escaped Venton. He held Mora's gaze, unshed tears glistening in his eyes.

"Guilt?" she said. "For messing up on Aosia?"

"It was my fault," Venton said. "In my panic, I used the wrong spell."

Mora shook her head and turned to Nameless. "Our Venton's not exactly known for his wisdom. You silly shogger. If anyone's to blame—*anything*—it's the dragon. It's not like you asked it to attack us."

"I should have been ready for anything."

"And so you made sure you were this time?"

"I've obsessed about it ever since we arrived in Gabala, imagined what I would do differently next time."

"And now we know," Gitashan said, "but Nameless is right: we still have this Jankson Brau to deal with, and we were counting on you."

"And we still can," Mora said. Something was communicated between her and Venton, and then she took a scarlet-capped mushroom from her pocket, bit off half of it and popped the other half in Venton's mouth.

As they both chewed, Mora took hold of Venton's hand and they locked eyes. No sooner had they swallowed their mushrooms, than Mora parted her lips and breathed out a stream of sparkling motes. Venton inhaled deeply. He stiffened. His eyes widened, burning with a fierce intelligence. And now it was his turn to hold Mora up as she sagged in his arms.

"Aren't we just exchanging one problem for another?" Nameless said. "I thought you were supposed to help free the dwarf-demons from infection by the Abyss."

"If I say I'll do something, I shogging well will," Mora said, though she looked ready to drop dead on her feet. "You do your part, and I'll do mine, right?"

Her cheeks were hollow, her eyes set in deep cavities. She had lost an incredible amount of weight in next to no time.

Venton seemed to come back to his senses—especially his sense of responsibility. He looked frantically around the beach.

"Has anyone seen Grittel?"

"Grittel invisible," Purg said. "How anyone see her?"

Venton let out an exasperated sigh. "Aren't you just the embodiment of logic!" The tip of his staff began to glow, and Venton cried out in a voice as loud as the dragon's roar: "Grittel!"

37

The dragon roared.

And Grittel ran.

Up the beach and into the jungle. She weaved around trunks, leapt over creepers and vines, and kept on running. Purg was the strongest, but she was the fastest.

She stopped to listen, panting for breath. Her ears twitched at the sounds of battle coming from the beach. She heard Mora cry Venton's name. The sky back the way she'd come flashed blue. A shriek rent the air. The ground shook beneath her feet, and she was off again, running for her life. Running blind.

She barely noticed the undergrowth she tore through. Her mind was filled with images from her past life on Aosia—images of the dragon diving down through the clouds, flame spewing from its maw. Images of Venton's staff blazing, of white fire erupting all around them, then nothing.

She paused beneath a massive tree to catch her breath. There was a hollow at the base of the trunk.

Never again. Death was the most terrifying thing she could imagine, and she'd not go through it again. She started to crouch down, intending to crawl inside the hollow trunk.

But Venton, a rogue thought objected. *Mora and Purg. Help them!*

She turned around. "Me coming!" she yelped.

But her legs were jelly, her tail hanging between them, limp.

Go! the rogue thought said.

"Me can't," she said through chattering teeth.

Quickly!

Grittel let out a miserable whine and took her first step back toward the beach.

Her only step.

There were paw prints in the ground near the tree roots. Big ones.

She stiffened and backed away to the trunk. The prints looked fresh, and now she thought about it, there was a stench: animal musk and something else... like the smell whenever Venton struck a firestick.

A hiss sounded from somewhere deeper in the jungle. It was answered by a deep and throaty growl.

"Grittel!"—Venton's voice, rolling like thunder through the trees.

Instinctively, she started toward the sound, but something brayed in the brush behind her, followed by the pound of feet or paws. The boughs of trees swayed, and the undergrowth shivered.

She flung herself to the ground and crawled inside the trunk. It was like a cave carved out of wood. It was like a den. The smell of rank meat filled her nostrils—a remembered stench. Mama and Papa. She wanted so badly to bolt from her hidey hole, but the pounding footfalls were right on top of her, and there was growling and braying and hissing.

She curled up inside the hollow and held her breath. If she stayed still, if she didn't make a sound....

A shadow fell over the opening. Grittel's hand went to her dagger, but her fingers froze on the handle as the head of a gigantic serpent darted inside. She squealed as it snapped at her and caught her by the scruff of the neck. Grittel kicked and thrashed and barked for all she was worth as the snake dragged her outside and dumped her on the ground.

She rolled to her feet and drew her dagger, and her jaw dropped open in shock.

It was no snake, not even a giant one.

The serpent head was at the end of a blue and sinuous tail that reared above the body of a lion. Wings like a bat's extended from the monster's back. Two other heads glared at her, each with its own neck protruding from the body: the head of a lion and the head of a goat.

"What have we here?" the serpent head said in a sibilant whisper.

"I can't see it," the goat head brayed.

Grittel held up her hand to check: She was still invisible.

"Me neither," the lion head said. "But I smell it."

"Oh, but I can see it," the serpent head said. "Clear as day."

Grittel started to back away, but the tail swept behind her, the serpent head baring its fangs and cutting off her escape.

38

Mora tripped on every root that crossed her path, stumbled more than stepped, bumped into every tree.

"Grittel," she called again, throat raw from all the shouting. "Gritty!"

She was so weak. She'd been a fool to donate so much essence to Venton. Give too much of yourself, and you'd never recover. You'd waste away until there was nothing left. But without Venton at his absolute best, she didn't fancy their chances against this Jankson Brau.

Curse Venton. He was a fool for facing off against the dragon, a guilt-ridden fool.

But Venton was special, even if beneath all the bluster he didn't believe it himself. She didn't know how she knew it, but she knew: Venton Nap, like the Nameless Dwarf, the king and hero of legend, was one of those people who made a difference, whereas she was nothing but a crazy woman dabbling with forces she scarcely understood. Or rather, drowning in them.

"Grittel!" Purg hollered. He was echoed by Nameless, Thyenna, and Gitashan.

"I'll try again," Venton said, the crystal atop his staff beginning to glow. "Gritt...!" He choked off mid-flow.

Dark shapes flitted through the intertwining branches above.

Mora glanced up to see bright eyes tracking their progress: tawny eyes, yellow eyes, red ones. Some kind of bird cackled and warbled, but when she looked in that direction, she couldn't see anything.

They continued on in silence, save for the crunch of deadfall beneath their feet.

When Mora started to lag behind, Purg dropped back to support her under the arm. Good old Purg, so dumb and yet so thoughtful. At once placid and dangerous, an eruption waiting to happen.

Ahead, she glimpsed the looming bulk of the mountain through a break in the trees.

"We have to assume Grittel will head there," Venton said.

But what if he was wrong? What if something had happened to Grittel, or she'd panicked when the dragon attacked and hidden herself away? She'd done it before, back when Venton and Purg first found her, and plenty of times since.

"We stop here," Purg said when they came to a clearing.

"We stop when we find Grittel," Venton said.

"Purg tired."

He wasn't even breathing heavily. Mora squeezed his hand in gratitude. He was doing this for her.

"Big strapping dwarf like you," Nameless said, "already in need of a rest?" But then he caught sight of Mora and realization dawned. "Now that you mention it, perhaps we could all use a break. Ladies, if you've business to take care of in among the trees, now's your chance."

"Business?" Thyenna said. "Trees?"

But Gitashan was already off into the undergrowth. "Thank shog for that. I'm bursting."

The glade they had stopped in was awash with the most brilliant orchids Mora had ever seen: vivid pinks, yellows, and violets. Blue and gold butterflies flittered in and out of the petals in search of nectar.

Venton stooped to examine a shrub with thick leaves and yellow flowers, and Mora had to smile.

"Trust you to find a tobacco tree," she said.

There were evergreens at the edge of the clearing, with clusters of orange seed pods.

"And this is cocoa," she said. "We should harvest some seeds for Grittel. You know how she loves hot...."

∽

She came to with Venton kneeling beside her.

"You collapsed," he said. "You gave me too much of your essence."

Behind Venton, she could see the blurry outlines of Purg, Thyenna, and Nameless. She heard the swish of vegetation as Gitashan returned from the undergrowth.

"You know what you must do," Venton said.

Mora bit her bottom lip. She'd resolved not to do it again. Stealing the essence from flora and fauna felt like a violation. Repaying the debt with her own blood, though, was more of a desecration.

"We need you," Venton said. He glanced at Nameless.

The dead dwarves who had become demons. Of course they needed her. She shut her eyes and sighed. "What if I can't do it?" she said. "What if I can't turn these demons back into dwarves?"

"All I ask," Nameless said, "is that you try. You can't do more than that."

Mora nodded.

She opened herself to the sounds and the smells of the jungle, to the flutter of wings, the pitter-patter of tiny hearts, the pulse of sap in stem and branch. If she had been more proficient, if she had practiced more, she might have learned to differentiate between the essence of plant and insect, bird and beast, but as it was, all she could do was cast a wide net and take whatever she could.

"Forgive me," she muttered.

Her veins prickled. Warmth effused her skin. Her heart skipped erratically, then settled into a deep and steady beat.

"It's working!" Venton said.

Mora's hands went to her cheeks. They were no longer hollow; they were fleshed out and full. She opened her eyes, and in a single timeless moment she saw flowers wilt and butterflies fall to the ground with desiccated wings.

She glared at Venton as he helped her up. "This is your doing," she snapped. "You just had to prove yourself against that dragon!"

He turned away, but she roughly pulled him back, let him see the tears in her eyes.

"I'm sorry," she said. "I shouldn't have said that."

He dabbed a tear from her cheek with his thumb. "No, Mora, I'm the one who should apologize. I'm sorry for putting you in this position—where you have to do this."

He reached into one of the deep pockets of his coat and handed her the little knife he used to scrape the bowl of his pipe clean.

Mora snatched the knife and walked in among the wilted orchids and the dead butterflies.

"Nobody look," she said, then checked to see they had their backs to her before she drew the blade across her palm and flicked hot blood over her victims: payment of her debt.

It made no difference. None of the butterflies moved. The plants were still faded and drooping. But she had taken and she had given. The law of reciprocity that governed not only this world, but Aosia, and perhaps all the others, had been adhered to. She would not sicken and die now, though she wouldn't have considered it an injustice if she had.

"Here." She handed the knife back to Venton.

"An exchange of blood for essence?" Thyenna said. "I learned of this but have never tried it."

"There is essence in blood," Venton said. "So it's a fair exchange."

"Try telling the orchids that," Mora said. "Try telling the butterflies."

"Some sorcerers are able to use their blood to restore the life of the flora and fauna they draw upon," Venton said. "An endless round of give and take."

"Well I ain't one of them," Mora said. She'd never considered herself a sorcerer. She was just... different, is all. And right now, not in a good way.

"Neither am I," Venton said. "I must confess, I have always been a taker rather than a giver in that respect. But I will learn the art sooner or later, I promise you."

"If we survive," Mora said.

"Yes, well, there is that to consider."

"And where, sister," Gitashan asked, "did you learn about this exchange of blood for essence?"

"Isn't it obvious?" Thyenna said. "I was possessed by the Witch Queen, remember? The rudiments of her sorcery still linger within me."

Gitashan snorted with disgust.

"Are you trying to tell me that Blightey taught you nothing, sister," Thyenna said, "while he whispered in your ear?"

Gitashan's eyes were locked to Nameless's when she answered. "What the Lich Lord taught me, I reject, as you, sister, should reject the magic of that vile hag."

"Aye, on that we are agreed," Thyenna said.

"I'm glad to hear it," Nameless said.

Mora turned at the rustle of leaves and saw Purg walking as if he were asleep into the undergrowth.

"Purg, where are you go...?"

Mora's tongue stilled as she heard singing—beautiful harmonies that came from the jungle. Soothing. Enticing. Arousing.

Her vision narrowed, until all she could see was a shimmering trail of silver motes leading into the trees.

And she had to follow it.

She was compelled to.

But at the same time, there was nothing else in all the worlds she would rather do.

39

Musk and sweat overwhelmed Grittel's senses. Pee and dung, fetid breath and sulfur.

The three-headed monster confronting her was massive, its lion's body the size of a horse. Bat-like wings fanned out, hemming Grittel in. The goat head moved from side to side, searching for her and not seeing. The nostrils of the lion head flared. Only the snake head at the end of the monster's long tail could see her, and so that was the one she snarled at and threatened with her dagger. The tail recoiled, and the snake-eyes narrowed to slits.

Grittel bared her teeth and growled. She hated being trapped. And she hated the way her hand holding the dagger shook.

"Smells like dog," the lion head said.

The snake head's eyes widened as it tracked Grittel's every movement. "There's a reason for that."

"I wonder what it tastes like," the goat head said.

"Trust you to think of our stomach," the lion head said. "Can you describe it?"

The snake head bobbed at the tip of the tail as it studied Grittel. "Two arms, two legs...."

"It is a human?" the lion head said.

"A human child, perhaps. With a dog's head."

"Dog's head?" the goat's head said. "That's disgusting."

"You still want to eat it?" the snake head said.

"Eat a child?" the lion head said. "You are joking, yes? At least, I hope you are."

"Can we keep it?" the goat head said.

"No one's keeping I," Grittel said. She thought about slicing a wing with her dagger. If the wing recoiled, if she dived beneath it, if she ran and tumbled and zigged and zagged…. Her heart pounded at the thought of all those "ifs."

"Keeping I?" the lion said. "That is so…"

"Wrong, is what it is," the snake head said. "Appalling grammar."

"I was going to say 'cute.'"

"I suppose that depends on your definition."

"Are you cute?" the goat head said, trying to locate her by looking in the same general direction as the snake head.

"Me just want to go," Grittel said.

"Me!" the lion head said. "How adorable."

"Why don't you show yourself to them?" the snake head said. "Or do you think they pose a threat that I do not." It darted toward her, jaws agape, fangs glistening.

Grittel backflipped out of the way, landing in a crouch and waving her dagger in front of her.

"Oh, you two have got to see what she just did!" the snake head said. "That was amazing."

"Show us!" the goat head said.

The lion head did a good impression of smiling. "You have nothing to fear. We will not hurt you."

"Try, and me stab you," Grittel said. "In the eye."

The lion head drew back at that.

"Know this, little one," the snake head said, swaying towards Grittel on the end of its tail. "If we wanted to harm you, there is nothing you could do to prevent it." Its fanged jaws opened as it breathed out fire, scorching the ground.

Grittel whined in misery, head down, tail between her legs. "Me believe you," she said in a shaky voice.

And so she saw nothing for it but to show herself.

"It *is* cute!" the lion head said.

"Cute with teeth," the goat head said. "And would you look at that wicked little knife!"

"It is just a surrogate claw," the lion head said. "Even cubs have claws."

"I would like to know," the snake head said, "what a little dog-girl like you is doing on the Isle of Mananoc. This is no place for children."

"Me not a child," Grittel said. "Me here with friends."

"Are you now?" she snake head said. "For what purpose?"

"Me don't know."

"You don't know, or you don't trust us enough to tell us?"

"Me not trust you."

The lion head let out a rumbling laugh. "She is a feisty little thing, is she not?"

"Feisty?" the goat head said. "The poor girl looks scared half to death."

"Me not scared," Grittel said through chattering teeth.

"These friends of yours," the snake head said. "Where are they?"

"Me don't know. Me lost. Me run away when the dragon came."

"Oh, so that's what all the commotion was about," the goat head said.

"You know the dragon?" Grittel asked.

"We know of him," the snake head said. "And we stay out of each other's way. So, what did you and your friends do to provoke the dragon?"

"Me didn't do it," Grittel said. "It wasn't I's fault."

"And now you want to find your friends?" the lion head said.

"If they're still alive," the snake head added.

Grittel's eyes welled with tears. All she could manage was a nod.

"We could help you," the lion head said.

The goat head stared blankly, as if it were thinking about something else. The snake head just watched Grittel, not even blinking.

"Go on," the lion head said. The beast crouched on all fours. "Climb on our back, and let us see if we can find your friends."

Grittel hesitated. The snake head and the goat head unnerved her. Was the monster toying with her? Playing with its food?

But what choice did she have? Refuse to play the game, and it would just kill her where she stood.

And so she climbed on the monster's back, gripping its fur with her fist as it stood to its full height. She swayed back as the monster ran between the trees and leapt into the air, borne aloft by the fierce flap of its wings.

40

A pleasant warmth flooded Nameless's veins and prickled his skin, the way it did when he was pleasantly drunk on mead. Singing filled his ears, sweet and alluring, drawing him on. Silver motes danced in the air before him, snaking away through the trees.

Undergrowth parted for him like the silk drapes around Dame Consilia's four-poster bed—a surprising intrusion from the locked strongbox of his distant memories.

Dame Consilia! Now there was a woman to put fire in your dwarfhood. For the briefest moment, he was back there in Brink, with his gym across the road from the whorehouse. He could feel a big, stupid grin spreading across his face. He loved that place.

Shush! Don't tell Cordy, a giggling thought said. Not that he'd been married back then, but some memories weren't meant for sharing, especially with your wife.

Hands touched him, spectral and unseen. Fingers not quite solid slipped inside his britches. Dimly, he registered the thud of his axe as it hit the ground. There were hands all over him now, urgent, demanding. He gasped as misty shapes materialized around him, swiftly growing denser as they took form. Dwarf women again, same as he'd seen under the spell of Elias Wolf's song. Naked, glistening with sweat, perfumed beards that fell in braids over massive breasts. And they were singing. Singing just for him. Enticing words, imploring. Words of lust and desire. Arms encircled him from behind. A golden-haired strumpet with a luscious beard leaned in for a kiss, but Nameless turned his face away: her breath stank of rot. The arms gripping him tightened into restraints. He started as the golden-haired woman hissed. Turned back to see the flash of fangs. She lunged for his neck—

And then she was gone.

All of them were gone, evaporated into the air like morning mist. And the singing had gone too. In its place, a chant, low and sonorous.

The jungle around Nameless rippled with blue light. He saw Venton shuddering on his knees, Purg embracing thin air, as if he'd not yet realized the spell was broken. Mora scowled and brushed at her clothes, as if they were infested with fleas. Gitashan stood there staring at him, cheeks flushed as she swallowed repeatedly.

And then he located the source of the chant: Thyenna, hands raised, blue light shimmering on her fingertips, already starting to fade. Her eyes were wide, her mouth agape as her chant came to a faltering stop.

"I did it," she said, as if she didn't believe it.

Gitashan narrowed her eyes. "What did you do, sister?"

"Saved your shogging arses," Thyenna said.

"Impressive," Venton said, climbing to his feet. "I, however, was not."

"I assume we have the Witch Queen to thank for your intervention," Nameless said.

Thyenna nodded, eyes never leaving her sister's.

"I..." Gitashan said.

"You would rather I left you to those... things?"

"Some kind of husks," Venton said. He looked visibly shaken. "Just goes to show, you can't let your guard down in this place. Not for a minute."

Mora spat out a wad of phlegm. "Husks, my arse. I ain't never been there, but this place is starting to feel like the Abyss."

"Agreed," Nameless said. "And I have been there. Briefly."

Venton nodded gravely. "Mananoc was exiled here by Witandos, before he fell through the Void. As a Supernal, he would have been more than capable of creating all manner of horrors out of this realm's essence. For all we know, the isle could have been a sort of proto-Abyss, his first experiment in becoming the god of his own domain."

Thyenna's eyes were still locked on Gitashan's. "I what?" she said.

"I…" Gitashan said again. "I was wrong… about the magic the Witch Queen left within you. If Thanatos taught me anything, it's that we must make use of every advantage, if only just to survive."

"I never asked for her magic," Thyenna said.

"No," Gitashan said. "You did not."

Thyenna doubled up and vomited, a gushing stream of foulness. When she'd finished, she wiped her mouth and chin with the back of her hand. "Just don't expect me to do anything like that again."

"Nor should you," Mora said, pointing out the brown and brittle vegetation around where Thyenna stood, and the half-rotted carcass of a squirrel that had fallen from an overhanging branch.

"Purg?" Venton said.

The big dwarf was lost in a daze. When he turned to face the wizard, a solitary tear rolled down his cheek.

"What is it?" Mora asked. "What did you see?"

"Ladies," Purg said with a bashful glance at Nameless. "Dwarf ladies. They like Purg. Now they gone."

"Aye, laddie, and a good job too, if you ask me. You obviously didn't see their teeth. What about you, laddie?" he asked Venton. "What did you see?"

"Nothing," the wizard snapped.

"Nothing?"

"I don't want to talk about it."

"Mora see dwarf ladies too?" Purg asked.

"What I saw was filth," Mora said. "A whole lot of filth that slopped from the arse of Mananoc."

"Not mushroom people with large appendages, then?" Nameless said.

"Go shog yourself."

∽

"You never did say what you saw back there," Nameless said as he walked alongside Gitashan.

The jungle had started to thin out as they entered the foothills that skirted the mountain.

She glanced at him but couldn't hold his gaze.

"Don't be bashful, lassie. I've told you what I saw."

"Pah! Inflamed by common whores! You are supposed to be Exalted."

"You sound jealous, lassie. There was nothing common about those beauties, I can tell you."

"Maybe I am jealous."

"Lassie, I was joking."

She grabbed his wrist, holding him back. Ahead, the rest of the group carried on, oblivious.

"Do I need to spell it out for you?" Gitashan asked. Her cheeks were flushed, her grip on his wrist uncomfortably tight.

"Me?" Nameless said. "You saw me?"

She released her grip and they continued walking.

"How many of me?"

"Just the one."

"More than enough to handle, eh?"

Again she stopped him.

"The others are getting away from us," Nameless said. He licked his lips. She was making him nervous.

"Good," Gitashan said.

"Lassie, it was an illusion you saw, nothing more. A trick of the mind, so those things could get close enough to bite."

"I know that." She stepped in close till her musk made his head swim. She glanced at his dwarfhood, which was shogging misbehaving again. "And I know you're interested."

Nameless swallowed. "I don't deny that…"

"But?"

"But I'm a married dwarf."

"And an honorable one," Gitashan said. He expected disdain, ridicule, but all he saw in her expression was a grudging respect. "You are a credit to your wife, but I must confess, it only makes things worse for me."

Nameless took her hand and lightly kissed it.

She snatched it back. "Do not toy with me!"

"Forgive me, lassie. I was just trying to show my gratitude."

"And you'd show it the same way, if I were a man?"

"Of course not!" And then he saw where this was going. "Ah, you got me, lassie. I'm being a shogger, telling you I can't and acting like I might."

"I know you are attracted to me," she said. "Do not deny it."

"And who wouldn't be? But that doesn't change a thing. At least… it shouldn't."

"What is it?" she asked. "What's the matter?"

"Cordy."

Gitashan's eyes narrowed as he explained.

"Before we met you on Kunagos, while we were still aboard the *Watchful Wake*, Mora gave me some kind of mushroom, so I could see what Cordy was up to."

"You spied on her?"

"No! Well, yes. I was worried. When I came to Gabala, Cordy was with me on Maldark's ship, until we reached the harbor. Then she just disappeared, and I've not seen her since."

"Witandos?" Gitashan said.

"Aye, using Cordy as a carrot to make me do his bidding."

"And you put up with it?" She started walking again, a haughty tilt to her chin, as if he'd gone down in her estimation.

Nameless scurried along at her side. "What choice do I have? If I want to see her again…"

"You think that shogger Witandos didn't make demands on me and Thyenna?"

"What demands?"

"Never you mind. What's important is that we told him to go shog himself. That's how we ended up on Kunagos, with all the other kings and queens who were too proud to bend the knee to that false god."

"So, I should have abandoned Cordy?"

"You should not let another dictate whether or not you will see her again."

Nameless shook his head. "Well, I did see her. In a mushroom-induced vision."

"And that was a bad thing?"

"To me it was. She was walking the Wayist maze. And she wasn't alone."

"Oh?"

"She was with her first husband, Thumil, who I killed at Arx Gravis."

Gitashan slowed her pace. He couldn't tell if it was sympathy or hope he read in her eyes. "You think she has been disloyal?"

"Cordy, disloyal! Of course not." But the way he'd felt when he saw her with Thumil, she might as well have been. "She'd never, never, never…"

Gitashan gave a condescending smile.

"You never really knew her," Nameless protested. "Trust me on this. Cordy wouldn't cheat on me. But…"

Gitashan's raised eyebrow invited him to go on.

"When I saw them together—innocently walking the maze, nothing more!—something changed inside me. I don't like the way it made me feel. It was like a boil being lanced and all the vileness and pus burst out. After… After she died on Aosia…"

And now Gitashan looked away.

"I tried to hold on to old memories. I idealized her, turned her into an angel—which she most definitely was not. I couldn't accept what Blightey did to her, the thing she had become."

His voice started to break, but he had to go on.

"How do you look at your wife the same way after seeing her as a rotting corpse, yet somehow still alive, and hungry for your flesh? How can I forget the feeling of smashing my axe through her ribcage to end it all?"

"And how can I forget," Gitashan said without looking at him, "that I was the one to cause it all?"

"Lassie…" Nameless said, but it was too late for words.

Gitashan stormed ahead, leaving Nameless lagging behind, alone with his thoughts.

∼

THE OTHERS WERE WAITING for him at the top of a bank of scree. The air was cooler here in the shade of the mountain, which loomed above them, its peak obscured by clouds.

"You see it?" Venton asked, tapping the rock face with his staff.

Nameless shrugged.

"No, of course you don't. A concealed door, you might see, being a dwarf, but this"—the tip of the wizard's staff glowed and the rock faded away, revealing a round opening in the side of the mountain—"is an illusion. A ham-fisted one, I might add. Careful!" he said as Purg strode for the entrance. "It's bound to be warded."

"Eh?" Purg said.

"Now, let me see," Venton said, looking around, then selecting a stone from amid the scree. He tossed it into the opening.

Nothing happened.

Purg started forward again.

"Wait!" Venton commanded. "Something heavier.…"

Gitashan passed him a sizable rock. Nameless tried to catch her eye, but she studiously avoided looking at him.

Venton threw the rock, and this time there was a crimson flash and the smell of brimstone. When the light died down, the rock was nothing but a pile of ash.

Venton gave a bored roll of his eyes. "Well, that was about as original as having a tentacled behemoth attack the ship. Whatever else he might be, Jankson Brau's no innovator."

"Is it safe now?" Purg asked.

"It most certainly is not." Venton turned around, rubbing his pointy chin as he considered. "What we need is something that absorbs force.... Aha!" His eyes came to rest on Gitashan's scimitar. "Just the thing: *ocras*."

"Oh no," Gitashan said. "This scimitar is a family heirloom."

"It will be perfectly all right," Venton said. "Chop, chop, now." He clicked his fingers. "We haven't got all day."

With a glance at her sister, Gitashan passed Venton the scimitar. "One scratch..." she warned.

"Watch," Venton said. "And learn."

He flung the scimitar into the opening. When it hit the ground inside, scarlet flared once more. This time, it didn't die down: it intensified, pulsing and flashing.

Nameless shielded his eyes against the blinding glare, but when he squinted through his fingers, he could see the dark outline of the scimitar, still intact. Crimson light converged on the blade, limning it in an abyssal glow. Sparks cascaded from the rock of the opening, swirled about the entrance, then streaked towards the scimitar, where they disappeared.

"Shouldn't be long now," Venton said, watching the display with a smug look on his face. "Here we go."

The scarlet light started to flicker as it faded. For a brief moment, it formed an aura around the scimitar, and then even that was gone.

Venton stooped and reached into the opening to retrieve the scimitar. "Not even warm," he said, handing the blade back to Gitashan. "*Ocras* really is a remarkable alloy. The bane of sorcerers, they call it. All safe now, Purg."

"Easy peasy," Purg said striding through the entrance, as if he had been the one to disarm the ward.

"Well," Nameless said, "it looks like Brau's no match for you, Venton. You'll beat him easily."

"At Empires, perhaps," Venton said—the game he'd been playing with Grittel Gadfly when Nameless first met him. "But I daresay we won't be playing Empires. Intelligence is all well and good, but there's more to sorcery than being clever."

They followed Purg into a tunnel that looked as though it had been bored out of the rock by some gigantic worm. Venton lit their way with the tip of his staff, bathing the group in a cone of pearly light that reflected from crystalline deposits in the tunnel walls.

Gitashan walked ahead of Nameless, and it was an effort not staring at her muscular arse. Any feelings she might have had for him had turned cold as a fish.

She was right to despise him, just as Cordy would be right to despise him, if ever he saw her again. He'd not given her a chance to explain herself. He'd been too quick to jump to conclusions. Maybe she needed the solace of the Way, after what Blightey had done to her. Maybe she needed Thumil to lead her back to the light. Because Nameless sure as shog couldn't do it. In the past, she'd been the one to help him claw his way back from the dark. How could he—the Ravine Butcher, the Corrector, the dwarf who'd slain her husband, her baby, and then slain her—show her anything but pain?

Purg brought them at length to a vast cavern with tunnels on every side. They walked in among the stalagmites, which exuded a soft, bluish glow.

"Scab lights," Mora said, indicating the pockets of fungal growth that coated the stalagmites. "First time I've seen them. They don't usually grow outside of the Abyss. Don't touch," she told Purg, slapping away his hand. "First they burn like acid, and then the rot sets in."

"Not edible, then," Thyenna said. "It's just like home on Thanatos." She nudged her sister in the ribs.

Gitashan didn't respond.

"Which way now?" Nameless asked. He sounded irascible, even to himself.

Venton eyed him curiously, then stuck out his bottom lip. "If Grittel were here, she'd be able scent our way."

"If," Mora said. "But she ain't here."

"You think we should wait for her?" Venton asked. "Or go back and search?"

"You might have wanted to consider that earlier," Nameless said, as shadowy forms started to emerge from the tunnels. There were hundreds of them. There were thousands.

"Demons," Venton said as the former dwarves came within the ambit of the scab lights.

Their corpse-flesh took on a cyanosed hue in the fungal light. Ragged mail and frayed clothing covered squat bodies, some with limbs set at unnatural angles from where bones had broken beneath the blades of the black axe. Wild hair, beards matted with ancient blood, teeth like cracked tombstones. The tatters of once red cloaks trailed from their backs. Some were black. They carried chipped swords and rusty axes, broken spears and battered shields. Ghosts from the past, as haunting as any *scadu*. Only, these former dwarves were solid, things of flesh and bone.

Purg growled, but that only made the demons hiss and groan.

"Don't hurt them," Nameless said.

"Maybe you should tell them the same thing," Gitashan said, as she drew her scimitar.

Thyenna's broad sword rasped as it came clear of its scabbard.

"Mora..." Venton said.

"I can't," she said. "There are too many."

Mora turned back to the tunnel they had entered by.

"Mora, please," Nameless said. He was about to add, "You have to try," but there was someone standing in the tunnel mouth, blocking their retreat.

A tall man, spindly, dressed in a red satin robe and a crooked, pointy hat.

His eyes were backlit by blue fire, ringed with a corona of yellow. He was thinner than when Nameless had seen him before. Skeletally thin. The blade of his curved nose almost met the tip of his equally curved chin. The imprints of his own hands were burned into his face, white and puckered. The skin was so thin, so taut, the skull showed through, reminding Nameless of Otto Blightey. Perhaps with good reason, for judging by appearances, Jankson Brau had been well on his way to becoming a lich when death had spared him from that particular path.

"You!" Brau said in a thin and rasping voice. "The dwarf with no name." He let out a grating laugh as he touched the burn marks on his cheeks. "Did Witandos send you? Remind me to thank him. And as for you," he said, sapphire eyes turning on Venton, "I'm not sure we need your help any longer. The first puzzle you set on the phylactery was tricky, but the second... already I've grown familiar with how your mind works. It won't be long now. So, no, I don't think we need you. I don't think we need any of you."

He nodded, and the dwarf-demons poured into the cavern.

And then a ball of fire streaked from Jankson Brau's fingers, straight at Venton.

41

Wind whipped around Grittel Gadfly as she flew on the monster's back. Bat-wings extended, the great beast crested the tops of the clouds, giving Grittel a glimpse of the peak of the island's lone mountain. And then they spiraled down through the cloud cover and glided above the beach. The stone ship Grittel had arrived on was bobbing back out to sea, now that the tide had come in.

"There!" the snake head said, dropping below the monster's body on its sinuous tail. "It looks like these friends of yours got the better of the dragon."

The monster swooped down, then spread its wings as it came in to land amid the scrunch of pebbles.

Grittel leapt off and ran toward the dragon's carcass. Its wings were shredded, and the stump of its neck oozed black blood. The dragon's severed head lay a few feet away, staring at her with dead eyes.

She got down on her hands and knees, scenting the ground. Purg's stench was unmistakable—the big dwarf seldom washed, and then only if Mora made him. She caught the whiff of Venton's tobacco-infused robe, of Mora's loam and mushroom scent, and the aroma of beer-sweat that clung to the other dwarves.

"I's friends went into the trees," she said.

"To look for you?" the lion head asked.

"Me don't know." Why had she panicked and run? Why had she hidden away like a coward? "Maybe they went without I."

"Went where?" the goat head asked.

Grittel pointed up at the distant mountain.

"Why would they go there?" the snake head asked as the tail brought it to rest between the goat and lion heads, and the three exchanged worried looks.

"Something was stolen," Grittel said, "from Witandos the One-Eye. He sent a dwarf to bring it back. Purg brought the dwarf home to see Venton..."

"Wait, wait," the goat head said. "Purg? Venton?"

"And Mora," Grittel said. "I's family."

"If they have gone to the mountain," the lion head said, "they are in great danger. I know the mountain of old. *We* know it. For hundreds of years, the mountain was my home."

"This isle is the embodiment of evil," the snake head said. "It attracts those who would be at home in the atmosphere of the Abyss. But the mountain: that is where Mananoc was first exiled by Witandos, before he fell through the Void. And that is where the Deceiver created us."

"Me," the lion and goat head said in unison.

"Me," the snake head concurred. "For we are three melded into one. A chimaera, our maker called me."

"What's your name?" Grittel asked. "Me Grittel Gadfly."

The goat and snake heads looked at the lion.

"When we were three separate beings, we each had a name, but two are not easy to pronounce." The snake and the goat chuckled at that. "You may call us—me—Igor."

"And Mananoc made you?" Grittel said.

"That fiend melded us into one," the snake head said, "in the bowels of the lone mountain. It is an obsession of his, to create monstrosities, but like all Supernals, he does not create out of nothing. He warps and shapes what is already there."

In her mind, Grittel was back in the den again, with the cold corpses of her parents.

"What is the matter, little one?" the lion head asked.

"Mama and Papa.... Venton said they were meldings made by people who wanted to be like Sektis Gandaw, the Mad Sorcerer."

Igor crouched, bringing the goat and lion heads down to her level, the snake head at the tip of its tail bobbing between them.

"Which makes you a melding too," the lion head said.

"Technically a chimaera," the snake head said.

"Just like us," the goat head added. "I mean, me."

Grittel blinked back tears. "Me am like you?"

All her short life on Aosia, and her long afterlife, she'd felt different, a freak. She suspected Venton and Mora only cared for her out of pity. It didn't help knowing that Purg was a melding too, albeit a half-finished one, if Venton were to be believed. Purg at least looked normal... for a dwarf.

Each of Igor's three heads nuzzled her, one at a time.

"Are us monsters, then?" Grittel asked. "Are us evil?"

"How so?" the goat head asked.

"Venton said Sektis Gandaw learned his science from the faen."

"Ah..." the goat head said. "I don't much care for the faen."

"The science people mixed dog and human to make Mama and Papa," Grittel said. "Venton thinks they added something else to I when me was growing in Mama's belly—some kind of husk."

"I see where you are going with this," the snake head said. "The faen are the spawn of Mananoc, so they were using this Sektis Gandaw to do their father's bidding."

"What was done to us doesn't make us evil," the goat head said.

"It makes them evil," the lion head said. "We are their victims. But we do not have to remain so."

"Much time has passed since Mananoc was driven from Gabala by the Archon and Etala," the snake head said. "Thousands of years in which we have had time to ponder what we are. What *I* am.

Mananoc created me for war against Witandos, and to that end he inclined me toward evil."

"And I *was* evil for a time," the goat head said. "I killed for Mananoc. Slaughtered."

"But left alone all these millennia, we did a lot of thinking," the snake head said, "each in our own way. The three of us thought and we talked, and slowly we began to concur. To become one."

"Evil is a choice we choose not to make," the lion head said.

Then all three heads together said, "I," and they laughed, a braying, hissing, rumbling sound that cheered Grittel's heart.

"It is a constant battle to remember that we three are one," the lion head said.

"Do you remember how we used to argue and fight?" the goat head said.

"Still do," the snake head said. "And it's still your fault."

"But where did you come from?" Grittel asked. "Mananoc didn't make you out of nothing."

"That is correct," the snake head said. "All Mananoc did was combine our original forms."

"You came from Aosia, like I?" Grittel asked.

"We did not," the lion head said, and now he sounded sad.

The tail holding aloft the snake head drooped, and the goat head closed his eyes.

"We came from the Pleroma," the snake head said. "When Witandos failed in his bid to become the supreme god, he breached the fabric of the Pleroma in a fit of rage. An ocean of essence gushed from the Pleroma to be lost in the Void. Within that flood, all manner of beings from the Pleroma were swept away. We were among them, rushing toward the oblivion of the Void. As were Witandos and his wife, Gabala.

"In a desperate last act of defiance, Witandos drew all the escaping essence around him to fashion this realm—a protective bubble against the emptiness of the Void. He trapped himself and Gabala within his own creation. And we three, like countless others, were imprisoned here too.

"For a while Witandos and Gabala were content. He even named his creation after her. She gave birth to three children: the Archon, Etala, and Mananoc. But as the centuries wore on, Gabala saw the Supernal Realm her husband had created as a prison. With all her being she strove to return to the Pleroma, but Witandos would not permit it. When Gabala took her own life, her youngest, Mananoc blamed Witandos. Ever since, father and son have been at war.

"At first, Mananoc was beaten back, exiled to this isle. In the roots of the mountain, he began to experiment with the shaping of essence, with the combining of forms. And he started to assemble an army of monsters and demons."

"Until he was driven out," the goat head said with a yawn. "Dragged through the Void by the Archon and Etala. Now, does anyone know: are dragons edible? I'm famished."

Grittel stared up at the distant mountain, once the lair of Mananoc. Once the abode of evil. And Venton, Purg, and Mora were going there, without her to keep them safe. She wished they had never come on this silly quest. Wished Purg hadn't been so stupid as to bring the Nameless Dwarf home.

"The dragon nested high up on the mountain," the lion head said. "We clashed when it first arrived from Aosia, for it had fallen under the sway of the new lord of the mountain."

"Kunaga?" Grittel said.

"Kunaga." The lion's head bared his teeth.

The goat head spat, and the tail grew agitated, thrashing the air while the snake head at its tip hissed.

"What is it?" Grittel asked.

"Kunaga," all three heads said at once.

"Like Mananoc," the snake head said, "he opposed Witandos, and he too was exiled here. I tried to prevent Kunaga entering the mountain when he first arrived. I warned him about the evil within, for Mananoc's taint lingers."

"What happened?" Grittel asked.

"We fought," the lion head said with a growl.

The goat head concluded with a nonchalant, "He won."

"It was Kunaga who took the phylactery," Grittel said. "He wants to bring Mananoc back from the Abyss."

Igor's three heads looked at each other, saying nothing.

"If Kunaga beat you," Grittel said, "I's friends are going to die! Me have to help them!"

She started back towards the jungle.

Igor launched himself through the air and landed with a thud in front of her, blocking her way.

"Don't try to stop I!" Grittel said.

The lion head tried to smile, but it was a poor mask. Grittel could smell Igor's fear.

The snake head whipped down and lifted Grittel to Igor's back.

"You're going to help?"

"We meldings should look after each other," the goat head said.

"Come on, my little chimaera," the lion head said as Igor leapt into the air.

First, at Grittel's urging, the chimaera flew out above the burning sea and shunted the stone ship back to shore; then he soared skywards again, bearing her toward the cloud-choked peak of the mountain.

42

Venton knew it was futile, but he still raised his arm to cover his face as Jankson Brau's fireball came right at him.

And veered away.

"What the blazes?" Venton muttered.

The fireball turned a half-circle and shot straight back at Jankson Brau.

Of course!

He took Coalheart's crystal from his pocket. Once again, it was glowing blue.

Brau shrieked and dipped his head, but before the fireball reached him, it reversed course and roared back towards Venton.

"Hah!" Brau cried, holding up an identical crystal.

A conundrum, Venton thought, willing himself not to blink this time as the fireball expanded to fill his vision and heat scorched his face. Mere feet from impact, it swung round and shot back at Brau.

Two spell-turning crystals, canceling each other out. Two wizards reduced to passive observers as the fireball bounced back and forth between the crystals. Another spell from either one of them would be wasted. Did that mean they were locked in an impasse? How did this end?

Venton risked a glance behind at the clash and clang of steel. A sea of demons engulfed his companions, but Nameless, Gitashan, and Thyenna were indomitable, smashing the demons back with bewildering speed and efficiency. And they were using the flats of their weapons. Even now, vastly outnumbered and demons without end still pouring into the cavern, Nameless refused to kill them.

Purg backed up beside Venton, protecting him as always. The big dwarf may have taken Nameless's concern for the demons too far, for he pushed and shoved, punched and kicked, but not once did he swing his axe.

The fireball roared back at Venton, and he moved to shield Purg, just in case. This time, when the crystal repelled it, he could see the fury and frustration on Jankson Brau's face, the slightest hint of fear.

And that gave Venton an idea.

Crystal held out in front of him, he took a step toward Brau. The fire ball came back his way. Rather than retreating, he advanced again, shortening the distance the fireball had to travel before it swerved and went back the other way. Brau hadn't cottoned on. He didn't seem to have noticed.

With quick pigeon steps, Venton continued to close the gap. Brau's pasty face was beaded with sweat. At last, the speed of the fireball zipping back and forth between them was too alarming not to notice. Brau went from a look of bewilderment, to realization, to outright shock in a fraction of a second. He'd worked it out. If the crystals came into close proximity—if they touched—the fireball would have nowhere to go. Its essence would compact, pressing in on itself, until it grew impossibly dense.

And then it would explode.

In a panic, Brau threw his crystal at Venton, then vanished into thin air.

Time seemed to slow as Venton flung his own crystal over his head, deep into the cavern. The fireball soared in its wake. And Venton realized his mistake.

There was no clear path between the crystals now.

The fireball struck a clump of dwarf-demons.

There was a blinding flash, a concussive boom. Blistering heat rolled over him. Bodies hit the ground in a succession of thuds. Acrid smoke billowed to the ceiling.

Venton coughed and spluttered, fanning his hand in front of his face. Purg was wide-eyed with shock, cheeks and beard blackened with soot. Nameless and the others stopped fighting as the demons scattered for their tunnels. A dozen demons lay twitching on the ground at the feet of the dwarves, battered, bruised, the odd broken limb, but nothing more serious.

But Mora…

He couldn't see Mora.

Please, no, Venton thought as he scanned the cavern, fearing she had been caught in the blast.

There! Tucked in behind Thyenna. *Oh, thank the Way!* Well, perhaps not the Way, but thank whatever it was—even if it were luck —that had spared her.

"We were trying not to kill them!" Gitashan snapped as she strode toward him.

"I'm sorry," Venton said. "I didn't mean to…"

"I know you didn't, laddie," Nameless said, and there was steel in his voice that made Gitashan halt. "It's Brau that did this. Where did the shogger go?"

Venton glanced around the cavern, seeing the last of the demons disappear back inside their tunnels. Plucking well-rehearsed calculations from his mind, he uttered an incantation and pulled essence from the injured demons through his staff—not enough to do them any serious harm, but enough to fuel his spell.

Glittery motes dispersed across the cavern, filling every inch of space.

"There he is!" he cried, as the motes on the far side of the cavern flared, and Jankson Brau was rendered visible, bustling toward the tunnel opposite the one they had entered by.

"Gah!" Nameless said. He had his axe drawn back, ready to throw. "I keep forgetting it's not the *Paxa Boraga*."

"Then you'll have to run, you lazy shogger," Gitashan said,

already sprinting after Brau, Thyenna on her heels, Nameless huffing and puffing behind.

Venton ran too... a couple of faltering steps that had his heart threatening to burst. He slowed to his usual long, loping strides, Purg stomping along beside him.

"What about them?" Mora cried as she struggled to keep up.

Gitashan, Nameless, and Thyenna turned back when they reached the tunnel mouth.

The demons were starting to creep back into the cavern, eyes burning, bashing weapons against shields. Hundreds of demons. Thousands. Hissing, groaning, snarling as they surged toward the tunnel.

"Mora?" Venton said, impatient to get after Brau, but worried about leaving the demons at their back.

She met his gaze briefly, then nodded as she faced the demons. "But I can't do this alone. I need time."

"Protect her," Venton said, and Purg stepped into the tunnel mouth, slapping the haft of his axe into his palm. Thyenna stood one side of him, Gitashan the other.

"Right," Venton said, licking his lips. "I suppose I'd better get after Brau." He didn't like it, but what could he do? The wizard was his responsibility. Who else could stand up to Brau's sorcery?

"Do you ladies need me?" Nameless asked. He winked at Venton, as if he'd realized how uncertain he was, how scared.

"What do you think?" Gitashan said.

"Good, then I'm going with Venton."

43

It was all very well being told how to do something, but actually doing it was another matter. Mora thought she had understood the Oracle's advice, but now she needed to put it into practice, the concepts slipped between her thoughts before she could lay hold of them.

It didn't help that the demons pouring into the cavern groaned and snarled and clashed weapons on shields, making it impossible to concentrate. It helped even less that Purg was all of a dither, standing with Gitashan and Thyenna at the mouth of the tunnel, all that lay between Mora and the horde. He kept looking over his shoulder at her, then toward where Venton and Nameless had gone.

"Go on, go," she snapped at him. When Purg started to object, she cut him off. "I know what Venton said, but I don't need looking after." —A lie if ever she told one. "He does. Especially if they run into Kunaga."

"But..." Purg said.

"Just go!" Gitashan growled. "She'll be safe with us."

"But there are hundreds of them!" Purg said, even as the dwarf-demons began to advance.

"More like thousands," Thyenna said. "But before they were

polluted by the Abyss, these were common blood dwarves." She winked at Purg. "My sister and I are Exalted. Now, get your common arse out of here!"

With a worried glance at Mora, Purg ran after Venton and Nameless.

Mora let out a sigh, part exasperation, part relief.

The clash of axe and sword on shield pounded at her skull, turned her thinking to spores of unrelated concepts. The Oracle had explained to her that fear was the catalyst that had opened Mora to the *feruveum* before, when she'd destroyed the kraken.

She stared dumbly at Thyenna's back, at Gitashan's, as the dwarf lords braced for impact. Beyond them, the demons were a tidal wave that swamped the cavern. Their animal cries grew to a bloodcurdling roar, and then they charged.

Mora should have been terrified, but all she felt was numb.

The demons hit, but the dwarf lords stood their ground. Gitashan's black scimitar was a blurry shadow as she smacked a demon in the face with the flat, then cracked the pommel into a second's skull. Thyenna flung out an elbow, splitting a demon's nose and misting the air with blood.

For too long, Mora was rapt by the chaos, the rage, the elemental fury of battle. She was overawed by the grace and efficiency of the dwarf lords' movements, the granite of their defense. They stood side by side, blocking the entrance, forcing the demons to come at them two at a time. And the demons were falling. Already a pile of the broken and bleeding formed a barricade between the dwarves and the rest of the horde.

"Whenever you're ready," Thyenna shot over her shoulder. "You wouldn't believe the effort it takes not to kill these shoggers."

And still Mora was numb. All those snarling faces, the blood, the spittle, the clashing blades—she should have been quivering on the floor. Perhaps if Venton, Grittel, and Purg had been here, threatened by the horde, it would have been different. Perhaps then she could have opened herself to the *feruveum*.

But surely fear wasn't the only way to get out of oneself, to grow porous to all that lay beyond. She'd heard talk of the ecstasy of love—though she knew next to nothing about it.

And then there was pain.

Mora raised her fist, considered splitting her knuckles by hitting the wall, but she couldn't bring herself to do it. She wasn't good with pain.

A demon flung itself between the dwarf lords, face contorted with rage, clawed hand reaching for her. Gitashan thrust it back into the screaming mass.

Think! Mora told herself. *Think!*

No, she was thinking too much. That was the problem.

She reached into her pocket for a piece of red-cap and shoved it in her mouth.

It wouldn't be enough. She'd built such a tolerance, she needed two pieces to settle her into that state where she felt at one with the world, three in order to hear the promptings of the great puffball in the sky, as Venton contemptuously called it.

She counted out the pieces she had left as she popped them in her mouth: two, three, four—enough to kill most people.

"Work!" she muttered. "Hurry up and work!"

The first time she'd tried red-cap, the effect had been almost instantaneous. But these days, the change came slowly. Much too slowly.

And so she took another piece, then another. Six pieces of red-cap. Then one more—her last.

Seven.

She almost giggled then. Forgot where she was. What she was doing. My, seven! It seemed funny to her, the idea of froth coming out of her mouth, of erupting both ends, of recovering briefly, only to suffer unimaginable pain and die.

Her vision grew blurry, till the dwarves and the demons were no more than a churning red haze. The clash of weapons, the screams and snarls were the breeze that blew between the stars. And she was cool and she was warm, and she was air and she was water.

Her heart thumped so loud she thought it might have burst.

She was a child now, in the dark of the closet, where she used to hide during thunderstorms. Her teeth chattered, and she trembled in the wake of each boom and rumble. She was covered in her own vomit, and there was hot wetness between her legs from where she'd pissed herself. Her pa found her that way, dragged her out by her earlobe, beat some shogging sense into her, then put her out in the storm. Decent folk didn't piss in their pants. Not in his shogging house! Mother stood by, nodding her approval, arms folded across her mean, flat chest.

Mora sheltered in the woods that night, startled by every lightning flash, haunted by the hoots and the howls, shrieking till her throat was roar, swallowing her snot and tears.

But stick with fear long enough, and it loses its grip. That endless dark night in the woods had cured her of her dread of thunder. Cured her of her desire to ever go home, too.

The visions gave way to reality once more. Gitashan stumbled back under a furious assault. A sword grazed her thigh, another came at her throat, but Thyenna blocked it with her own blade, then brought the broad sword down with such force, she clove through the demon's skull.

And Mora understood then: the sisters had looked indomitable, and they had done all they could to honor Nameless's wishes and not kill his former victims. But there were too many, and the sisters were starting to tire. It was no longer Exalted against common bloods: it was kill or be killed.

And Mora was to blame.

Her impotence hit her then—almost sobered her. Would have done, save for the fact she taken enough red-cap to kill a roomful of people. Dither too long, and she'd be dead before the *feruveum* entered within her. Gitashan and Thyenna would be buried beneath an avalanche of demons, and the demons would swarm after Venton and Nameless and Purg.

She focused in on the clash and clangor of battle, the snarls and the growls. Every blow was a boom that split her skull and left her quivering. It was her old dread of thunder reborn, and she was a child again. She couldn't think, couldn't move. All she felt was the pressure in her bladder, the thready patter of her heart.

Thyenna cried out as a sword bit into her shoulder. She hacked through the wrist holding the blade. Blood spattered her face. The demons shoved forward, driving the sisters back, forcing them against the walls either side, surging through the middle, straight at Mora....

And she saw them in that instant. Saw them as they once were: dwarves, frightened dwarves, some of them armored, some of them not. Red cloaks and black, or no cloaks at all. Soldiers and assassins. Brewers, miners, tinkers, tanners, cobblers, mothers, fathers—there were even children!

The motes of the *feruveum* winked and sparkled all around her, glittering in place of flesh and bone—and even the rock of the cavern. But the demons who had been dwarves didn't shine silver like everything else. The motes that defined them were tainted with red.

And she *knew* that redness. Could see each speck as if it were as big as her fist.

Spores.

Crimson spores that repelled her with their wrongness. They shouldn't have been here in this realm. These spores had their origins in the Abyss.

Now she understood the Oracle's instructions, the direness of her warnings.

She could feel the prickle of the *feruveum* in her skin, her bones, her marrow; saw it as a scaffold of interconnected spores, silver and glinting. She had no flesh now. She was essence alone. Everything outside of her too, nothing but essence pulsing through the patterns of gossamer thread determined by the *feruveum*.

And at the heart of all that essence, a pit of blackness, a hollow space she'd not been aware of before. Was this the *well* Venton spoke about, the reservoir of essence that existed inside all beings, though usually in an atrophied state? Essence kept on gushing into the black pit, limitless essence, too much to contain. The blackness stretched—

it felt almost painful. It swelled within her, growing harder, more dense.

And then, like a puffball ripe for spawning, it burst, immolating Mora in a coruscating blast of white fire. Burning motes swarmed like lightning bugs out into the tunnel and the cavern beyond, torching everything in their wake. Thyenna and Gitashan were incandescent, white flames leaping from them to demon after demon, until the entire cavern was ablaze with blinding light and blistering heat.

But no one screamed.

All was silent.

All was still.

White.

Only white.

And then darkness.

Stillness.

An inhalation.

The susurrus of the tide in retreat.

Then a driving roar as the ocean came crashing back in. It hit with concussive force, slamming Mora to the ground, flat on her back.

Her lips started moving of their own accord, as she uttered a ceaseless stream of names and words and concepts:

"Sleepy sleeper Venton Nap sends them to sleep with a sparkly clap. Gor-Skag Muncreekin and Barfan Frothbeardson, an ogre and a dwarf makes a very strong dwarf. Nameless no name, no name at all. Taken out of time, but not out of the puffball's mind. Who is Carnac Thayn? Never heard of him. Gitashan, so sad. So sad, poor Gitashan. Thyenna weeping. Gritty Grittel Gadfly. Where's my Gritty Grittel? Mother, father—bastard, shits. Demons and frights and gods and sods. Nemus. Go to Nemus? Where the shog's Nemus? Mushrooms. Gills and thrills and sacks and bowls. Don't eat the scaleskins, just sniff the spores. Venton's hives. Little lives inside. Don't neglect them, you hear? Wizards and their work! And who do you think's going to gather the honey? Oh, my bees, do you miss me? My busy buzzy—"

Thwack!

Mora saw stars. Her cheek stung, and there were bells ringing in her skull.

"Cease your prattle," Gitashan said, hand raised to strike again. Her expression softened as Mora's head cleared and she focused. There were tears in Gitashan's eyes.

Mora's brain still fizzed with half-formed ideas, sentences that ran this way and that. But the slap had jumbled them up into disparate streams of thought that slowly congealed into one.

"It's left me," she said, grinding her teeth, then running her tongue over them, not quite understanding what they were. "I can't feel the *feruveum*."

It was a hazy observation, numb and disinterested.

She was empty.

A shell.

Just a gossamer thread of essence running through her that was even now starting to fade.

"Oh," she said, not quite caring. "I think I'm dying."

And not on account of the red-cap she'd eaten, either. She'd used up every last dreg of essence within her. She'd be dead before she erupted both ends and felt the onset of incalculable pain. Now, that was something to be grateful for.

Thyenna knelt at her side, gripped her shoulders, as if she might impart some strength.

"It healed me," the dwarf lord said, indicating her shoulder. "Whatever you did, healed me. Healed Gitashan too. And look, it healed them."

Thyenna held her upright, and Mora squinted at the mouth of the tunnel, packed with squat figures: men, women, children, all of them bearded.

"You did it," Thyenna said. "Gods of Arnoch, you did it."

"They're dwarves," Mora muttered. "Dwarves, not demons."

And the dwarves were looking round at one another, confused, relieved, sobbing, laughing, shrieking with joy. Then all of them were singing.

All save one.

One that rose into the air on a silver disk, attempting to flee.

Gitashan took two strides and hurled her scimitar. It whistled end over end, impossibly fast, impossibly accurate, and it smacked into the dwarf, who plummeted from his disk. The dwarf hit the ground with a cry and a thud, and the disk dissolved into the air.

The sea of dwarves stopped their singing and parted for Gitashan, heads bowed in deference, as if they recognized her status, or scented her Exalted blood.

She grabbed the fallen dwarf by the scruff of his neck and hauled him to his feet.

Only, it wasn't a dwarf any longer.

He was smaller—the stature of a dwarf child. Grey face. Pebbly black eyes. Silver hair, braided tightly to his scalp. Skin-hugging clothes that shimmered with all the colors of a rainbow.

"A faen," Gitashan growled. She smashed its face into the ground until the faen was limp in her grasp. "I shogging hate faen."

The dwarves who had been demons cheered, then resumed their song, thousands of voices come back to life.

And Mora smiled then as Thyenna gently laid her back down.

She'd always wanted to see a faen. Perhaps not beaten to death by an angry dwarf lord, but all the same....

"You saved them," Thyenna said, voice thick with emotion.

Mora smiled. "Nameless will be happy."

"He will be proud."

"Venton..." Mora gasped. "Purg...."

"We'll follow them," Thyenna said. "We'll keep them safe."

"Promise?"

"My word of honor," Gitashan said, standing over Mora, wiping the faen's blood from her hands. "As a dwarf lord."

The last thread of essence keeping Mora in this phony life shivered and vanished.

And Mora was all right with that.

Because she knew.

Knew that on Aosia she'd lived in a world dreamed by the son of Supernals. Knew that Gabala was no different, except for the fact that

Witandos had consciously willed its creation. They were all the same: Gabala, Aosia, the Abyss. How many worlds were there, like air bubbles in the sea of everything?

She gasped, arched her back, then slumped down with a sigh as her body started to crumble and dissolve.

She could hear the puffball calling her, urging her on, bringing her home to... where? The Pleroma?

Not yet, it seemed to say. *There are other ports along the way.*

44

In the fight circle, you advanced with caution and a tight defense, or you risked getting knocked out. And yet Nameless still ran ahead of Venton along the tunnel.

He rounded one corner only to see a flash of scarlet disappear around another—Jankson Brau's robe.

"Keep going!" Venton called, dropping further and further behind. "Don't let him get away."

Sucking in great gulps of air, Nameless sprinted as fast as his stumpy legs could carry him. The tunnel twisted and turned like an agitated snake, but no matter how fast he ran, he couldn't close the gap. When the tunnel straightened, Brau was still a hundred yards ahead, walking briskly with his stiff gait.

Nameless slowed to a jog, and the distance between him and Brau remained the same. Slowed again to a walk. No change.

"Why are you stopping?" Venton said, coming up from behind.

"It's a trap," Nameless said. "No matter how fast I go, how slow, the shogger's always the same distance ahead of me."

"Leading us on," Venton said. "I wonder what spell he's using. I agree with you: it's a trap. But what choice do we have?"

"This one," Nameless said. "We can spring the trap while exhausted and out of breath…"

"Presumably what Brau's hoping for," Venton said.

"Or we can conserve our energy and make the shogger wait."

"I like that option better."

"Comes from experience in the fight circles," Nameless said, realizing now what his intuition had been warning him. "You have to pace yourself."

Still a hundred yards ahead, Jankson Brau vanished into the gloom of a massive hall.

Venton's staff flared, the crystal at its tip sending a cone of pearly light into the dark. Where the cone shone, it revealed walls of cut stone, giant letters carved into them. Old dwarven letters. The few words Nameless recognized were curse words.

As they advanced into the hall, he could make out fluted pillars, their tops swallowed by the darkness beneath the ceiling.

"I'm going to try something," Venton said, "see if I can't disrupt his spell so we can catch up to him."

"Don't bother," Nameless said. "I think we've arrived."

Brau had stopped before the denser darkness on the opposite wall. With his back to them, he looked up and spoke in a low voice, as if he were conferring with someone, then stood to one side.

A rumbling chuckle came from the darkness, causing the floor beneath Nameless's feet to vibrate.

"Laddie," he said, "can you give us more light?"

"I'm not sure I want to," Venton muttered. "And there's so little essence here, other than our own."

"Then take some of mine."

"Oh, well," Venton said. "Here goes."

Nameless's skin tingled, and then the cone of light coming from the tip of Venton's staff burst apart into thousands of burning motes that spattered the walls, ceiling, and floor and clung there, filling the hall with a wavering radiance. Nameless felt a little queasy, but it swiftly passed.

The space ahead of them was truly vast, a mighty hall with a flat stone ceiling held up by row upon row of pillars.

On the opposite side of the hall, Jankson Brau stood before an immense figure seated upon a throne that looked to have been carved out of the very rock of the wall: a man, proportionately a dwarf, though three, maybe four times the height of a regular dwarf, and three times again as wide. Mountainous shoulders, thick neck, corded with veins, face like an escarpment, at once broody and simmering with barely suppressed rage. Eyes of crimson lightning glared from beneath a craggy brow. His black beard was braided into dozens of ropes that were threaded through the eye cavities of skulls. Beneath it, he was bare-chested, riddled with scars and tattoos. He wore no armor. Perhaps he didn't need any. One gigantic hand rested on the haft of an enormous warhammer.

Beside the throne, fiery motes outlined an arched opening onto a tunnel beyond. The other side of the throne there was a gaping hole of blackness that swallowed all the light that touched it. The darkness tugged at Nameless, compelled him to throw himself into its infinite emptiness and lose himself forever in the Void.

But the figure on the throne was even more compelling. It demanded his attention. Commanded it.

"Kunaga," Nameless muttered. His teeth chattered, and it felt as though his leg bones had melted into soup; he didn't trust them to hold him up if he moved.

"It's a glamor, nothing more," Venton whispered in his ear. "Daemonic dread, a portent of doom and foreboding. All the Supernals possess it."

All that time working with Witandos, perhaps the wizard had developed a tolerance. But to Nameless, it was like standing on top of a volcano, waiting for it to erupt.

"Not so tough now, are you?" Jankson Brau said, coming to the front of the throne, Kunaga's great bulk looming above him.

The sorcerer was like some of the kids Nameless had faced growing up in Arx Gravis: weedy, pathetic bullies who brought their older friends to back them up.

"I haven't forgotten, dwarf, what you did to my face."

At first, Nameless couldn't reply, not without plunging to his knees and begging Kunaga for mercy. But then Venton touched his arm and whispered, "Courage," and just that one word sparked something deep inside of Nameless. His veins grew molten, his skin taut, his muscles pumped and full. He breathed in a lungful of stale subterranean air, swelling his chest.

"You've only yourself to blame, laddie," he said. "Next time, I'll shove your blazing hands up your arse."

Brau's hand came up wreathed in flame, but instantly went out in a puff of smoke.

"What!?"

"A wizard should try not to be too predictable," Venton said. His staff shimmered with an icy blue aura.

"Speaking of predictable," the figure on the throne said, the boom of his voice like a kick in the stomach, "Witandos, of course, did not come to retrieve this himself."

Kunaga turned his fist over and opened it. There, tiny on his massive palm, was a shadow-woven cube.

"The phylactery," Venton breathed.

"Witandos is a busy man," Nameless said. "Big realm like this to run, you know what it's like."

"And so he sent you," Kunaga said. "The one he used to gloat about. The one who was supposed to end his war with Mananoc."

"That's news to me, laddie."

"Actually, Witandos did go on about you all the time," Venton said.

"Aye, and I bet he was disappointed."

"Not entirely..."

"The Ravine Butcher," Kunaga said with a chuckle that evoked a landslide. "The Corrector. The abdicant king of Arnoch."

"You're forgetting Champion of the Ballbreakers drinking contest in Bucknards Beer Hall," Nameless said. "Not a thing to be sniffed at."

"You think this is a joke?" Kunaga said, lifting the haft of his hammer and pounding the head into the floor. A shockwave rolled out across the hall, causing Nameless to stumble and Venton to pitch to his arse.

Kunaga's eyes briefly rolled up into his head, Nameless noted as he helped Venton to his feet.

"You're making him angry," the wizard warned in a whisper.

"What would you rather," Nameless whispered back, "a virtual Supernal, a dwarf lord of Exalted blood, in possession of all his faculties, or an enraged baresark?"

Either way, they were shogged, but perhaps if Kunaga went berserk, an opening would present itself.

Or perhaps it wouldn't.

"On your knees, dwarf with no name," Kunaga said, rising from his throne and thrusting the phylactery into the pocket of his britches. He towered above Jankson Brau, who scurried out of the way, as if he feared what was coming. "Or do you wish to fight your god?"

"My god?" Nameless said, making a show of looking around. "Oh, that's you, is it?"

"I heard your prayers from Aosia," Kunaga said. "You called upon my name!"

"I'd hardly call them prayers. Drunken songs, maybe, no better than the ones about big-bottomed girls. I must admit, I did bellow your name as a desperate battle cry on occasion, but that was before."

"Before what?"

"Before I got to meet you and realize you're nothing but a big, fat, ugly shogger."

Kunaga's lips curled back, baring his teeth. Foam leaked from the corner of his mouth.

"He's trying to rile you, oh great one," Brau said.

"You think I don't know that? You think I'm stupid?"

"Forgive me, great one. But if I may... The phylactery is all that matters. A little more time, and I would have opened it, but seeing as its principal creator is standing right in front of us, perhaps we could expedite matters...."

Kunaga swiveled his mighty head and glared at Brau as if he were a turd clinging to the arse of a battle goat.

Slowly, those crimson eyes came to bear on Venton.

"Come here, little man," Kunaga said.

Venton didn't move.

"I said…"

"I heard you the first time," Venton said. "But I am disinclined to comply."

"Open the phylactery, and I might yet let you live."

"Open it yourself."

Kunaga snarled and took a lumbering step toward Venton. He reached down, but Nameless stood in the way.

"Insolence!" Kunaga roared. "Where are my demons?"

Brau cast a nervous look back the way they had come.

"I believe they might have been otherwise delayed," Venton said. He sounded far more confident in Mora's abilities than Nameless was. And yet, no demons had come.

"Big strapping dwarf lord like you," Nameless said, "and you need all those little demons to do your fighting for you? Is that why you've done nothing but talk? What is it you're scared of, laddie?"

He did his best to sound intimidating, to sound like the Butcher, but he was fooling no one, least of all himself. Perhaps with the Axe of the Dwarf Lords… and the Lich Lord's Armor, the Shield of Warding, his ma's *ocras* helm…. But even with the power he'd possessed when he returned to the ravine for his second massacre, he doubted it would be enough to beat Kunaga.

"You dare to insult me? A tiny insect like you!"

"I've beaten bigger," Nameless said. "The fire giant Sartis, for one. Now, he was a big shogger. He'd have thrown you over his knee and spanked your hairy arse raw."

"Hah!" Kunaga said. "And yet you claim to have beaten him!"

"To a pulp, laddie, and the way you're going, you'll be getting the same treatment."

"He's goading you, great one," Jankson Brau warned. "I tell you, this dwarf is dangerous."

But Kunaga was too far gone. Foam drenched his beard, and his eyes rolled up into his head, all the way this time, till they were white and incandescent with rage.

Nameless was ready for a lumbering attack, not the one that came—blisteringly fast. He felt the wind of Kunaga's hammer coming down before he could move his feet; but then lightning ripped through his veins and his Exalted blood made him move faster than he could think. He dived and rolled and came up swinging almost the same instant the hammer head struck the ground. Chunks of stone flew into the air and fractures spread across the floor. Kunaga grunted in surprise, and Nameless's axe bit deep into the meat of the giant's thigh.

Blood sprayed. Kunaga roared as he countered with a deft reversal of his hammer's arc that sent the head straight at Nameless's face. On instinct, Nameless ducked and the hammer clipped the top of King Arios's stone helm. The chin strap pinched Nameless's neck, and one of the horns went skittering across the ground.

Nameless tried to reset, make room for a second swing, but Kunaga was as relentless as he was fast, pounding the ground with hammer blows that barely missed the mark. Nameless hopped and jumped out of the way, dived and rolled, never given time to attack.

Through the rent in Kunaga's britches, where Nameless had scored his first and only hit, he expected to see blood gushing, but there was none, just a hairline scar where the wound had already healed. Impossible! Not to mention unfair.

Something distracted Kunaga—a flash of scarlet rushing past. Nameless barely had time to snatch a lungful of air when the hammer came at him again. He swayed to the left, but it had been a feint, and Kunaga crouched as he stepped in and punched him full in the chest.

Nameless flew back against the wall, axe clattering away from him. He couldn't breathe. Glanced down, expecting to see a hole in his breastplate, the protruding ends of broken ribs; but the breast plate had held. It wasn't even scratched.

There came a flash and a blast, the stench of sulfur. He glimpsed the red of Brau's robe, the black of Venton's coat as the wizards clashed, but already Kunaga was charging, hammer raised for the killing blow.

And then Kunaga flew sideways as something smacked into him with unbelievable force. The hall shook when Kunaga hit the ground. Dust spewed into the air, masonry cascaded from the ceiling.

Nameless forced himself to his feet, grunting with pain as he stooped to retrieve his axe. Shoggers like Kunaga never stayed down, he knew that from bitter experience.

But down he still was, roaring in rage and pain. Something flashed through the dust cloud drifting to the ground—an axe blade that came down with a pulpy splat.

And then the air cleared and Nameless saw Purg, astride the giant, swinging for all he was worth. But before he could strike again, Kunaga swatted him across the hall, and Purg hit the floor hard.

Kunaga roared as he climbed to his feet. He glanced at Nameless, then at Purg. Decided Purg was the greatest threat, and advanced on him with thunderous strides.

But Nameless was already running, bellowing a song, doing his best to ignore the crushing pain in his ribs.

"Baresarks have a father, from way back in the past,
A shogger called Kunaga,
Who takes it up the—"

Kunaga turned, and Nameless hurled his axe. It spun head over haft, whistling through the air as it hurtled towards Kunaga's face.

A massive hand caught it.

Crushed it.

Dropped it to the ground.

"You stupid shogger," Nameless said. He was talking to himself. "How many times! It's not Paxy!"

Kunaga pounded towards him.

45

Anticipation was the name of the game. Read what your opponent was about to do, then counter it before the spell could take effect. And that's just what Venton did. He had prepared for such an onslaught as Jankson Brau now slung at him, and that's what enabled him to keep his calm and wait for the storm to pass. Read the signs, attune yourself to the changes in the local *feruveum*, and if you'd done your homework, you could tell what was coming before the sorcery was made manifest.

Brau might have been halfway to becoming a lich, might have wielded sorcery powerful enough to control a kraken, but he lacked the subtleties of true proficiency. Every spell was preceded by a telltale sign—a raised eyebrow, a waggle of fingers, a curling of the lips. And Venton had the better of him, could read him like a book—or at least a well pored-over scroll.

It was all about who could most effectively and efficiently repurpose the *feruveum* to give shape to the essence. After that, it came down to who had the biggest well, for there was so little essence in the hall to draw upon, and Venton had no intention of taking it from his comrades. He'd tried snatching essence from Kunaga, but the giant dwarf was as warded as Brau—most likely he was warded *by*

Brau. Venton's staff was next to useless with no external essence to mediate, and his well was emptying rapidly. Much more of this, and he'd be reduced to dredging up his own essence—from his organs, his marrow, his veins—just to stay in the fight. But use too much, and there was no coming back from the depletion. He would simply sicken and die.

Another spell, another counter, and he felt his well contract within his mind. It started to spasm. Brau attacked again—a waft of essence designed to put Venton to sleep, but Venton had mastered just about every combination of sleep spell. He countered with ease, but not without pain, for his well ran dry and essence bled from his body instead. He felt instantly scraped out, hollow. The skin of his cheeks stretched taut, and his spine wrenched and twisted.

Brau, on the other hand, showed no signs of fatigue, and he grinned to show he had recognized Venton's depletion.

The floor beneath their feet shook, and Venton flung his arms wide for balance. Brau did the same, and both wizards turned, momentarily distracted, as Kunaga pounded across the hall towards Nameless. Venton winced. That didn't look good. But then Purg charged in and caught Kunaga by the ankle.

Venton wrenched his eyes away before Brau could take advantage. He was almost too late.

As Brau's cheek twitched—another telltale sign—and black vapors effused from his eyes, Venton abandoned magical defense and instead cracked him in the temple with his staff. Brau squealed and staggered back, clutching his head, all trace of the necromancy he'd been about to unleash gone. The glare he flashed Venton said it wasn't fair, that this was meant to be a duel of sorcery. Venton gave an apologetic shrug, then smacked him in the face with a second strike of his staff. Blood sprayed from Brau's mouth, and he spat out a tooth.

Lightning burst from Brau's fingers as he roared in rage, but Venton saw it coming a mile off. Wincing against the pain in his head, the twist of his guts, he displaced his location with the merest nudge of the *feruveum*. The lightning scorched past him and hit the wall in an explosion of rubble.

Brau gaped with confusion, and so Venton swung for him again, but this time it was Brau who anticipated, and he caught the end of Venton's staff and ripped it from his grip, slinging it away across the hall.

Venton backed away. Brau was stronger than he looked. Preternaturally strong.

Brau's fingers splayed, and Venton readied his counter—only, the fingers had been a feint this time. Instead of discharging sorcery, Brau pounced.

Venton shifted to one side with a quick two-step, pivoted, and caught Brau with a jab as he came in. Brau's head snapped back, but he quickly recovered and came at Venton again—on a straight line, not even thinking of moving his head. Venton hit him with another stiff jab, stepped off to his left and cracked him on the nose with a right cross. Brau shrieked as blood poured from his nose. Shrieked again as Venton's left hook plastered his nose across his face.

Venton skipped back nimbly, keeping a high guard. Thank goodness for Grandpa Purg's boxing lessons. The problem was, he only had the stamina for perhaps thirty seconds, and then he was done for.

It was a wonder he'd lasted as long as he had.

When Brau recovered and leapt at him, Venton couldn't manage a nimble step-step- pivot. Instead, he lunged to get out of the way, but Brau was quicker and caught hold of him by the throat.

Venton fought Brau's hands, but he could find no purchase. Brau was too strong, his grip like a vise. Venton started to choke. His legs buckled, leaving him hanging limply in Brau's unremitting grasp. His vision blurred, but he could swear something massive flew out of the passageway beside Kunaga's throne, wings beating up a storm.

Nothing good, he thought as he started to drift away. *Probably another bloody dragon.*

But a dragon with three heads?

46

Grittel clung to Igor's back as he hurtled along corridors that looked to have been made for giants. The chimaera had lived in the halls and passageways beneath the mountain for hundreds of years—before his maker, Mananoc, had passed through the Void millennia ago. He still knew every way in and out.

She smelled sulfur first, and then she could hear shouts and cries, the pound of massive feet, the fizz and bang of sorcery.

"They're here!" she yelled, and the goat head nodded that he'd heard.

The lion head growled as Igor redoubled his pace.

Pillars and arches, bearded faces of carved stone in bas-relief, statues in alcoves all raced by her in a blur. Igor's paws barely grazed the floor in between bounds and leaps, and then he sprang through an opening and spread his wings, soaring through the dust cloud in the midst of a great hall.

Grittel gripped Igor's lion body with her knees, clung onto a fistful of mane.

A huge, bearded man with a hammer strained toward Nameless, while Purg clung to the giant's leg, holding him back.

"There!" Grittel cried, and the snake head saw what she was

pointing at from where it bobbed beside her at the tip of its tail. "Venton! Help him!"

A man in a scarlet robe and pointy hat had his hands wrapped around Venton's throat. It made Grittel's blood boil to see Venton grey-faced and choking, eyes bulging from their sockets.

The wizard strangling Venton turned in shock as the lion head roared and Igor hurtled straight at him. He flung up his hands in a vain attempt to ward himself, and Venton dropped to the floor.

Grittel blinked as the goat head butted the red-robed man and sent him flying across the hall. But the wizard didn't hit the ground hard, he drifted down light as a feather. Sparks danced on his fingertips as Igor charged him, but before the wizard could unleash his spell, Igor's tail whiplashed toward him and the snake head spewed fire in his face.

The wizard screamed and collapsed to his knees, flesh sloughing from his face amid plumes of smoke.

Igor landed with a snap of his wings, then reared up on his hind legs. The lion head roared as it came down, jaws engulfing the wizard's head. There was a muted scream, a crack and a crunch, and the wizard's body toppled to the floor, blood gushing from the stump of its neck. Igor spat the head out with such force, it hit the wall with a pulpy splat.

Grittel leapt from the chimaera's back and ran to Venton, rolling him onto his back. Venton's cheeks were hollow, his eyes sunken and dull.

"Gritty," he rasped, rubbing his throat.

She helped him to sit, but he pushed her away.

"Leave me," he croaked. "Kunaga. Phylactery. Trouser pocket."

"Me fetch," she said, turning invisible and running toward the giant fighting Purg and Nameless.

"And for goodness' sake, be careful!" Venton called after her.

She'd gone barely five yards when something slammed into her, knocking her from her feet. She tumbled and came up with her knife in hand. Igor's snake head bobbed above her.

"Not you, little chimaera," it said, and then Igor launched himself at Kunaga.

As the giant turned, the snake head sprayed him with fire. Flesh sizzled and bubbled. Igor's front paws hit Kunaga in the chest, knocking him flat on his back, the great hammer crashing to the floor. The lion head bit into Kunaga's shoulder, rending and ripping. But the giant grabbed hold of the goat's horns and wrenched with such force, Igor fell off to one side. Kunaga rolled on top of the chimaera, snarling and pounding the lion head with his fists.

"Igor!" Grittel squealed. She ran in and plunged her dagger in Kunaga's spine. The giant roared and tried to swat at her, but she tumbled out of the way.

Igor's tail thrashed, and the snake head sunk its fangs into Kunaga's neck. The giant ripped it from him, blood gushing from his ruined throat.

Then Grittel saw: the stab wound she'd made in Kunaga's back had stopped bleeding, and his charred and melted face shone with new skin, as if he had never been burned.

Kunaga smashed the snake head into the floor, and the tail went limp. As the lion head roared, he hit it with a thunderous punch then surged to his feet, no sign of the gaping wound to his throat. Two long strides, and Kunaga retrieved his hammer. He turned back to finish off Igor.

Grittel tumbled between his legs, dragging her blade across the back of the giant's ankle, slicing deep into the tendon.

Kunaga bellowed and stumbled back.

"Axe, laddie!" Nameless cried, and Purg threw him his axe. With bewildering skill and timing, Nameless caught the axe by the haft even as he was spinning to swing it.

The axe hewed into Kunaga's good leg, stripping his base away, and the giant toppled to the ground with a colossal impact. Dust spewed into the air, the floor bounced, and masonry cascaded down from the ceiling.

Nameless was immediately astride the giant, smashing the axe into Kunaga's face, shattering teeth. Purg kicked the fallen giant in the head so hard, he left a crater in the skull.

With a bellow of rage, the giant flung Nameless from him, then back-fisted Purg across the hall. Both dwarves went down hard. Neither moved.

Kunaga pushed himself to his knees, swaying as his wounds healed over, and even his teeth grew back.

Before he could stand, Grittel darted in and, gently as she could, slid her hand into his trouser pocket. Nothing. There was nothing there. She withdrew her hand as Kunaga made it to his feet, towering over her. She must have picked the wrong pocket, but now he was too tall for her to reach. Kunaga started towards Nameless, who still wasn't moving.

There! On the floor where Kunaga had lain: a black cube that looked as if it were woven from shadows, small enough to fit into the palm of her hand. Small enough for Kunaga not to have noticed when it fell out of his pocket during the fight.

As Grittel reached for the phylactery, she saw movement out of the corner of her eye: Venton standing, retrieving his staff.

"Kunaga!" the wizard cried, and Grittel's heart turned to stone.

It was Venton's pompous tone of voice, the one he used for boasting. Or bluffing. He was weak, close to death, more bones than flesh. But he was trying to draw Kunaga away from Nameless.

"I have been more than patient with you," Venton declaimed. "But now, prepare to face the wrath of Venton Nap!"

47

Purg was hurting. Hurting all over. Hurting bad.

"Mora," he muttered.

He needed someone to tell. Mora would fix him with something mushroomy. She always did.

"Mora," he called. He tried to yell for her, but he might just as well have whispered. "Mora..." Now it was barely a rasp.

Purg poorly! A thought this time, no sound. *Purg dying.*

That made Purg scared, but not for himself. Scared for Venton, for Grittel. Scared for Nameless. They'd hit Kunaga with everything they had. They'd even hurt him, but his wounds kept healing. It was magic or something—Purg didn't understand. But it wasn't fair. Purg was the strongest there is, but it didn't matter. Kunaga was cheating.

Purg could still hear the giant stomping around. And there was the sound of something big gurgling as it breathed. He craned his head to see the three-headed monster that had knocked Kunaga down, shuddering as it lay there, broken and bleeding.

"I have been more than patient with you."—Venton, in his best telling-off voice.

Purg flinched, as if he'd done something wrong. Wincing at the pain in his ribs, he pushed himself up on one elbow.

"But now, prepare to face the wrath of Venton Nap!"

Kunaga bellowed with rage as he turned away from Nameless and charged at Venton.

Lightning streaked from the wizard's left hand, then his right. Then fire. Then spears of ice. Left, right, left right. So many spells in so little time, the fastest Purg had ever seen.

Odd... Venton's staff didn't shimmer like it normally did. The crystal at its tip remained dull. But the air around Venton himself grew hazy and sparkled with motes, and the wizard grimaced with each spell that left his fingertips. His knees buckled, his spine twisted. His shoulders bunched around his ears. And he grew visibly thinner second by second, as if each use of magic came at a terrible cost.

Spell after spell found the target, but Kunaga continued to cheat, his wounds healing almost instantly.

Kunaga's hammer went up, started to come down. Venton raised his staff in a futile effort to protect himself, but Kunaga suddenly screamed, and his hammer thudded to the floor. Blood sprayed from the back of his leg, where an angry red slash appeared.

As he slumped to one knee, Kunaga lashed out with his hand and hoisted something into the air. Something Purg couldn't see, until Kunaga shook it and there she was: Grittel Gadfly, held aloft by the scruff of her neck. She yipped and she barked, and she flung something to Venton, which the wizard caught in one hand and shoved in his coat pocket. Already, the wound in Kunaga's leg had healed.

"My phylactery!" Kunaga bellowed. "Give it back! Now! Or I rip this dog-headed freak limb from limb."

"Would you listen to that!" Nameless said. He was up and staggering toward Kunaga, trailing Purg's axe behind him. "Laddie, you're a shog-arse, not a god. Picking on little girls and skinny old men! And even when you face real competition, you cheat with whatever poxy sorcery heals you as soon as you're harmed. Your father was a turd-eating goat-shagger, and your mother was a drinker of Ironbelly's. You scut. You shogger. You skronk!"

Purg had never heard that last word before, but it must have been bad. Kunaga took two thunderous steps and kicked Nameless across the hall.

The clatter and clang of Purg's axe hitting the floor caused the three-headed monster to stir. Its wings shivered as it rose to its knees.

Kunaga snatched up his hammer and stalked toward it.

The goat head spat—a sticky stream of goo that spattered the giant's face. As the monster made it shakily to its feet, the lion head growled.

The snake head at the end of the tail rose up, picking out Venton with its slitty eyes. "My essence is yours, wizard," it hissed.

Kunaga's hammer came down—a one-handed blow that struck home with a terrible impact. The lion's body slumped, its three heads hitting the floor, *thud, thud, thud.*

And the crystal atop Venton's staff blazed into life.

Kunaga turned back to face the wizard, then with a wicked grin tossed his hammer aside so he could hold Grittel out by the arms.

"The phylactery," he said. "I won't ask again."

Grittel snapped her jaws and kicked her legs, but it was useless. Kunaga was too massive, too strong. Kunaga was a big, fat bully!

Red hazed Purg's vision. Pins and needles pricked his veins. He sucked in air through his teeth, each breath coming faster than the last. His heart fluttered then pattered then started to pound. His nostrils flared. He could smell meat, raw and bloody. Saliva spilled from the corners of his mouth, soaking his beard.

"Skronk!" Purg growled, pushing himself to his knees, then surging to his feet.

The giant looked towards him.

And Purg charged.

Kunaga hesitated, as if he didn't know what to do with Grittel. But Purg didn't hesitate. Purg was hungry. Purg was fast. Purg was strong.

He threw a punch at the giant's guts, but Kunaga was too tall, and Purg hit him in the fruits instead. Kunaga gasped and doubled up, and Purg ripped Grittel from the giant's grasp and flung her aside, expecting her to flip in the air and tumble when she hit the floor, but she was limp as a rag-doll. Purg cried out in despair, only to see the three-headed monster surge forward with a grunt of effort, one wing extended, catching Grittel as she fell, then the great beast slumped down, exhausted.

"Purg, down!" Venton cried.

Down? Purg was too angry to get down. Too hungry to....

A sheet of flame burst forth from Venton's staff, and Purg threw himself face-first on the ground. Scorching fire passed overhead. Kunaga roared in pain. Purg could smell smoke and sulfur and melting flesh. He shielded his eyes so he could see. Kunaga staggered back, thrashing at the flames consuming every inch of his gigantic body. Blisters erupted and immediately healed. Erupted and healed, over and over.

"I've always wanted to try this," Venton said, "but could never muster enough essence. I call it Abyssal Fire. Regenerate all you like. The flames will not go out."

"So long as you live!" Kunaga roared.

Ablaze from head to toe, blistering, melting, alternately healing, the giant thundered across the floor toward Venton, who just stood there, frozen with shock.

Purg surged to his feet and threw himself at Kunaga. Flames scorched, but he snarled at the pain. And then he tackled Kunaga to the ground, both of them burning, only Purg wasn't healing. He screamed in torment, even as he roared with fury and fear and hunger and hate.

And he was on top of Kunaga, holding him down. Kunaga was bigger by far, but Purg was the strongest, and only getting stronger the more his skin bubbled and blistered, the more he raged.

"Run!" he yelled at Venton. They had the phylactery. There was no need for anyone else to die. "Run!"

Kunaga arched his back, trying to buck Purg off. The giant smashed fists wreathed in flame into Purg's burning face, but Purg was above him and the blows lacked power. Not Purg's, though. He hammered an elbow into Kunaga's face, then threw a punch that bounced Kunaga's head from the stone floor.

He glanced to one side as Venton started to run—not towards the tunnel they'd entered by, but toward the throne and the circle of emptiness beside it.

What was he doing?

Howling in agony, Purg tried to get up, go after Venton and leave Kunaga to burn, but arms like tree trunks wrapped around him and squeezed, and Kunaga started to laugh. "I will survive the flames," he said. "You will not!"

Skin sloughed from Purg's bones, rage the only thing keeping him alive. He strained to break free, but he was wrong: he wasn't the strongest. Kunaga was stronger, and Purg's struggles were growing weaker.

"Venton!" Purg screamed.

The wizard stopped.

Turned back.

He hesitated for a second, torn between staying and going, and then the crystal atop his staff flared blue, and the flames died.

Too late for Purg.

He might have been daft, but he wasn't that daft. His skin was melted like candle wax, his fingers no more than bony claws. It hurt even to breathe, each inhalation a choking gasp, the out breath a gurgling shiver.

Kunaga shoved him off, and Purg just lay there, twitching. Already, the giant's skin was healed, shiny and new, though he was naked now, his clothes burned to ash. Every inch of Kunaga's massive frame was etched with scars and inkings: jagged lines, feral eyes, skulls and bats and ravens.

Kunaga moved out of Purg's line of sight. There came the thump of giant feet, the scrape of stone on stone. Then, as if through a dark and blurry cloud, Purg saw Kunaga looming over him once more. He had retrieved his hammer.

48

"Get up, you shogger, get up!"

Nameless shook with the effort of trying to move. It felt as though every bone in his body was broken.

Across the hall from where he lay, he could see Purg on top of Kunaga, pounding away with fist and elbow. They were both on fire. Purg was screaming in rage and pain, his blows growing weaker.

"Stand up!" Nameless grunted. "Gods of Arnoch, let me stand!"

He raked his fingernails across the floor in an effort to crawl. Purg was dying! Tears of frustration stung his eyes. How had he grown so weak? He was nothing without Paxy. All those high-sounding ideas of saving the dwarf-demons from the ravages of the Abyss! Even if by some miracle Mora achieved what he could not, the thousands he'd slaughtered at Arx Gravis would die again, this time at the hands of Kunaga, once he realized he'd lost control of them.

It couldn't end like this. He wouldn't allow it. All he had to shogging do was get up! He'd done it before when he'd been beaten down in the fight circles. Done it in the taverns, too, when he'd had too much grog.

And then the flames engulfing Purg and Kunaga went out.

Venton Nap stood there, the tip of his staff blazing blue. The wizard must have changed his mind. He'd been halfway to the throne when Purg told him to run. Why the throne? He should have gone the other way. Unless Venton had succumbed to a despair deeper than that which Nameless felt. Unless he'd planned to throw himself into the Void, taking the phylactery with him.

Even now, the wizard could have run, if not to the circle of Void stuff beside the throne, then back the way they'd come. Nameless wouldn't have blamed him. Venton had the phylactery. When all was said and done, that was all that mattered to Witandos.

But the wizard stayed, staff radiant as he walked towards Purg and Kunaga, and that told Nameless all he needed to know.

Kunaga stood and went to retrieve his hammer, leaving Purg charred and melted, quivering on the ground.

"Stand!" Nameless growled, bashing his face into the floor. "Shogging stand!" He butted the floor again, and his vision blurred. White fire sparked in his depths, rose to his skull, then exploded.

And he stood.

Still weak, still wavering on his feet and good for nothing, but he stood.

And he filled his mind with rage. Anger at Witandos for getting him into this mess, and for keeping him apart from Cordy. Anger at Cordy for becoming a Wayist. Anger at Thumil. Anger at Paxy for breaking in two and not being here when he needed her. But most of all anger at himself, for not being the Butcher anymore.

"Hey, skronk face!" he yelled.

But why would Kunaga pay attention to him, a failure?

"No!" Nameless cried as Kunaga towered above Purg and his hammer came down.

In the same instant, Venton swept his staff out, and some unseen force shoved Purg across the floor, away from Kunaga.

Towards Nameless.

Behind the wizard, the three-headed monster shuddered as it seemed to contract. In the space of minutes, it had grown skeletally thin.

Grittel scampered away from the beast, coming to stand with Venton. She held the wizard's hand.

Kunaga flashed Venton a glare. "You think you can save your friend with puny magic tricks? He is strong, I'll grant you, but not strong enough. Now you will watch him die."

Hammer held two-handed. Kunaga strode across the hall toward Purg's prone body. But Nameless stood over Purg. He'd not let that shogger kill this dwarf, his friend, even if it was the last thing he did. And he still had hold of Purg's woodcutting axe.

"You want to be first, Nameless weakling?" Kunaga said as he advanced.

Gone was the rage of the baresark. He was calm now, eyes once more blazing and red.

Nameless let the axe head rest on the ground. He lacked the strength to hold it up. Kunaga saw and grinned, quickened his pace as he prepared to swing.

A huge cry went up, and Nameless's heart hit his throat. A great battle roar that crashed against his skull—or was that the impact of Kunaga's hammer? He thought for a second he was hearing things as he plummeted toward the second death.

But it wasn't the hammer—that was still held over Kunaga's head as the giant stared open-mouthed at the tunnel Nameless had entered by with Venton.

Dwarves.

Hundreds of dwarves, pouring into the hall with axe and sword and shield. Men and women, some mere children. And with them, at the front, Thyenna and Gitashan.

Mora must have done it! Nameless was too shocked to move, as dumbfounded as Kunaga. It was a stampede. No, this was an army. It was a full-on charge. Thousands of dwarves, hurling insults, bellowing songs.

Tears bled from Nameless's eyes. Tears of relief, of guilt. Tears of grief. Because these were the victims of the black axe, and they were charging headlong into a second slaughter.

Kunaga recovered from his initial shock and set his feet, bracing for battle. Laughter, rumbling and derisive, rolled up from his guts to echo around the hall. He didn't even see the dwarves as a challenge. And why would he, when any wound they could inflict on him would heal in an instant? No challenge at all. This was sport.

Nameless opened his arms in an effort to stem the tide. "Stay back!" he cried. "Stay back!"

One or two in the vanguard recognized him and faltered, the masses behind slowing to a halt. Thousands of eyes turned on him, drank him in. Condemned him for what he had done to them in life. Feared him, even now.

"What are you doing?" Gitashan snarled.

"I can't, lassie," Nameless said. "I can't let them die again."

"Are you Exalted or a mouse?" Thyenna said. "If you've not the guts to finish this, out of our way. My sister and I will put this shogger down."

"Please," Nameless said, "you can't win. None of us can. Kunaga can't be hurt."

"And you've just realized that, have you?" Kunaga said. He slapped the haft of his hammer into his palm, eyes roving the thousands of dwarves, challenging them to come on.

Nameless faced Venton. "Laddie, you have the phylactery. Get out of here. Use sorcery, if you have to, but go. We don't all need to die. You too, Grittel." He turned back to the rows upon rows of dwarves. "All of you."

"Hah!" Kunaga laughed. "And you'll hold me, will you? For all of two seconds."

"Go!" Nameless cried.

No one moved.

"If I go, Purg will die," Venton said.

If the big dwarf wasn't already dead. He was red raw, blistered all over, oozing pus.

"You can't save him," Nameless said. "Or are you a healer now?"

"Mora!" Venton said. "Mora can heal him. She'll know what to—"

"Mora's gone," Thyenna said.

"Gone?" Venton said. "Gone where?"

The wizard's chin quivered as the blood drained from his face.

"Dead," Gitashan said. "But she did what she agreed to. She dispelled the taint of the Abyss."

"Oh, Mora." Tears streaked down Venton's face. He leaned on his staff, as if without it he would fall.

"And she revealed a faen that wore the illusion of a dwarf," Thyenna said. "Likely the source of the infection that made demons of dwarves."

"A faen?" Nameless said. He glanced at Kunaga. "You have a faen?"

"Not any longer," Gitashan said.

"Is that how Mananoc got you in his clutches?" Venton snarled at Kunaga. "By using the faen who came to Gabala and offered their lore to Witandos?"

"You know nothing, wizard," Kunaga said.

"Whatever he knows or doesn't," Nameless said, "it's plain you're being used. Trust me, laddie: I know."

"You were used because you are weak," Kunaga said.

"What's Mananoc offering you, Kunaga?" Nameless said. "Because whatever it is, he's lying, and you're a fool if you believe him."

"He needs me," Kunaga said. "Same as I need him."

"So you can defeat Witandos?" Venton said.

"Crush him," Kunaga said. "Take possession of this realm."

"And what then?" Nameless asked. "You think Mananoc will be happy sharing power with you? Please don't tell me you're going to marry and live happily ever after!"

Kunaga growled. Took a step toward Nameless.

Thousands of dwarves raised their weapons and glared.

"You would fight for *him*?" Kunaga asked. "The butcher who slaughtered you in your thousands!"

A dwarf in a red cloak stepped forward. Nameless vaguely recognized him from one of the beer halls, though they'd served in different divisions.

"Aye, he slaughtered us," the Red Cloak said. "And we died with terror in our hearts, futility, hatred."

A black-cloaked Svark came to stand at his side. "Mananoc touched us after death. We didn't warrant the Abyss, but he staked his claim, and Witandos was powerless to refuse."

"The rules of their blasted game!" Venton said.

"The Deceiver possessed us," the Red Cloak continued. "Changed us." He addressed Nameless directly now. "Just like he changed you."

But not Thumil, Nameless thought. He'd been the black axe's victim—or Nameless's, depending on how you looked at it. Witandos had said Thumil was protected. By the Way?

"We had no choice but to do Mananoc's bidding," the Red Cloak said. "We don't hate you, dwarf with no name. We pity you. We understand you. And now, we are free like you."

"Free to choose how we live," the Black Cloak bellowed, and cheers went up from the army behind him. "And how we die a second glorious time!"

Thousands of voices roared as one, and the army charged, Thyenna waving them forward with her broad sword, Gitashan streaking ahead, scimitar a blur of blackness as she struck at Kunaga with impossible speed.

But the hammer came down faster.

Crushing her from her feet.

Leaving her broken and wheezing on the floor.

Such was the ferocity of Kunaga's strike, the power, the speed, that the army's charge petered out. They knew what they were up against now. They had seen it. And all thoughts of a glorious second death were banished by the stark reality.

There was nothing any of them could do.

Thyenna's broad sword dropped from her grasp. She went to her sister. Knelt beside her. Cradled her head as she wept.

"No one else need die," Kunaga said, sweeping the dwarves with his crimson eyes, "so long as—"

"Silence!" Nameless barked, as if he were still a king. As if Kunaga were as lowborn as his baresark descendants who used to live in the filth at the foot of the Ravine City.

Nameless's blood was on fire. He felt only numbness, where before there had been an agony of breaks and bruises.

He jabbed Purg's axe at Kunaga. "Shut the shog up and show some respect. That woman is a dwarf lord, one of the Exalted, not some overblown lackey of the Abyss like you."

Kunaga looked too stunned to say anything, and before he could, Nameless turned on his heel and strode toward Thyenna and her dying sister.

He dropped the axe and knelt. Gitashan reached for him with a shaky hand. He took it, held it in both his own. Forced himself to look upon her shattered face, her crushed skull. Her neck was horribly twisted from the impact, her spine broken. Blood seeped from her ears and her nostrils, and there were chunks of gore in her hair.

She tried to speak, but no words came out. She swallowed and tried again, but Nameless pressed a finger to her lips as he looked into her eyes, shutting out the rest of her broken body. Just her eyes, locked to his, and then even her eyes grew blurry through his tears.

What could he say? That she was magnificent? That they would have been good together, if he'd been free to love again? He had to say something to mark the passing of this most exquisite dwarf lord, this hero, this queen.

She squeezed his hand, and her eyes seemed to say, "No words are necessary. I know."

She shuddered once, and then she was gone.

Thyenna sobbed as her sister's body crumbled into dust that dissolved into the air. The only thing left of Gitashan was her scimitar.

Nameless stood, not even bothering to pick up his axe. What would be the point?

"As I was saying," Kunaga said, and something like sadness had crept into his voice, "no one else needs to die."

He advanced on Venton, and Grittel growled.

"Open the phylactery, wizard," Kunaga said. "Travel inside it to the Abyss."

"So Mananoc can use it to come here?" Nameless said. "Don't do it, laddie. We'll all die then. Every last soul in the Supernal Realm. Either that, or he'll turn us into demons."

"Very well," Venton said, "I'll go."

"Laddie!"

"You've had your say, Nameless Dwarf," Kunaga said. "Now it's you who should be silent. If you had not killed Jankson Brau, wizard, he would have been the one to use the phylactery."

"A bit late to worry about that now," Venton said. "But I do have one condition."

"Venton!" Nameless started toward the wizard, but Kunaga blocked him with a massive hand.

"What condition?"

"First, you allow me to help my friend." He indicated Purg, writhing and twitching on the floor, moaning in agony.

Kunaga nodded his consent.

"I'm no healer," Venton said as he knelt beside Purg, "but I can stop the pain." He lay a hand on the melted flesh of Purg's forehead. Lime-colored motes surrounded his fingers and Purg's breathing eased, grew regular with sleep. But whatever he had done seemed to age the wizard, and there was a pronounced stoop to his shoulders when he stood.

"Now the phylactery," Kunaga said.

Venton caught Nameless's eye before he nodded.

"Very well." The wizard reached into his coat pocket and withdrew the shadow-woven cube. "Don't worry, Grittel," he told the dog-girl. "I'll find you. Somehow, I'll find you. Look after Purg. He has the blood of an ogre. Who knows, he may survive, and if he does, he's going to need you more than ever."

"Me go with you," Grittel said.

"To the Abyss? I don't think so." He released her hand. "Besides, only one at a time can travel in the phylactery. We should move to the Void portal," he told Kunaga, then headed toward the throne and the circle of emptiness beside it, leaving Grittel standing there, tail between her legs.

Kunaga followed the wizard.

Nameless hesitated, pondering the look Venton had given him. Something had been communicated, but he had no idea what. A trick? Venton had a plan?

Purg let out a groan and his hands shot out, fingers scratching for purchase on the floor. With an effort that sent shudders through his ruined body, the big dwarf dragged himself forward an inch, then another, and another.

And Nameless went with him, edging forward at Purg's side. Why, he had no idea. But something compelled him, even if it was only the beckoning of the Void.

Venton stood in front of the hungry dark of the portal.

"I must concentrate," he explained, and Kunaga frowned. "In order to forge a link with my destination through the Void, I must construct an image of my destination."

"Jankson Brau never mentioned this," Kunaga said.

"Because Brau was a second-rate wizard with a high opinion of himself," Venton said. "Why do you think he took so long to solve the first puzzle I placed on the phylactery? It's a good job we came along when we did. Do you seriously think he could have solved the second? Could you?" he asked Kunaga, and the giant narrowed his eyes. "Could anyone, but me?"

"Do what you need to do," Kunaga growled. "But how do you know what the Abyss looks like? Have you been there?"

"A wizard does not divulge his secrets, Kunaga. Even to you. Even," he added quickly as Kunaga started to froth at the mouth, "on pain of death. Now, do be a good chap and be quiet. Goodness knows what will happen if I don't get this right."

Kunaga stiffened but remained silent. Everyone was silent as Venton, staff in one hand, phylactery raised in the other, faced the Void portal, muttering under his breath.

First there was a swirling of the dark, then an image appeared inside the mouth of the portal: the coal-black walls of an immense cavern. Twin crescents of violet glared from within a rapidly forming structure of crystal... or ice.

A chill worked its way up Nameless's spine. He'd seen this cave twice before. Seen the gigantic figure taking shape within the ice.

"Mananoc!" Kunaga said in an awed whisper.

"Shush!" Venton snapped.

"No..." Nameless muttered. He'd been wrong. Venton didn't have a plan. The wizard had given up hope. He'd succumbed to despair.

"Don't do it, laddie. This won't save anyone!"

Least of all Venton, who faced an eternity in the Abyss, tormented by demons.

Ignoring him, Venton brought the phylactery to his face, uttering words in a language Nameless had never heard—they might have been made up, for all he knew.

The vision of Mananoc dissolved into the blackness of the Void. But Venton had his destination now. He was ready to go.

There followed strings of numbers, snatches of chant. The wizard tapped the top of the phylactery with the tip of his staff, then each of its sides, and when he'd finished, he held the cube out towards the utter blackness of the Void portal.

"Someone stop him," Grittel Gadfly said, appearing at Nameless's side. "Me frightened!"

The cube rose into the air, and its lid opened like four triangular teeth.

"Goodbye, Grittel," Venton said, without looking round. "Goodbye, Purg. Nameless."

The wizard's fur hat grew misty as it was drawn into the interior of the cube. Venton's head followed, his arms, his staff, his torso, and legs.... Then he was gone. The phylactery snapped shut and shot forward into the Void.

"Venton!" Purg rasped, crawling toward the portal.

Kunaga's foot came down on Purg's back.

"Shogger!" Nameless roared.

Before Kunaga could recover his balance, Nameless slammed into him from behind, knocking him screaming into the Void.

But Kunaga was fast, and he twisted as he fell, snagging Nameless by the wrist and dragging him after.

49

On the other side of the darkness, Nameless plunged into a cold so absolute that he lost all sensation. Ahead of him Kunaga thrashed for an instant, then grew still, one hand locked around Nameless's wrist.

Blackness gave way to a crepuscular grey with no up or down, no left or right. A myriad ghostly forms drifted in the sea of twilight, tatters and rags of humans and dwarves, slathians, cat-people, lizard men, and faen; all manner of bird and beast and insect, swirling into one another, dissolving into the featureless grey.

And Nameless drifted toward them, towed in Kunaga's wake, filled with the knowledge that one collision, one touch would mean oblivion. Yet he was powerless to move, to do anything but watch and wait, a passive observer of his own demise.

But then he did feel something: a tug on his beard as a fist closed around it—a misshapen fist, melted like wax. It yanked him free of Kunaga's grasp, and then he was hurtling backwards through the grey, till with an audible pop he tumbled out of the portal to land on top of something solid but giving.

"Purg got you!" the big dwarf said from beneath Nameless.

"Thank shog," Nameless gasped. "Thank shog, thank shog, thank... Laddie?"

He rolled off of Purg and teetered as he came to his feet.

Purg was so still, Nameless thought he was dead. And he should have been. His body was charred black in places, red-raw in others, glistening with pus. But when he pressed his ear to the big dwarf's lips, he felt the faintest tickle of breath, rhythmic and steady. Purg had fallen asleep.

"By shog, you're a strong one, " Nameless said. "The strongest there is."

Grittel had hold of Purg's foot. She'd anchored him and stopped him from joining Nameless in the Void.

"Venton?" she asked.

Nameless shook his head. If the phylactery had done as it was designed to, and saved the wizard from the Void, then he was in a far worse place by now. Venton Nap had gone to the Abyss.

"And Kunaga?" Thyenna asked. She stood glowering at the Void portal, as if her hate could still reach Kunaga, still make him pay for what he'd done to her sister.

"Gone," Nameless said. "Forever."

"Then Gitashan is avenged." She extended a hand to clasp Nameless by the wrist. "You have my thanks."

"Aye, well let's not celebrate too soon. There's still Mananoc to worry about."

∽

"We should go," one of the Red Cloaks said. "Flee the isle. This doesn't concern us. It mustn't."

"How so?" another said. "If Mananoc comes, do you seriously think he'll leave us alone? War is coming, I tell you. Terrible war."

"A war we can't win!" one of the Black Cloaks said.

"We stay!" Thyenna said, and the hall hushed at the authority in her voice. "We are dwarves. We fear no one and no thing."

Thousands of eyes were drawn to the corpse of her sister

Gitashan, lying beneath a red cloak someone had mercifully thrown over her. They seemed to say, "She could do nothing against Kunaga, and she was Exalted. What do you think any of us—all of us, even—can do against the Lord of the Abyss?"

Thyenna was no fool. She knew, as well as they did, there was nothing they could do.

No one spoke after that, the only sounds Purg's snoring and the gurgling breaths of the three-headed beast as it lay shuddering, ribs protruding along the flanks of its lion's body.

Grittel Gadfly crouched in front of the Void portal, ears twitching as she waited for the end they all knew must come.

And Nameless... he was too far gone for worry. He'd fought too hard, taken too many breaks and bruises, and they hurt like shog now his Exalted blood had cooled off. He could almost hear Cordy in his head, goading him on, urging him not to give up hope, to fight to the last. But there were limits to what a dwarf could do. He'd met those limits against Kunaga. What he'd done at the end was the desperate act of a beaten man. To tackle an enemy from behind wasn't exactly honorable, but there had been no other way to even the odds. Even Purg—strong, fearless Purg—had been unable to stop Kunaga.

But Mananoc, the Deceiver, the evil that had cursed Nameless from the start, the mastermind behind the twin slaughters at the ravine.... Mananoc, the errant son of Witandos, a being so ineffably powerful he might just as well have been a god. What could any of them do against a god?

And so they waited, more than an hour, until Nameless couldn't take it anymore.

"Perhaps Mananoc's not coming," he said. "In any case, we should leave."

"And go where?" Thyenna asked.

"Back to Witandos? If Mananoc ever turns up, maybe he'll follow us, and the two of them can fight it out."

"While we sit idly by and do nothing?" Thyenna said.

"We could drink beer and watch from the sidelines."

Thyenna sneered, but before she could reply, Grittel began to bark and back away from the Void portal.

Nameless snatched up Purg's axe, and Thyenna drew her broad sword. All around the hall, dwarves overlapped their shields as they formed defensive lines.

Out of the darkness of the Void, the tiny cube of the phylactery emerged and drifted lightly to the ground beside the unconscious Purg.

Nameless glanced at Thyenna, and together they crept forward, then stopped abruptly as the phylactery opened.

Nameless held his breath, heart pounding in his ears as he waited for something to emerge. Waited for the gigantic horror from his vision. For Mananoc.

A fine mist plumed from the cube. Grittel whimpered. Thyenna stepped back, pulling Nameless with her.

The mist flared white, and Nameless shielded his eyes. Something clattered to the floor. When he looked, the mist had gone. In its place there was a pipe with an *ocras* stem and an ivory bowl carved with strange letters and symbols.

"Look Purg!" Grittel cried, shaking the big dwarf till he groaned and forced open one sticky eyelid. "Look!"

Purg's exposed teeth and gums twisted, as if he were trying to smile. "Venton," he rasped.

"What?" Nameless said.

"Me steal that pipe for Venton's ninety-seventh birthday," Grittel said. "Well, not I... someone who look like I."

And now Purg was alternately laughing and coughing.

"Purg dig big hole in ground before we went away."

"To hide us's things in, till us returned," Grittel said. "Only, us not go back."

"Because you died?" Nameless asked. "But why? What does this... Oh! Venton dug up the stash and sent the pipe through as proof he's all right! He didn't go to the Abyss. He returned to Aosia! But that means he must have known Kunaga was dead...."

"He is a clever man, your wizard," said a voice with a sibilant hiss.

Nameless turned to see the three-headed beast roll to its knees. It shook with the effort.

"Igor, you're awake!" Grittel said.

The snake head spoke again. "When your wizard friend drew upon my essence, I felt the touch of his mind."

"But the face of the Void portal," Nameless said. "Before Venton entered the phylactery, he had to forge a link with his destination. I saw Mananoc encased in ice. I saw the Abyss."

"Perhaps that is what you were supposed to see," the snake head said.

Purg snorted. "Venton such a trickster!"

Grittel folded her arms across her chest and let out a huff. "Venton cheat at Empires."

"You mean it was an illusion?" Nameless said. Some kind of manipulation of the *feruveum*? Of course! Any wizard capable of manipulating the local *feruveum* to create a perfect facsimile of his smallholding on Aosia would be able to alter the image on the face of the Void portal. He'd tricked Kunaga, shown him what he expected to see.

Venton had tricked them all.

"But how?" Thyenna asked. "If he's never been to the Abyss? If he had no idea what Mananoc even looked like?"

"Ah, but he did, lassie," Nameless said. "Back at his smallholding, Venton read my mind. He saw my vision of Mananoc in his cavern of coal. But, hang on a minute... if Venton tricked us all, tricked Kunaga, did he plan this all along?"

"Venton would never leave I," Grittel said, though she sounded far from sure.

"But leave you he has," Thyenna said.

"Come here, little one," Igor's lion head said. "All will be well. You will see."

Nameless finally plucked up the courage to broach the subject that had been bothering him: "Gitashan...."

"Will not be forgotten," Thyenna said. "There will be a memorial on Kunagos, with all the pomp and ceremony becoming a queen. And we will also remember Mora."

"Aye," Nameless said. "That we will."

"What about Purg?" Grittel asked.

The big dwarf was snoring once more.

"There's nothing anyone can do for him, Thyenna said. "Purg is dying."

Tears spilled from Grittel's eyes. "But Venton's gone. Mora.... Me alone. Me have no one."

"No, little chimaera," Igor said, and it was all three heads that spoke. "Not alone. We meldings must stick together."

"But..."

"The dwarf lady is right," the goat head said. "There is nothing you can do for Purg. Stay here with me, for a while. Help me to recover, and I will help you bear your pain."

"Me like that, but me can't leave Purg."

"Good girl," Nameless said. "Don't give up on Purg yet. Anyone else would already be dead. Perhaps the Oracle on Kunagos can do something for him. In any case, I intend to take Purg with me to see Witandos, to confront that shogger with the cost of his games. Come with me, if you like, lassie," he told Grittel. "And bring your new friend. Kunagos first, then on to see Witandos."

He picked up the phylactery, and his guts clenched. The dark cube seemed to shiver, and pins and needles ran through his hand to his arm. He thrust the phylactery into his pocket, and the sensation ceased.

"You think the ship will hold Igor's weight?" Thyenna asked.

"Once I have eaten and regained a little strength, I will fly," the lion head said. "It will be good to stretch my wings."

"I was created by Mananoc in order to wage war on Witandos," the snake head said, "but in the millennia since Mananoc's departure, I have changed a good deal, learned much about myself and who I really am. Perhaps it is time Witandos and I spoke face to face."

"Or rather, face to faces," the goat head said.

"Me fly with you!" Grittel said, hopping from foot to foot.

"And us?" one of the Red Cloaks asked. "What's to become of us?"

"Wait for me on the island," Thyenna said. "I will return with a fleet of stone ships and bring you to Kunagos, under my protection."

"You think the other kings and queens will agree to that?" Nameless asked.

"They had better do."

∼

NAMELESS CARRIED Purg from the tunnels beneath the mountain, through the jungle, all the way to the stone ship beached on the shore. It didn't matter that his legs were numb, his arms aching with effort, he refused to set Purg down. Call it penance, call it a matter of honor, all he knew was that it was the right thing to do.

Thyenna carried her sister's scimitar with the same reverence she would have carried her body, if it hadn't crumbled into dust.

Thousands of dwarves trailed them all the way from the mountain, and when they reached the beach they split into groups and gathered wood for fires. It might be some time before enough stone ships arrived to ferry them to Kunagos.

Igor swooped overhead with Grittel riding on his back, then came in to land with the flap of huge wings. The beastie had been off hunting beneath the mountain and had clearly found something to eat. He was still ribby, still drained and exhausted, but he'd turned a corner, and quickly.

"The ship is where I left it," the lion head said. "This is good, no?"

"Obliged to you, laddie," Nameless said. "I'd be even more obliged if you could give me a hand getting Purg here aboard."

"It would be my great honor," all three heads said in unison.

"And we could use a quick nudge out to sea."

After that, a quick layover on Kunagos while Rabnar finished repairs to the *Watchful Wake*, a few flagons of ale, and then off to see Witandos with the phylactery, penance done, and Cordy waiting as his reward.

Only, that last bit Nameless wasn't too sure about.

50

Heads turned as Nameless carried the unconscious Purg through the Feasting Hall of Witandos. Dwarven heads mostly, but someone else might have seen something different. The Isle of Mananoc had been stable by comparison. All the shifting and changing out in the streets and here in the hall was a shogging headache waiting to happen.

Wide-eyed, fearful of the second death Purg seemed to represent, the dwarves looked down into their beers as Nameless passed.

And Purg wasn't even dead yet, but he was good as. The Oracle had done what she could for him, stabilized him for the return journey on the *Watchful Wake,* but Purg's injuries were beyond even her powers.

Grittel followed Nameless, visible for once.

Last came Igor, nudging tables and spilling beer, but no one raised an objection. And why would they? The chimaera had feasted on fish all the way from Kunagos, and though his ribs still showed, he was a formidable beast.

Nameless didn't hesitate when he reached the door at the end of the hall. He kicked it open and went straight through.

A moment's disorientation—no visions this time—and he found

himself in a pool of wavering light amid the gloom. Above his head, the lone miner's lantern he'd seen before. In front of him, one-eyed and glowering, the gigantic form of Witandos seated upon his wooden throne.

Nameless felt rather than saw Igor's great bulk behind him. Grittel Gadfly moved to his side. Her tail was between her legs, and she trembled.

Beside the throne there was something covered with a sheet. A statue perhaps? Head height to a dwarf.

Nameless set Purg down on the floor, then he reached into the pocket of his britches and held up the black cube.

"You have done well," Witandos said, snatching the phylactery and holding it up to the light. "The lid is open. It has been used?"

"Twice," Nameless said. "Kunaga defeated us. He forced Venton to enter the phylactery and take it to the Abyss."

"But Mananoc—!"

"Didn't return. Show him."

Grittel held up the ivory-bowled pipe. "Venton tricked Kunaga," she said.

"Venton didn't go to the Abyss?"

"He went to Aosia," Nameless said. "I don't think he liked it here very much."

"And Kunaga?"

"He had a little fall," Nameless said. "Into the Void."

Witandos swallowed. Covered his one eye with his hand. "Kunaga was once a hero. He would have been the greatest of the Exalted, but for his rage. He fell, you say?"

"I might have given him a hand," Nameless said. "I'd have been lost to the Void myself, if Purg here hadn't pulled me out by the beard."

"Purg saved you, did he?" Witandos gave an enigmatic smile. "That is interesting." He touched his eyepatch as he peered at Purg's ruined body.

"This is what happens when you refuse to fight your own battles," Nameless said. "When you let mortals do the work of gods."

Witandos's good eye blazed red. He started out of his throne, but Grittel stepped in front of Nameless.

"Can you help him?" she asked. "Can you help Purg?"

Witandos glared at Nameless for a long moment, then sat back down.

"Purg's injuries were foreseen." Again, that telltale touch of his eyepatch. "Provision has been made."

"Provision?" Nameless said. "You knew this would happen? You can see the future?"

"Not every future. I did not foresee Venton entering the phylactery and going to Aosia. I had chosen another for that task, one who knows the land of Sahul, where my daughter is to be found. Without a clear mental image of one's destination, if I understand Venton correctly, one cannot predict where the phylactery will exit the Void. With Venton gone, the person I have chosen will not know how to enter the phylactery, let alone direct it."

"Baz could work it out," Grittel said. "Baz is clever, just not quite as clever as Venton."

"Perhaps," Witandos said. "He did work on the phylactery with Venton for years. I will speak with Baz. A setback, yes. An inconvenience. But the important thing is, we have the phylactery back."

Witandos closed his hand around the black cube. There was a shimmer of blue light, and when he opened his hand again, the phylactery was gone.

And now he looked past Nameless's shoulder.

At Igor.

"Come forward," Witandos said.

Heads dipped in obeisance, Igor edged closer to the throne.

"Before you go doing something we might all live to regret," Nameless said, "know this: Igor helped us. Without him, I doubt we'd be here right now, and nor would the phylactery."

"Igor is I's friend," Grittel said.

"Igor has nothing to fear from me," Witandos said. "Not any longer. You are much changed since last we met on the field of battle, chimaera."

"I have had millennia in which to think," the snake head replied, "since Mananoc fell through the Void."

"Indeed," Witandos said. "And did you think about those you slaughtered on Mananoc's behalf?"

"I was wrong," the lion head said. "I believed his lies."

"You're not alone there," Nameless said. "It's what he's good at."

"I should have hunted you down," Witandos said. "Killed you for what you did."

"I would have welcomed it," the goat head said. "Why did you not?"

Witandos sighed. "If not for me, you would have remained three instead of one."

"You are not responsible for what your son did to me," the lion head said.

"It was my actions that brought you here to Gabala. My pettiness. My rage. My exile."

"An accident," the serpent head said.

"No, it was a crime," Witandos said. "My crime. Which is why I did not hunt you down. Once Mananoc was out of the way, there was no need, and you had already suffered enough.

"For the part you played in retrieving the phylactery, you have my thanks. It was an act of great bravery to pit yourself against Kunaga. What is it you desire from me? Why have you come?"

"For peace," the goat head said. "I wish to leave the Isle of Mananoc."

"And live here? Why?"

The lion's head nudged Grittel. "This little one is alone now, and that should not be. We meldings should look after each other."

"This is what you want?" Witandos asked Grittel.

"Me do."

"Then stay, Igor, and be reconciled. All of you"—and now he took in Grittel and Nameless—"have acted with great courage."

"Good," Nameless said. "Then my penance is done? I can go find my wife now?"

"Not just yet."

Nameless opened his mouth to protest, but Witandos silenced him with a raised hand.

"First, your friends must go."

The door they had come through opened of its own accord, not onto the Feasting Hall, but onto trees and pasture, and a yard bright with bloom and buzzing bees. And there, through the hedge maze, was the cottage where Nameless had first met Venton.

"Go with my blessing," Witandos said.

The doorway seemed to widen to admit Igor's bulk. On the far side, the chimaera turned, all three heads looking expectantly at Grittel.

"Not without Purg," Grittel said. "Make him better."

"Purg stays," Witandos said.

He flung out his hand, and Grittel flew through the open door. The door slammed shut behind her, leaving Nameless alone in the gloom.

Alone with Witandos.

And Purg.

Whatever was about to happen, it didn't feel good. It was like standing on the top tier of Arx Gravis during a thunderstorm.

"Now," Witandos said, hand hovering above the sheeted statue. "We must discuss your final penance."

"Must we?"

"In the service of Aosia. And your wife."

"Cordy? What's she got to do with it?"

"Everything. Ask her."

The door opened again, this time onto a corridor with walls, ceiling, and floor of mother-of-pearl.

∽

NAMELESS FOUND Cordy seated on a bench at a crossroads within the maze. She watched him approach, not the faintest bit surprised to see him.

"Sit with me, husband," she said, patting the bench beside her.

"Husband? Is that what I am?" Nameless asked as he sat. It was good to take the weight off his feet after carrying Purg all the way from the harbor.

"What else would you be?"

"Not sure, lassie. Perhaps we should ask Thumil."

"And why would we do that?"

"I saw, lassie. Don't ask me how, but I saw the two of you together in the maze."

"Did you now? And what exactly did you see? Nothing I'm ashamed of, that's for sure."

"I know that, lassie. I didn't at first, but you know what a shogger I can be."

"Aye, a paranoid one." She smiled and placed her hand on top of his. "Thumil's your friend, above all else. Always was. And besides, he's changed. Death has changed him. He has a one-track mind now."

"How's that different to before?" Nameless asked.

Cordy gave him a playful slap. Once upon a time it would have been a punch. The fact that it wasn't made Nameless sad.

"He's obsessed with helping me find a way out of here."

"You don't want to stay? But lassie, you can't go back."

"Nor would I, if I could."

"What is it?" Nameless asked. "What's wrong?"

Her chin quivered beneath her beard, and she could no longer meet his eyes. "I can't say his name... in case he hears me."

"Blightey?" Nameless spoke in a whisper.

Cordy nodded. Squeezed his hand as she trembled. "What he did to me..."

"Lassie, it's over. He can't harm you now."

"He told me he could, that he'd find me, even here, just to get at you."

"Two hundred years ago! If he was going to do something..."

"He was weak. I felt him, Nameless, even here. His taint will never leave me. For a while, he disappeared altogether. No trace, not here, not on Aosia. Anywhere.

"But he's back. Just before you arrived, I felt his evil clawing its way back. Still feeble. Unformed. But it is growing.

"Witandos sees more than anyone else—with his blind eye. He says a shadow is coming, one that will imperil all of Aosia. He cannot say what it is exactly, only that it involves... *him*."

"And this is why you're here in the maze? You're looking for some way to move on, beyond Blightey's reach?"

"The Pleroma. If I can reach the Pleroma...."

Nameless stood. Held his arms out to her. Embraced her.

"My wife, a Wayist! I suppose I have Thumil to thank for that."

"You must think me such a coward," she said.

Nameless shook his head. He'd seen the thing she'd become, the horror Blightey had made her into. "No, lassie, you're no coward. But I think I know now what must be done, the penance Witandos has laid out for me. He wants me to destroy Otto Blightey, for good this time."

How could he and Cordy ever be reunited with the threat of the Lich Lord still hovering over them?

"Witandos has taken steps," Cordy said. "The threat is not just to me. Aosia itself lies under a dark cloud. You will have help. From an Exalted."

"Thought I was the last of the Exalted."

"You were, but Witandos sent another."

"Sent? You mean another Exalted was born?"

"Not this one."

Cordy pulled away from him, hands going to her belly.

She had been pregnant when she died. With Nameless's baby. Her eyes were bright with either hope or madness.

"Witandos fashioned her a body from clay—the very same clay he used to create the first Exalted. And he sent her through the Void. To Arnoch. Our daughter, Nameless. Our daughter!"

"I have to go," Nameless said. "Now!"

"Witandos is not what you think he is," Cordy said. "He strives to become better than he once was."

"Aye, a better tyrant. A better manipulator of other people's lives."

He turned from her and almost walked into Droom.

"I'll keep her safe, son," Droom said. "We both will."

Thumil stepped out of the corridor behind Droom. A dwarf girl of perhaps four or five was holding his hand. Pretty little thing. Golden hair, a tuft of beard, dress the color of the sky on Aosia.

"Laddie." Nameless acknowledged his old friend with a stiff nod.

"The Way willing," Thumil said, "I'll get Cordy to the Pleroma. She'll be safe there. It's a realm of unparalleled peace and beauty."

"Is it now?" Nameless said. "Then how come Witandos managed to get himself exiled from there? Peace and shogging beauty! What about adventure and fighting? What about beer?"

The little girl holding Thumil's hand flinched at Nameless's tone, then ran to Cordy.

"Is this...?" Nameless said.

"Marla." Cordy hugged the girl tight. "See how she's grown. One of the blessings of Witandos. I tell you, he's not as bad as he seems."

Nameless knelt in front of Marla and touched her cheek. She'd been a baby when she died. When he had....

He stood and turned away.

"I have to go," he said. "Witandos is waiting."

"Be safe, son," Droom said.

"Ah, you know me, pa. There's as much chance of that as of you laying off the Taffyr's."

51

When Nameless came back through the door, it wasn't the dingy room with the miner's lantern he entered, it was a sweltering smithy.

Witandos was waiting for him beside an iron table, upon which Purg lay, unmoving. A dwarf woman with silver hair stood with her back to Nameless. She held something in tongs over the glowing coals of a forge.

The heat was unbearable. Nameless was drenched in sweat the moment he arrived, and every panted breath scorched his throat and lungs.

"Paxy?" he said, and the dwarf woman turned and smiled.

"You still think of me as an axe," she said. "My true name is Hucca Hogshead."

"I like it," Nameless said. "A good dwarven name."

"You don't mind that I am lowborn, the daughter of a brewer from the time Arnoch was young?"

"Lassie, I married a brewer's daughter, if you remember. There's no more honorable a trade. Speaking of daughters," he said, turning to Witandos, "I've a bone to pick with you, laddie."

"Be mindful of your tone," the Supernal Father said, towering above him.

But Nameless was beyond caring.

"My daughter, laddie. You've no right!"

"Is that so?"

"She was a baby, for shog's sake. An unborn baby!"

Witandos turned to inspect a wooden haft on one of the workbenches that lined the walls. Dark wood, polished. It might not have been wood at all.

"You would deny her a chance at life?"

"Yes!" Nameless said. "No. I don't know. But did she have a choice?" How could she have, when she'd died in her mother's womb?

Witandos turned back to him. "Do any of us have a choice when we enter into life?"

"No, but…"

"Enough buts," Witandos said. "You have spoken with your wife. You know what you must do."

Nameless would have spat, if he'd had anything to spit. He wiped his sweat-soaked brow, wrung moisture from his beard. "Aye, I know. And I'll go. But I'm doing this for Cordy, not you, not Aosia."

"You are going to need this," Witandos said.

Paxy—Hucca Hogshead—stood aside from the forge, and Nameless gasped.

There, on the coals, white hot and smoldering: the broken halves of the Axe of the Dwarf Lords.

"Do you have no shame?" Nameless said to Witandos. Then to Hucca, "Lassie, you don't need to do this! You've already sacrificed so much!"

She looked as if she wanted to say something, then deferred to Witandos with her eyes.

"Hucca Hogshead will remain here with me," Witandos said.

"Oh, and why's that, then? So she can become a Supernal, like my ma?"

"I want this," Hucca said.

"Lassie, whatever he's offering—"

"I'm not a child."

Nameless closed his eyes and shook his head. "No, Hucca, you're not. And I'm sorry. Whatever you want, I hope it works out for you. I'll never forget the things we did together." He thumped his chest, above the heart.

"Nor I." Her eyes glistened, and then she turned back to the forge.

"But the axe blades are too hot," Nameless said. "They should be glowing yellow, not white."

"Then you have no experience forging divine alloy," Witandos said. "This is not steel."

Hucca was wracked with shudders as she used the tongs to remove one of the broken blades from the hearth and carried it to the anvil. Under Witandos's watchful gaze, she took up a heavy hammer and began to beat it, sniffing between strikes, wiping her eyes on her sleeve.

"You're changing its shape?" Nameless asked. "Why?"

"The time of the *Paxa Boraga* has passed," Witandos said. "This will be a new Axe of the Dwarf Lords, for a crueler, more brutal time."

Hucca did the same with the other half, pounding on the blade with the hammer.

Hours passed, though they seemed like minutes, as Hucca repeatedly heated and pounded each blade, and Nameless feared he would grow deaf from the clangor.

When she'd finished at last, Hucca took each half and plunged them into the slack tub, to cool them for inspection.

Witandos held them up and ran an appraising eye over Hucca's work—his only eye. "Fit for purpose," he grunted. "But not exactly a looker."

Before, the Axe of the Dwarf Lords had been elaborately cast, the divine alloy of its blades shining and golden. Now, the twin blades were dull and grey.

"If you are satisfied..." Witandos said.

"I am satisfied," Hucca replied.

Witandos carried the blades to the workbench, and set them either side of the haft. With his back to Nameless, he raised his eye patch. Lightning forked from whatever lay beneath, striking each of the blades. There was an explosion of blinding white brilliance, and Nameless turned away, shielding his eyes. When the light died down, he looked again, and the blades had fused together around the end of the haft.

Witandos stood back, nodding at this new creation as he lowered his eye patch in place.

Hucca put on some heavy gloves then lifted the axe and plunged it into the slack tub. The water fizzed and sizzled, sending up great plumes of steam. And then Hucca held up the axe before her, tears making tracks through the soot on her cheeks.

"It is done," she said.

Witandos took the axe from her. "Not quite."

Purg let out a rattling breath as Witandos moved to the iron table and placed the axe on his chest. Again, Witandos raised his eyepatch, and this time Nameless saw a radiant gem where the eye had once been, glowing silver and blue and gold. And within the gem, fiery letters—Old Dwarvish—in perpetual motion, swirling around each other, mingling, merging, dispersing.

"Do not look at the gem," Witandos commanded, "else your mind will be lost."

Nameless wrenched his eyes away as Witandos began to chant words he didn't recognize—the language of the Pleroma?

The axe on Purg's chest pulsed with golden light as, beneath the chant, Hucca Hogshead sang a gentle threnody, a song of death and mourning that brought tears to Nameless's eyes.

Silver motes effused from Purg's body, converging on the axe, dissolving wherever they touched. Purg's ruined flesh lost substance, and beneath the skin Nameless could see the flecks and the filaments, the intricate web of the *feruveum* that gave form to his essence.

The axe flared golden, causing Nameless to look away.

And when he looked back, Purg was gone.

Witandos replaced his eyepatch, then took hold of the axe haft and lifted it from the table. "You did well, Hucca. It may even be better than before."

"Certainly duller," Nameless said. The axe had returned to dull grey, no better, no worse than any other axe. Ubiquitous. And perhaps that was the point.

"Are you disappointed?" Hucca asked.

"It's going to take some getting used to, lassie, but I think I rather like it. No offense, but the old one was all frills and fancy."

"The axe and the soul that inhabits it are one," Witandos explained. "It might lack the finesse, the subtlety that Hucca brought, but this axe is a formidable weapon, and far, far stronger."

"Purg strongest there is!" the axe said.

The axe!

Hucca beamed like a new mother.

"Purg?" Nameless said. "Can you hear me?"

"Course Purg hear you! Purg not deaf!"

"But I can hear him..." Nameless said, looking at Witandos for an explanation. "Through my ears. With Paxy—when you were in the axe," he told Hucca, "your voice was in my head."

"As I said," Witandos said, "this new axe lacks subtlety."

"Stands to reason," Nameless said, "given who's inside."

"Come now," Witandos said. "It is time."

Hucca looked almost bashful as she smiled. "Farewell, my Exalted," she said.

"Lassie... I don't know how to... Och, you know."

"I know," she said.

"Thank you, lassie. For everything."

The smithy faded from view, taking Hucca Hogshead with it. Gone was the heat, the smell of molten metal. Nameless was back beneath the miner's lantern.

Witandos leaned on the new Axe of the Dwarf Lords beside his wooden throne.

"So, what now?' Nameless asked, trepidation gnawing at his guts. "Just magic me back to Aosia?"

"If only it were that simple."

Witandos stood aside, revealing the sheet-covered statue.

"I learned that Venton was making this for himself," Witandos said as he pulled away the sheet. "Baz has a careless tongue."

It was the statue Venton had been working on when Nameless first met him, made from red clay, lumpy and featureless, save for rough legs and arms. But the arms were different to how Nameless remembered. They were extended in front of the body, as if carrying a tray. He remembered Venton saying the statue was supposed to be human size, but due to a lack of clay it was only the height of a child.

Or a dwarf.

"Oh no, laddie! No!" he said, wanting so much to back away, only, his legs wouldn't move.

"Clay or divine alloy," Witandos said, patting the haft of the axe. "Besides the phylactery, there is no other way to survive the Void."

A circle of blackness appeared around the base of the statue.

Witandos lay the Axe of the Dwarf Lords atop the statue's outstretched arms. He lifted his eyepatch and Nameless averted his gaze from the scintillant gem and the swirling script.

"Wait," Nameless said. "If you send me back, won't that cede an equal move to Mananoc?"

"It will not. Mananoc has already made his move. You are my counter."

This time, as Witandos began to chant, it was Nameless who lost substance, not Purg. He felt lighter than air, and when he raised his hands they were mist, streaming away from him toward the statue. He was a ghost, a *scadu*, and then he was....

"I can't see!" he said. His voice came out a muffled echo that reverberated around his mind. Could anyone hear it?

"You will, soon enough," Witandos said. "Once you arrive, the clay will conform to the pattern of your soul. Your body will be new, like the axe, but its essence will remain the same."

"But how will I get back?"

"Be honest with yourself," Witandos said. "Would you really want to wander the Wayist maze in search of an eternity in the Pleroma? I am doing you a favor."

"But Cordy!"

"Good luck, Nameless Dwarf. Farewell."

And then Nameless was falling, his cry an infinite wail, stretching out above him:

"Shog-og-og-og-og-og…!"

EPILOGUE

Venton took a long drag on his weedstick as he gazed up at Aosia's three moons and breathed in the cool night air. He was tired from digging, but at least it was done.

Once he'd passed through the Void, the phylactery had sprung open and he'd re-formed atop the tree-ringed hill that overlooked his smallholding—the very spot he had visualized, not the Abyssal scene he'd reconstructed from Nameless's vision in order to trick Kunaga.

And it wasn't a new body that had been formed, it was the same one. Regurgitated was the only way he could describe it, by the fungal fabric of the phylactery. What an invention! He should be proud of himself. Even the clothes he wore had come with him: his favorite black coat and his fur hat. Even his staff.

His digging had left a barren rectangle of mud in the ground, but it would soon grow over with wild, unruly grass, given it was spring—the position of the stars told him that.

Beside his abandoned shovel was the one book he'd retrieved from the strongbox buried underground: a dogeared copy of Bellosh's *Husk Life of Cerreth*. It was one of the first batches of books to come off the newfangled printing presses in Maranore, when printing presses were a thing. He'd bought it for an arm and a leg at the author's emporium in Malfen, more years ago than he cared to remember. About the only good decision he'd made when he set out on that last, fateful quest, was to memorize as much as he could, then bury the book in the ground.

He'd also retrieved a coin purse, a backpack filled with clothes, a crystal-powered lighter from the time of Sektis Gandaw, and a box of weedsticks. Quality weedsticks, he thought as he breathed out a plume of smoke. Oh, how he'd missed them. Somehow, they tasted different in the Supernal Realm. Not quite genuine.

It was a good thing to know that, in all the time he'd been away, no one had found his secret stash. There was a small library buried down there, a fortune in trinkets and hard-earned shekels, jars of tobacco, Mora's dried mushrooms, Grittel's spare blades, and Purg's favorite flagon. All the things they dared not leave in the house while they were away.

And a good job too.

He'd not entered the cottage when he'd gone to the shed to fetch a shovel. He was afraid of what he might find inside, and sure that anything of value would be long gone. The roof had collapsed in the center, the thatch black with mildew. The windows were all broken, the front door hanging from its hinges.

The yard hadn't fared any better. The hedge maze was… well, one giant overgrown hedge. Venton's beehives had been reduced to sawdust by termites and rot. Mora's crops had gone to seed decades ago, and were indistinguishable from the underbrush. There were mushrooms, though—an abundance of mushrooms for this time of year. Sight of them had brought a smile to his lips, but recollecting it now brought tears to his eyes.

Mora was gone.

He liked to think she'd gone somewhere, but he wasn't convinced. The second death had a certain finality to it, marked by absence and ashes.

And Purg. Poor, silly, dumb old Purg, burned to a cinder and still clinging to life. But not for long. Purg was just too stupid to realize he was dead.

It had been no consolation to Venton when the phylactery had shown him Kunaga's fall into the Void as it sped him on his way. Nameless had fallen too. A victory perhaps, but a bitter one. He'd seen no more than that, but what else was there to see?

That left only Grittel, afraid and alone, no one left to take care of her.

It's why he'd sent the ivory pipe back in the phylactery. Grittel had stolen it for his birthday present. What better way to let her know that he was all right?

If there was any possibility of bringing Grittel back to Aosia, he was going to do it. Quite how, he wasn't yet sure, but he had the inkling of an idea—Bellosh's book had given him that.

But he needed more information, a copy of the companion volume: *Roots in Both Worlds*—an account of Bellosh's encounters with the fabled lily cats of Rhylion.

Bellosh would have been long dead by now, but perhaps someone else had taken over his emporium. Because there was nowhere else he could think of that might have a copy of any of Bellosh's works. The adventurer had fallen out of favor due to his association with the Ant-Man of Malfen, and his books had gone out of print.

Venton thought about returning the shovel to the shed, but instead took it in among the trees, where he covered it with deadfall. He couldn't bear seeing the smallholding again. He'd sooner remember it as it was: buzzing with bees, blooming with color, Mora picking mushrooms and placing them in a basket, Purg coppicing trees, Grittel making mischief—all the sights and sounds of happiness he never realized he had, until it was gone.

He took a last puff of his weedstick and ground the stub underfoot. Shouldering his pack and taking his staff in hand, he turned his back on the home he'd shared with his strange little family and headed north, towards the looming dark of the Farfall Mountains.

THANKS FOR READING

The story continues in...

ANNALS OF THE NAMELESS DWARF

BOOK NINE

TOMB OF THE WITCH QUEEN

Please share your thoughts on DEAD DWARVES DON'T DIE by leaving a review.

Stay in touch at www.dpprior.com where you can sign up to my mailing list for new releases and special offers.

Facebook@dpprior

ALSO BY DEREK PRIOR

ANNALS OF THE NAMELESS DWARF

1. Ravine of Blood and Shadow
2. Mountain of Madness
3. Curse of the Black Axe
4. Land of Nightmare
5. Skull of the Lich Lord
6. Fate of the Dwarf Lords
7. Last of the Exalted
8. Dead Dwarves Don't Die
9. Tomb of the Witch Queen

TEMPLUM KNIGHT

Origins 1. Ward of the Philosopher
Origins 2. The Seventh Horse

1. Sword of the Archon
2. Best Laid Plans
3. The Unweaving
4. The Archon's Assassin

SORCERERS' ISLE

1. The Codex of Her Scars
2. The Hand of Vilchus

Blood Trail

www.dpprior.com